Books by Edwin O'Connor

THE ORACLE

THE LAST HURRAH
(*Atlantic Prize Novel, 1955*)

BENJY

THE EDGE OF SADNESS
(*Pulitzer Prize for Fiction, 1962*)

I WAS DANCING

ALL IN THE FAMILY

All in the Family

EDWIN O'CONNOR

All in the Family

An Atlantic Monthly Press Book

LITTLE, BROWN AND COMPANY • BOSTON • TORONTO

The author wishes to thank the *Atlantic*, in whose pages the first chapter originally appeared.

ATLANTIC-LITTLE BROWN BOOKS
ARE PUBLISHED BY
LITTLE, BROWN AND COMPANY
IN ASSOCIATION WITH
THE ATLANTIC MONTHLY PRESS

Published simultaneously in Canada
by Little, Brown & Company (Canada) Limited

PRINTED IN THE UNITED STATES OF AMERICA

To

Arthur Thornhill

I

one

ONE year, when I was a boy—eleven, going on twelve—my father took me to Ireland. We went because of a tragedy, a family tragedy which was really my first experience with sadness of any kind. We arrived there early in April and stayed the rest of the spring and all of the summer. It was the first trip we had ever taken together, for although my father was a great traveler, before this he had always gone off alone with my mother, leaving me at home with my younger brother Tom, a housekeeper named Ellen, and a small, neat red-faced man who could do anything—fix a car, fly a plane, shoot a rifle, build a tree-house, whistle through his teeth, and walk like an Indian. His name was Arthur, and he had been with my father for years. He was a man of unusual appearance: his face, which was the color of a bright cherry the year round, was also strangely smooth, looking always as if it had been freshly waxed, and his hands, I remember, were astonishing. They were freckled and very large—for someone of his size they were enormous. Enormous, and powerful: one night, one great night, when I was about eight, I had their power demonstrated for me in the most dramatic way imaginable. I had been asleep; I was awakened by a series of loud noises coming from somewhere in the house. I listened, frightened; Tom was in bed beside me, still asleep, and in any case too small to help. The noises continued, and finally—and fearfully—I got out of bed, crossed the room, and opened the door the smallest possible crack. Through this opening nothing much was visible to either side, but straight ahead I could see down the stairs leading into the front hall, and there, at the bottom of the stairs, just at this moment and as if for my exclusive benefit, Arthur and a man I had never seen before came bursting into view, moving swiftly but oddly across the dark parqueted floor, and all at once I realized that they were fighting! It was a thrilling sight, but an alarming one, too, for the other man was much bigger than Arthur—to me he seemed at least twice his size. Suddenly, however, Arthur stepped back, very quickly, and his right foot shot out, kicking the other man savagely just below the knee. The other man's arms dropped and he doubled over; at this Arthur moved in and with a forward sweep of one arm brought the flat edge of his huge hand smashing high and hard against the other man's face. From where I crouched I could hear as well as see the blow: the sound was not loud—a thin sharp *splat*—but the man instantly collapsed and fell to the floor, one leg jerking up and turning as he fell, so that his toe caught and was held in the neck of a large Persian vase. For a moment he lay there, motionless and silent on his stomach, one leg up in the air behind him, and then, amazingly, he began to cry! I was terrified, but also astounded: I had never seen a grown man cry before; I had never seen Arthur like this before. The ferocious kick, the slashing smash to the face did not belong to the Arthur I saw every day; moreover, they were not at all like the squared-off stance and the manly closed-fist attack which, I knew, was the only fair way men and boys fought each other.

This troubled me, and later, when Ellen had telephoned the police and they had come and taken away the intruder—whom, to my surprise, they seemed to know quite well: they even laughed and made jokes with him, in which he did not join—I asked Arthur about it. To my relief he agreed with me at once. "Don't you go by what I done, Jackie," he said. "That's no way for nice people to fight. It's more what you could call a shortcut, like. A little joke I play sometimes on people that's bigger than me."

When my father and mother came back a week or so later and learned what had happened, my mother, who had been an actress before she married my father—she was tall and very pretty and smelled like flowers, and she had soft, pale gold hair and extraordinary eyes that sometimes looked gray and sometimes very green—wept and hugged us hard, first Tom, then me. After we were out of the room and, supposedly, out of hearing, she began to talk excitedly of kidnappers and ransom and declared that she would never again go off and leave us without what she called "adequate protection." My father, who had disappointed me by receiving our great news with his usual calm, laughed and said that of course she was right. He added that this was why we were so fortunate in having Arthur.

"He's as good as a regiment," he said, and when my mother protested that this was not at all what she had meant, he simply nodded and said, "I know. But what would you rather have? Two state cops in the living room? Burning holes in the rug and shooting the mailman by mistake? No, we'll stick with Arthur. He's small but he's tidy. And he's very very tough."

The thrill of this night was never repeated. My mother and father continued to travel, just as before, and we continued to be left with Ellen and Arthur, just as before. There were no more breaks, no more fights, no more summoned police; as my father had predicted, we could not have been safer.

We were very happy. Ellen and Arthur, who must then have been in their early forties, had no children of their own—Ellen was a widow, Arthur had not yet married—and possibly because of this they gave us great affection as well as excellent care. We responded, naturally, inevitably. Tom, who was five years younger than I, and still not much more than a baby, preferred to stay close to Ellen, but I had some time ago begun to slip away from such placid company and now spent every possible moment with Arthur. This kept me busy, for Arthur was never idle. We lived in a large, old-fashioned house, always painted freshly white, with big round pleasant tower rooms and, up above, a steep crowning cupola with a golden rooster weathervane. We had space to spare, inside and out: there were wide lawns and maple trees and, in the back, some distance from the house, a combination stable-garage which also, at one point, had served as a hangar. My father had owned a small, single-engine plane—silver, with a red, jagged streak of lightning painted on each side—but my mother, who had always objected to his flying, had finally persuaded him to sell it a year or so ago, and now the building housed two cars, my father's horse Sinbad—a powerful, inky, restless animal I feared and avoided—and my own version of a horse: a docile and nearly motionless pony named Theodore. All of this was Arthur's territory: he made his rounds every day, walking briskly and sometimes almost running, but always looking all around at everything, his sharp blue eyes searching for soft spots, for the first signs of damage or decay.

"You got to hop on it before it hops on you, Jackie," he said to me one morning. There had been a thunderstorm during the night, and a cellar window had cracked; sprawled out on the warm summer grass I watched him as he worked swiftly and expertly with his glass-cutter and his putty knife. "You let it get a head start on you, and you know what happens? You wind up livin' like them Lynches!"

I grew up with all the Lynches and never saw one. I met them only in Arthur's stories: a large and very dirty family who had only to move into a house—a good house, Arthur emphasized, a *new* house—and that house died, simply crumbling to pieces in no time at all around its awful tenants. Arthur never told me exactly what the Lynches looked like, but I thought I knew: they were huge and smudged and covered with hair; they threw bones on the floor and circled each room slowly all day long, rubbing against the walls like cattle, their massive shoulders slowly *erasing* the house away. The Lynches must have been very much on Arthur's mind, for he talked about them a great deal, and whenever he set out on his daily tour of inspection, with me at his side, I felt satisfaction and pride in knowing that I was helping him to preserve us all from similar disasters.

I followed him everywhere. If he left the house for so much as an hour—to drive in to the center of the city on an errand, say—I was on the front seat beside him, pelting him with questions, listening to every word as he answered in his high and rather solemn voice. It was the same voice he used to everyone, to my father as well as to me, and it was for me—at least in my father's absence—the voice of authority and adventure, everything it said being one more link to the fascinating world which Arthur knew so well and which I was burning to know:

"Arthur, did you ever shoot a tiger?"

"Only the one I told you about, Jackie. When I was with your dad out in India, there."

"Was that the man-eater?"

"The man-eater, that's right, Jackie."

"Did you ever shoot an elephant?"

"Your dad wouldn't shoot elephants, Jackie. Still, there was one he did. On account of it was crazy. What they call a rogue. They're bad actors, them rogues."

"Are they man-eaters, too?"

"No, elephants don't eat anybody. Not even rogues. What they'd do, they'd spear you with the tusks and then jump on you till you was jelly. . . ."

"Arthur, are you rich?"

"I wouldn't say that, Jackie."

"Is Dad rich?"

"Some people of got more money than other people, Jackie. That's what it all comes down to."

"Buster Mahoney says Dad has millions of dollars. He says my Uncle Jimmy is the richest man there is."

"There's people in this town of got nothin' to do but talk about this family. I wouldn't pay them no mind, Jackie. Mostly they don't know what they're talkin' about. You listen to your dad on that one. . . ."

"Arthur, did you fight in the war?"

"That's right, Jackie."

"Did you kill lots of people?"

"Not many, Jackie. Not many at all. And they was Germans, mostly. They call them Huns."

"How did you kill them? With your rifle?"

"Different ways, Jackie. Different ways. . . . "

I had a marvelous time with Arthur. If I wasn't with him all day long it was only because by now, unlike Tom, I was old enough to go to school. There was a public school about a mile from our house, and I went there from the first grade on. I liked this school, I liked the teachers—or most of them—and I made good friends and had a fine time, but it always seemed to me that I had a far better time when, at the end of the day, I got home and ran to find Arthur and talk to him and listen to him and join him in whatever fresh and exciting project he had found to do that day.

He could make anything, even painting a wall, seem exciting to me, and the only people I knew who could make all parts of life even more exciting were my father and mother. When they came home, everything and everyone else, even Arthur, slipped into the background—not forgotten, but diminished temporarily—for once at home our parents filled our lives. We never talked or wondered about this; it was simply taken for granted that when they came back, they came back to us. They seemed to do nothing without us, and yet, of course, this could not have been so—they were young, they were popular, they had a great many friends here in the city. They must have had a thousand things to do which had no connection with us at all, and I suppose they did them, but I have no memory of this. All I remember is that they seemed to be with us, not just at odd hours or in their free moments, but literally all the time. And they arranged this so easily, so naturally, that each time they came home we slid without awkwardness or hesitation into the family routine which had been suspended from the moment they went away.

Exactly what we did depended on the time of year. In the summer we often drove into the country for long, all-day picnics, or else we went to the ocean—not far away there was a broad, gently sloping beach which stretched straight as a string for miles in both directions, and which by some miracle was nearly always deserted—and here we swam and played in the surf and, when the tide went out, built our moist, doomed castles in the sand. In the fall and spring—and in the winter, too, if the weather was clear and the roads were open—we went on weekend camping trips to a cabin my father owned, only two hours from our house in the city, but so cleverly isolated in a dark pine woods that whenever we were there I felt as if we had been dropped mysteriously into the middle of a distant northern wilderness for which there were no maps and which no one but ourselves had ever seen.

I loved this cabin. My mother, who always enjoyed herself up here, but probably found life a good deal more comfortable in our house in the city, never called it anything but "your father's log cabin," although actually there were no logs at all. The building was long, low, shingled, and because of the pines all around it rather dark even in the brightest daylight. It had one central room with a huge stone fireplace, and two small bedrooms; it was situated on the end of a point of land which reached out between small twin lakes. These lakes were blue-black and very clear; except for some weeks from late spring to early fall they were too cold for leisurely swimming. A weird, chilling cry sometimes came floating across these lakes at night, and it was my father who told us that this was a loon. And often around sunset we would see two large domed shells appear suddenly and side by side, to ride sedately and heavily on the surface of the water; they belonged to a pair of enormous turtles who apparently always swam together. My father said that they were very old.

"How old?" I asked.

"Older than anybody," he said. "Anybody you know, that is."

"Older than Grampa?" I mentioned my grandfather—who was always being mentioned by other people—not because I thought about him a lot, or because he was a favorite relation, but only because he was certainly the oldest person I had ever met. I barely knew him: he was my father's father, but he was not a great visitor—I had seen him in our house only a very few times—and my mother told me that he was now almost never in the city and lived mostly abroad.

"Older than Grampa, even," my father said. "If that's conceivable, and I guess it is. Although maybe not to him. Look, give me a hand with this rope, will you? I want to rig a hammock for your mother."

Since so few people came up here during the year, the country all around us was pretty much let alone—particularly the lakes, which were said to be bursting with fish. This would have delighted me if I had been more of a fisherman, but I was not. I hated fishing, and I hated it from the first. One spring, when I was still quite small, my father took me out on the east lake in a large flat-bottomed rowboat he had shipped up to the camp for just this purpose. It was ugly and clumsy, but it was also just about untippable, and this was a condition my mother had insisted on. We rowed slowly out to what my father said was a likely-looking spot, near a patch of lily pads; I had with me the shiny black fishing rod which my Uncle Jimmy, of all people, had sent me a birthday or so ago and which until now I had never used. We anchored, and my father showed me how to bait my hook, how to cast, how to reel in after a strike; then, in silence, we began to fish. And I remember that, sitting there, hunched down in the bow of the boat, a bottle of rapidly warming ginger ale beside me, with the smooth blue monotony of the sky doubling itself in the still water, and the faintest drowsy breeze bringing the first smells of summer through the piny air, and the gentle tugging at the line informing me that soon now one more small perch would either be brought into the boat or else would get away—I did not in the least care which—I decided that fishing was the greatest waste of time I had ever known, and I began to fall asleep. I opened my eyes to find my father looking at me; he nodded encouragingly and said, "This is the life."

"It's swell," I said politely. "Really swell."

"I'm glad you like it," he said. "I had an idea you might not, but some of my friends told me I was missing a real bet, having a place like this and not taking my boy out to fish with me. They said that's all a real boy wants: to be taken out in a boat with his dad, with his fish pole in his hand. As I say, I had my doubts, but now that I know you like it so much we shouldn't have any trouble catching ourselves a couple of hours this way every morning. And maybe in the afternoon, too. How about it?"

I said cautiously, "I might not like it all that much."

"No? Well, that's all right. The problem would be if you didn't like it at all. Then we'd really be up a tree. I suppose then we might just have to try the other way."

He paused thoughtfully. After a moment I said, "The other way?"

"The emergency way," he said. "It's what you do if you find that one of the people in the boat really can't stand fishing. There's only one thing you're allowed to do in that case. You have to row in to shore, bore a few holes in the bottom of the boat—not too big—and then row out again and sit there while it sinks under you. Boat, bait, fish poles and all. Then you swim back to shore and never bother with anything like it again. But of course that's an extreme measure; you do it only if someone doesn't like fishing at all. I wouldn't think of doing it to you. Why, do you know what it would mean? It would mean *no more fishing for the rest of the summer!*"

I stared at him, not really believing that I had heard what I had heard, and then I saw that he was smiling, and I felt like yelling because I knew that he not only realized how much I hated it, he hated it just as much himself. And later, after we had sunk the boat—in just the way my father had said—and were swimming back to the shore, with my mother standing on the little dock, just looking at us, he said to me, "You never know till you try. Later on, there's a kind of fishing you could enjoy. But this is for sleepy old men with pipes. You might just as well be knitting."

I said, panting as I swam, "I just remembered—the fish pole. It was a present from Uncle Jimmy."

"I've been wondering what to do about Uncle Jimmy's presents for years," my father said. "I guess we've just discovered the ideal solution. Come on, over on your back, float a little. Keep on with that dog paddle and you won't last another ten seconds."

So the fishing stopped for good, and we passed the time in far better ways. We swam whenever we could; we shot across the lakes in a long, dark green canoe which, strangely enough, my mother (who was always worried about boats collapsing or turning over) loved, and handled expertly; we skated in the winter; we trooped after my father on expeditions through the woods, over narrow trails which had been broken long ago, by whom we did not know. Pine needles had been dropping on these trails for years and had not been disturbed; they formed a thick dry cushion on which we could walk in silence, frequently surprising birds, snakes, rabbits, squirrels, and even deer. Once my father stopped abruptly and simply pointed to the sky; there, taking off from the top of a tall dead tree, his wings moving up and down with a powerful lazy majesty, was an eagle! To me it was like seeing a dinosaur or a roc. I had read all about eagles, but I had never seen one before—and I have never seen one since.

There was a cave at the end of one of these trails; we entered it through a small opening in the side of a hill. It was gloomy and damp and just large enough for my father to stand up in it, but people had lived here—maybe, I thought, Indians. The roof had been darkened with smoke, there were rough scratchings on the walls, and when I began to dig around in the dirt floor, I found an arrowhead. We dug some more: we found another arrowhead, a piece of colored glass, and an old and very large bone. We wondered excitedly about this bone. To what had it belonged? Or to whom?

"A bear or a buffalo, I imagine," my mother said. "It's certainly too big for a man."

"Too big for a man, yes," my father said, looking significantly at Tom and me, "but ask yourselves this: *is it too big for a giant?* Think about that for a minute!"

I thought about it for much more than a minute; I thought about it for days. It seemed to me that as usual my father was completely right.

Often, when we came back to the cabin after one of these expeditions, tired, not talking much, and thinking of many things but most of all of supper, it was quite late and sometimes it was dark. Then there was a different, quieter kind of excitement, for after dark the cabin was a mysterious and even a romantic place. We had no electricity up here: the cooking was done on an oil-stove, and the only light came from kerosene lamps and the big fireplace. The fire was seldom allowed to go completely out, but every once in a while it died, and then, if we begged him hard enough, my father would restart it Indian style, using no matches, but twirling a bow with a leather thong rapidly back and forth across a wooden spindle, while we watched breathlessly for the first thin curl of smoke from the little pile of shavings he used for tinder.

After supper we usually went right to bed, and as the final treat of the day my father came into our room to tell us a story. He always waited until we had washed up and said our prayers, and then, as we lay in bed waiting, with the blankets pulled up hard around our necks, he would come in, sit on the bed, and begin. He must have had hundreds of stories; I don't remember ever hearing him repeat one. A few were familiar—I had read them in books, or heard them in school—but only a few; the rest he made up himself, and these, for me, were by far the best. My mother always came in with him and sat on the bed, too, and I think he must have told the stories to her as well as to us, for although she did not listen in the same way we did—she might suddenly laugh where I could see nothing funny at all, or else she might ask a question just as he came to the most exciting part—still, most of the time she listened with great attention, and if the story was an especially long one, and if in spite of everything we could do we sometimes fell asleep before it was over, the last thing I always saw was my father looking down at us, still talking, and my mother, seated beside him with her arm around him, still listening.

This was the cabin, with my father in charge. At home, in the city, he was still in charge, but here it was more my mother's world, and here more time was given to the things she really liked. The theater was one of these. Although she had left the stage for good when she married my father, she was still very fond of anything connected with it, and she kept in close touch with all of her old friends. Whenever a new play came to the city, some of the people who were in it were quite likely to come out to our house for dinner, and one who did so very often was an English actor they called Dickie. He was a great friend of both my mother and father. He was small and bald, with large horn-rimmed glasses and funny teeth; when I saw him he usually had a cold, and he ate very little because of what he called the Old Intestine. I liked him because he was always nice to me and brought me a present whenever he came, and also because he could pop his eyes and play the banjo and sing sailor songs.

One night, shortly after one of his visits to us, my mother and father gave me a surprise treat by taking me to the theater with them, and as I sat between them, not really enjoying or very much understanding what was happening on the stage, suddenly, in one corner of that stage, there appeared a tall man in a long black robe that reached to the floor. His face was dark and evil; he had long black hair and a small pointed black beard. As soon as he took a step forward there was an absolute silence in the theater, a silence which was broken only when his voice screamed out: a malignant, paralyzing howl that seemed to shake the building, then dropped away to the thinnest of whispers that was somehow more frightening than the howl. I sank back against my seat, petrified, and it was a moment or so before I realized that my mother was patting my hand and murmuring that it was all right, that this terrifying figure was really only Dickie! I did not believe this simply because I could not believe that such a thing was possible, and it was not until later, in Dickie's dressing room after the performance, that I was at last persuaded. And it was not until many years later that I learned something which would in any case have meant nothing to me as a child: that our friend Dickie, with his popping eyes and his Old Intestine and his sailor songs, was usually spoken of as one of the few really great actors of that day.

But the theater I liked best was the theater we had all to ourselves. My mother enjoyed family theatricals, and we were always rehearsing and presenting special versions of plays she had selected for us. Whatever these plays may have been in the beginning, by the time they reached us they had been considerably changed to fit our talents. There was always an infant and often nonspeaking part for Tom, and always an older and more heroic role for me. My mother and father doubled in brass, each of them always playing at least two parts, and sometimes three or four, and my father, who was very good at doing magic tricks, found that more often than not a magician was an important figure in our plays. Then he, with my mother as his confederate—he in white tie and tails, she in a long white evening gown—would miraculously change one card into another before our eyes, pull colored flags out of the air, make tennis balls appear and disappear, and once produced, from an obviously empty hat, a small white rabbit for me!

If there was music in the play, as there sometimes was, we all took turns at singing, but it was really only my mother who sang well. She had a pretty voice, light and sweet and true, and I loved to listen to her sing. For years, whenever I thought of my mother I thought of her as standing on the small improvised stage in the music room, holding Tom by the hand on one side of her and holding me by the hand on the other, trying to keep us swaying back and forth together in rhythm while she sang to my father a song which went, in part:

. . . cannot tell you whether
We'll sail off together
To the golden dreaming sands
Of Zanzibar . . .

The rest of this song, or even the show in which it was sung, I cannot remember at all.

We were never entirely alone at these family productions. Since my mother firmly believed that no play should ever be without an audience, no matter how small that audience might be, Ellen and Arthur were invariably called in to watch us. They always applauded loudly, and on several occasions Arthur told me in confidence that I was a very good boy actor, and that if I ever decided to go on the stage to earn my living, he would be enormously surprised if I did not get famous and make a huge fortune.

We had an interesting, a happy, and a wonderful childhood. More than most children, I think, we had a *family* childhood, and in a way this was strange because our parents were away so much more than other parents. But this seemed to me to make no difference. We knew that whenever they went away they would soon come back; we knew that we were loved; I think we may have been *surer* of our parents than most children. And in the meantime, of course, we had Ellen and Arthur. So that when I look back upon my childhood—or at least upon this part of it—in spite of school and the good times there and all my friends, I'm always tempted to think of it as exclusively a family time, a time in which there were my father and mother and Ellen and Arthur and Tom and me and no one else, a time in which I was as happy as a boy could ever be, a time which was so marvelous that day after day I hoped with all my heart that it would never end.

It did, of course. It came to an end on a morning in March, when I was eleven years old. It came to an end most sadly and most unexpectedly; it came to an end in an instant.

We had gone up to the cabin for the weekend. March was always unreliable, and the winter had been bad, but for more than a week there had been a warm spell, and when we reached the cabin, late on a Friday afternoon, the ice which had edged the lakes on our last visit was gone, the sharp wet smell of winter had left the air, the ground was soft, birds we had not heard in months were chirping away somewhere in the trees, and out on the water a fish jumped. Spring had not really and firmly begun, but winter was over, and when we woke the next morning the air was very warm and slow and slightly hazy, as though we had skipped a season overnight and were now in mid-July.

After breakfast, wearing only our shorts on this extraordinary March morning, my father and I went outside and began to work around the cabin, doing the little things that always needed to be done at the end of every winter—there were screens to be replaced, shingles had blown off, paint had flaked away in spots, and a squirrel had started a hole in the back wall near the fireplace. My mother, who always cleaned the cabin each time we came up as if no one had been here for years, stayed inside and, with Tom as an unreliable and occasionally disappearing helper, opened windows, aired bedding, and swept dirt that I could not even see off the floor. When she began her cleaning she usually stayed with it until she finished, but this morning she surprised us by suddenly joining us in the yard. More surprising still, she was wearing her bathing suit.

"Ha!" my father said. "Who's rushing the season? Don't let that sun fool you—the last thing in those lakes was an iceberg."

"I'm having spring fever," my mother said, "for the first time in years. It's all so beautiful I'm taking time off. No swimming, just the canoe. The first ride of the year. Want to come?"

"All right," my father said. He began to get up—he had been plugging the squirrel hole—but then he stopped and said, "On second thought, no. I'd better wait for this stuff to dry. Otherwise I'll have to start all over again. Take Jackie with you: he's a good man in a canoe."

But I was my father's helper; loyally I said, "I want to see this stuff dry, too."

"I can go," Tom said. He was now six years old, a round-headed little boy who came up to my shoulder, with blond hair so light it was almost white, and gray-green eyes just like my mother's. For a long time now I had been making bets—sometimes with Arthur, but mostly with myself—that whenever people came to our house and met Tom and me for the first time, they would always say that Tom was the image of my mother, just as they would always say that I was the image of my father. Tom had been wandering in the woods on the other side of the cabin, and when he came walking toward us now he held in his hand a very small box turtle. "Look what I found," he said. "I could take it in the canoe."

He went over to my mother, who put her hand lightly on his

head and mussed his hair a bit. "Good for you, Tommy," she said. "That gives me one customer. That's all, is it? Just the one?"

"And a turtle," my father said. "Don't forget that. And look—don't be too long, will you? I'd like to drive in to the village sometime before noon."

My mother had already started for the lake, with Tom at her side. As they went around the corner of the cabin Tom turned and held up his turtle to show me once more, and my mother, with a little wave of her hand, called back, "We may surprise you: we may never come back!"

And as she called this out to us, her voice was light and very gay. It was almost as if she were singing.

We were working away about ten minutes later when my father paused and said, "Wait: listen. Did you hear anything?"

We both listened; we both heard a shout. My father jumped up and ran down to the point; I followed as fast as I could. We looked out on the east lake, which was the one my mother liked best, and there, some distance out and closer to the far shore than to us, we saw the dark green canoe. We could see it very clearly. It was floating upright, and it was empty. Of my mother and Tom there was no sight at all. My father called my mother's name three times, very loudly; there was no answer. There was no sound of any kind: I don't think that at that moment we even heard a bird. We simply stood there in the complete stillness of the beautiful morning: I, not yet realizing just what had happened, and my father, who must have realized it from the very first shout.

Suddenly my father went "*Aaaggghh!*" It wasn't a call, it wasn't a shout to my mother, it wasn't anything: just a loud and terrible sound. Then without even looking at me or asking me to follow him—but I did anyway—he spun around and ran for the little boathouse, about fifty yards away on the shore of the lake. Here there were a small rowboat and a blue canoe, neither of which had been used since last year; my father began to tug at the rowboat and pulled it into the water. Still without looking at me, with his eyes out on the lake, he said, "Hurry up, get in. Take this can: you'll have to bail. This thing can't be tight. Hurry up, hurry up, *come on!*"

So I jumped in, and by now I was frightened. I had never heard my father like this before, I had never seen him look like this before, and now at last I knew what must have happened. My father began to row very fast, and water began to seep into the boat through the seams—not much, but I had to bail. We moved out over the water, the spray from the oars sometimes hitting me in the face, and as I felt the icy drops I knew how cold the water really was. I thought of my mother and Tom in that water, and suddenly I began to cry. At first my father paid no attention to this, merely keeping on with his rowing and looking constantly over his shoulder at our target: the dark green canoe which continued to float and swing gently about, not moving much in the still morning air. I continued to bail and also to cry, and my father continued to pay no attention, but at one point he looked up from his rowing and stared at me with such a strange expression that for a moment I was sure he was terribly angry with me. But he was not, it must have been something else, for he closed his eyes tight, then opened them and said in a quiet voice, "Don't cry, Jackie. Don't cry. It'll be all right. You'll see. We'll both see. It'll be all right." After this he seemed to row faster than before, breathing quite hard now, and still looking back over his shoulder at the canoe as if he were afraid it would go away before we reached it.

I don't know how long it took us to get there: probably no more than a few minutes, but it seemed a very long time. We came alongside, and my father reached over and grabbed the canoe, pulling it right up against us, and there, on its floor, we saw the pale blue kerchief that my mother had worn around her head, and we saw also, carefully crawling its way across the varnished ribs, Tom's turtle. So the canoe had not turned over: we knew that much. My father stood up in the boat; I started to do the same, but he said, quickly and harshly, "Sit down! And stay down! Don't move until I tell you to!" I sat at once and began to look over the side of the boat, more frightened than ever by the thought of what we were looking for and what I might have to see. The water was dark but quite clear, and although we must have been several feet over my head, I could see to the bottom, but I could see nothing except sand and dark patches of leaves and weeds and a couple of large smooth shapes which I knew were rocks.

My father now knelt in the bow, his head bent forward as if he were trying to reach down through the water with his eyes. Straining to see, he was so close to the water that he seemed to be mostly out of the boat, and suddenly I had the terrible feeling that at any moment he might topple overboard and get lost, like my mother and Tom, and in that case what would become of me? It was a thought that filled me with panic, but I didn't dare to say a word, and after no more than a few seconds my father straightened up and, without taking his eyes from the water, reached around behind him and grabbed one of the oars. Using it as a paddle he began to send us forward quickly but not too quickly, dipping the oar each time very carefully so that it made no ripples to interfere with our seeing. We went in straight toward the shore, then came back out; we zigzagged; we swung around in a big circle, then came back to the center in smaller circles. We covered all the nearby water, with my father kneeling in the bow and with me seated on a thwart in the stern; we saw nothing. Once I asked my father a question, but he gave no sign of having heard me. He continued to paddle, never missing a stroke, and as I sat there behind him, seeing only the blank and silent surface of his slim, strong, freshly sunburned back, my own hope died away, I knew at last that my mother and Tom were gone for good, and I began to cry again, but this time to myself.

My father was paddling faster now, taking less care not to disturb the water, but this did not matter much any more, for while we had been looking a wind had come up out of the north. It was a cold wind, the kind of wind that brings clouds, and these were now scattered all over the sky, huge and gray, all rushing together to block out the sun. The still lake was now fairly rough, the boat began to bump along, and while we continued to search, I realized all at once that with the choppy water and the loss of sunlight I could no longer see the bottom—I could barely see to any depth at all. My father could have been no better off, for suddenly he jumped to his feet, threw the oar down on the floor of the boat, and stood looking all around him, out over all the lake, and then back into the boat and right at me, but looking at me in such a different way that I wasn't even sure he saw me. Then, without a word, he dived over the side and disappeared in the cold dark tossing water!

I screamed at him, but I don't think he heard me. I stood up, still screaming and at the same time crying, for I was terrified now: too much had happened that I did not understand, and I had no idea what was going to happen next. Then, just as suddenly as he had gone, my father was back, pulling himself over the side, standing, breathing deeply, and diving over the side again. I looked over after him, saw him swim down and out of sight, and knew now that he was not leaving me or swimming away: he was going down to the bottom himself to try to find my mother and Tom.

This knowledge was of no help, however, because for the first time it had occurred to me that I was going to drown. The wind had become stronger and the water rougher; the boat was rocking badly, and except for my father's frantic reappearances, I was alone: I was certain that within the next few minutes the boat would capsize and I would be dumped into the freezing water and would never come up again. Meanwhile, my father kept on diving from the boat and a minute or so later scrambling back in—clearly not in answer to my screams, for each time he came back he said nothing to me and didn't even seem to know I was there.

The pattern was always the same: my father throwing himself over the side, the splash as he entered the water, my screams, my father bobbing up on the other side and then pulling himself in, waving me away, almost *pushing* me away if I tried to help. Each time he climbed in, the boat tipped more dangerously than before, and twice I slipped and fell to the floor, sprawling out on my back in water which had leaked in through the seams or come in over the sides, while my father stood over me, ignoring me, and breathing in and out noisily, filling his lungs before he hurled himself into the water again. It got worse and worse, and I remember screaming and crying and yelling "Dad! Dad!" whenever he came back in the boat, and thinking that at any moment now we would both go over and that would be the end of me. I was so frightened by my own danger that I could think of absolutely nothing else, and from the beginning to the end of this awful interval I completely forgot the reason, the terrible reason, for our being out on the lake in the first place. I did not once think of my mother or of Tom.

Then, at last, my father climbed into the boat once more, but slowly this time, and very carefully, as if it had only now occurred to him that he might tip the boat over. I had slipped and fallen again and was lying on the floor; my arm hurt where I had cracked it against one of the oars, and I was cold. My father stood over me, dripping water on me, just as before, but now he seemed more like himself, and instead of looking all around him in a wild way and breathing in and out in great harsh gasps, he just stood still, breathing deeply but quietly, his shorts soaking wet and torn by something—a nail in an underwater board, maybe, or a branch. All at once he said loudly, but mainly to himself, "Nothing. Nothing nothing nothing."

At this I sniffled, and he looked down at me with a funny expression on his face; he said, "Jackie."

"I'm cold," I sobbed. "I'm freezing."

"You're freezing?' he said. And he said it almost with surprise, as if he didn't even know that it was cold. Yet the wind was very strong now, there was no sun at all, the temperature must have been dropping all the time; like me he had on only his shorts, and he had been in the icy water. When I looked up at him for comfort I saw that he was shaking and that his skin was pinched and blue. I was shaking too, trembling all over: my teeth had started to chatter and I couldn't stop them. My father looked down at me, and all at once he bent over and lifted me up and held me very close to him, hugging me against his cold wet chest. He held me there for a few seconds, and I could feel him shivering. Then, very gently, he put me down in the stern, propping me up against a wet cushion.

"All right, Jackie," he said. "We're going in now."

And so we went in, with my father rowing as hard as he could, and being helped by the wind which was blowing strong behind us. It must have been a fast trip; it seemed very slow. There were little whitecaps on the water now, the sky was completely covered with low thick dull gray clouds, and it had begun to feel like snow. The beautiful March morning had gone in an hour, and I was so cold I ached. I was still shaking, I kept rubbing my arms and legs, and every second the cold seemed to get worse: great layers of it that passed right through me, freezing the inside of my bones. I could think of nothing but this cold, the warm cabin seemed a very long distance away, and I wondered miserably if I would be frozen to death in the boat before we reached the shore.

My father spoke only once, and that was when he stopped rowing for a moment and looked across at me as if he had just hurt me. "Jackie," he said. "Jackie, I . . . good God forgive me, I don't know what to say to you!"

I said, lying bravely, "It's all right. I'm not so cold any more."

But he just looked at me with the same hurt look and said nothing to this; he went on with his rowing. It didn't dawn on me that he hadn't been talking about the cold at all.

When we got to the shore my father leaped from the boat, picked me up, and carried me to the cabin, running all the way. He ripped my shorts off and, with a heavy, rough bath towel, began to rub me dry. He rubbed so hard it hurt, and then he dried off too, and we both put on heavy winter clothes. All this time he was silent; finally he looked at me and said, "You ought to be in bed, but I can't—come on," and we ran out and got into the car and drove to the village.

Here, while I sat in the car, warm and safe now, my father hurried about, gathering people together, pulling them along with him: the priest, the doctor, the man with no jaw who ran the gas station. I watched all this, and as I watched, the odd and awful thing was that I couldn't feel what I should have felt at all. By now I understood everything that had happened, I knew just what my father was doing and what he was going to do, but it was as if a part of me—an important part of me—had not been able to catch up with what the rest of me knew. What I felt was mainly suspense, a kind of excitement: I was like a spectator at some game which was interesting but with which I had no great personal connection. As yet I had not begun to feel anything more than the faintest trembling beginnings of what I was to feel so devastatingly, and for the first time in my life, later in the day.

My father jumped into the car, bringing some of the men with him, and we drove back to the cabin, more men following us in two trucks loaded with some kind of equipment. When we reached the cabin my father took me inside; he built up the fire and told me to stay in front of it until he came back. Then he went off to the lake with the other men.

I stayed in the cabin all afternoon. Most of the time I was alone, and most of the time, as my father had directed, I stayed in the main room near the fireplace. Obedience was easy; there was really no place else to go. Once I went outside, into the clearing in front of the cabin, but the weather was worse now, a cold drizzle had begun to fall, and when I peered through the mist across the lake all I could see was men in boats over near the far shore where my father and I had been. And inside, beyond the main room, there were only the two bedrooms. I went into mine briefly. It was just as it had been when we had got up that morning: Tom's pajamas were still on the bed, and his lopsided fort, which he had made out of pillows and blankets, was still standing. I left the room quickly and did not go back. Later, reluctantly, but somehow feeling that I ought to, maybe even that I *had* to, I went into the other bedroom. The first thing I saw, directly opposite the door and hanging over the back of a chair in front of my mother's dressing table, was a bathing suit—one she must have taken out, then decided not to wear: in that moment it looked to me exactly like the one she had worn. On the table was a scattering of her things—combs, brushes, little white jars of face creams, a slim gold bottle of the perfume which she liked best and which my father, for some reason, always called One Night in the Alps—and on the edge of the mirror, stuck in under the frame, was the birthday card from me. It was the first card I had ever sent her, long ago, before Tom was born, and I remember that my father had guided my hand while underneath the printed greeting I wrote a message of my own: *Dear Mom I love you and hope you have a very good birthday. Your son Jackie.*

And so I left this room quickly too. I sat by the fireplace and wished my father would come back. I started to read a book, I pushed around the pieces of a huge family jigsaw puzzle called Big Game of North America, I picked up a pack of cards and began to scale them, one by one, across the room. I did all these things halfheartedly, in fact without any interest at all, because by now I had begun to feel quite different: uneasy, very strange. Here by myself in the silent cabin where I had never been alone before, where nothing I touched or even looked at was all mine but was a part of my father and mother and Tom as well, where into my head now came not vague and passing thoughts but a sudden succession of hard and marvelously clear pictures of things we had all done together and could never do again—here, now, I felt as if something had begun a slow incessant twisting inside me, like a key which was winding me up, turning and turning and turning, tightening me more every second, and this was all so real that all at once the tension shot me out of my chair and I sprang to my feet, stiff and trembling a little and waiting apprehensively for the one final twist that would surely be unbearable. But suddenly it stopped, the tautness let go completely, and when it did it seemed that everything that was in me, even my breath, left me in a single great gushing rush, and I stood there boneless and helpless and absolutely empty. And it was in this desperate, desolate, *total* way that the death of my mother and my brother came home to me at last, and in this awful, cataclysmic misery I thought my heart would really break.

Strangely, I did not cry. I sat back in the chair once more, very lonely and full of a great dull swelling ache. After a while—it might have been minutes, it might have been an hour—my father came back. He came into the cabin alone, he came over to me and hugged me hard again, and then, quietly but very quickly, he told me that a few minutes ago they had found my mother and Tom. And when I heard this it was just as if I had been expecting to hear it, and it made no difference: it just landed in the empty ache, and I didn't feel any worse because, I suppose, I couldn't feel at all. Then the priest came in and took my hand and patted it a few times.

"A brave li'l boys like you," he said, "he don' wan' to cry, eh? You know what for? Because dat brave li'l boys, he know his mama and his li'l brudder, dey're wit' de angels now!"

His name was Father LaPlante; he was a French-Canadian priest who sometimes in the pulpit on Sunday talked English, but most often did not. Everybody else came in then, and some of them said things to me and some of them just looked, but in a little while everyone went away, and they took my mother and Tom with them. I asked my father if I could see them before they went, but he said it would be better a little later.

And so my father and I were alone in the cabin again, but not for long. He went into his bedroom and I heard him moving about; when I looked in I saw him putting some of my mother's things into a suitcase. After this he came out and took me by the hand, just as if I were a baby, and led me out to the car. It was dark, and the cold drizzle had changed to a light and lazy snow. We drove off, and as we took the first turn on the dirt road I looked back through the slow flakes at the cabin, and I saw that my father had not even closed the door.

I never saw the cabin again.

We drove toward the city: a long, silent, immensely sad drive. To my surprise we did not go home; instead, about twenty miles from the city, we left the main road and turned into a small seaside town and stopped in front of an old hotel. My father said simply, "We're going to stay here. Just for tonight."

I had never been in a hotel before, but I knew that this was not a very good one. At the desk downstairs a thin, tired-looking man with watery eyes watched my father sign a big book; over his head was a card which said: PEOPLE *may come and* PEOPLE *may go, but the* BULL *in this place goes on forever.* Upstairs, our room was big and dark and smelled of the sea. There was a wide brass bed, everything was old but looked clean, and on the floor, underneath one of the windows and attached to the foot of the radiator, was a coil of thick rope with big knots in it. Above the rope was a sign in big red letters reading: IN CASE OF FIRE.

It was late, I hadn't eaten since morning, but I wasn't hungry at all; my father said it was time to go to bed. I undressed and knelt by the bed and said my prayers, and I think that this was the worst part of all. For the prayers for the dead were familiar to me, I had said them every night since I had begun to pray, but they had never been in any sense *personal* prayers: no one I knew had ever died. Suddenly I was saying them for my own mother and for Tom, and even now I found this impossible to believe, even though I knew it was agonizingly, shatteringly true.

Finally I got into bed, and after a minute my father got in too. We lay there in the dark and the silence. There were no night noises from the streets of the town; the only outside sound was from the sea: a dull and regular thudding as the surf broke on the hard shore. There was a thud, then silence, then another thud, then more silence, and in between I could hear only the beating of my heart, which seemed to me very loud and very fast. My father said nothing. He was lying on his back, looking straight up at the ceiling. Suddenly I felt his hand touch mine, then take it and hold it, very lightly and tenderly, and when this happened something seemed to turn completely over inside me, and I twisted around in bed and flung myself up against my father, clinging to him desperately, and as he quickly put his arms around me and held me, I cried for the first time since my father had told me that my mother and Tom had been found.

I cried and kept crying: very hard, and for a very long time. My father just held me, not saying anything, not trying to comfort me with words, and when at last I stopped—or at least gave signs of stopping—he still held me, but he began to talk, and to talk only about my mother. He went back to the beginning: he told me about how he had met her, how she had looked on the stage, where they had been married, and who had married them—the bishop had been at the reception, my mother had been thrilled by the telegram of congratulations from the President, my mother had been terrified when my Uncle Jimmy (at the time, my father explained, a drinking man) had first threatened to punch the governor of the state in the nose, and then in fact had done so. My father told me about their life together before I was born and afterward, of their trips and travels, of the wonders they had seen and the love they had shared. He talked and talked about my mother, and he seemed not to be able to stop talking, and I listened, hanging on every word, just as I had always listened to his stories at night in the cabin, and then, imperceptibly, I began to grow drowsy, and finally—again, just as I had done so often in the cabin—I simply collapsed into sleep with his words still sounding in my ears.

At one point during the night I woke and realized with sudden fright that my father was no longer in bed with me. But then I saw him: he was on the far side of the room, but I could see him clearly. The weather must have broken, for there was a moon, and in its pale light I could see that my father had thrown open the window wide and was in front of it, not standing but kneeling, motionless, his hands joined, and looking out into the still, dark, windless night. I watched him for a moment, and then I must have fallen asleep again, for the next time I saw him he was back in bed and it was morning.

We left the hotel and went home. Ellen and Arthur were waiting for us: Ellen was weeping, Arthur was pale and very quiet. Later in the day my mother and Tom were brought home, and I saw them at last. During the next two days, until the morning of the funeral, I saw them often. Sometimes I was by myself with them, sometimes I was with a crowd of people who came to the wake. On the third morning we all went to the church and from there to the cemetery, and at last it was over, and I knew that from now on I would see them only in my memory.

One week later, my father took me to Ireland.

two

OF Ireland itself I remember best Dublin and the very green and hilly country a hundred miles or so to the southwest where, to my great surprise, my Uncle Jimmy and his family turned out to be living at the time.

My father was now much quieter than he used to be, and on the boat going over he stayed in our cabin most of the time, reading or smoking cigarettes or maybe just thinking, but never saying very much. Every once in a while, though, he would look up suddenly just in time to see me looking at him, and whenever that happened he would jump to his feet and come over to me and pick me up and laugh and whirl me around and tell me over and over again that once we got to Ireland we would have great times together, just the two of us. We would buy a car and go all over the whole country; we would see castles and ruins and all sorts of places with strange and marvelous names: the Devil's Punch Bowl, the Giant's Causeway, the Poisoned Glen; we would meet people called tinkers who were like the gypsies and traveled around in caravans; we would ride in donkey carts and camp out in tents on the sides of mountains; we would move on to the west to a little fishing village my father knew where all the men went out to sea with harpoons in their hands.

"Because, you see, they're after sharks!" my father said. "And they go out after them in these little boats you'd swear the first big wave would chew to bits! Oh, I tell you, Jackie, just wait till you see them!"

And when my father talked like this his voice sounded just the way it always used to, full of excitement and all kinds of promises, and I could hardly wait until we got to Ireland.

The funny thing was that when we did get to Ireland, none of these things my father talked about ever really happened.

We left the boat and went by train directly to Dublin, where my father took me to a hotel. This hotel was not at all like the only other one I had ever been in, the one at home, by the sea, where I had spent that night with my father. This one was almost like a palace, and when I went in through the big front doors I stopped still, seeing all at once the long high lobby, all white and dark red and gold, with mirrors all the way down both walls, and chairs that looked like thrones underneath them. It was crowded with people, mostly men, laughing and smoking pipes and cigars, and talking loudly and quickly but in such a different way that for a minute I didn't realize that what they were talking was English. Just at this moment the crowd of men seemed to split apart in front of us, to separate into two equal halves, leaving a space like an aisle down the middle of the lobby, and there, in the exact center, I could see a great pile of suitcases and trunks, at the foot of which lay a long and strange-looking dog, apparently asleep.

"Wolfhound," my father said. "An Irish wolfhound. They're trying to revive the breed."

A very little and very old man with a derby hat and bright yellow gloves was standing next to the luggage, slowly rubbing his small feet against the wolfhound, as if he were trying to get a shine on his shoes. We walked past him, and as we did he nodded to my father and spoke to him in a loud gargly voice. My father nodded back, and when he spoke to the man I heard him call him "Lord" something. I thought he was joking, but when I looked up at him he didn't seem to be, and after a couple of steps he said to me,

"Lord Ivermorris. No one you have to remember, especially. I wouldn't think you'd be pals."

I said, "But he's not a *real* lord, is he?"

My father stopped and looked at me, then he turned back to look again at the little man. "I see your problem," he said. "But he's real enough. The genuine article, by the grace of His Majesty. He's English, but he's over here most of the time. I imagine the English see to that."

Even though my father said this, it was hard for me to believe. I could remember my mother reading to me, even before I could read for myself, stories about England and great kings and their knights and lords who always went out to battle bravely with their lances and their shining armor. And now I had seen a lord in person and he was a little dried-up man in a derby who shined his shoes on a dog. It was one of the biggest disappointments I had ever had.

By this time we had reached the main desk of the hotel, and here my father seemed to know everybody and everybody seemed to know him—he told me, later on, that he and my mother had come here on their honeymoon and had been back here many times since. They all shook hands with me and said that they were glad to see me and that I looked just like my father, and after this the manager of the hotel, who was named Mr. Guilfoyle and who was an old friend of my father's, took us upstairs to our rooms.

We had three large rooms in the front of the hotel with high wide beds and big worn-down leather chairs, and in the bathroom was the biggest bathtub I had ever seen: it was old and yellowy, but so long and smooth that you could slide into it and then down along the bottom, almost like a chute. From the front windows of all the rooms we could look out over a great green park, and in the distance we could see mountains.

"The celebrated Wicklow Hills," Mr. Guilfoyle said, pointing them out to me. He was a big bald man with watery eyes and a funny little square of brown moustache that looked as if it had been stuck onto his face with glue. He had a high laugh that came jumping out of him just when you didn't expect it, even when nothing funny had been said at all. My father said that this was just his habit. "We have a saying about the Wicklow Hills," he said to me now. "We say that if you look out your window and *can't* see the Wicklow Hills, then you know it's raining. But if you look out your window and you *can* see the Wicklow Hills, why then you know it's *going* to rain! That's the secret of Holy Ireland, young man: the magnificent climate, the envy of the Western world. Ah ha ha ho." He turned to my father and said, "Isn't that right, John? Or do I exaggerate the charms?"

"You never exaggerate," my father said, sounding as if he weren't really paying attention. He was standing in the center of the middle room, slowly looking all around him, as if he were trying to memorize everything in the room. "Everything's great in this country, Dan. You know that."

"Right you are," said Mr. Guilfoyle immediately. "Oh indeed. A little bit of heaven fell from out the sky one day: we're all familiar with that one, John. Fundamental dogma. Ah ha ha ho. Well," he said. "I must go now and leave you to become accustomed to the home away from home. Goodbye, young man. Come in to see me while you're here and I'll tell you fascinating tales of the Blessed Isle. Mother Machree and the Rose of Tralee. Ah ha ha ho!"

After he left I told my father he sounded like a very strange man, but my father said he was really one of the best, and only talked like that in front of his old friends. Then he looked all around the room once more, and went over to the window to look out at the celebrated Wicklow Hills.

"Home away from home," he said. "Well, all right. You can't hang a man for trying to be nice."

And we started in to live for a while at the hotel. It was all new to me, all different: I had never been anywhere like this before. I woke up early to mornings which might be sunny but most of the time were not, and which always smelled faintly and pleasantly of smoke—this came, I learned, from the turf which people burned in fireplaces all over the city. I would dress quickly and go downstairs to have my breakfast by myself, for my father liked to sleep late these mornings; it was so early that I was almost always the only one in the dining room.

I liked it here in the early morning. The big dining room was my favorite place in the hotel: like the lobby, it was high and long and rather narrow, with an immense chandelier hanging from the middle of the ceiling. There were silver bowls and plates and trays everywhere; the chairs were made of an old dark wood and were always so highly polished you could see your reflection clearly in their arms; the tablecloths reached all the way to the floor and were very white and so heavy and crisp that when you snapped them with your fingertips they gave off a sharp cracking sound, not like cloth at all. I thought it was the most elegant room I could imagine, and so I was startled and even shocked when one night, as my father took me in to dinner, he took a good look all around before he sat down, and then shook his head and said that it was a pity that everything seemed to be getting a little shabby around the edges.

I sat at the same table every morning, next to a deep bay window, eating thick oatmeal and thick bacon and cold toast with mountains of orange marmalade, and looking out at the horses and carts and the few automobiles that by now had begun to move through the soft moist morning. The waiters had come into the room and were standing near the door to the kitchen, dressed in their long black tailcoats and their white bow ties, talking together in low voices and sometimes yawning or rubbing their eyes. They were all very nice to me and usually came over to say hello and to talk a little. Some of the older waiters would tell me that they had waited on my mother and father for years, and would tell me stories about them and ask me questions about myself, but the younger ones—a couple of them not much older than me—talked to me mainly about going to the United States some day, and asked me questions about it that I couldn't answer and that the older waiters laughed at—questions such as whether there was good pay over there, or whether there were lots of dances.

After breakfast, when the room started to fill up and the waiters had to get busy with their tables, I would go out into the lobby and across into the lounge to wait until my father came down. On some mornings Mr. Guilfoyle would come out of his manager's office and stop me in the lobby and ask me if I wanted to walk around the hotel with him.

"It would be of the greatest assistance to me, young man," he always said. "The fresh young eye, you know, on the vast managerial problems: that's what's needed here. Could you possibly do it, I wonder?"

And of course I could—I had nothing else to do—even though I knew that this was just his way of talking and that I wouldn't really be helping him at all. We made several tours together and he showed me all the parts of the hotel, beginning with the tiny bare rooms up under the roof, the smallest rooms I had ever seen, where maids and some of the other help lived.

"Old World, Old World," Mr. Guilfoyle said cheerfully. "The snug accommodation for the loyal employee. That's the way we do things in the Blessed Isle. Ah ha ha ho."

He took me down a secret back stairway, narrow and full of cobwebs, which opened at the bottom into a dusty room packed with shelves and shelves of old glasses and dishes that looked as if they hadn't been used for years.

"Treasure trove," Mr. Guilfoyle said.

He took me into the main offices of the hotel, where there was a huge safe you could walk right into; he let me go inside while he closed the heavy door behind me: it was very quiet, so quiet you could hear your heart beat, and rather scary. After this we went down into the laundry, which smelled of hot water and soap and wet cement, and where red-faced women with big freckled arms scrubbed away and kept yelling at each other. He took me to the carpenter shop, where an old man with very blue eyes put broken chairs and couches together, and where the smell of varnish and the sound of the old man humming as he measured and glued and painted made me think of Arthur and all the times I had been with him while he fixed things around our house. One morning Mr. Guilfoyle announced that he had a special treat for me and took me into the kitchen: a huge and noisy room with lots of white tile and a row of long black iron stoves. Here everybody seemed to be arguing with everybody else; two boys in their undershirts were running around carrying great pots from one place to another; next to us a man in dirty white pants was chopping up vegetables, his big broad knife flashing up and down so fast you could hardly see it moving. A tall fat man who seemed to be the boss was cooking something in a pot and smoking a cigar at the same time.

"Artists all," said Mr. Guilfoyle. "Of a sort, you know, of a sort. Ah ha ha ho."

There was a table in front of me that was covered with different kinds of meat: steak, lamb chops, ham, bacon. One kind, however, I had never seen before: it wasn't cut up like the rest, but seemed to be a small whole animal that had been skinned; because the legs were stretched out in front and behind, it looked quite long and lean. I couldn't imagine what it was, and so I asked Mr. Guilfoyle.

"The mortal remains," he said, "of our old friend bunny rabbit!"

And suddenly I felt sick at my stomach and wanted to leave the kitchen right away; I must have showed this because Mr. Guilfoyle grabbed my hand and quickly took me out, asking me anxiously if I was all right, and telling me that it was undoubtedly the atmosphere that did it. After this I went to other places with him on other mornings, but I never went back to the kitchen.

On those mornings when I didn't go with Mr. Guilfoyle I went directly into the lounge, where I sat down to read one of my books, or else I went over to the writing desk to write postcards until my father was ready. I wrote these cards to my friends at home and also to Ellen; to Arthur I wrote mostly letters, telling him how we were and what it was like at the hotel and what we did every day, and asking him to write to me and tell me how he was and what was happening at home. By the time I finished, my father usually had come down and was walking quickly into the lounge, looking as tall and neat and fresh as he always did—only now, of course, on account of my mother and Tom, wearing a dark blue suit and a black tie instead of the light gray ones or the sport coats he usually wore in the mornings. I was always happy and proud when he came in, because he always looked better than anyone else in the room (once, at our house a couple of years ago, I had heard a woman say, "I think John Kinsella is the handsomest man I've ever seen. He's the only man I know who looks as if he got a haircut every day!") and because he always came straight across the room toward me, smiling a little, and then saying good morning by lifting me clean off the floor with a great bear hug through which I could feel his strong arms and smell his good clean after-shaving smell.

He would sit down beside me and ring for a cup of coffee right there in the lounge—he never went into the big dining room for a regular breakfast. After this he would put his cup down on the table, rub his hands together, look at me and say, "All right. On your feet: we're off."

And we were. The only surprising thing was that we were never off to any of the places I expected us to be off to. For some reason, ever since we had come to the hotel my father hadn't said a word about getting a car, or about our trip to the castles and the tinkers and the shark-hunters out in the west. Instead we went off every day, sometimes by taxi but usually just walking, to places which were all different, but which were all right in Dublin. After a while I wondered if my father might not have forgotten that he had promised to take me over all the whole country, and finally, one day when we were walking along, I decided to ask him about this. When I did, at first he stopped and looked as if he were completely taken by surprise, as if what I had just asked him were something he had not considered or even heard mentioned before. But then his look changed, as if he had just remembered, and he nodded and smiled and told me not to worry, that we would get going any day now, but that there were just a few things he wanted to clear up first.

He didn't tell me what these things were, but after a few days I thought I knew: he wanted to see again all the special places he used to visit with my mother, and he wanted me to see them, too. Every day we would set out from the hotel and after a fairly long walk—and sometimes a very long walk—we would reach the place my father had been thinking of, and then he would explain to me what he and my mother did here years ago. One day, for instance, we walked for quite a while along the bank of the Liffey River, and at last we crossed to a spot which my father said was the exact spot where he and my mother used to stand and watch the neat blue barges go up the river, the very same barges that we were watching now.

"Look at them!" my father said. "Beautiful, aren't they? A toy navy, neat as a pin. And all they do is cruise back and forth, up the river about a mile, taking barrels of beer from the brewery down to the ships in the harbor. That's something your mother could never get used to: pretty boats like that carrying beer. She said they ought to be loaded with pearls!"

On another day we stopped on a back street in front of an old Dublin theater. It was dark and dirty and looked as though it hadn't been used for a long time, but my father told me that it was here that my mother had gone back on the stage for just one night, because he and some of their Irish friends had dared her to. On still another day we found ourselves in the middle of a field, with stands and fences all around it; it was empty now, but my father said in late summer every year a tremendous horse show was held here which my mother had loved, and which had always been followed by a series of balls and wonderful parties. And then on one rainy day—a Saturday, I remember—we walked all the way out to the zoo, which was located in the biggest park in Ireland, and after going all around the zoo and seeing all the animals, we went to a little restaurant and had tea and cakes, and my father told me how he and my mother had found out that it was right here in this zoo that they bred—of all things—lions, and that when they were full-grown they shipped them off to—of all places—Africa!

There were other days on which we wound up at no particular place, but just kept walking around the streets, with the rain stopping and starting, and very few people walking along the old brick sidewalks, and my father stopping every now and then to point out some old house where some famous man had been born, and telling me that he and my mother often used to walk around Dublin like this, going nowhere special, but just walking and looking and stopping to talk to people, and somehow having a marvelous time.

"And God knows why," my father said. "Because there's no use kidding ourselves: as a city dear old dirty Dublin is no great shakes. I mean, compared to London, say, or New York. Not to mention what Dan Guilfoyle would call 'our old friend Paris.' It's small and it's dingy and it's down at the heels and you'd have to be half mad to claim it was the amusement capital of anywhere. But I don't know, there was always something about it. . . . And of course," he said, pointing at me with one finger, as though to tell me that here was something I should particularly remember, "of course there was this: the timing was right. It came right at the first. For both of us. Young dreams, and all that. Rainbows in the sky and here we were in Dublin and wasn't everything grand? I suppose you never quite shake anything like that, do you? Anyway, we never did. Never, never, never!"

I couldn't completely understand all this. Lately, my father had taken to talking to me at times in this strange way, which seemed to say that he was telling me things which we both knew. The only trouble was that usually I didn't know them at all, and half the time, as I looked at him while he talked and saw that he was looking right at me, I still wondered if he was really talking to me, or was just talking to himself but saying what he had to say out loud. Whenever this happened I never knew what I was supposed to say, and so I didn't say anything. My father didn't seem to mind. At least he didn't say anything about my silence, and I'm not sure he even noticed.

We went around the city like this for two weeks, going to a different place every day. In a way I didn't mind, because I liked being anywhere with my father, but in another way I did, because the places we visited—except for the zoo—were not very interesting or exciting to me. And not only that: every one of them made me miss my mother more.

I missed her, and I missed Tom, very much every single day. Right after they died, and in the days following the funeral, I had missed them all the time, without stopping. Now, however, I missed them in a different way. Quite a long time might go by—hours, even—and I might not think of them even once. Then, just as I might be doing something that wasn't connected with Tom or my mother and couldn't possibly have reminded me of them, all of a sudden I *would* be thinking of them, and thinking of them so powerfully and so completely that I couldn't think of anything else at all. This never happened slowly; they always came into my mind very quietly but like a flash, without the slightest warning. It was like staring at a drawing on a piece of paper, then blinking your eyes, then staring once again only to find that the drawing is now totally different. Except that here I didn't even have to blink my eyes; no matter what I was looking at, suddenly I would seem to be staring at a small but very clear, bright, and familiar picture: my mother coming into my room on a hot summer day, wearing a light blue dress and looking almost like a girl, telling me to hurry up because we were all going off to Dabney's (a kind of farm out in the country where they made all sorts of delicious ice cream, which we ate on plank tables under great shady trees); my brother looking helpless and upside down, his short fat legs poking out of a snowbank into which he had fallen while coming down No Man's Hill on his first Flexible Flyer; my father all dressed up in a stage costume, with a straw hat and striped jacket, singing to my mother a song called "Tell Me, Pretty Maiden, Are There Any More at Home Like You?"; my mother and father stealing silently into our room late at night after they had come in from a party, to give us a goodnight kiss. And more than once I saw the picture of my mother in her bathing suit, waving as she went around the corner of the cabin, trailed by Tom, who was still holding his turtle in his hand.

All this happened in the daytime, while I was wide awake. At night I usually dreamed, and this was worse, because the dreams seemed to last a lot longer and because of course while they were going on I didn't know they were dreams. All my dreams were now unwelcome, and the good dreams—or the dreams that once would have been good—were the most unwelcome of all. The bad dreams frightened me, but the good ones, those dreams in which we were all together again, doing all the things we used to do, were much more terrible, because I would be happy in them, and then suddenly in the middle of this happiness I would wake up to the pitch-black quiet night. When this happened there would be just a moment when I couldn't take it all in, when I would lie there with my eyes open, hearing nothing and smelling the faint smoke that was always in the air, still more in the dream than out of it. Then I would hear a noise: it was a soft noise—my father sighing in his sleep—but the instant I heard it the dream vanished, I knew just where I was, I felt lonely and terrified, and in spite of all I could do I very often began to cry again, covering my head with my pillow so that my father wouldn't hear me.

So that every day and every night I remembered my mother, and when my father started to take me around to all the places she had liked so much, at first I was eager to see them because I thought that they might make everything better. But they didn't, and partly they didn't because of my father. Because in these places, when he talked about my mother, and told me when she had been here and what she had seen here and just what she had said here, he began to talk about her in such a strange way that sometimes he sounded as if he thought that she was right here with him, that she was still alive. Of course I knew he didn't really think so, but all the same when he talked like this he was different than I had ever seen him, and it gave me a funny feeling. After he finished and we started on our way back to the hotel he was even more silent than before, occasionally squeezing my hand or putting his arm around me, but never saying more than "It's all right, Jackie," or "You're a great little soldier." And again I wouldn't say anything, because I didn't know what to say.

This went on, as I say, for about two weeks. Then one night, just as we were going in to have our dinner, my father said, "Ah, I nearly forgot. Tomorrow's the big day. We're leaving."

I was delighted; I said, "For the castles?"

"Well, for one castle, anyway," he said. "You might even call it a family castle. For the time being. Your Uncle Jimmy's living there. With his family. So at last you'll have someone your own age to fool around with." He looked at me and smiled. "Just for a change," he said.

And I was surprised by this, because up till then I had no idea that my Uncle Jimmy was in Ireland or that he had a castle. Also, I didn't dream that my father knew that even though he was with me, I had missed quite badly having someone to play with.

The next morning we left the hotel in a kind of car I had never seen before; my father said it was made in England. I said goodbye to all my friends in the dining room, and then Mr. Guilfoyle came out of his office and walked out to the car with us.

"You'll be back, young man," he said to me. "They all come back to the celebrated hostelry. A breath of Paris in the Blessed Isle." He looked gravely at me, and his square brown moustache wiggled; he said, "Ah ha ha ho."

As we drove off I turned around in my seat to wave at him, and at that moment Lord Ivermorris came walking slowly out of the hotel with his wolfhound beside him. It was a windy day, very windy, and the last thing I saw, before we turned the corner away from the hotel to go off into Ireland, was this little old man holding on to the dog's collar for dear life, as if the wolfhound were some sort of anchor without which he would blow away.

three

OUR car was smaller than the ones at home, but my father said it was just what we needed for the roads over here; he drove quickly through the light Dublin traffic and in no time at all we were out in the country. Suddenly it had become a beautiful day—the best we had seen since coming to Ireland. The low rolling clouds that had completely hidden the Wicklow Hills this morning and then had brought rain had now completely disappeared, the sun poured down through the clear washed air, the wind that had threatened to blow Lord Ivermorris away was now a gentle breeze, and we rode along with all the windows down, feeling the shining warm day all around us and smelling the fresh grassy smell from the greenest fields I had ever seen. The roads were much narrower and curvier than they were at home, and every so often the hedges and stone walls on both sides were so high I could hardly see over them. We drove along on what still seemed to me to be the wrong side, but it didn't make any difference because we had the roads practically to ourselves: in the first half-hour I saw only one other car. We took our time, because my father, who ordinarily drove quite fast, slowed down as soon as we got outside of Dublin, saying that nothing on earth could make him hurry through a day like this.

"Not even your Uncle Jimmy," he said. "Paralyzing though the thought may be."

My father, when he talked about my Uncle Jimmy at all, often talked about him in this funny, half joking way, as if he and everybody else were supposed to be afraid of him. I didn't know why, but that might have been because I didn't know my Uncle Jimmy any better than I knew my grandfather: neither one of them had been very much around. I knew that he was married to my Aunt Mary, and that they had three boys who were my cousins and were somewhere around my own age. Their names were Phil and Charles and James, and I could barely remember them; I had only seen them two or three times and in the last couple of years I hadn't seen them at all. Now, riding along with my father, I asked him more about my uncle. I told him what Buster Mahoney had said: that he was the richest man there was.

"That's not true," my father said. "Or maybe I should say that it's not true yet. But it *is* true that they're never going to have to hold any tag days for your Uncle Jimmy."

"Is he richer than you?" I said.

"Much," my father said.

"But are you richer than a lot of people?"

"That's right," my father said.

I felt better at this; I said, "Will I be rich some day?"

"I wouldn't think there was too much danger of that. Unless we have what the experts call a 'gratifying upswing.' Do you know what that means?"

"No," I said.

"Good." Then he looked over from the steering wheel at me in a curious way and said, "This sudden interest in family finances: it's a little new, isn't it? What's up?"

"I just wondered," I said. "I didn't know."

He looked at me again in the same way and then he said slowly, "Well, maybe it's high time you did know. I don't know why we never talked about it before—except that neither your mother nor myself ever went in much for family trees. And then I guess we figured you just wouldn't be interested. However, a few facts about the family can't hurt you. Especially since we're about to visit Jimmy."

So then, while we drove closer to my Uncle Jimmy's castle, going up higher into hillier, barer, almost mountainy country, where occasionally we could see men digging with spades—my father said that these were peat bogs, and that the men were cutting turf—I heard about my great-grandfather (my father's grandfather), who had been born not far from where we were driving now in a cottage with a dirt floor and a roof made of straw, and who had come to America as a very young man and had got a job putting down railroad tracks; about his son, my grandfather, who had left school before finishing and had run away to sea, and then, a few years later, had come back home wearing a very handsome suit and with more money than an ordinary sailor could have hoped for. And as it turned out, my father said, he had *not* been an ordinary sailor.

"Was he a *pirate?*" I said. I had known my grandfather only as a very old gray-faced man who was quite deaf and had a bad limp. Now, suddenly, he had become more exciting: a boy who had run away to sea, and whose limp might have come from a hair-raising wound.

"Not in that sense," my father said. "Actually he wasn't at sea very long. He jumped ship in California, worked at different jobs out there, and finally got enough money together to buy a little land. This seemed to work out quite well, so he bought some more. Then somehow he joined a bank in some small way and bought even more land. Before you knew it he was doing very well. Then, one day, unexpectedly and rather hurriedly, he came back home."

"Maybe he got homesick," I said.

"That must have been it," my father said. Here, he said, my grandfather had to start all over again—why, I didn't understand—

but before long he was buying land again, and after a while he got back into the banking business again, and in a couple of years he was doing even better than before.

"By that time," my father said, "he had married your grandmother and they had the three children: first Jimmy, then Gert, then me. Now you see, if this were the typical Irish-American story of those days, here is where I'd have to stop and tell you about the other children who were born but didn't survive. That's what used to happen then. All the time. But not with us; we were lucky. There were just three of us born, we all lived, and we all flourished. And so did your grandfather, who continued to prosper."

"How rich was he by then?" I said. "Did he have a million dollars?"

"I don't know," my father said. "I never had what seems to be your passion for such details. But we were better off than the neighbors. Considerably better off, although you wouldn't have known it. We still lived in a three-tenement house. The main difference was that now your grandfather owned it, along with a good many others just like it. So that— Ah!" he said suddenly, pointing straight ahead of us. "There they are, Jackie!"

We had just come up over the top of a hill, and there in front of us, on the other side of a great broad valley and still quite some distance away, was a range of mountains. Not huge mountains, like the pictures I had seen of the Alps, but big enough—much bigger than the Wicklow Hills—and with white patches right at the top looking very bright in the sun.

"Snow, this late in the season!" my father said, looking surprised. "Fair enough. Anyway, there it is. That's Kerry, Jackie. That's where we're bound."

Down in the big green valley I could see cows, lots of them, moving around. Up in the sky it was very blue, with not a single cloud anywhere to be seen, and out in front, rising up toward the blue sky, was the long row of mountains with their white tops. It was all very beautiful; I said to my father, "But didn't you even know you had lots of money?"

"What?" he said. He had stopped the car and was looking out into the distance. After a minute he turned back to me and said, "Oh. Yes, we knew. After a while. By the time we went off to school we had a fair idea that we weren't exactly poor." He started the car again, and we began down the other side of the hill, going toward the mountains, with my father seeming to drive even slower than before. For a little while he didn't say anything but just kept looking around at the scenery in the same slow way he had looked around the hotel room when we first arrived in Dublin. When we got to the bottom of the hill and into the valley he began to talk again and tell me some more about my grandfather. He said that when they were old enough, my grandfather had sent Uncle Jimmy and himself to good colleges that nobody else in the neighborhood went to, and that in fact my Uncle Jimmy had had to go to three of these colleges because he wouldn't do what they told him to. My father said that my grandfather had been blazing mad at this, but that he stopped being mad as soon as my Uncle Jimmy got out of college for good and started up in business on his own.

"Because that's when he began to remind my father—your grandfather—of someone," my father said. "He began to remind him of himself. Your grandfather felt rather sentimental about anyone who did that."

"Didn't you remind him?" I said.

"Not very much," my father said. He drove along for a few seconds without talking, and then he said, "Years ago I once heard a man say something about your grandfather I've never forgotten. He said that he had a rat's nose for money. Now, you may not think that's a very elegant thing to say and I don't suppose it is, but it was said with great admiration, and the man who said it meant it as the highest compliment. All he really meant was that your grandfather had a way of finding money in places where other people didn't even suspect it existed. And that was perfectly true. When it came to that your grandfather was a very gifted man. What surprised everyone about your Uncle Jimmy was that once he left school and began to fly a little on his own, he turned out to be even *more* gifted."

"Did he have a rat's nose too?" I said.

"I'll tell you what we might do about that rat's nose," my father said. "We might forget it. Particularly since we're going to be dropping in on Jimmy very shortly. You see, I know it's a compliment, and you know it, but there's always the chance that Uncle Jimmy might not know it. So we'll just let it go, if it's all the same to you. Meanwhile, since you asked the question, the answer is yes. He did. And does. Your Uncle Jimmy is a rather remarkable man, and do you know why? *Because he understands money*. He knows all about it. And that's very rare. You see, quite a few people have money, and quite a few more know a little bit about it, but you could put in a pup tent all the men who know *all* about it. The way Arthur knows about birds, for example, or about fixing things. Well, that's the way your Uncle Jimmy knows about money."

"Is that why he has more money than you?" I said

"That's right," my father said.

I said, "I bet you could know all about it if you wanted to."

My father laughed and reached over and grabbed the back of my neck in his hand and rubbed it up and down, the way he always did. "I'd love to get the odds you could pick up on that one," he said. "But what's wrong with having a cheerleader for a son?" And now, unexpectedly, he stopped the car again, and this time we were about in the middle of the valley, near a small stone bridge that crossed over a brook. The brook was very clear and running fast through the fields, which looked just as green down here as they had from the top of the hill. I looked all over but I couldn't see anyone: there was nothing but the fields, and up ahead the mountains with their snow, and over on the right the cows, which were slowly munching around. The air was very warm now, almost like summer at home; the little breeze had gone completely. Up overhead a few big black birds flopped across the sky; my father said they were called rooks. There was not even a sound. I leaned back against the car seat, feeling sleepy; my father was sitting straight up, looking down the fields a way. All of a sudden he said, "This is too good to miss. Come on!"

Quickly he got out of the car; sleepily, but not wanting to miss anything, whatever it was, I followed him. He cut out across the fields along the brook, walking fast, and in a few minutes we came to a little pool where he stopped. To my surprise he took off his shirt, then his shoes and socks; he said, "Your first swim in Ireland: a clear puddle in a cow pasture! But at least it's wet. And cool. Come on!"

We didn't even have our bathing suits. I hesitated and looked around; my father laughed and said, "It's all right; this is birthday suit territory. For this afternoon, anyway. Come on, hurry it up: there's no one around for miles!"

So I got out of my clothes and walked down to the edge of the water, and my father and I jumped in together. It wasn't just a puddle, as my father had said: it was more like a small pond, but very shallow, not even up to my shoulders all the way across, and it was freezing cold. We splashed around as fast as we could and ducked under a couple of times, and then we ran back up onto the bank, a little out of breath, and began to jump around, the cold water drying off our bodies in the warm sun. It was fine. Pretty soon my father went over to his clothes and got some towels he had fished out of the back of the car, and we dried off the rest of us. Then we put on our clothes and went back to the car, with my father racing me and winning by only a few steps. We got all set to go again, and just before we started my father passed me his comb and watched me while I combed my hair in the car mirror. He said, "Well, how goes it?"

I said, "Swell." Because it really was. My father nodded and smiled and then he started the car again and once more we were on our way to my Uncle Jimmy's.

After we had been going a few minutes my father said, "I suppose we should have one last word on this subject of money which you suddenly find so fascinating. I think I want to tell you how I feel about it. I think it's great. I think it's great to have, and I think it's great to spend. I've always had plenty—all the credit for that goes to your grandfather—and I've always spent plenty: I guess all the credit for that has to go to me. But the thing is, I've enjoyed it. We've never lived inexpensively, and we've always had a great time. I've enjoyed having the money, I've enjoyed everything it's brought me, and I'd hate like poison to have to do without it. There's a fellow on the stage who says, 'I've been rich, and I've been poor, and believe me, rich is better.' Well, I believe him. On the other hand, if I woke up tomorrow morning and suddenly I didn't have any money, I wouldn't lose my mind. Or I don't think I would. And I *know* I wouldn't spend the rest of my life hightailing it down the pike with my tongue hanging out, shaking all the bushes along the way because you never can tell, one might turn out to be the money tree. That always seemed to me to be a pretty dull way for a human being to put in his time. And the people you meet, all doing the same thing, are about as grisly a bunch as you could ever find. Like so many anteaters: uninteresting, you know. Well, that's understandable—because money—just plain money, all by itself—is pretty uninteresting. That doesn't happen to be the majority opinion in our family, but it's the way I've always felt and it's the way your mother felt, and as for you . . . well, how you'll feel is something we won't know for quite a while yet. But I don't know, I think I might be willing to take my chances on that. Despite this little question bee today. Which is now ended, by the way," he said. "I hope that's all right with you. No more talk today about high finance and the family: do you think you can manage to survive that?"

I said I could, of course, and from then on until the end of the trip we didn't talk any more about money or my grandfather or my Uncle Jimmy. In fact we didn't talk much about anything at all. I didn't care. I just sat there, thinking of what my father had said to me, and of how it was different from anything he had ever said to me before. And I wondered if maybe all of a sudden he had made up his mind that I was growing up, that I had stopped being small, and that from now on he would talk to me in this older and more important way. The more I thought about this the better I felt, and not just because of this, but also because it was good just to be sitting here next to him, and to be having swims with him, and to be riding around with him all through the country.

We rode for maybe an hour more, going up into the mountains, but turning off onto a dirt road long before we reached the top and the snow. My father said that this road, which was winding and very bumpy and only a little wider than our car, was not much used but that it was a good shortcut, and pretty soon it took us down into another valley which was just as broad and just as green as the one we had left. My father drove faster now, and we passed two very long and very blue lakes, and then we went into the first big woods I had seen in Ireland. On each side of the road were tall smooth trees with green vines like ivy crawling all over their thick trunks. My father told me that sooner or later these vines would kill the trees by just winding around them and slowly strangling them to death. I kept looking back at these trees and wondering why somebody didn't come along and cut off the vines, and just as I was thinking this my father said, unexpectedly but quietly, "Coming up dead ahead: one castle!"

And I whipped around in my seat, to find that we had come to the end of the woods and were at the front edge of a wide clearing. Right ahead of us, in the middle of this clearing and about a hundred yards away, was what I had been waiting so eagerly all day to see, and now that I saw it at last I could just stare at it and wonder if my father was playing a joke on me. Because this couldn't be my Uncle Jimmy's castle, since it wasn't even a castle at all! A real castle, I mean, that looked the way all castles were supposed to look and that had what all castles were supposed to have: things like moats, and great high stone walls all around, and towers and turrets and battlements, and banners flying from the roof, and an enormous heavy front door that could swing down slowly to let the soldiers come charging out across the drawbridge. And while of course I didn't expect to see soldiers come charging from my Uncle Jimmy's castle, I did expect to see the rest, and instead all I saw was this very old building that looked like a tall stone box. It was thick and square and ugly with no towers or anything; there were no windows but just a few wide slits which let in the light and through which maybe they used to shoot arrows. Vines, the very same kind of vines that had been choking the trees, were creeping all over it; everything looked silent and deserted. I remember thinking that this would be a terrible place to live in, and I wondered how my Uncle Jimmy, if he was as rich as everybody said he was, could do it. Then, suddenly, as I looked more at the building, I saw that he *couldn't* live there, and in fact nobody could, because I could now see that the whole building was crumbling in the back, that the whole roof was gone, and that one of the sides had fallen down almost to the ground! I turned around to my father and said, "But it's all wrecked!"

"That's right," my father said, not seeming at all surprised. "That's what it is: a wreck. Or, more properly, a ruin. A very respectable one, too. It's a kind of national shrine. It's Jimmy's, but he has to behave himself around it."

I couldn't see what there could be to behave about around something that was so old and broken down; I said accusingly, "You said it was a castle!"

"It is," my father said. "Or was. It's been one, or part of one, for six hundred years. It's a fairly typical example of the—" Then he stopped and didn't say anything for a minute; he almost seemed to be laughing. "I apologize," he said finally. "I should have realized that this wasn't quite the kind of castle you had in mind. You see, you've been brought up on all the right books: you know what a real spit-'n'-polish castle is supposed to look like. The Irish didn't have your advantages. They *didn't* know. So most of the castles they built—with a few exceptions—were pretty much like this one. Small, you know, and by your standards fairly dowdy, but still they did the job. So I guess they just kept on building them that way, and I'm afraid we're stuck with them. Or at any rate, Jimmy is."

I could hardly take my eyes off the castle, it looked so collapsing and awful; I still couldn't believe that anything like this was really a castle. And then I thought again of what else had bothered me, and I said, "But I thought you said Uncle Jimmy lived here."

"He does," my father said. "They all do. For the time being, anyway. Or until Jimmy gets tired of it. But obviously they don't live right *in* the castle. The castle's supposedly the great attraction, and they call the place by the castle's name, but they live in the house. Over there."

He pointed off to the right, and for the first time—because up to then I had been looking only at the castle—I saw a big whitewashed spick-and-span house not very far away, with long windows reaching all the way down to a neat green lawn, and beds of yellow flowers just outside the windows. There was a big circular driveway going up past the house, and a man was standing in the middle of it, waving. Three boys about my size were standing next to him, just looking, and not waving. And this was how I first saw my Uncle Jimmy and his family together in Ireland.

We drove up right away, and I didn't even bother to look back again at the castle. My Uncle Jimmy started to walk toward our car, waving us to a stop. When we did, my father got out and my Uncle Jimmy ran over to him and they shook hands. My

Uncle Jimmy started to talk very fast, and I heard him say, "I would have gone over as soon as I heard. But they didn't get in touch with me in time; I heard too late. So then, what was the point of going? To cheer you up? Foolish, hah? I never cheered anybody up in my life. Especially you."

"That's all right, Jimmy," my father said.

"How are you?" my Uncle Jimmy said. "You look great. Look at me. This climate is driving me nuts. I have chilblains and gooseflesh every day until noon. My teeth are going and last month I spit up blood. I'm an old man thanks to Ireland. Uncle Dan died at eighty-three and when he'd been dead a week he looked better than I do now. Hello!"

This was said to me; I got out of the car and went over to him and said, "Hello, Uncle Jimmy."

"How do you think I look?" he said. "As good as your father? Come clean: who looks better, your father or me?"

I didn't know what to say, because I didn't expect to be asked any question like this. Especially since it was such a funny question, for my father, who was so tall and straight and had lots of black hair, was a very good-looking man, and while I had forgotten how my Uncle Jimmy really looked, I saw now that he was quite homely. He was much shorter than my father, and you could see the skin through his thin, slicked-down yellowy hair. He had a small face with round cheeks and a small sharp curved nose, and when I saw this now I suddenly remembered that once, years ago, when he had come to our house and was sitting at the dinner table talking, I kept watching him and playing a game with myself, trying to decide what he looked like most. The answer turned out to be a canary. A kind of fierce canary, with his little beaky nose always shooting out at you as if he might be ready to poke you to pieces with it. He wore glasses with metal rims that somehow made him look quite old, even though he was only two years older than my father, and even though his skin was so pink and white it was almost like a baby's.

"Come on!" he said, shooting his nose out at me now. "Let's have it: who's the better looker? Hah? No bull, now! If there's one thing I hate, it's bull!"

I could see that the three boys—my cousins, that I hadn't even said a word to yet—were grinning, as if some sort of big joke were being played. I looked at my father for help, still not knowing what to say, and he said to my Uncle Jimmy, "You ought to make a chest protector and shin guards standard equipment for all your guests. How about taking it easy for a few minutes? Or at least until he gets used to the climate. Or until we both do."

"Listen," my Uncle Jimmy said, "I don't have to pull any punches with this kiddo. He can take it. I knew that the first time I saw him. I took one look at him the day he was born and I said, 'Whatever you do, don't throw this one back. This one's a winner!' And he is. Just like my three here." And he turned to glare at the boys standing beside him. "What's the matter with you?" he said. "Can't you talk? How do you like that: three dummies! In a country where every feeble-minded little bum can get up on his two hind legs and spout poems, all these three can do is clam up! A swell ad for America you are! Come on, snap out of it! Say hello to your cousin, show him around. Give him some real Irish hospitality: a glass of milk, a piece of bacon. Spare no expense. Do you want him to think we're a bunch of cheapskates? Hah?"

My father had never yelled at me in my life, and I had never heard anybody talk to his own boys like this. And even though part of what he said sounded almost like a joke, he said it so loudly and so ferociously that I was sure that at any minute he would go over and grab each boy and begin to punish him for not saying hello to me. But instead he just turned his back on all of us and started talking to my father as though the three boys and myself had suddenly disappeared. My father winked at me, so that I knew everything was all right, and then the three boys came over to me, still grinning, and not seeming at all upset or frightened by what their father had been shouting at them in his powerful voice. The biggest one—I knew that he was James—said to me, "He was just kidding, you know. He does that all the time."

"Well, not all the time," the middle boy said. He was Phil, and as soon as he spoke I remembered a rhyme my mother had made up for me when I was about seven and my Uncle Jimmy was coming to our house with the three boys I hardly knew at all:

There's James and Charles, and then there's Phil
Who's in between the two.
And James is nine, and Charles is six,
And Phil's as old as you.

I remembered that she also said that Phil and I had even been born in the same week, so that now, like me, he was almost twelve, and James was nearly fourteen. James had gotten quite tall since the last time I had seen him, and now had a different, deep voice, almost like a man's; he had dark brown hair which he combed very neatly, and he wore gray flannel pants and a blue coat with bright brass buttons. I thought he looked very elegant. Of all the boys he had changed the most, while Phil didn't seem to have changed at all. He was still a little fatter than me, but just about my size, with red hair and a snub nose and large dark blue eyes; he always looked as if he might start laughing at any second. As for Charles, who was always the smallest, he now seemed even smaller than the last time I had seen him, and I wondered if he had grown at all. He was going on eleven, but he was so much littler than the rest of us that he seemed almost babyish. Also, he was now wearing glasses, so that while in a way he still looked like Phil—with his red hair and blue eyes—he now looked a little bit like my Uncle Jimmy. He had stopped grinning and was now staring at me in a rather solemn way, still not saying anything.

"Sometimes," Phil said, still talking about his father as we walked away, "sometimes when he's not kidding you ought to hear him yell."

He said this as though he were very proud of the way his father could yell. James nodded and said, "Yes, but today he was only kidding. You can always tell." He said to me, "Would you like to go into the house, or would you like to see the castle first?"

"I don't care," I said.

"We'd better go to the castle, then," James said. "Actually, it's not very interesting, but Pa always likes people to look at it right away."

So we went over to the castle and climbed in through a hole in one of the crumbling walls, and it didn't look a bit better from the inside. It was all shadows, and moss was on the stones, and the ground was wet, and even though we were still out of doors—because there was no roof and the walls were falling down—it seemed much colder here.

"Actually," James said, "it's over five hundred years old. It was built before Columbus discovered America, so you can see that it's very historic. And of course piles of people were killed here. Actually most of the nobles who owned it were horribly destroyed."

Phil said, "We sometimes play that there's a curse that goes with the castle. We made up a good curse once. It goes that the youngest member of any family living on the castle grounds will be stolen from his bed in the dark of the night by wild beasts who will eat him without making a sound."

Charles spoke for the first time; he said, "Nobody's ascared of that. Anyway, there aren't any wild beasts in Ireland. I looked it up in a book."

"They probably forgot about the foxes," Phil said. "We've seen lots of foxes, remember? Sometimes quite big ones. I saw a huge one looking in the window the other night. With red eyes. And foam on his mouth."

"Nobody's ascared," Charles said again, very quickly.

"Well, let's go," James said. "There's no fun here. Actually we hardly ever come out here anyways. The house is much better. Unless you smoke, of course. Do you smoke much?"

I had never smoked at all. I had never even thought about smoking, but I didn't want to say this to James now, so I said, "Not too much."

"James smokes," Charles said. "He smokes like mad."

"Not any more," James said. "I *used* to. Actually I used to come out here by myself and sometimes the air would be blue with smoke. But now I hardly smoke at all."

"Pa caught him," Phil said to me, "and walloped him good."

"That's only partly it," James said. "Actually, the real reason was that it was getting dangerous. I was becoming a slave to it. So I gave it up. Or I practically did. Actually I wouldn't recommend smoking to anyone who didn't have tremendous will power."

I wasn't sure whether I had tremendous will power or not, but I thought I probably didn't. I also thought that James probably did. He was the most grown-up boy of around my own age I had ever met, and I could hardly believe that my Uncle Jimmy had really walloped him.

"James says 'actually' quite a lot," Phil says. "That's because Mr. Clendennin used to say it all the time. He was our tutor until Pa caught him reading his mail."

"He was quite a nice man," James explained to me, "but he was very poor, and so he thought if he read Pa's mail he'd find out how to be rich. But he didn't have time before Pa caught him. Actually it was too bad, because he was the best tutor we ever had. He had a fantastic vocabulary. He told me once about a secret test they conducted and found out that he had one of the ten most fantastic vocabularies in the world."

"In all languages?" Phil said. "Or just English?"

"He didn't say," James said. "But I imagine it was all languages."

"I didn't like him much," Charles said. "He was a show-off." He looked at me and said, "Would you like to see me stand on my hands?"

"No, he wouldn't," James said. "No one wants to see you stand on your hands. You're always doing that silly trick and half the time your glasses fall off and get smashed. Then we catch heck for letting you do it. Anyway, there isn't time because we're all going in the house now. Ma's awake and she'll want to see Jackie."

And suddenly I realized that this was the first time since I had come to my Uncle Jimmy's that anybody had said my name, and somehow I felt good about this, and I felt good, too, that James had been the one who had said it.

We ran back across the lawn to the house, passing on the way a couple of men who were mowing the lawn and weeding the flower-beds. Out in back I saw horses, and James said that everybody rode a lot here and that maybe we would go riding ourselves later if there was time. Then we went into the house, which inside seemed to be all white stone and very light with all the windows open wide. The floors were of stone, also, with not many rugs, and as we came in a maid, all dressed in white and with a funny kind of white cap like a nightcap, was polishing the front hall floor. About halfway along the righthand wall I saw a small shrine to the Blessed Virgin; it was set back into the wall and had a little lamp burning in front of it.

"We have our own private chapel," James said. "We have special permission. We all go to Mass there on Sundays, and Ma goes every day. She's exceptionally devout, you know."

But more than the shrine, what caught my eye was the sight of our bags—my father's and mine—lying on the hall floor at the bottom of a staircase. Someone had brought them in from the car, and what was so strange was not the bags themselves, but the fact that right next to them stood a dog which looked exactly like the dog that had been next to all the luggage in the hotel lobby in Dublin! For just a moment I thought that maybe little Lord Ivermorris might have come down to see my Uncle Jimmy too, but then I realized that it was just a coincidence, and that of course it was a different dog, but of the same breed. As we passed by it I said to James, "I see you've got a wolfhound."

"Yes," he said. "His name is Barney." And he looked at me in a different way as he said this, as if he were surprised that I knew about wolfhounds, and this gave me a good feeling, too.

We went into a long living room, which turned out to be the room with the tall windows going all the way down to the ground. It was a room I liked right away, with no crowding and plenty of space, but still lots of light-colored comfortable chairs and couches that looked as though you could sit in them or push them around any way you wanted to. There was a very old blue cloth with faded gold all through it hanging on the main wall—I knew this was a tapestry. At one end of the room was a piano; at the other end was a fireplace in which, even though the day was so warm, a big fire was going. Over the fireplace was a painting of a man in a queer kind of uniform with a cocked hat; when I got closer to it I saw that it was a painting of my Uncle Jimmy—as what, I didn't know. Right under this painting, and in front of the fire, was my Aunt Mary.

"Dear Jackie," she said, coming over to me and bending down to give me a kiss on the cheek. "We're so glad to have you here!"

She had a very nice voice, which was low and almost sounded as if she were singing. We looked at each other, and if I hadn't been expecting to see her, or if we hadn't been here in her house, I don't think I would have remembered her at all. She was tall and not very good-looking, with a long smooth quiet face and a rather big mouth. She had light red hair and blue eyes, like Phil and Charles, and I saw that on both her hands she wore big rings. She asked us all to sit down, and just as we were doing this a maid came into the room carrying a large tray which she put down on the table in front of us, and it was now that I saw that my Uncle Jimmy had really been joking when he talked about giving me a glass of milk and a piece of bacon, because here on the tray were plates of ham sandwiches and chicken sandwiches and cookies and little cakes as well as pitchers of milk and a pot of tea.

"I know the boys are always hungry," my Aunt Mary said to me, "and I know you must be simply famished after such a long drive.

So why don't we eat while we talk? I think we might manage that, don't you?"

She smiled as she said this: a kind of large, soft smile which somehow went with her voice. With the plates of food before me I suddenly realized that I hadn't really eaten much all day, and so I began to eat now very hungrily, and I was glad to see that the others did, too. The boys did, that is; my Aunt Mary didn't eat anything, taking only a cup of tea, and I noticed that while Charles and Phil and I drank glasses of milk, James was allowed to drink tea, too. As we ate, we talked—or at least my Aunt Mary did. She talked mostly to me, telling me how she and my Uncle Jimmy and all the family were very pleased that I had come here with my father, and how they all hoped I would like it here. Then she talked about the house and the castle and when they were built and what had happened to them, and after this she talked about what she and Uncle Jimmy and the boys did here every day, and what they planned to do now that I was here. The three boys said a few words every now and then, but mostly they just ate and listened, and so did I. It was all interesting enough for a while, but then, what with the eating, and also because there was something about her low voice as it kept talking that made me feel a little sleepy, I must not have paid attention all the way, for suddenly there was a silence and just as I was lifting my glass of milk again I saw that they were all looking at me, and I knew that my Aunt Mary had probably said something to me that I should have answered. I was embarrassed; I blurted out, "Excuse me: what?"

It was a clumsy thing to say, and impolite, too, and I knew this as soon as I said it, but my Aunt Mary just smiled another soft smile and said, "Poor Jackie. Here we are, talking away about ourselves, and he's so sleepy from his long day that he can barely sit up straight."

"No, I'm fine," I said, trying to wake up. "It's very interesting. I'm really not sleepy at all."

My Aunt Mary smiled again, and then I saw her give a little

nod to the three boys. They stood up and looked as though they were ready to leave, but when I started to get up too she put out one hand and motioned me back into my chair.

"Go along, boys," she said. "Jackie will be with you in just a minute, and then you can show him where his room is. I want to have a few words with him alone."

The boys went out, and my Aunt Mary and I were left sitting alone in front of the fireplace. The fire was still going, and even though the windows were open I was beginning to feel uncomfortably hot—maybe it was the heat as well as the food and the talk that had made me so sleepy. But my Aunt Mary didn't seem to mind this heat at all. She sat looking at me, her hands just touching each other in her lap, her rings catching the light from the fire. Her big smooth face was very still, not moving at all, and as she got ready for her few words with me and I kept looking at her I had the funny feeling that in a way it was really like looking at some painting.

"Poor Jackie," she said again. "I simply wanted to tell you that all of us are so terribly sorry at what happened to your mother and your little brother."

Since my mother and Tom had died a lot of people had said this to me, and I knew they meant it and that they were really sorry, but whenever they said it I always wished they hadn't. Because it never really made anything better, and I could never think of what to say back. So usually I just thanked them, which is what I did with my Aunt Mary now.

"I only wish I had known your mother better," she said. "You see, your Uncle Jimmy has always moved around so much because of his business that we've never settled anywhere for very long, and so I've never had a chance to know the other members of the family at all well. And I would have liked so much to know your mother really well, because I always thought of her as someone very rare and special. All that marvelous lovely gaiety, and then of course she was so beautiful—I'm sure I envied her. I think almost any woman would have envied her very much."

And her big and not very good-looking face changed just a bit now and seemed to me to look a little sad. I just sat still, not really wanting to look at her but not feeling that I could look away. I wished that she would not talk about my mother much more.

"I know how much you must miss her," she said. "And I know how queer and cruel it must seem to you that all this could have happened to someone as sweet as your mother, and as innocent and as helpless as your brother. But this is a mystery, Jackie. This is one of the great mysteries to which none of us, no matter how smart, knows the answer. One day we'll all know the answer to that mystery, but not now. And not here. We'll know in Our Blessed Lord's good time. Whenever He chooses to tell us. And not until then. Meanwhile, we must just go along, not understanding it, and trusting in God's goodness and mercy and justice. It's very hard sometimes. Very very hard. But this is what we must do. And we must never, never, not even for a minute, be tempted to blame God for what happened. That would be very wrong. You understand that, don't you?"

She still looked sad, but very serious now, and I nodded, feeling sad myself—I couldn't help it, because just the solemn way she talked about my mother made me feel sad—but also puzzled, because I didn't at all understand why she was talking to me about mysteries and about blaming God. I had never thought about blaming God. Why should I?

She nodded back at me as if she were satisfied, and then she stood up. I stood up too, wondering if I could go now. She stepped over toward me and stood in front of me with a funny kind of almost wondering expression on her face, as if she weren't quite sure what she was going to do next, and then all of a sudden she reached out and took me in her arms and pulled me to her, holding me very tight. At first I started to pull back, not wanting her to hold me at all, but then I heard her make a little sound, as if she were crying, and all at once I put my arms out and around her, just the way I used to around my mother, and I wanted her to hold me and I held her just as tight as she was holding me. I cried a little, too, and for some reason, standing here with my Aunt Mary whom I hardly even knew, it seemed all right to do this now and I didn't even try to stop myself.

In a few minutes this was over. My Aunt Mary moved back, touching the corners of her eyes with a small white handkerchief, and now that all the crying and holding was done I felt embarrassed again and wondered what she would say. But her face was smooth and quiet again, just the way it was when I came into the room, and she said in her low voice, "Well, Jackie, I think you can join the boys now. I know they're expecting you."

"Yes, Aunt Mary," I said.

"We love having you here," she said. "All of us. And we hope you're going to be with us for a good long stay."

I thanked her again and said that I was glad to be here too, but that I didn't know how long I could stay because my father and I still had to travel in our car all around the country and see all the different sights of Ireland.

"I'm sure you'll enjoy that," she said. "Still, some of the most beautiful sights are very near here. This is said to be the loveliest part of Ireland." She walked with me to the door of the room, and just as I left she said, "And people do change their plans, you know. Perhaps we can persuade your father to change his."

"Maybe," I said politely, but I was sure she couldn't, because I knew that my father would rather be traveling all over the country with me instead of staying here with my Uncle Jimmy, whom he never really wanted too much to see.

And yet my Aunt Mary turned out to be right: my father did change his plans, and our tour of Ireland ended right here at the castle. My father never at any time told me that we weren't going on; we simply didn't go. And he never really told me why, although one day, after we had been here about a week, he stopped me as I was running through the front hall, chasing after James and Phil and Charles. We were all on our way out back to go riding; my father said to me, "Hold up a minute; I won't keep you. You're having a good time?"

"Swell!" I said. I was out of breath from running.

"And the boys: you like them?"

"They're really great!" I said. I saw them leave the house by the back door; I said to my father hastily, "We're going riding now!"

He just nodded and let me go and he never said anything more about it. So we just stayed on, and even though I had been looking forward to our trip, I now found I didn't miss it at all. I was too busy. For the first time since we had come to Ireland—in fact, for the first time since my mother and Tom had died—I was mostly with boys around my own age, and we played together all day long.

What we did, or how we played, depended on the weather. It often rained here, just as it had in Dublin, and when it did we usually stayed indoors, spending most of our time in a big room where the grown-ups almost never went, and which James called the game room. Here we had a table for pingpong and one for pool, and we also played games like darts and Parcheesi, and punched a big leather punching bag. When we got tired of this, if it was still raining we could sometimes get Teddy, my Uncle Jimmy's chauffeur, to take us for a ride in the big car, and then we would drive through the pouring rain out to the ocean to watch the great black clouds come sweeping in at us from the sea while the surf smashed away at the cliffs underneath us. Once we were there in a big storm and it was wild and even frightening, with the ocean just as black as the clouds and the rain banging down on the car like hail and the wind screaming in to flatten out the yellow gorse and the few little white houses with their straw roofs looking gray and lonely and lost in the soaked dark green fields.

Up on the side of one of the hills we always passed was a queer group of small stone buildings called the beehive huts. Each one was only a few feet high, and it really was shaped like a beehive.

We often stopped and crawled into them: they were old and dark and cold and not big enough for me to stand up in; it was hard to believe that hundreds of years ago they had been lived in by grown men.

"Actually it's all a very deep mystery," James said. "Nobody knows for sure who built them. Most people say they were built by the monks, don't they, Teddy?"

Teddy nodded slowly, and after a moment said, "I t'ink dere was midget monks in dose days."

Teddy was an Irishman with a long sad face who had not been working for my Uncle Jimmy very long. I don't think he liked his job much. At least he never seemed very happy, and he talked mostly to himself. My Uncle Jimmy called him Sad Sam and used to scream at him for his bad driving. He got lots of flat tires and twice he hit things; finally, toward the end of the summer, my Uncle Jimmy fired him and Teddy left silently, not saying goodbye to anyone. My Aunt Mary said that in a way it was a shame, because he had a family of ten children, but my Uncle Jimmy told her not to worry, because now Teddy could probably go into the hardware business.

"Why not?" he yelled. "While he was driving for me that chump must have picked up every nail in Ireland!"

But all this happened later, and meantime Teddy drove us around on rainy days, and we all had a good time. Not as good as when it didn't rain, however, because in clear weather we went out right after breakfast and spent all day in the fields or the woods near the castle, playing ball or follow-the-leader, or building treehouses—I showed them all how to do this, the way Arthur had showed me—or going swimming or exploring or riding. I liked the riding best of all. The horses we had here were far different from the pony I had ridden at home, and at first I was a little afraid, but in no time at all I got used to a big, swift, gentle horse named Boy, and we would all ride off single file to a wide meadow and then, lining up, we would all race across it, with James usually winning, and either Phil or myself in second place, and Charles behind all of us. But not too far behind: he rode the smallest horse, and two or three times he fell off, but he always got right on again and he never seemed hurt and he never complained. And what I remember best of all those horseback rides is riding along and turning to look back over my shoulder and seeing Charles with one foot in a stirrup, scrambling up fiercely into the saddle while his little white horse stood waiting patiently, probably not at all expecting the excited kicks that came in a second as Charles, all scrunched down in the saddle, his small body bucking back and forth and the sun glinting brightly off his glasses—which somehow never seemed to be broken in these falls—tried frantically to catch up with the rest of us.

That was the way we spent the summer. It was a good way, but later, when I thought back on it, I realized that it must have been a strange way too, because Ireland made no difference to us. I mean the fact that we were *in* Ireland, because what we did there was not a bit different from what we would have done at home. We didn't play any Irish games, and we didn't play with any Irish boys—we didn't even meet any. They were around, we knew that, because sometimes we saw them watching us as we rode or swam or played ball, but we never said more than hello to them, and none of them ever joined us in our games. I don't know whether they ever wanted to or not, and maybe they didn't, but as things turned out they were never asked. Once, I remember, I thought it would be good if we could have a regular ball game, with a full team of players on each side, so I suggested that we could ask them, but James said no. He said that they didn't know the game, that we would only have to teach them, and that anyway it was more fun the way we were. Phil and Charles agreed with him at once. I noticed that they almost always agreed on something like this. Among themselves they argued as much as anybody, but this was all in the family; whenever anything outside the family came up they were all very loyal to each other and always stuck together.

So we played only by ourselves while we were here, and I didn't mind at all, because I had a marvelous time. I got to like all three of my cousins very much, and I think that they liked me. Often as we played we had arguments and fights—sometimes quite big ones—and once I had a real fistfight with Phil about something, in which he got a cut lip and I got a black eye. But this fight and all the rest were over very quickly, we became friends again, and we went on liking each other and having lots of fun together.

I liked each one of them in a different way. I still admired James more than any boy I had ever met, not only because he looked so fine and could talk the way he did and always knew what to do whenever the grown-ups were around, but also because even when he was bossing the rest of us around he was somehow nice about it, and even when he was lecturing me about something he thought I ought to know he always seemed glad that I was here. I felt that if I ever got into any trouble I didn't want to tell my father about—although what kind of trouble that could be I didn't know—I could go to James and he would help me. And it was just the other way around with Charles. As I got to know him I began to realize that he looked up to me almost as much as I looked up to James. He was always following me around, asking me questions, and asking them in a kind of little-boy way, so that when I answered him—if I could, which wasn't very often—he would just look serious and nod and then he would ask me another question which usually didn't have any connection at all with the one I had just answered. One day when he had been asking me a lot of these—James and Phil had gone down by the river, and the two of us were playing catch—he said suddenly, "Do you think I'm a pest?"

Sometimes I did think he was one, but I said, "No, Charles. You're not a pest."

"I don't think I am either," he said. "James says I'm not yet, but I'm going to be one if I don't watch out. So I keep on asking people, just to find out."

"Well," I said, "you're not one yet. Throw the ball here, Charles."

He threw it and said, "Are you ever going to get married?"

"I don't know," I said. "I might. Some day. When I get out of college or something."

"But you don't *have* to get married, do you? I mean, if you don't want to?"

"No, nobody makes you. There's millions of people that don't. But most people do."

"I might not," he said. "I might be a priest, maybe. Priests can't get married ever, can they?"

"No. Come on, Charles, throw it."

He threw it again and said, "Why not?"

"Because they promise they won't."

"What happens if they break their promise?"

"Then they stop being priests, I think."

He nodded his head in that slow satisfied way, and then he said suddenly, "You want to see how long I can hold my breath . . . ?"

Lots of talks with Charles ended like this. He spent a lot of time worrying about what he was going to be when he grew up, or about whether he was going to stay small, or about whether he would always have to wear glasses. Phil and James used to tease him sometimes, and so did I; you couldn't help it. When you teased him enough he got mad, but he never stayed mad very long, and pretty soon he was asking some more questions. I usually liked him very much, and I thought that probably some day I might be able to help him, just as James might be able to help me.

But of all the boys I liked Phil the best. He became my special friend almost from the start, and I was with him more than with the others. This was mainly because I shared his room with him—it was where the three boys had taken me right after my talk with my Aunt Mary on that first day. I found out later that Phil had the biggest room of all the boys; James explained to me that when they went to a new house they always tossed up for rooms, and that Phil had won here. It was a nice room on a corner of the second floor, with so many windows that if the sun came out, it could be sunny all day long. There were two beds with thick quilts and great soft mattresses you could sink down into, and when I first moved in—in late spring, when the weather could turn quite cold at night—we always had a fire in the fireplace when we came up after supper, and in each bed there was always a long heavy stone jar full of hot water, around which our pajamas had been wrapped. And it was always good to undress very quickly and jump into the warm pajamas and then into bed, huddling next to the heavy jugs which were always so nice and hot at night, and were always ice-cold if they were still in your bed by morning.

This room was full of Phil's books and toys and interesting things that he had made himself. One of these was a radio, a crystal set to which we listened at night through big earphones. I never heard anything but a kind of static, and Phil said we were really wasting our time listening, because there were no radio stations around here anyway. But we listened, hoping that something might happen, and later, after we were supposed to be asleep, we drew all the curtains so that no one could see the light, and then we turned the stereopticon on and looked at pictures of the Alps and Brazilian jungles and palaces in India. Or else we just talked, lying in bed in the dark, except sometimes in the summer when the days got to be very long and it was still light outside until late at night. Then we might get up and crouch down by the open windows and look out over the sill into the long-fading day, and see my father and my Uncle Jimmy and my Aunt Mary sitting out on the lawn underneath our windows, where they often liked to sit and talk until it got too dark. And we would stay there at the windows, watching, and breathing in the deep, different smells of night and the slow smoke from my father's cigar coming up through everything, and listening, as what they were saying would come up too, but sometimes loud and sometimes soft and sometimes hardly at all, so that we never really heard what they were talking about.

But this was only on some nights, and mostly we just talked by ourselves, lying in bed and getting ready to go to sleep. Phil liked to talk then, and he talked mainly about his family—James and Charles and my Aunt Mary and my Uncle Jimmy—and the way they lived and traveled around, and how much fun they had together. It was all very different from the way we lived—or had lived—and I supposed this was because my Uncle Jimmy had so much money, but some of it didn't sound like so much fun to me, and I was surprised to find out that Phil had never done some things that I thought everyone did. For example, he had never been to school.

"To a regular school, that is," he said. "We haven't any of us ever been. On account of traveling around so much, I guess. That's why we've always had tutors. We'd have one now only he just got fired before you came and Pa couldn't find anybody else right away."

I remembered hearing about Mr. Clendennin, who had wanted to get rich by reading my Uncle Jimmy's mail. "Have you had lots of tutors?" I said.

"Piles," he said. "Mostly they don't stay too long because Pa gets mad at them when they do something wrong. But James says we're very well educated, just the same. And anyway, when we go back home in the fall Pa says we're going to have to start in school, so I guess Mr. Clendennin was the last one we'll ever have. I thought maybe he was going to come back to America with us, but then Pa caught him with the letters." Suddenly his voice changed and he said very loudly, "Don't try to con me, Clendennin! You're standing right next to the jar and you've got jam all over your dukes! For two bits I'd kick your can all the way to Japan and back! Then I'd stash you away in the hoosegow for thirty years! Come on! Amscray!"

And although it was very late, and we were supposed to be asleep long ago, I couldn't help laughing out loud because it was such a perfect imitation of my Uncle Jimmy: his voice, and the kind of words he used, and even the way he looked. Phil was very funny and could do imitations of lots of people, but this one was his best. The other boys were always asking him to do it and sometimes, when he felt like it, he would. One rainy afternoon when we were in the game room, not doing anything special, Phil started doing his imitations, and just as he got to his father, who should walk into the room but my Uncle Jimmy himself! He came in through the back door, behind Phil, so that Phil didn't know he was there, and it was too late to warn him because by now he was already doing one of my Uncle Jimmy's speeches, with my Uncle Jimmy just standing there, not very far away, looking at him. Phil was very funny, but I didn't laugh and neither did anybody else; I was sure that at any second my Uncle Jimmy would let out a bellow and run across the room and grab Phil and wallop him right in front of all of us. But instead of that all he did was laugh. He just kept looking and laughing, and then we all did too, with my Uncle Jimmy laughing harder than any of us. He seemed enormously pleased, and even gave Phil a dollar.

"Go buy yourself a yacht," he said.

I couldn't understand my Uncle Jimmy at all, and I was always a little afraid of him, right up until the time we left. He was always nice enough to me, and never even yelled at me very much, but I could never tell when he was going to get mad at one of the boys or at one of the people that worked for him. Sometimes when he was mad he just hollered, but other times he did more than that—while I was there he walloped all the boys at least once, even James, for different things they had done. Usually he took them into his private office to do this, but once he walloped Phil in our room; he did it right in front of me and didn't even seem to notice I was there. Late one afternoon he came rushing in, his canary-bird face all red, and I could tell right away that this time he wasn't pretending to be mad, he really meant it. Barney, the wolfhound, who slept with Phil and me most nights, slid under one of the beds as soon as my Uncle Jimmy burst in, and Phil jumped up, because he knew right away what was coming. This time my Uncle Jimmy didn't yell at all. He just ran over to Phil, grabbed him, plunked down into a chair and pulled Phil across his knees and whacked him hard about ten times with a broad brown strap he was carrying. It must have hurt very much, because Phil tried not to cry, but I could see he was crying a little. Then the funny thing was that as soon as this was over my Uncle Jimmy didn't seem to be mad any more, and talked in a calm and even friendly voice to Phil, just as if he hadn't been walloping the daylights out of him a second ago.

"Now you know why you got it," he said. "No baloney or fake excuses: right?"

Phil nodded slowly, not saying anything; he was rubbing where he had been whacked. Earlier that afternoon, when Teddy the chauffeur wasn't around, Phil had sneaked into the big car and turned the key and somehow started it. The car had jumped forward and banged into the corner of the garage and if it wasn't for that it would have kept on going, because Phil didn't know how to stop it. But just then Teddy came back and turned everything off, and I guess he must have told my Uncle Jimmy about it.

"One," my Uncle Jimmy said to Phil now, "you made a dope of yourself this afternoon, and you know how I hate dopes! Two, you did what I told you not to do. You could have been hurt, you could have been killed. I'll always wallop you for that, and you know I will. So smarten up! Get wise to yourself! You're not one of these hay-shaking boobs that slinks around here with a clover hanging out of his mouth! You've got a head on your shoulders. A kiddo with all the brains and the moxie that you've got, I shouldn't have to say a word to you. Let alone lay a finger on you. So don't do it again. Now: you want to shoot a game of pool?"

And Phil nodded again, and he went out of the room with his father kind of privately, just as if everything had been settled between the two of them and I hadn't even been there. Later Phil talked about this to me, and while of course he wasn't glad he got the walloping, he wasn't mad either at his father for giving it to him. He talked about his father in the same admiring way he always did, in the same way all the boys always did. I never heard any of them say a single word against their father. They never did against their mother, either, but they talked about her in a quieter way, and even though you could see they loved her, you could see too that it was my Uncle Jimmy they all looked up to in this special kind of almost worshipping way.

"Because actually," James said to me once, "he always makes you feel he's really very proud of you. Even when he's just whacked you hard."

And I remember that Phil could hardly believe it when, that night, he asked me how often my father walloped me, and I told him never.

"Golly!" he said. "You better be careful, Jackie—you might grow up to be a . . . a *slob!*"

Because that was what my Uncle Jimmy was always yelling at them: that he wasn't going to have any of his family grow up to be slobs or weak sisters. I didn't see what walloping had to do with that; in fact I thought it probably didn't have much to do with it at all, because if it did I was sure my father would have walloped me at least a few times. But when I said this to Phil he didn't seem to think it made any difference, and he warned me again that I had better be careful.

We used to talk in bed at night about lots of things, though—not just wallopings—and when he told me about his family and what they did, I told him all about mine and what we did. Not so much about what we did now, of course, but more about what we used to do: about Ellen and Arthur, about the time the burglar broke into our house, about the exploring expeditions we made, about the beach we went to, about school and my friends there, about the parties my mother and father gave, about the plays we put on and my mother singing, and about the cabin and the lakes and the woods. And as I talked about these things I kept remembering my mother and Tom more and more, and I felt bad again, the way I always did, but this time I suddenly felt a little ashamed of myself, too. Because all at once, as I was telling Phil about Tom and about my mother, I realized that lately I had hardly thought of them at all. Compared, that is, to the way I used to. Not that I'd forgotten them or stopped missing them, but it just seemed that I hadn't been remembering them as much—I suppose because I was playing so much now, and having so much fun. And as soon as I realized this I stopped talking and for a minute I just lay there, blaming myself and feeling awful and promising I would remember them better from now on. While I was doing this Phil said out of the darkness, "Your mother and brother drowned, didn't they?"

It was the first time any of the boys had said anything to me about this. (I found out later from Phil that they all knew all about it, but that my Aunt Mary had told them not to mention it to me.) And nobody had ever asked me the question right out like this. So I just said, "Yes. They were in a canoe and it tipped over."

"Couldn't they swim?" he said.

"Of course they could swim," I said. "We all can swim. My mother was the best swimmer I ever saw. So we don't know what happened. Nobody ever found out. Maybe it was because the water was so freezing. . . ." And then I told him all about it: about my mother and Tom going away from the cabin on that warm March morning, about the shout, about my father and me running for the rowboat, about going out on the lake and circling around and around, about my father suddenly jumping overboard again and again while I was so frightened. I told him what happened later, too: about coming back to the cabin and driving fast into town with my father, and then coming back and waiting all by myself in the cabin while my father and the others searched, until finally my father came back with the priest Father LaPlante, and told me that they had found my mother and Tom. I had never even thought about telling all this to anyone before, but it seemed all right to tell it to Phil now, because he was my friend and I liked him a lot. And somehow telling it to him like this now didn't seem as bad as when I used to go over it all the time just by myself—I don't know why. Anyway, he listened to me right through without even making a sound, without hardly moving; when I finished he said, "Boy! That's really terrible! That's worse than anything that ever happened to me!"

But of course I knew this, because both his mother and my Uncle Jimmy were still alive, so how could anything as bad as this have ever happened to him?

Phil said that he remembered my mother from when he had last visited our house, a couple of summers ago, with my Uncle Jimmy. He remembered just what she looked like, and that James had said she was the prettiest lady he had ever seen; he remembered that one afternoon she had taken them out to the kitchen and given them glasses of ice-cold lemonade and dark brown cookies that tasted like burned sugar and that were filled with a good kind of jam; most of all he remembered the way she had acted toward my Uncle Jimmy. Because she never seemed to be at all frightened of him, and she was always teasing him in a way that nobody else ever dared to. Once, Phil said, he had seen her reach out and actually tap my Uncle Jimmy on the top of his head and call him Shortcake, and one night after supper, when someone had put a record on the victrola, he remembered that suddenly my mother had jumped up and grabbed my Uncle Jimmy by the hands and danced with him all around the living room, going faster and faster and laughing all the time, while my Uncle Jimmy, who always hated to dance, finally started to laugh and danced right along with her and had a marvelous time. And as I listened to him tell me the way he remembered my mother, it was as if I remembered all over again and in a fresh way just how beautiful she was and how she looked, and I could almost taste the jam-filled cookies —it was raspberry jam—that Phil was talking about, and I could see her tapping my Uncle Jimmy on his half-bald head in a gay laughing way and then dancing around the room with him—I could see it all just as if she were here and doing it now. It was the only time in talking to Phil about her that I felt like crying.

"Boy!" he said again. "She was great. I bet you miss her like anything!"

I said I did, that I missed her very much, and he said he would, too. Then, suddenly, I didn't feel like talking about this any more, so I was quiet, and so was Phil, and after a while we went to sleep. We didn't talk about Tom or my mother again while I was there, but somehow I was glad that we did talk this once.

One night, near the end of our stay in Ireland, a strange thing happened while we lay here in our beds. It was quite late, long after we had had our supper, which on this particular evening had been different for us because there were guests in the house. My Uncle Jimmy and my Aunt Mary didn't give anything like parties while I was there, and they never really invited guests very much, but every once in a while people would drop in to see them, sometimes staying for a couple of hours or for dinner, and sometimes—although not so often—staying in the house overnight. There were never any people from the neighborhood; I don't think I ever saw anybody who was Irish come to call. They were mostly people my Uncle Jimmy knew or had done business with, and while two or three of them were English, the rest of them were travelers from America, like ourselves.

But on this night the guests were special, because they were members of the family: my grandfather and my Aunt Gert. My grandfather was of course my father's father and my Uncle Jimmy's, and my Aunt Gert was their sister. I had almost forgotten my grandfather since the last time I had seen him—the way he looked, I mean—and I was surprised that he was not only so old but also so small. I don't think he was much bigger than me; he wore an old blue suit and a black tie and funny square-toed black shoes; in his vest pocket he had a large gold watch that he kept on taking out and looking at while other people were talking. They didn't seem to mind; at least they didn't seem to pay any attention to this but just kept on talking all the same. My grandfather didn't talk at all. He didn't say a single word all through dinner, but just kept looking around the table and at his watch, and a few times I saw him looking right at me with his old blue eyes that watered a lot and that were all red around the edges. Even when he had arrived at the house with my Aunt Gert and we all came in to say hello to him, he just shook our hands and bobbed his little head—the top of which was bald and bumpy and shiny, with big brown spots on it—and kind of moved his lips in a hello, as if he had said hello to so many people so many times before that he had got tired of saying it to anyone any more. Toward the end of supper, though, when he still hadn't said even a word, I began to wonder whether it was just because he might not feel like it, or whether it was that he really *couldn't*—I thought that when people got that old maybe they might lose their power to speak. But this turned out to be wrong, because suddenly my grandfather did say something. He had finished the last speck of food on his plate—I noticed that he had a huge appetite and ate everything—and he sat for a second looking straight in front of him; then he pushed his chair back from the table and slowly got up on his feet.

"Gas," he said. "It's all gas." His head was shaking a little, and his voice was dry and whispery, but astonishingly loud. "The whole wide world is nothing but gas."

I didn't know what this meant at all, and I looked at the other boys and they looked back at me. My Aunt Gert got up now and said, "Pa's tired and no wonder, God love him. It's been a long long day!"

My Aunt Gert was a great surprise to me. I had heard a lot about her but I had never seen her until tonight. She had never come to see us in our house, not because we didn't want her to, but because she lived out near San Francisco, where her husband was in some sort of business. He had died a couple of years ago, and since she didn't have any children she was now all by herself and traveled around a lot. Once a year or so she went to visit my grandfather, and when she did she usually went traveling with him, and I remember once hearing my father say something about this to my mother. He said it was a good thing.

"Greek meets Greek," he said.

Later I asked my father what this meant, but he told me not to worry about it, that it was just a way of saying that my Aunt Gert was another one in the family who was very interested in business matters. Somehow from what he said I had always had a picture of her as a kind of thin little woman with a narrow face and glasses who kept on shooting looks at you and asking you quick questions. Instead she turned out to be tall and very fat, with a round jolly face and lots of brown hair which she wore tied up in a bun at the back of her head. She had a huge necklace of pearls and wore a hat at the supper table, and while my grandfather didn't talk at all, she did just the opposite: she talked most of the time, telling us stories of where she had been and what she had done since her husband had died. Mostly, it seemed, she either went to different shrines in Europe or America, making pilgrimages and watching the sick people who hoped that miracles would make them well, or else she went to Paris or Rome and bought lots of clothes and jewelry for herself. She seemed to have a good time wherever she went, because she laughed a lot whatever she talked about, even the shrines.

"Crutches flung all over the place like toothpicks," she said. "God bless us, I don't know who they belonged to, but whoever they were they haven't got them now. I suppose they're all cured. Or else. Well, I went up to Saint Anne de Beaupré in Canada with Alice Leary. They wanted us to climb the steps on our knees and it's halfway up a mountain. God help us, I could no more do that than I could fly, but Alice, poor dear, big as she is, said she had to get to the top. She said she had a special favor to ask from Saint Anne. I don't know what it was, of course, and she wouldn't tell me, but I wouldn't be surprised if it wasn't about

Joe. He was mean as a panther, you know, since he came down with the bad heart, and poor Alice didn't know which way to turn. The worst of it was he told her he was going to put the money into government bonds and Chicago wheat. Well, I told her right then and there the man was going out of his head, nothing could be clearer than that, and she'd better do something about it. So she got this funny look on her face, you know, and up the mountain she went on her knees. All I could do was put two and two together and guess that she'd gone up to ask Saint Anne to speed poor Joe along. One way or the other."

"Lucky Joe," my father said, "to have someone praying for him like that."

"Joe Leary was a chowderhead who got lucky," my Uncle Jimmy said. "I knew him from the day he was born and he was always a chump. He belonged playing pinochle in Station Three every Tuesday night, shooting the breeze about Al Smith with a lot of hook-and-ladder boobs. Instead he got into the big leagues by an accident and he's been three and a half feet from the bughouse ever since."

"Well," my Aunt Gert said comfortably, "he's gone now, poor dear. And Alice has moved into the Plaza. Four lovely rooms overlooking the park." And she went on, telling more stories and laughing most of the time, but getting more serious when she started to talk about herself and how hard it was to be a widow with no husband to advise her any more, and with all kinds of people coming up to her with different schemes to get her money away from her. And as I listened to her I thought that it must really be hard for her with her husband dead like that, and I got so interested that even though none of us as a rule interrupted the talk when we had guests, I suddenly asked her if she had been cheated out of much money by these people. She stopped and looked at me as if she were surprised by this question, and then she laughed again, this time harder than before.

"No," she said. "No, dear, I haven't. And aren't you the good boy to be thinking of your Aunt Gert all alone in the world! But

God has been very good to me. He hasn't let any of them cheat me yet. Of course," she said, "they haven't really been very smart about it, either."

At this I saw my father look over at her in a way that made me think that for some reason he was going to laugh, but all he did was to say, "Good old Gert! And of course her partner, God."

My Aunt Gert just laughed again, and then everybody began to talk about different things, and pretty soon we—the boys, that is—left the table to go upstairs, because by now it was quite late. On our way up James told me that I shouldn't feel sorry about my Aunt Gert and her money, since he had once heard his father say that he pitied the man who ever got mixed up with her in a business deal, because he would come out of it all ground up like a plate of hamburg.

"Actually," James said, "I wouldn't be a bit surprised if she wasn't quite a financial wizard. Almost as big a one as Pa."

When Phil and I were in bed we talked for a while about my Aunt Gert, and Phil imitated her long looping laugh and kept on making up things to say like "God love you, I stubbed my toe!" or "God bless us, dear, is there anybody in the bathroom?" After this we talked about my grandfather, and Phil, who had seen him many more times than I had, told me that usually he was just the way he was tonight, not talking much, but every once in a while he would suddenly start in talking in a loud buzzing voice and he would keep right on talking, with no one—not even my Uncle Jimmy—daring to interrupt him at all. Because, said Phil, if he *was* interrupted, he would start to shout, and then the boys would be sent from the table because there would a lot of swearing and sometimes dirty talk as well.

"One time," Phil said, "they forgot to send us out while he was talking like that, and that night there was a friend of Ma's staying for supper. I forget what her name was, but she was the skinniest lady I ever saw. Anyway, she didn't know about Grampa, so when he stopped just for breath or something she began to talk and say what she thought. And you know what Grampa did? He just looked at her and yelled, 'I've let farts that weighed more than you!' Boy, you should have seen the way she looked! It was awful, but it was kind of funny too, and Charles started to laugh, and then I did too, I couldn't help it, and then she began to cry, and then we were all sent out of the room so we didn't hear any more. But that's what Grampa does sometimes. Things like that. James says he's really crazy but we can't say so on account of who he is."

I thought it was awful too, because I had never heard anyone say anything like that to anyone—I didn't dream they could. All the same, I would like to have seen it. But it made me think of my grandfather in a different way: for the rest of the time he was here, whenever I was in the same room with him and saw him looking at me with his watery eyes, I remembered what Phil had said about him being crazy, and I wondered what I would do if one day I were all alone with him in the house and all of a sudden he went crazy and started to scream and maybe run around with a knife in his hand, looking for me. Nothing like this ever happened, of course, and after a couple of days my grandfather went away with my Aunt Gert without saying any more than goodbye to me and—again—not really saying that.

But on this one night when we were talking about him, Phil told me a little bit more about him and things he had seen him do, and then he was quiet, and I knew that he had gone to sleep. I was tired, so after a few minutes of just thinking about my grandfather and my Aunt Gert, and looking up at the ceiling and out through the window at the black night sky, I must have fallen asleep too. How long I stayed asleep I don't know, but suddenly I was awake again, and what woke me was the sound of somebody talking. I looked over at Phil, but he was all bunched up in his bed, still sleeping. Then I heard a voice again, and then another voice, and this time I recognized them: one was my father's, the other was my Uncle Jimmy's. The funny thing was that they seemed to be right here in the room, but I could see for myself that there was no one here but Phil and me. I listened harder: even though I couldn't hear every word I could still get most of what they were saying quite plainly, and as I looked around, trying to see how this could be, I finally discovered that the sounds seemed to be coming from the fireplace! I got out of bed, went over, and listened: sure enough, here I could hear the words much louder and clearer, and then I knew that my father and my Uncle Jimmy were probably in the small room underneath ours—a kind of second office for my Uncle Jimmy which I had never seen used before—and that through some trick in the fireplace, or from something being left open downstairs, everything that was said in that room came shooting right up to us.

I didn't know what to do. I had never listened in on what my father was saying before, and I didn't think I should do so now. I went back to my bed, but either they were talking louder or I had got used to the voices, because now, even from here, I could hear every single word very distinctly. I didn't want to go downstairs and tell them; I thought of waking Phil up, but then I decided not to; I put my head under the blankets to block out the sound, but after a few seconds I came up again because I couldn't breathe very well. So in the end I listened, at first not really wanting to and feeling kind of guilty, but after a while, in spite of telling myself I didn't want to, I got really interested, because what they were talking about, among other things, was me.

". . . leave him with us," my Uncle Jimmy was saying. "Why not? Hah? The best thing in the world for him. Look, we're going home in a month, six weeks. I had some business in London, Paris—that's done. And I'm about fed up with these home-grown Micks: there's not a quarter in the crowd. So when we go let your kiddo come along with us. He gets along great with my bunch. They all like him and I do too. So does Mary. She's nuts about him. So what's the problem? What do you say? Try it out: what can you lose?"

"Nothing," my father said. "Except, of course, my boy. No thanks, Jimmy."

"Bunk," my Uncle Jimmy said. "What's that supposed to be:

dramatic? Lose your boy: how could you do that? What am I going to do: sell him to the gypsies? Talk sense, Buster. Use your squash. Here's a great kiddo, all of a sudden his mother's gone, so's his kid brother. Now, what's better for him: to be with a family with a woman to take care of him, with other kiddoes, horsing around the way he should, the way all kiddoes should? Or to be spooking around this way with you? Hah? Come clean: which one?"

"You're a busy man, Jimmy," my father said. "You lead a very complicated life, and now you want to lead mine too. No dice. I know what you're trying to do, and believe it or not I even appreciate it. But I don't want it. This is my business. And this is my boy. He's not up for grabs by Kinsella, Inc. What I don't need at this point is any of the famous family help. I'm doing just fine."

"Says who?" my Uncle Jimmy said. "Don't con me. This is Jimmy. I know how fine you're doing. You come to life about twenty seconds a day. The rest of the time you're flat on your tochus blowing smoke rings at the sky and feeling sorry for yourself because the world went all lobbo for you one day three months ago. All right all right, you got belted. But people that get belted snap out of it. They don't quit. They don't take the gaspipe. They keep on living, they come out punching. But what about you? Hah? You don't even put your dukes up! You droop around here like a one-man graveyard. You're doing fine: I guess so. Tell it to Sweeney, Buster, but don't hand me that bushwa!"

And out of all this loud talk, which was so unexpected and so strange and in some ways so alarming to me, what really seemed stranger to me than anything else was my Uncle Jimmy calling my father "Buster." Maybe it was a name he had always called him since they were boys together, but I had never heard him call him that before, and I couldn't even imagine anybody calling my father by a boy's name like that. And of course I couldn't imagine either that anyone would ever talk to him in the hard swift way that my Uncle Jimmy just had. In fact, when I heard my Uncle

Jimmy start in on this I thought at first he was only joking, the way he did sometimes with the boys, but then I saw that this wasn't his joking way at all, and when he finally finished I just lay there in bed, holding my breath and almost afraid to hear what would come next, because I was sure that now my father would get angry, and that he and my Uncle Jimmy might start shouting at each other, and then I wouldn't know what to do. But nothing like this happened. At first there was a silence, as if my father were making up his mind what to say, and then, when he did begin to talk, it was as though my Uncle Jimmy hadn't yelled at him at all.

"I suppose they'll do a biography of you some day, won't they?" he said, talking in a friendly voice. "What will they call it, I wonder? *Gaspipe on the Bushwa?* Or *Don't Con Me?* I used to wonder how a man who'd gone to so many schools—some of them pretty good ones—could come out talking like a second-rate act on the Gus Sun time. You do it on purpose, don't you? Why?"

My Uncle Jimmy laughed. "I'm supposed to bite at that, right?" he said. "The old swerve? Get Jimmy talking about himself and maybe he'll forget what he's after? Cut it out, Buster. I've had experts pull that stuff on me. If you really want to know, I talk this way because I like to talk this way and that's that. And it comes in handy sometimes. You'd be surprised how many of the smooth pedigreed jokers fall flat on their striped pants when they hear a little southpaw lingo. They're all out after the fast buck; they think they've got themselves a real live country boy they can peel like a grape. And by the time they find out they've made a little mistake, then it's too late! So never mind the way I talk. What we were talking about was you."

"Correction," my father said. "What *you* were talking about was me. Don't get the idea that that was a conversation. Come on, Jimmy, let's have a little peace. I'm only going to be here a few days more. I'll let you alone if you'll let me alone. What about it? Fair enough?"

"Don't be a sap," my Uncle Jimmy said. "What do I care whether you let me alone or not? Hah? Okay, so you've always got the needle ready. So what? People needle me all the time. I let them do it. Then one day I take a little look down the drain and there they are. Right down there at the bottom. And I'm not. But there's where you're going, Buster, whether you know it or not, unless you get on your horse and start moving. I've checked on you. I know just where you stand. You're up to your collarbone in your capital: you think I don't know that? You think I don't know about all those hotshot theater pals that gave you those big tips in the market? Don't fob me off with that everything's-roses malarky! Unless you wise up, one of these days all you'll be leaving that kiddo of yours will be three cheers and a deck of cards. Meantime, handing him over to us for a while would be the smartest thing you've done in ten years!"

"Forget it," my father said. "Just forget it."

"Baloney!" my Uncle Jimmy said. " 'Forget it'—what does that solve? People like you are always running around saying bughouse things like that: 'Forget it,' 'Everything's all right,' 'I'm just fine.' Kiss it and the pain will go away, hah? Applesauce! Okay, suppose I do forget it? Then what? What will you do? You'll bring your kiddo back home with you, right? *Then* what? Who brings him up? Who handles the show? You? By yourself? With that toolshed gangster Arthur? And that fat dame that looks like an old milkmaid? Is that it? The whole setup just the way it was before? Only with just one little difference: now there's no mother, no brother? And you think that's going to work out? In the same house where your kiddo lived all his life with them? Is that what's supposed to be good for him? Hah?"

I heard my father give a big sigh; he said, "Jimmy—"

"And you," my Uncle Jimmy said, not paying any attention. "What about you? Hah? How long do you think you'll last? I'm not even talking about your dough now, I'm talking about *you*. All by your lonesome in that big house every day? With no wife and no more fancy long trips to get you away? Just sticking around the house every day, getting a big charge out of watching that jujitsu champ mow the lawn while you wait for the kiddo to get home from school? Spending all your time in that deadhead burg they would have given back to the moths fifty years ago only the moths wouldn't take it! With those cold codfish Yankees that have to be warmed up before they can even be buried! And all those cornball Harps that keep moaning about what the APA's did to poor old Al in the last election, and about how John Jo Donovan could become Sewer Commissioner if only his brother the foot doctor would play Waltz-Me-Around-Again-Willie with fat Billy O'Brien, and about how Sister Mary Theresa of the Holy Angels gave the back of her hand to the bishop when he opened the new parish hall last Saint Cantaloupe's Day! I can hear it all now, right down to the last thick Mick syllable! And that's the way it's going to be with you, is it? Right there in the old home town, happy as Larry with that crowd of apple-knockers? Don't make me laugh! I'll give you two months before you go clean off your rocker!"

"There's only one word for this kind of talk," my father said. "Refreshing. I don't know, Jimmy, there's just something about you that makes me feel glad all over. I think it's probably the delicate way you have of muscling in on everything that's none of your business."

"That's supposed to make me feel crude, right?" my Uncle Jimmy said. "Vulgar? Ashamed of myself? Come on, come on! You talk about my own business—whose business do you think *this* is? You think you've got an exclusive here? Well, get that out of your squash right now. This is my business too. Why? Because it's *family* business, that's why. And with Pa soft as a Chinese slipper half the time, I'm the head of the family!"

"Ah well, then," my father said politely.

"Big laugh, hah?" my Uncle Jimmy said. "Well, it's no laugh to me. The family never meant anything to you. You always went your own sweet way and made a lot of fast cracks about the rest of us. The money-grubbers: Pa, Gert, me. Especially me. Okay. That never made any difference to me because it didn't matter. Talk's cheap. And you couldn't hurt me no matter what you said. The people I work with would think you were bats anyway. So I never gave a hoot. But Pa did. He used to get sore as a boil."

"Really?" my father said. "Pa did? That's strange: all I remember is this pleasant, even-tempered man who hardly ever raised his voice."

"Cut the clowning," my Uncle Jimmy said. "And he got sore not because you laughed at the dough he made, but because you laughed at it and then took it!"

"That's right," my father said. "I took it. Cheerfully and greedily. And if he'd given me ten times as much I would have taken it the same way. As a kind of reparations. War damages. A part payment in return for the warm and charming childhood I was given."

"Bushwa!" my Uncle Jimmy said. "What was there, something special about your childhood? Hah? You didn't have it a bit worse than the rest of us. He was a hard nut."

"He was all of that," my father said. "Do you remember old Father Coffey who used to be pastor of Saint Anne's? I saw him about a year ago. He was reminiscing about the old days, about the people in the parish, and of course about us—do you know how he referred to Pa? As 'a stern parent'! How's that for a euphemism? Incidentally, you're wrong if you think he was sore at me because I laughed at the money and then took it. He was sore because of what I did with it after I got it."

"Sure," my Uncle Jimmy said. "Why not? You blew it!"

"I spent it," my father said. "There's a difference. Although maybe not to you, and certainly not to him. Anyway, that's what really did the job. I spent the money. Or most of it. If I'd hung on to it and dug it and raked it and manured it and watched it grow nice and fat and tall—the way you and Gert did—I could have laughed like a hyena and he would have put up monuments to me. But I didn't. I laughed, I took, I spent. And that was that. I suppose it nearly crucified him. At least he told me often enough it did."

"What did you want him to tell you?" my Uncle Jimmy said. "'Good luck, Buster, here's another bundle: let's see you try it again'?"

"I didn't want him to tell me anything," my father said. "I didn't want him to talk to me at all. Because by then he'd said about everything he could say, he'd pretty well boxed the compass with me, and I was just about fed up to the teeth with him. Is that a harsh, an unfeeling thing to say? I guess it is. And do you know something? I couldn't care less."

"The trouble with people like you," my Uncle Jimmy said, "is you never learn to forget things."

"I forget all the time," my father said. "But I do remember certain things. For example, I remember always being cold when we were small, except when I was in bed or it was summer. Really cold, freezing, all because the stern parent was too miserable to put a little more coal in the furnace and howled like a maniac if anyone else did. I remember bending—or being bent—over that dark green plush chair in the parlor while the stern parent got his exercise larruping me with a belt strap because I left the kitchen door open—remember the fiction that good, warm, almost tropical air thereby escaped from the house?—or because I forgot to turn off a light when I left the room: forty golden watts wasted for a full ten minutes! And I can remember Ma in the kitchen, on her hands and knees—literally—scrubbing away at that cheap linoleum he treated like Carrara marble. No maid, of course. No help of any kind. Ever. That's the warm, traditional touch, isn't it? Ma in the kitchen, scrubbing away? The familiar trademark of poor Irish immigrants everywhere? The only difference being that all the time this was going on, all the time we thought we were just skidding along with the rest of them, our dear old stern parent had more than one million dollars in the kitty!"

"A hard nut," my Uncle Jimmy said again. "But so what? It's all over now. He's an old man. You want to go upstairs and bust him in the snoot and say, 'Here's one from the coal bin'? Don't forget he had a tough time himself. That's the way he lived when he was a kiddo. All right all right, he could have been better to us, but he loosened up later on. You got yours, the same as we all did."

"That's right," my father said. "He loosened up. He invested in us. He sent us to first-class colleges, and we all know what you're supposed to make there: first-class contacts. It all pays off in the end. And then of course there was the famous cash settlement. Accompanied by those famous last words: 'I've done all a man can do and more. Now go out and fly on your own. Say hello to a few of those fancy friends you made at school. Show me what you can do for yourself!' "

My Uncle Jimmy gave a little bark of a laugh. "You showed him, all right," he said.

"Yes," my father said. "It must have been a cruel disappointment. Still, he had you and Gert, and two out of three isn't bad in any league. And we can't take away from him the fact that he did loosen up. With us, of course, not with Ma. Although there really wasn't much percentage in loosening up with Ma, was there? I mean, by then she was a little too old to be much of an investment for the future, wouldn't you say? Come to think of it, she didn't have much of a future left at all, did she?"

"You don't give him a break, do you?" my Uncle Jimmy said.

"I'll tell you what," my father said. "I'll let you do that, Jimmy. It can be a private joke between us: the well-known hard-boiled member of the family being the one who shows compassion for his Pa. But then you understand him better than I do, don't you? You even have a little sympathy for what he is. Or was. And for what he was after. Maybe you have even more than a little sympathy."

"You think I'm like Pa, right?" my Uncle Jimmy said.

"In one way," my father said. "Admittedly, it's a pretty important way."

"And that's the real reason you don't want your kiddo to stay with us?" my Uncle Jimmy said. "Hah?"

"No," my father said. "It's a reason and not a bad one, but it's not the real one. The real reason is just what I told you it was: I don't want my kiddo staying with you or anybody else, because, after all, he is *my kiddo*. Now that apparently is incomprehensible to you, Jimmy, and I swear to God I don't know why!"

"All right all right," my Uncle Jimmy said. "I get all that, I'm not a dope. But so what? That's not the point. The point is the kiddo and what's best for him, right? Now you listen to me: I don't care what you think about the family, but—"

"Well, that's good," my father said, cutting in, "because I don't think anything about it. What is all this talk about family, anyway? You lose me very easily there, Jimmy. Because I'll tell you what I think of as family. One wife, dead. One little boy, dead. And one little boy, alive. That's my family. The only one. And I'll take care of it, or what remains of it. It's true, as you suggest, that I'm not in the best shape I've ever been in, but I'm not broke, I can limp along. And if anything happens to me, Jackie's all taken care of—your intelligence system broke down there, by the way; with all the spending, I did manage a few prudent touches. So there you have it: that's what I mean by family. Anything beyond that doesn't interest me at all. Especially what you seem to be getting at: some sort of romantic notion of the descendants of Pa Kinsella all closing ranks and sticking together through thick and thin. Is that it, Jimmy? Are you going to start a dynasty? Onward and upward with the once humble immigrant family, each generation greater than the one before? Are you going to have a family crest? How long before the first aristocrat?"

"One big laugh after another, right?" my Uncle Jimmy said.

"No, no big laughs," my father said. "Just nothing. I don't care. If you want to establish your own royal line, if you want to be a kind of paramount chief of all the export Irish over here, that's all right with me. What will they call you, I wonder? Super-Harp? No matter; if that's what you want, good luck to you. Only deal me—deal *us*—out. For good."

After that no one said anything for what seemed like a long time, so long that I thought they might have left the room. But then suddenly I heard my Uncle Jimmy say, not shouting, but in an even quieter voice than he had used so far, "Okay, Buster. That's the way you want it, right?"

"That's the way I want it, right," my father said.

"Okay," my Uncle Jimmy said again. "Then that's the way you've got it. As far as I'm concerned. Only get this straight: if I really wanted to put the squeeze on you, I could, and don't get any funny ideas that I couldn't. But I don't want to. Why should I? Hah? Why should I break a leg doing you a favor? You're a proud guy, Buster, and in my book a proud guy is usually a dumb guy. You can't do him a favor because he doesn't know what a favor is, even when it smacks him right in the puss. He thinks it's an insult! So okay. I'm done. I'm through horsing around with you. Go chase yourself, Buster. Right over the hill to the poorhouse."

"I hear the sounds of hands being washed," my father said. "Of me. All right, Jimmy. That's all I asked you for in the first place, isn't it? To be let alone. So let's call it a day. Or a night; I'm tired. And thanks for trying. One day I'll tell Jackie what I passed up for him. He may even be angry. I hope not."

"Before we break this up," my Uncle Jimmy said, "you want to answer one question for me?"

"If I can," my father said. "Let's hear it."

"Okay," my Uncle Jimmy said. "What's eating you? No no!" he said, suddenly getting loud again. "Cut that stuff out! Don't hand me that surprised look! If there's one thing I don't need it's any more of that empty urbane baloney! You know what I mean all right. I mean you're different, you've changed. I spotted it the minute you walked into this joint and I've spotted it every day since!"

"For example?" my father said. "The difference, I mean?"

"You're not even here with us," my Uncle Jimmy said. "You're not even anywhere that's real. You're in some half-baked cloud of your own. People talk to you, you talk to them, what does it all add up to? One big zero! You don't pay an attention to what they say, you don't pay any attention to what *you* say. All you're doing is going through the motions. You don't even pay any attention to your dirty digs at me, and for you that's real bad, because you always got a big bang out of that. They all had you pegged wrong, Buster: Charlie Charm, the easygoing sport with the tennis racket and the ice cream pants and the big hello for everybody, right? Strictly for the bluejays, that one! You were always a sour-apple guy who got his big kicks out of jabbing away at his own family. Well, you still jab away, but now it's just out of habit. You don't even care if the needle goes in or not. You don't care about anything that happens. I said you walked around here like a spook, and by God you do, but that's not the whole story. You're a nervous spook, you're worried, you're thinking about something all the time and it's got you! So what I want to know is: what is it?"

After a second my father said, "Of course there's always this possibility: I had a slight misfortune recently. I thought you'd heard."

"You can't even be real about *that!*" my Uncle Jimmy said. "And I'm not talking about that and you know I'm not! So let's not kid around. Don't try to con me out of this; you're wasting your time. You can't do it. Look, I do business every day with guys who are a lot tougher and smarter than you. And some of them even have better manners. What do you think of that? And every last one of them is trying to con me into the boneyard. Well, they haven't. Not yet. And the reason is because I'm really a very hard guy to con. That's my racket, Buster. That's what I do for a living.

I don't get conned. Not by them, and certainly not by you. I know you, Buster, I know you like the back of my hand. And I know that something's at you, that it's something you haven't told me about, that it's something you probably haven't told anybody about. Don't ask me how I know: I just *know*. I know you've kept it all inside you. And now it's getting you, right? Well, why not spit it out? Come clean with Jimmy! I'd like to know!"

"You would," my father said. "I suppose you even have a right to know? A family right?"

Now it was my Uncle Jimmy's turn to give a big sigh. "Who's talking about rights?" he said. "Listen, if you want to keep it all buttoned up inside you, what am I going to do? Rip it out of you? If you don't want to say anything, forget it. But I had an idea you might be better off if you spilled it to someone."

"That someone being you, of course," my father said.

"Yes, me!" my Uncle Jimmy said. "Just me. Nobody else but. And you know why? *Because you can trust me*. You may not like me much, but you know down deep on something like this you can trust me all the way. Now, how many of your flashy pals can you say that about? Hah? You know the answer to that one. So why not give me a try?"

My father didn't say anything. Neither did my Uncle Jimmy. Once more there was the silence, but this time for some reason it didn't even occur to me that they might have left the room, because I knew they were both just sitting there, looking at each other and waiting for something. It was all so still I didn't dare to move. No sound at all came up through the fireplace now, yet the funny thing was that somehow I thought I could hear them breathing, and breathing deeply. Suddenly, from the next bed, came a groan; Phil said loudly and very distinctly, "The anchor! Who's got the anchor?" I almost jumped out of bed, I was so startled, and I began to wave frantically at him to stop before I realized that of course he was only dreaming and had been talking in his sleep. He mumbled something and then turned over in his bed and was quiet again; he didn't wake up at all. I was glad of this, not only because they might have heard us downstairs if he had kept on talking, but also because by now I didn't want anyone listening with me, not even Phil. I didn't know what was going to happen, but for some reason I had a growing feeling that whatever it was, I didn't want anyone else to hear it, and maybe I shouldn't even hear it myself. Yet all the same I kept on waiting and listening; I couldn't help it.

It was my Uncle Jimmy who spoke first. He said, "It's that accident, right? But not just what we know: something else happened. What?"

My father said, in a funny flat voice, just as if he had been reciting some lesson in school, "My wife fell out of a canoe. So did my boy. They fell and were drowned."

"Fell," my Uncle Jimmy said, just repeating my father.

"Fell," my father said again. "She slipped, and fell. That's what happened. That's the only thing that happened. That's the only thing that could have happened. Anyone knows that."

There was another silence. Then my Uncle Jimmy said, "Ah. That's it. That's what's doing the job on you. Right?"

Once more my father didn't answer right away, and this time there was the longest silence yet. Then, suddenly, he began to talk, and when he did, what he said came out clearly enough, but oddly, too: it was as if something was hurting him while he talked, as if he would rather not have said anything at all, but that the words just came pumping out anyway.

"I don't know," he said. "There it is, the whole thing: I don't know. I go over it every day—good God, every *hour!*—and all I come up with is the same answer: I don't know. And that's what's so terrible, Jimmy. Don't you see? It's not just that I don't know; it's that I can't even seem to get close to knowing!"

And what was as strange as anything else in this way of talking was that my father now seemed to have changed toward my Uncle Jimmy, so that he wasn't arguing with him any more, or joking or trying to get away from him, but instead seemed to want something from him.

"Always supposing there's anything to know," my Uncle Jimmy said. "Don't get subtle, Buster. Subtle guys are a dime a dozen. All they do is make trouble. For themselves and everybody else. They see a barn full of hay, they see some rube drunk walk into the barn with a can of kerosene and a box of matches, they see the barn burn down to the ground, and what do they do? They start checking the weather reports to see if it couldn't have been started by lightning! Nothing's ever the way it looks, right? Forget that stuff, Buster. That's for amateurs. You play games like that, you'll wear holes in yourself. What's wrong with a little common sense? You said it yourself: she slipped, she fell. Well, I'll buy that. What've you got that says anything different?"

"The canoe," my father said. "It was dry, Jimmy. The canoe was bone-dry."

"Okay," my Uncle Jimmy said. "The canoe was dry. So what's your pitch: you can't fall out of a dry canoe?"

"Not and leave it dry," my father said. "It's not very likely, anyway. And this one didn't have a drop of water in it. The queer thing was that I didn't think anything of it at the time. And then of course later I realized—"

"Bushwa!" my Uncle Jimmy said loudly. "You realized. You realized *what?* And *from* what? What are you: Sherlock Holmes? 'There's a smudge of chalk on the end of your nose: I can tell by that you teach fifth grade in parochial school!' Hah? Don't make me laugh! You and your dry canoe!"

"It's not just the canoe," my father said. "I'm not a fool, Jimmy. It's Chrissie too. There's a history there: I don't have to spell it out for you. You know . . . what she was like."

"I know I know," my Uncle Jimmy said.

There was a pause, and then my father said slowly, "That's what kills you, you know: the *unfairness.* I mean, just take Chrissie, and then just think of all that warmth and beauty and goodness—it's a funny thing, but in a way, Jimmy, she was a plain old-fashioned *good* girl—and ask yourself how often in a dozen lifetimes you'd run into a combination like that. So you have all that, you know how lucky you are, and then, every once in a while, just long enough after the last time so that you'd almost have forgotten there *was* a last time, suddenly you're just looking at her and you see something in the eyes, or the way the hands move, and you know the first shadows, the clouds—it's coming again. . . ."

"Okay okay," my Uncle Jimmy said. "You're always punching yourself in the gut. She had her ups and downs, I know that. But what about then? Up at the lake? The way I got it, she was in good shape then. Right?"

"Fine," my father said. "She never seemed better. And for a long time. The longest, in fact. There wasn't a trace, not even a hint . . . if there had been," he said, "naturally I wouldn't have let her go. But this time it had been so long and she looked so great that I guess for once in my life, just once, it wasn't even in the back of my mind. Good God, it was even my suggestion that she go out alone! Or with Jackie or Tom. *My* suggestion, Jimmy! So you see—"

"So I see nothing!" my Uncle Jimmy said. "That's what it all adds up to in my book: *nothing!* What's your big clue? A dry canoe? That could have been dry all the time? Or that could have been wet and dried out by the time you got there: you said the sun was out, it was a hot day, right? Use your squash for something besides a hatrack, Buster! The only thing is Chrissie and you said she was fine! So what have you got? I'll tell you what you've got: *you've got an accident.* And that's all!"

"Jimmy, I don't think I've ever caught you trying to be kind to me before," my father said. "And thanks, but no cigar. Because you just don't understand. Not only about canoes, but about Chrissie. And about what was wrong. I do, because I lived with it a long time. And I put all this together and it doesn't add up to nothing to me, Jimmy. I wish it did, but it doesn't."

My Uncle Jimmy said, "The kiddoes: they ever know anything about this?"

"About Chrissie? No," my father said. "No. I could usually see it coming long enough in advance, and then we'd go away and stay away until it was over. Most of the time we stayed longer than that, so that Chrissie could have a good time traveling around when she was well, too. She was a great traveler, Jimmy. Good to be with, you know."

"She had a lot of spark," my Uncle Jimmy said. "But I don't get this. If you're such a hawkeye and could always spot this thing coming on, how come you missed it this time, hah?"

"I don't know," my father said wearily. "I just don't know. It could have been a hundred things—"

"And it could have been that it wasn't there at all!" my Uncle Jimmy said. "Hah? How does that strike you? Not subtle enough? Just maybe you didn't spot it because there wasn't anything to spot? Just maybe she was fine all the time? You ever think of anything straight like that? You said there was always a warning every other time: well, where was the warning this time? Why don't you ask yourself that question?"

"I've asked myself all the questions," my father said. "It's true there wasn't any warning. Or it's true that I didn't see one. But you don't understand: these things don't always happen the same way. There didn't *have* to be that warning. It could come on in an instant: I was told that. And I was told it so that I could guard against it. But it never had happened, and I guess maybe I thought it never would. I guess I got lax. I used to let her do things which were all against the books. Nothing ever happened. And yet I knew, or should have known: I've been through all this with a hundred doctors. I suppose I know as much about this kind of thing as any layman does. But that didn't help Chrissie much, did it?"

"You drive me bananas!" my Uncle Jimmy said. "Now listen to me! First, this canoe business. You're not trying to tell me it's *impossible* to fall out of a canoe and leave it dry, are you? You're not saying that nobody's ever done it, nobody ever could do it? Listen, I'll guarantee you I can get fifty palookas, right now, to fall out of fifty canoes, and when they're all out half the canoes will be dry! So what are you really saying? All you're saying is it's *hard* to do, right?"

"No," my father said. "All I'm saying is just what I said before, and that is that it's unlikely. And when two people are involved, and when one of them is a little boy, then it becomes extremely unlikely."

"Okay," my Uncle Jimmy said. "Let's call it *unlikely*. And what does that mean? It means that it might not have happened, but on the other hand it just might have. Right? It might have. So that's one thing. Then we go on to Chrissie, and that's where you're walking around with your thumb in your mouth, Buster! Because you've got nothing! You're tearing yourself to bits, and why? Because you're playing a game of eenie meenie minie moe! You're guessing, Buster! You don't know that a single thing was wrong with her that day, right? I mean, *really* know?"

"You're always asking me to listen to you," my father said, "but you never listen to me. I'm not complaining, but it would make it easier if you did. Now look: you're telling me that I really don't know. But isn't that exactly what I said to you in the beginning: *I don't know?* And don't you see, can't you see, that that's the trouble? Can't you understand that, Jimmy? What are you trying to prove to me: that it's not a certainty that Chrissie did this, that it's just a possibility? Don't you think I know that? It's the one thing I do know. And I know just how strong the possibility was, and I know it a lot better than you. And I know that because I lived with Chrissie and I loved her and I know what she could do and what she couldn't, and I know what happened before and I know better than anyone on earth just what could have happened that day. I *don't* know that it actually did happen that way, but the *could have* is enough, believe me. Because as long as I live I'll never know anything more than that, there's no way I can. Is there? So this is the way I live now, Jimmy. Not knowing exactly how it happened, but knowing how it might have happened, how it possibly happened, how it probably happened. And knowing too just one more thing: that if it did happen that way, it had no right to. Because it could have been stopped, it should have been stopped! And by me, Jimmy! By *me!* I should have stopped it, I'm the only one who *could* have! But oh my God my God!" my father cried, his voice suddenly suddenly going way up almost to a scream and reaching out and soaring up through the fireplace right out to me in a great wild desperate shout, "I *didn't! Jimmy Jimmy Jimmy, I didn't!*"

And even after he finished, his voice still seemed to hang in the room, shaking through it and filling it, and I remember that even in the midst of everything I looked over at Phil in a panic, afraid that he might have awakened and heard everything. But he hadn't; he was still sleeping away. By now I was sitting at the foot of my bed, having gone little by little toward the sound as I had been listening, and now I sat there absolutely still, as if I had been frozen there and couldn't move until something else happened. After a while I realized that the echo of my father's cry had gone, and that now there was nothing but the silence again. Then, from downstairs, I heard a small and different sound: not clear, but muffled, the sound of someone who might have been crying but who was trying not to cry. And I knew this couldn't have been my Uncle Jimmy, because now I could hear him speak over the sobbing sound.

"You poor bastard," he said, kind of softly. And even though it was a swearword, it didn't sound as though he were swearing. It sounded as though he were talking to my father in the best way he ever had.

"Come on, Buster," he said, after a couple of seconds. "Come on now. It's getting late."

And then I didn't hear anything more, no words and no more sobbing, and after a little while I knew that they had left the room and had gone to their beds for the night.

I sat there for a while at the foot of my bed. It was raining hard outside now—it must have started some time ago, but I hadn't even noticed it—and the room was damp and cold. I felt chilly, and suddenly I began to tremble; I got back in under the covers, pulling them all up over me, even the big brown downy puff that was used mostly in winter. Pretty soon I felt warmer, but the funny thing was that the trembling didn't stop right away. I closed my eyes tight, not to try to go back to sleep—I knew I couldn't do that now—but mostly to help me think about all the different and confusing and even frightening things I had just been listening to. I tried hard to remember everything, not just every word but even the way it had been said, because I had the idea that if I could only remember enough and put it all together and go over it by myself I might be able to understand it—or at least to understand it a lot better than I did right now. But all the words kept whizzing around and sailing through my head in no special order at all, and whenever I tried to stop and think of any one of them and what it meant, the very next second I would be thinking of something that wasn't connected with it at all: my grandfather and how mean he was to his family, my Uncle Jimmy and my Aunt Mary and how they wanted to take me with them and bring me up, my father and how he didn't any longer have as much money as he used to have. These things, all of them, came as a surprise to me, because nobody, not even my father, had talked about them to me before, and now that I had heard about them I almost wished I hadn't heard anything. Because it seemed to me that all these things, everything that my father or my Uncle Jimmy had talked about tonight, were in some way sad and unhappy. It was as if whatever they had done or been through had for some reason not turned out the way they hoped it would but instead had got all tangled up or twisted around, so that in the end almost everybody wound up being disappointed or miserable or in some dreadful kind of trouble.

And this made me feel awful, partly because I didn't want to believe that things were like this, but mostly because it was my father who seemed to be saying that they were. In all the time we had spent together, he had never talked to me in this gloomy way, not even right after my mother had died, and when I heard him tonight I didn't know what to think. At first I thought that maybe he didn't really mean it, that while he might not actually be joking—I could tell from his voice that he wasn't doing that—still, he might be just talking for the sake of arguing or of trying to make my Uncle Jimmy mad. But then, when he began to talk about my mother, I knew that this was wrong, because he never would have done that about her. Still, what he *did* say about her was even more confusing than anything else he had said, because he seemed to be telling my Uncle Jimmy that maybe the accident in the canoe hadn't been an accident after all! This didn't make any sense to me, because of course I *knew* it had been an accident: I had been there! And so had my father: we had both gone out on the lake together, we had found my mother's empty canoe, and there had been nobody but ourselves for miles around—so then, what else could it have been but an accident? It was all very baffling, I couldn't understand anything about it or why my father was talking like this, and I couldn't understand why—a minute later—he had talked about my mother as though she had been sick a lot, when I knew perfectly well that she had never been sick at all! I knew this not only because I never saw her sick, but because she told me so herself. Doctors sometimes came to our house to see Tom and me, and a couple of times they came for my father, but no doctor had ever come to see my mother, and I remembered now that one day I had asked her why this was. She had just laughed and said, "What would a doctor come to see me for? Doctors only come to see sick people, Jackie, and you know me: I'm Sweet Sunshine Susie Brown, remember?"

This was from a song she used to sing:

I'm Sweet Sunshine Susie Brown,
I'm the healthiest happiest gal in town. . . .

But then I remembered my father saying to my Uncle Jimmy that my mother had been sick only when they were away on their trips, and that sounded funny to me, too—I mean, that you would be sick only away from home. And also, even if she *had* been sick sometimes and hadn't wanted to tell me about it, that couldn't have had anything to do with her accident in the canoe, because on that morning I had been with her, or at least near her, most of the time, and so I knew for sure that she hadn't been sick then. She had been just as happy and gay as she always was, maybe even more so, and I remembered that once during the morning, when I left my father for a minute and went inside the cabin to get a drink of water from the pump over the sink—there was no running water in the cabin—my mother saw me and suddenly stopped her cleaning and came over to me. I don't know where Tom was, but he wasn't around right then: there were just the two of us. And my mother reached over and sort of lifted me, as if I were as little as Tom, not all the way off the floor but up to the tips of my toes, and said, in a whispery singing voice, "Oh Jackie boy, Jackie boy, where have you been?"—just as if it were a part of another song. Then she looked at me and gave me a hug and a kiss and took me by one hand and twirled me around in a kind of dance step before she laughed and let me go and then went back to her work. I went back out to my father, and started to tell him what had happened inside, but then I didn't, because we both got busy nailing on some of the new shingles. But that's how I knew that on that morning my mother was just fine.

So, then, I lay in my bed now, worried and wondering because my father and my mother had seemed to say such very different things, and I couldn't see how this could be. I didn't even know if I would ever find out now, because of course I couldn't ask my father, since then he would know that I had been listening. And then, just before I fell asleep, I began to wonder if he might not know anyway, if maybe he might not be able to guess from something I might say without meaning to, or from some different way

I might act. I hoped he wouldn't, not just because he might get mad, but because he might think I had been sneaky or spying on him and then maybe he might change his feelings toward me. And more than anything else I didn't want that to happen, because he was my father, and because it seemed to me that too much had changed already.

But the next day everything went along all right. My father and my Uncle Jimmy behaved just as they usually did toward each other, as if they hadn't had their long talk at all, and my father was just the same as ever to me. I guess I must have been just the same to him—and outside of being puzzled, I of course felt just the same—because he didn't say a word to show that he had noticed anything special or different about me. It was only two days later—early in the afternoon of the day before we were going to leave my Uncle Jimmy's castle to start out on our way home—that he came up to me, all alone, in the front hall, and said, "How's it going?"

"Good," I said. "Just swell."

He looked at me for a couple of seconds without saying anything, and I was afraid that somehow he had found out and was going to say something about what I had done, but instead all he said was, "I thought you were looking a little thin in the face these days, that's all. However . . . you're not too sorry to be going home?"

"No," I said. "I'm glad."

And I was. I knew that I would miss James and Charles and especially Phil, and that I would even miss my Uncle Jimmy and my Aunt Mary. But I was glad to be going back with my father after such a long time away from home. I wanted more every day to see our house again, and to be in it, and to see Ellen and of course Arthur and to tell them all the things that had happened to me since I had been away.

My father nodded. "All right," he said. "I just wanted to know.

Make sure you're all packed by tonight, now, because we want to leave first thing in the morning."

So I played the rest of the day with my three cousins, and that night after dinner my Aunt Mary came up to my room and helped Phil and me pack all my things. Then James and Charles came in to see me and to give me going-away presents, which turned out to be things they already owned themselves.

"We wanted to get you something brand-new," James explained, "but we couldn't find anything. They don't have very good stores to buy things in over here."

"Except sweaters and belts and junk like that," Charles said. "And they're not presents because you get them anyway."

So Charles gave me his best model airplane, and James gave me a big leather wallet which had his initials stamped on it in gold, but that was all right because luckily they were my initials, too.

"Actually," James said, handing the wallet to me, "it's a better present than it looks because I think it's made out of quite rare leather. You can tell that when you feel it."

So I felt it, and then I thanked them both, and after this Phil gave me his present, which was the best of all: it was the crystal set that he had made himself.

"When you get home," he said, "you'll be able to get millions of stations on it. It's really a swell radio!"

I thanked him, too, and then we all talked for a while, and pretty soon, because we all had to get up very early on account of my going, James and Charles left and Phil and I got ready for bed. We didn't go to sleep for a long time, though. We stayed awake in our beds, talking about the good times we had had this summer, and remembering some of the funny things that had happened to all of us, and guessing about what we would do now when we got home. Phil didn't know exactly where he would be, because my Uncle Jimmy had a couple of houses in different parts of the country and he hadn't made up his mind which one he was going to yet. But wherever he went, Phil and I agreed that we would fix it so that we would still see each other a lot, and it was after talking about this for a few minutes that Phil said maybe we should sign a Pact.

We got out of bed and turned on the table light, and on a piece of letter paper we found we made up a Pact. It went:

A PACT
between
THE FIERCE AND FRIENDLY TWO

(1) We will stay friends our whole lives no matter what happens.

(2) No matter how far away we are we will meet each other at least three times a year and probably a lot more.

(3) If anyone harms or wounds either one of us the other one will revenge him.

We signed this and made a copy of it and signed that too, so that we each could have one, and then we went back to bed. Phil went to sleep almost right away after this, and even though I was still excited about going home and everything, in a little while I did, too.

The next morning, very early, we all had breakfast, and then my father and I went out to the little car that we had come to the castle in a couple of months ago, but that I hadn't been in much since. Our bags had already been put in, so we just said goodbye to everybody once more, my Aunt Mary kissed me and cried a little, and my Uncle Jimmy gave me a hard handshake and said, "Stay in there swinging, Jackie! Don't let us down! I'll be watching you all the time! And remember: no baloney!"

I promised him that there would be no baloney, and he nodded and walked over to my father and began to say something to him in a low voice. I shook hands with James and Charles and Phil, and then I got into the car, with my father getting in beside me in the driver's seat.

"All set," he said. Then he waved, and I did too, and we drove off down the big circular driveway. The sun was pretty far up now, there was a little mist coming over the pond, some birds were singing, and it was another good day. As we reached almost the end of the driveway I looked back and waved again, and the three boys waved at me, and we all kept waving until I couldn't see them any more.

We rode through the country, not the way we had come but more to the south, to where we could catch the boat for home. My father didn't talk much on this ride either, but every once in a while he would ask me some questions about how I had liked this or that at my Uncle Jimmy's, and I would answer him and tell him about how much fun we had had, and about all the things we did, and about how of all the boys I liked Phil the best. I didn't tell him anything about the Pact, because that was supposed to be just between Phil and me. He didn't say anything, ever, about his talk that night with my Uncle Jimmy, and of course I didn't, either. But now and then, after driving a long time without saying anything, he would just reach out with one hand and grab me by the back of the neck and muss my hair the way he always did. And I felt good, because even though I missed the boys some already, it was still fine to be driving along here and to be alone with my father again.

We got on the boat and started on our way back to America. It was all very much like our trip coming over: our cabin was almost the same, and the ride was very smooth, with no big storms to bother us. My father still stayed mainly in the cabin, reading or smoking, and I went all over the ship by myself, sometimes talking with other passengers, sometimes going up with some of the officers, who let me watch the way they ran the ship, and sometimes playing with other boys I met on board. I ate all my meals except breakfast with my father, though, and at night we were always together, talking about the different things we always talked about. Then one night—it was the night before we landed—we were talking about what we were going to do, and about the house and Ellen and Arthur, and suddenly I thought my father was looking a little sad—or maybe not sad so much as far-off, as if while he was talking to me here he were really thinking about something else. We went on talking, and pretty soon he said, "Let me ask you a question: do you know anything about boarding schools?"

"Not very much," I said. "Hardly anything."

"Any of your friends ever go to one?" he said.

"Only Charlie Hughes," I said. "His father and mother took him out of our school last year and sent him away to one."

"And did Charlie like it there?" my father said.

"At first he hated it," I said. "But now he likes it okay. Why?"

"No special reason," my father said. "It's just one of those things you happen to think about, you know." Then he went on and started to talk about something else, and we didn't come back to the boarding school subject again. And I didn't know—I guess maybe I couldn't have known—that something terribly important to me and to what I was going to do had just been said.

One month later, I went away to boarding school. For the first time in my life I was away from everybody I had always known, for the first time I was with nobody but strangers: strange boys, strange teachers, in a world that was completely strange to me. And with that the whole first part of my boyhood—my childhood, really: the happy time spent with my father and mother and Tom and Ellen and Arthur—came to an end forever, and I began what I suppose was the business of growing up.

II

four

On the first Tuesday of November, my cousin Charles was elected governor of the state. His election came as a surprise to many: I think perhaps to most. To most, but not to all: months before Election Day the bishop of our diocese—a shrewd, ancient crag of a man, circumspect almost to the point of meaninglessness in public speech, blunt as a club in private—reportedly had said, "I've known Jimmy Kinsella all my life. *And* his sister Gert. It's been my experience that they usually get what they go after. This boy is just like them. They try to tell you he isn't, but he is. So I think he'll be governor. One way or another. Matter of fact, I think if he wanted to be one of the Trinity he might make it."

This was the bishop; it was a minority opinion. For the rest, Charles was a possibility, no more. And so when he won there was at first the surprise, but then, once the victory had been established as official, and once hindsight had been given its usual chance, there was common agreement that he had won easily, indeed almost without trying. To be sure, this was the view of the political amateur—the voter—but it was not without professional support. One of Charles's more conspicuous aides—from the practical (politician) rather than the theoretical (professor) wing: he had both—said comfortably, "A piece of cake. He had it all the way."

Had Charles believed this? I doubt it; he was far from being an optimist, and he was seldom casual about what concerned him most. Certainly from all I could learn—and this was largely at second hand, from the reports of others: I had been away from the city for a long time, and had come back just before the election—there had been nothing in the least casual about his campaign. It had been meticulously planned and tirelessly conducted; more to the point, it had been extremely expensive. Like many men with money, Charles was a guarded spender, yet suddenly in the campaign there had appeared that long string of ads, terse but full-page ("Integrity: KINSELLA!" "Dignity: KINSELLA!" "Leadership: KINSELLA!"). There had been the billboards, springing up to border superhighways (same message), the radio jingles, the banners, the posters, the bumper stickers by the thousands. And there had been television.

It was on television that Charles had come into his own. The rest—the ads, the signs, the jingles—were faultless but routine: no candidate in his right mind would have come before this particular electorate without that magical "Leadership." But television, for Charles, was something different. It was as if he had recognized at once that this newest route to the public belonged to him in the same way that the torchlight parade had belonged to older and earlier men. He had used it well. He was photogenic; his speech, casual, rather spare, and unremarkable in a ball park or an auditorium, was curiously impressive on this intimate medium: it became almost imperative to believe that he believed in whatever he was saying. I saw him only twice in this way, during the final week of his campaign, but I discovered that he had been appearing regularly and very often from the beginning, and that each appearance had been prepared and filmed in advance by a team of experts brought in from the outside. As a candidate Charles had naturally come out strong for all local industry, but as a prudent man he had excepted television. The local brand was abundant but unsteady, vacillating between the competent and the bizarre; Charles, who liked to be sure, had decided to import reliability.

None of this had been free: he had spent hard. And he had worked hard. Little known in the small towns and the rural areas, he had set out to become known. Motorcades had crisscrossed the state daily; Charles had led them all, in rain or shine marvelously visible in the long open Cadillac: very tall (six feet three), light red hair and dark blue eyes, the long and rather watchful face smiling slightly, one hand raised and occasionally dipping in a dutiful and not quite unselfconscious wave. (Unlike his opponent, Charles was not by temperament a waver; it was only for the smallest fraction of his life that he had been saluting—in this or any other way—crowds of total strangers.) In this personal approach to the voters he had refused to deputize. The result had been a schedule which must have been punishing and which had in no way suggested overconfidence.

He won. Perhaps it was the size of the victory rather than the victory itself which surprised so many, for he had always been given that outside chance. His opponent, the incumbent governor, was a formidable politician and deeply entrenched in office, but on balance Charles was at least a respectable candidate. He had the liability of his limited experience—one four-year term as mayor of the capital city—but against that he offered certain strengths. He was young—thirty-nine, intelligent, attractive, ethnically correct. He was a Democrat—far rarer for us, a Democrat untouched by scandal. Thanks to his father, he was rich. He had married a handsome woman who had managed to avoid the dislike of other women. His political record, though short, was good: as mayor he had started cautiously, but firmness had come fast, and in City Hall circles there had even been complaints that his tactics were unfair.

"I've got only the one rule when I shake hands with the mayor," one veteran city councilman was alleged to have said, "and that is to keep the iron jock on at all times."

Imperfect protection, apparently: the councilman had been in jail when he said it. But whether merited or not, these grumbles seemed not to have damaged Charles. By the end of his term he had drawn praise and—far better—support from groups which did not otherwise agree.

He was a fresh face on a tired scene; his image, as they say, was good. Moreover—although this was perhaps not widely recognized at the time—he had the luck which those who are destined to be successful sometimes seem able to manufacture for themselves. Toward the end of the campaign, the governor—a persuasive Italian confidence man, currently working as a New Republican—made the first really serious mistake of a long and uncannily sure-footed career: he trusted an ally. Incredibly, he wrote a letter which no one a week in politics would have written; worse, he signed it. There was an argument; bitterness flashed, persisted; old cronies fell out; the letter was produced and made public. There were threats of investigation; the governor howled forgery; and Charles—Charles worked harder and spent more. The New Republican was buried; Charles won by the largest plurality ever recorded in the state.

I saw him on the night following his election. There was a victory party; I had been invited. It was a gesture pleasantly, perhaps even automatically, extended to a relative, for while Charles and I had always been friendly and once had even been fairly close—although never as close as, say, Phil and I had been—that had changed over the years, and now when we met it was casually, agreeably, and not very often. There had been no quarrel, no formal break of any kind: simply a gradual and probably inevitable growing apart. There had been marriage, new demands, new friendships; our work was different and so were most of our interests; and Charles, with his now very considerable income, lived and moved on a scale far more luxurious than mine—there had even been a brief period of glamour when he and Marie had figured in the gossip columns as minor members of the international set. In all of this I had had no part—just as, later, I had had no part in his political rise. I had written no speeches, made no broadcasts, pushed no doorbells; I had not raised funds. I had given him the support of my vote: that was all. And never once, not event at the very beginning, did he even suggest that I might help him in any other way.

It had been Phil, in fact, who told me the news. He had said to me one night, with no preliminary, "Jack, I'll give you something you haven't heard before: Charles is going to run for mayor."

This had been five years ago, at a time when no one even dreamed of anything like this for Charles—no one, that is, except his brothers and my Uncle Jimmy. And, of course, Charles himself. The family cohesiveness had grown with the years, and they took few steps without a family council. They did not surprise each other. But as for me, if I had been told that Charles was shortly to become an astronaut, or that he was soon to produce a fresh translation of Proust, I think I would have been less astonished. For there had never been any connection between Charles and politics of any kind—let alone our local variety. The city had been his birthplace and had remained his home base, but he had always been away from it more than in it, and I had never known him to show the slightest interest in its operation. I remembered this for a particular reason, because years ago, shortly after leaving college, I had been in and around City Hall for a brief period myself. The old mayor of the city, Frank Skeffington, had always shown great friendliness toward my father—in a sense this was odd, because I don't believe they knew each other well, and there had certainly been no professional tie: my father, who frequently forgot to vote, would have been a poor political worker—and it was undoubtedly due to this that one day, out of the blue, he had called me to his office and asked me if I would care to become his secretary. It had been a flattering offer; I had at that time no definite plans of my own; I had been curious; I had accepted in an instant. I had been the last of his secretaries to be employed by this extraordinary old man before his death. Necessarily, through him, I had come to know City Hall well, and I remember that occasionally I had talked to Charles about what went on in that shabby, sordid, hilarious place. I remembered too that while he had sometimes been amused by these stories, more often, I think, he had been a little bored. Because it was not his world: it was simply not his world at all. And now, suddenly, it was. He had decided to join it, and more than that, he had decided to join it as its chief. It was not a modest proposal.

On the night that he had told me this, Phil and I had been sitting, very late, in a nearly deserted and very bad restaurant. It had been a Sunday at the end of the summer; my wife and I had been spending a weekend with Phil and his family at their place on the island. At the last moment Jean had decided to stay on for a few more days, and so I had driven back to the city alone with Phil. It had been a hot drive and a slow one in heavy Thruway traffic, and by the time we reached the city Phil was ready to stop for food before going home. Because of the hour and the day few places were open, and in the end we had gone to an all-night cafeteria. I remember very clearly Phil sitting there opposite me, rapidly eating thick pancakes soaked in a thin imitation-maple syrup.

"Yum yum," he said dryly. "This is where all the truck drivers eat. I guess we can believe that, hey?"

I remember that the only other customers were four deaf-mutes, seated a few tables away, conducting what appeared to be an agitated conversation in their speedy pantomime. The counterman had pointed them out to us when we had given our orders.

"They's dumbos," he had said.

I remember exactly how Phil looked, what he was wearing: a light tan tropical worsted which he called his Hong Kong suit, and for which he claimed to have paid eleven dollars and a half—it was a souvenir of his trip to the Orient the previous winter. It was a strange suit: fresh from the iron it was handsome, worn for an hour it was wrinkled rubbish. According to Phil it was a unique fabric of Chinese invention.

"Half wool, half Kleenex," he had said. "They saw me coming."

And on that night, listening to him as he told me the surprising news about Charles, looking at the tall body bending slightly forward as he told me, and seeing the dark blue eyes in the bony intelligent face watching me with amusement at my surprise, I remember that I had felt a fleeting but curious sensation: it was as though I were not only listening to talk about Charles, but that it was really Charles himself who was doing the talking. It was the sort of thing that had happened to me before with the two brothers, a special kind of momentary confusion, and I knew that others had felt this, too. For Charles and Phil, as they had grown older, had come more and more to look like each other, and now, although the resemblance was hardly breathtaking, still it was close enough so that strangers—or those who did not know that Charles was a year or so younger—normally assumed that the two were twins. Neither had James's elegance, his peculiar *distinction* of appearance, but they had their own good looks—Charles in particular had come a long way: the little fat boy with the glasses had been left far behind, vanishing forever during one six-month period somewhere in his middle teens—and with their height and slimness and red hair and blue eyes, they were extraordinary-looking men, in no danger of being passed by. An old man I know once said to me, "By God, Jack, you'd look at them even if they were poor!"

Apart from their looks they were not much alike, and yet there were those moments when something seemed to happen, to click and to connect the two in some mysterious subsurface way, and when it did—as it had on this night—for just a second or two there was likely to be a flash of uncertainty, a sense of bafflement among even those who knew them well. This moment always passed quickly, an oddity which was never fully explained or understood, because in fact we knew—or I knew—that the two were really poles apart.

I had said, "*Charles?*"

He had nodded. "Charles."

He was serious; I could tell that. I said, "That's a strange one: does anyone actually think he has a chance?"

"Sure," Phil had said. "I do. James does. Pa does. And then of course there's Charles. Does that sound arrogant? I guess it does. I guess it is. But anyway, here's the main thing: want to hop on board? We have a few vacancies at the moment."

"I'll bet you have."

"What do you say, Jack?" he said. "I'd love to have you with us. Charles would too. You know that."

I shook my head. "No thanks. I've been to the zoo. I've had it."

"That was a long time ago. Stone Age stuff. This is going to be different."

"No, it's not. And I'll tell you why."

And then, for a few minutes while he listened with surprising patience—because he was essentially a talker rather than a listener—I had talked from the only platform I could: that of my own short political experience. I talked about the small, inbred, incredibly complicated world of the local politician, about the practical experience needed even to begin to spar with those soiled but crafty veterans, about the scars, the dirt, the damage that would inevitably come from the kind of campaign that would inevitably be fought, about the difficulty of changing or affecting the ancient, massive, corrupt and rusted machinery of the city's government, about the impossibility of even getting in to try.

"Because he can't do it, Phil. He's bright, he's honest, he's a good lawyer, but that's not enough. He's rich and he's Jimmy Kinsella's boy—that's better, but even that's not enough. He'll get slaughtered; he won't get past the primaries. They just won't let him in."

And Phil had laughed. He seemed in the best of spirits, as if he had enjoyed my bleak recitation and indeed had expected it. "Good for you, Jack," he said. "It's all true, every word of it. Except for one thing: it doesn't matter. It really doesn't. Not any more. Oh I know, I know," he said, "you think it does because it always has: Big Dad Skeffington and all that hoo-ha. But no more; it's all different now. Or it's going to be. Because we're not going to wait for them to let us in. We're going in anyway, even if we have to blast. We're going in and we're going to take it away from them and they won't even know what hit them until it's all over." He leaned toward me, a familiar look in his eye: it was boyish and bold and merry, a look he'd had ever since he was small, ever since I'd known him—at this moment I could never have mistaken him for Charles or for anyone else. "Oh come on!" he said eagerly. "They're such a scaly bunch: let's take it all away from them and drive them back under the ground or wherever they came from. We can do it. This whole place is aching for something new. Come on, Jack, and we'll have a ball. What do you say? It'll be great fun!"

He was off and running; he was describing an exciting game. I said, "Just for kicks?"

"Well, kicks *and*," he said, more soberly. "A little principle got mixed up in it somewhere—I tried to stop it, but it did. You see, I know the wicked flourish and all that; what kills me is the really crummy grade of wicked who flourish around here. This gang of shanty clowns has been playing the city like a slot machine for years. You can't sit still for that forever, can you? It's humiliating. It's like being goosed by the garbage man every day!"

"And you think Charles is going to change all that? Incidentally, why Charles? I mean, of all of you?"

"He was the logical one," he said. "Always supposing it had to be one of us. And I guess it did—anyway, it was our idea and we're running the show. But Pa's too old and too busy, and James obviously couldn't do it, and I didn't want to—to be the actual candidate, that is. And Charles *did* want to."

"How did he do that? Was there an acceptance speech? Did he say, 'All right, it's settled: I'll be the mayor. I think we're all agreed that I want to be'?"

Phil laughed again. "No, it wasn't much like that. You might say he had the honor thrust upon him. You might also say that we didn't have to thrust very hard. But that's all right. You haven't seen much of Charles lately, have you? He might surprise you, Jack. He's really pretty good."

"You'd know about that better than I would. You both work the same side of the street."

"No, I don't mean as a lawyer. Good lawyers are a dime a dozen. He's something else—or he's getting to be something else. At least it seems that way to me. There have been times lately when Charles has impressed the hell out of me."

"In what way?"

He gestured vaguely. "Just generally. He's a very cool customer, you know. And he knows how to handle himself—in a way he's like Pa. Only with manners. Anyway, think it over. I wish you'd come along."

"Well, thanks, but I don't think so. I'll give Charles a ring and wish him luck. And if there's anything special or occasional he needs, all right. If I can help, I will. But I don't want to get in on the whole picture. Once was enough. And I don't think this is going to be all that different. I know you want to make it different, but I don't think you can. And I don't think Charles can. I just don't think he's the answer." He didn't say anything to this; I looked at him and then, puzzled—because, after all, I had known him a long time—I said slowly, "But you do, don't you?"

He nodded. He pushed his plate away from him, and as he did a thin trail of the fake maple syrup dribbled down across the table, and a few drops fell onto the pants of his Hong Kong suit; he didn't bother to blot them up. The restaurant was now strangely quiet. No further customers had come in out of the hot night; up behind the rows of fruit cups and butterscotch cookies and plates of cold pale meat the counterman diverted himself by balancing a floor mop on the end of a forefinger; at the corner table the mutes continued to sip iced coffee and to sustain their furious still eloquence. The only sound I could hear was the troubled whining of the air-conditioning. Phil stopped nodding and said, "I guess I do. I guess I even think that Charles might be the answer to a lot of things. That's kind of funny, isn't it? But I do. I really do." He pushed back his chair and got up. "I'm ready if you are," he said. "I find as I get older than I need that good, solid, one hour's sleep. Isn't that what you find?"

We left the restaurant, and he drove me home. And that was the way I first heard that Charles was considering a political career. And now, five years later, I was driving through the city on my way to the governor's house.

five

MORE than a year before he entered his first political campaign, Charles had made a necessary preliminary move: he had established firmly and unmistakably the fact of his legal residence. He had moved from his apartment—which he and Marie and their three children had used as a headquarters whenever they happened to be in the city—and had bought a private house. The apartment had been pleasant but cramped, and also, in a curious way and despite its years of use, somehow impermanent, as if it were a high-rent bivouac; the house, on the other hand, had room to burn and was undoubtedly here to stay. It was the old Burroughs house: an impressive, gloomily handsome Georgian mansion, tree-shadowed and built like a fort. When I was a boy I had often bicycled by this house, and peeping in through the tall hedge, I had sometimes caught a glimpse of Amy Burroughs—who seemed ancient even then—tottering slowly across the lawn, her long purple dress brushing the tops of the grass, her cane poking the earth ahead of her, while behind trailed a vast and spreading retinue of cats. She was the last of her family; they were now popularly believed to have been old-line aristocrats of faultless pedigree, but this was not true. Her grandfather had in fact been a druggist, who after protesting violently had been dragged off to the Civil War, from which he had emerged as a captain, and then had gone on to make a fortune in nose drops of his own invention. It was he who had built the house, which for some time afterward had been known as Catarrh Castle. The name had died with the captain, the house had acquired a somber majesty over the years, and Charles owned it now.

And now, tonight, this old house, where lonely, palsied Amy Burroughs had never entertained, and where Charles and Marie had given only their small and rather elegant dinners—tonight it was breaking with its tradition of seclusion, and it was breaking with a bang. It was wide open, literally, for the night was very warm—Indian summer, the last gasp—and the celebration had reached out onto the deep green lawn where tables had been set up, gay with paper lanterns. It was light and loud and festive, and through the open windows music sprang into the still night air; coming toward the house I had heard it blocks away.

I arrived late, but even so the traffic jam near the house had not broken. The section in which Charles lived was one of wide, pleasantly curving, carefully patrolled streets, and these were now so crowded with people that all cars could do no more than inch along. For a moment I thought that the official party had overflowed into the streets, but then I realized that the crowd out here was entirely different: they were sightseers rather than invited guests, they were mostly young people who were eager for a glimpse of the new young governor at play. Charles had great strength among the students; there were half a dozen colleges in or near the city, and it seemed that they all had representatives here tonight. I drove through them very carefully; the police were on hand but had little to do, for this was a friendly crowd: they had come to cheer. Many of them seemed too young to vote—I'm sure they were. There were boys and girls dancing on the sidewalk to the music of a portable radio; under one of the simulated gas lamps which illuminated this district a well-dressed young man with a guitar was singing the song of a depressed worker; others were cheering and beating rhythmically with their hands and calling for Charles, hoping to coax him into an appearance. There was only one dissident note: a tall elderly tattered man wearing sneakers and a World War I overseas cap stood on the curb, facing Charles's house and waving his arms; he was shouting, "I hope it thunders and lightnings and rains like the hammers of hell, Charles Kinsella, all over you and your damn garden party!" This was greeted with loud mock cheers and hurrahs which seemed to further enrage the old man. The police watched, but did not interfere.

Finally I got through enough of the crowd so that I was opposite the driveway. A state trooper—symbol of Charles's new station—requested identification; I showed my invitation, and while I was not recognized, my last name of course was. The magic "Kinsella" whisked me, with another state trooper as escort, to a preferred parking space at the edge of the lawn.

The state trooper looked as young as some of the students; he jumped down and held my car door open for me. He said, "It's a great night for all of us, sir. Your brother's a wonderful man. He's really wonderful! A great man to travel around with. Very very considerate!"

"My cousin," I said.

"Oh," he said. His interest diminished, but did not disappear.

I walked toward the house across the lawn, stepping among the tables, occasionally stopping to talk as I recognized a face in the lantern light. At last I reached the house and went in. It was crowded and very noisy, for while many of the guests had gone outside, the main body of the party had preferred to remain indoors—near the food, the liquor, the music, and of course, near Charles. They were gathered mostly in the great long room to the right of the front hall. This had been the old ballroom—question: had Amy Burroughs ever danced?—and I had seen it once many years before: it had been formal and forbidding, massive with dark mahogany. Now it was all cream-white and gold: Marie's touch. As I entered, the orchestra was playing and a chunky blonde girl was singing the simple dreadful song that had accompanied Charles everywhere throughout the campaign:

Kinsella!
Kinsella!
He's the man for me!

Kinsella!
Kinsella!
It's on to victory!

He's marching marching marching
to the governor's chair.
Goodbye corruption: Kinsella's
on the square. . . .

I saw Charles; he was surrounded, on the far side of the room. They were laughing, he was smiling. A heavy perspiring man in a very blue tuxedo came up to me, a plate of food in his hand; he said, "Correct me if I'm wrong, but you're the Governor's brother, right?"

"His cousin," I said.

"Good for you!" he said promptly. "You've got a real sweetheart there!" With his free hand he tapped the plate of food. "Lobster!" he said. "That's the way you can always tell a real big-leaguer. Hey, Walshie!"

He grabbed the coat of a man who was about to pass without seeing him; the man stopped, turned, and delightedly called, "Edso! Whaddaya say?"

He was very small and very thin, with yellowish eyes and an astonishing set of false teeth which were much too large for his little face; he could hardly have looked less like the man who had stopped him, yet somehow there was a resemblance so strong it was remarkable.

"Happy days are here again!" Edso said. "Walshie, say hello to the Governor's cousin, who's a top-notcher in his own right. Let me see now, the first name is Ralph, am I right on that?"

I corrected him; he accepted the correction joyously. "*Jack!*" he cried. "Of course it's Jack! Don't tell me I forgot that! What the hell am I thinking of: it's a name I know as well as I know my own! How goes the battle, Jack?"

Ritual questions, ritual answers; I said, "Fine, fine."

"You're doing a great job there," he said vaguely. For a moment I wondered what would happen if suddenly I asked just what job it was that I was doing so well, but then of course I knew what would happen: nothing. The question would have been resented as being deeply unfair and antisocial. He said, "Jimmy's your uncle then, am I right on that?"

I said that he was right, and Walshie said, "God bless Jimmy. He's a credit to his people and someone the whole country can be proud of. He was always a good friend to me. And God bless the Governor and his lovely wife as well. You can tell him I said that, Jack. You can tell him it came right from the heart!"

"Right from the heart of a man that's looked death in the face and licked it!" Edso said. "Don't forget to mention that to the Governor while you're at it, Jack. Don't forget to mention that one of his very top campaign workers, Leo J. Walsh, got up off his ass and licked the deadliest enemy of modern times: cancer of the bowels!"

"After all the finest doctors at the Mother Cabrini Hospital had given me up for dead," Walshie said. "I fooled them all!"

"I tell you, whenever I hear a story like that," said Edso, speaking with difficulty, for his mouth was now full of food; he had resumed his eating from the plate he was carrying about with him, "I feel like saying a little prayer. Walshie, did you get any of this lobster? It's positively the greatest!"

Walshie said that he had, and that in fact he was now on his way back to the buffet table for seconds. "By God, a man that serves food like this can't help but be a great governor," he said. "I been in politics all my life, and I always say you can tell a man by the food he serves. Nothin' kills a man faster than servin' bum food. Look at Dan Cohalan. D'ye remember him, Edso? Down at the Department of Health?"

"Big Dan," Edso said. "With the cockeye. Retired now on a three-quarter pension."

"That's him," Walshie said. "Well, one time he decided to go for the City Council, so he gave a little party for himself over in the old Shore Gardens Hotel that's now the parkin' lot. Everybody was there, you know, and pretty soon Dan comes edgin' over to me and he says, 'Well, Walshie, how does it look from where you sit?' I says to him, I says, 'Dan, I got to tell you the truth: you're all done. You haven't got a Chinaman's chance. After servin' food like this you couldn't get elected dog-catcher!' Well, he gets right up on his high horse, you know, and he says, 'What the hell's wrong with this food? The trouble with you is you don't know classy food when you see it! You prob'ly think this is creamed chicken! Well, I'll tell you what this is: *it's genuine creamed capon, that's what it is!*' 'It is, is it?' I says. 'Then it's a damn funny kind of capon, that's all I've got to say. And if you want to know what I think, I think it's the kind of capon they spell s-e-a g-u-l-l!' "

"Good for you, Walshie!" Edso said. "Right smack on the button: it served him damn well right!"

He now decided to join Walshie in the search for seconds; they left together, with Edso winking a broad farewell at me, and punching me playfully on the arm as they moved away.

"Over the river!" he said jauntily. "And give my very best to His Excellency. Be sure you tell him that Edso Monahan is behind him all the way!"

I watched them go off into the crowd, Edso's blue tuxedo serving as a vivid, inescapable marker. I had never seen either of them before, but I felt as if I had known them forever and had heard this conversation a thousand times before. The time was the present, the scene had changed, but it was obvious that certain great constants in the political life of the city remained. I wondered exactly how Charles fitted Edso and Walshie into his announced program of the New Look in Government.

Looking across the room once more I could see that Charles was still standing on the far side of the room, his position unchanged, and still surrounded. Just at this moment, however, he looked up and over in my direction, and from the quick smile and the slight beckoning movement of his head I knew that he had seen me. I began to move toward him, but progress was slow, for all at once a great many more people seemed to have come into this room, which was already unpleasantly crowded. They must have come in from the lawn: possibly because a night wind had come up, possibly because they sensed that at any moment now the Governor would speak. It was out of the question to move in any straight path; I tacked my way back and forth among swirling groups of people, and as I did so I noticed for the first time the peculiar nature of this gathering. It was not like the old political crowd—not at all. It was noisy, happy, even jubilant, but it was not a *crowd*. It was, instead, a large grouping of independent knots; walking through them, I saw that although the pressure of too many people in too small a space had forced these knots together, each knot had a life of its own and did not mix readily with its neighbor. They were adjacent islands, not a continent—the tie was Charles and that was all. Some of them I knew quite well, others I knew slightly, most I did not know at all. As I edged my way through them and past them I paused at times to exchange a shouted word, but for the most part I just moved along, and as I did so my pace was so slow and the voices were so loud that for moments I would seem stalled in the middle of a conversation in which I had no part, and every word I overheard seemed to emphasize still further the heterogeneousness of Charles's support. . . .

". . . we flew up yesterday morning. Nick stayed behind to come up with Davy, but that didn't matter because he couldn't vote anyway."

"What's the matter with Nick? Not registered?"

"Sweet, he hasn't registered for *ages.* Not since we bought the place on Cat Key. We're there all the time, we never see anyone any more. Of course it's an absolute dream, but who wants to be stuck there forever? But it's all because of taxes. . . ."

"Poor Polly. Tell Nick when he comes to write to Archie Tolliver. Archie has an arrangement in Switzerland which is practically bomb-proof as far as the IRS is concerned. It might be just the thing for you."

"I doubt it. Nick *loathes* Switzerland and I'm not mad about it either. I thought I might ask Charles: he's always so clever. And of course now he's in a position to help, isn't he . . . ?"

". . . you're attempting to tell me that alienation wasn't a factor in this election? Is that what you're attempting to tell me?"

"I'm not attempting to tell you anything. Why should I attempt to tell you a single word? You've got your own personal dialectic, anybody who doesn't agree one hundred per cent is automatically a *schmo.* So all right, I'm a *schmo.* Why should a *schmo* attempt to tell *you* anything?"

"You're a very resentful person, Bernie. The pathetic thing is you don't realize how resentful you are. Believe me, you could use some help. You could use a lot of help. . . ."

"Please, *fellas.* We won, right? So stop *arguing.* . . ."

". . . five hundred bucks a plate. A heavy tab, but a sellout from the word go. I'll tell you who the toastmaster was: Father

Artie McGuire. You know? From the Hill? He's just back from Rome. Vatican Council. He did a hell of a job. A million laughs, but something you could take home with you, too. Frank Regan got him for us."

"There's the boy that's loaded these days. Frank Regan. He's got nothing but money. Wall-to-wall. They say he's got all Jimmy Kinsella's insurance."

"And the boys' as well. A real shrewdie, Frank. And JoJo's up for the Federal bench. That's not bad, either."

"The only judge in the state who can't spell 'attorney.' But a prat-boy for Jimmy for years. He was damn near indicted on that finder's fee business. Georgetown, isn't he?"

"The Cross. . . ."

"Har har har! *Hey, Guido . . . !*"

". . . a fair student, no more. I remember a long paper he wrote on Charles James Fox. Not good, not really bad—just undistinguished. That was typical of all his work."

"Yes. I always thought the older brother was the brighter of the two."

"Phil, yes. I had them both; I wouldn't have picked either of them to do much of anything. Two more rich boys who did just enough to slide by, and why bother to do anything more? No, Charles is a great surprise to me. And a very welcome one. You see, what no one could have predicted was the *growth.* He's liberal, he's open-minded, he works hard at all the right things. And he has a quick, complete grasp of whatever you tell him: I found him very impressive all through the campaign."

"No reservations? I must say I'm not entirely happy about that Inner Guard."

"The ex-altar boy types, yes. I agree. But I think they're more a concession to the father than anything else. Charles is something else again. He's not an intellectual, despite all the claims. But he has a respect for those who are; I find him extremely sympathetic. I think you'll find that as time goes on a certain amount of jettisoning will be done, and that you'll be much happier with the replacements. I think that's inevitable. . . ."

". . . so I said, 'You fired this waiter. Why?' He said, 'Because he's not a good waiter any more. He mixes thing up, he drops things, he upsets the dining room.' I said, 'Okay. Now: was he ever drunk on duty?' He said, 'No.' I said, 'Okay. Now: did he swear or use bad words to customers? Did he insult them?' He said, 'No, he didn't do that.' So I said, 'Okay. Then I'll tell you what's gonna happen. You're gonna hire this man back as of now, or else I pull him and everybody else out of this hotel by tomorrow morning, and when all your fancy guests wake up there won't be a waiter or a maid or a bellhop in the joint. So make up your mind!' So they hire him back. They had to. What else could they do?"

"Don't tell that to the Governor. He stays in that hotel lots of times."

"Yeah? Well, maybe he should start stayin' in another hotel. . . ."

". . . trust him? That's what I'm asking you right here and now: *what makes you so sure you can trust him?*"

"And once again I answer you: I would rather trust him than the other."

"You think he understands? You think a rich white man with a million dollars in the bank, you think he even *begins* to understand?"

"I think if we supported only those who understood, we would support nobody. This is a practical situation, it is a situation of relatives, it is not a situation of absolutes. If you ask two men, 'Have we here *de facto* segregation?' and the one man says, 'No, we do not have *de facto* segregation,' and the other man says, 'Yes, we do have *de facto* segregation and it is a bad thing which I promise to do something about,' then it is not a question of absolute trust or of absolute anything but of accepting the better of the two. . . ."

And all this was a long long way from those shouting, cheering, unified throngs of only a few years ago, which as much as anything else, I suppose, were in reality clan rallies honoring the chief. But this was a gathering of disparate social, racial, and intellectual forces which would have been unthinkable behind any one candidate then, and while I had suspected something of this, it was not until I saw the victory party in action that I realized how effectively Charles had cut across the old established lines. So that while the old remained, something new had been added; Edso and Walshie were but a part of a far more complicated spectrum.

The orchestra had continued to play without interruption; directly in front of the musicians a space was being used as a dance floor, but this was pure farce; any sort of rhythmic movement was impossible. The curtains at the sides of the long open French windows began to blow in strongly as suddenly and blessedly the cooler air came into the room. I was close to where Charles had been standing, but now he was no longer there; looking around, I couldn't see him anywhere. Congratulations would have to wait. Still, I kept moving forward slowly—it was as good a direction as any—and as I came almost to the point where Charles had been, a hand touched my arm, tapping it twice, and when I turned I saw Marie.

"Charles was looking for you," she said. "I have a message to give you."

It was a gracious and rather formal statement; I knew that it had been meant not for me, but for the women to whom she had been talking. They were together in a clump, rather alike in appearance: in late middle age they were pale and fat-featured and laughed a lot. I knew that they were the wives of heavy contributors; for their part they would have given "at homes" and "bridge benefits" throughout the campaign. "Will you excuse me?" Marie said to them now. "Just for a minute? More family business."

She smiled at them; they laughed back; they laughed at me: I was lucky, I was family. Marie took my hand and led me a short distance across the room. For the first time that evening I could move quickly, for the crowd parted to allow her smiling passage. We got to a small alcove off the main room where, surprisingly, there were only three or four others, and where, even more surprisingly, the sound from the main room was somehow diminished, so that for a moment I had the impression of being in a place of great and sudden silence.

"No message," she said. "I just wanted a breather. How goes life, Jack? Isn't this a great night?"

She was a big woman, but not in the least bulky or buxom: she was just big and smooth and beautifully made. She was very fair, with large smoky-gray eyes and a full attractive mouth; her skin was marvelously clear and fresh and her hair was so blonde that when Jean had first seen it she had declared that it couldn't possibly be natural—and yet I think it was. There was something in her appearance which suggested the outdoor girl, but then there was something else which suggested a much more feminine side, and in fact that was much closer to the truth. She was very much an indoor girl, she was not fond of golf or tennis or riding or long brisk walks in the country. She paid close attention to her appearance and had a great sense of style—she was one of the best-dressed women I had ever seen. Charles was reported to have said, just before the election, that he considered the greatest contribution to his campaign to have been made by Givenchy.

Men found her very attractive and yet, as I've said, women liked her too. I think this may have been because she treated them not with mere politeness, but with a genuine friendliness. She liked people to like her, and while she had her party manner, she had a great naturalness too, and this kept breaking through. I had not known her before her marriage to Charles—indeed, who had?—but I liked her from the first, and I think that she liked me. At any rate, we had always been easy with each other. She said to me now, without waiting for an answer to her other questions, "How about it, Jack? Am I your first First Lady?"

"I met a queen once, but I'm not sure she counts. She'd been deposed for quite a while, and I guess she hadn't been much of a queen anyway. Besides, she was old and limped and had one eye. So I much prefer you. How are you bearing up?"

"Oh, you know me. I love it. Or most of it. It's exciting and wonderful—Jack, nobody ever won by such a margin before: did you know that?"

"Oh, I did indeed. There's not a loose marble left in the state; Charles has them all today."

"He has, hasn't he?" she said happily. "And the great thing is that nobody thought he could do it. Or almost nobody. For instance, you. You didn't think he could, did you?"

I shook my head. "I thought he'd carry the city easily enough, but I was sure Consolo would have too much strength up north. Not to cop a plea, but remember I'd been away."

"Well, when you got back you should have come to me," she said. "I'd have set you straight in a minute." She was a strong partisan of her husband and could be rather chilly with any of his friends or acquaintances who gave him less than all-out support, yet for some reason I had always been saved from this. Maybe it was because I was a relative for whom special rules applied, maybe it was because Charles himself had never seemed to mind in the least that I hadn't worked for him, or maybe it was simply because she knew that I really liked him—at any rate, all she said now was, "Poor Consolo. Or no, *not* poor Consolo, because he's really rather a dirty little man. He spread all kinds of stories about Charles—and about Charles and me. I'm used to that by now, but these were a little nastier than most. And he could have stopped them but he didn't. So I don't care what happens to him. I'm just happy for Charles." She gazed out into the big noisy crowded room and said, "If I lived to be a hundred and ten I don't think I could ever be any prouder!"

She looked it; I said, "You might even be a little proud of yourself, too."

"I am," she said frankly. "I helped a lot, I think. I went on television and that was all right, and I met old biddies and young biddies and old pols and young pols and people who'd known Charles since he was a baby and people who *said* they'd known Charles since he was a baby and I shook hands and I danced the basic box step with every dreadful dancer in the state. And I went to field days and cookouts and ball parks and rallies and reunions of Charles's old Air Force buddies, and some of it was wonderful and some of it was just so plain unbelievably boring that you'd want to shoot yourself that minute. But I did it, all of it, and I wouldn't *not* have done it for the world, and I know that in the end it helped. So in a way it's my night, too." Then she smiled and said, "And I'll tell you what I did. Tonight: just before I came downstairs. I'd finished dressing, and my maid had gone out, and I was all alone in the bedroom. And I stood in front of the mirror and just looked at myself for a long time. I thought I looked pretty." She glanced down at herself now with satisfaction. "Pretty enough to be the Governor's wife. And then do you know what I thought? I thought, 'Well, not bad for a little Pole from West Nowhere!' And it isn't, is it?"

"It's not bad for anyone from West anywhere," I said, and I meant it. But she meant it, too. She had been a poor girl, her parents had been born in Poland, and she herself had in a sense come from nowhere—certainly nowhere that my Uncle Jimmy had been willing to recognize. Charles had met her shortly after getting out of college, and what had happened then had been a genuinely romantic story. Because, where Phil had only the year before married Flossie, whom he had known all his life—a very fancy and glamorous wedding, with guests flown in from everywhere, and my Uncle Jimmy presiding loudly and proudly and lavishly—and I had just become engaged to Jean, whom I had known for most of mine, Charles, usually so much more watchful and prudent than either of us, fell in love with a complete stranger the very first time he met her. Love at first sight—and yet with Charles, of all people, it had happened. And I had been there when it had: at one of those huge charity balls held for the armed forces during the first year of the war. I had come home from the Navy and so had Phil—we had been able to arrange our leaves together—and Charles, as it happened, was to go into the Air Force the very next day: the ball was his last civilian fling. We had all gone together; I had danced mostly with Jean, Phil mostly with Flossie, and Charles—Charles, after the first dance, very little with the girl he had brought: I even forget now who she was. He had danced with Marie—and by what route Marie Granowski had got there, or with whom she had come that night, I never knew. I did know that she left with Charles, and that he went into the Air Force the next morning. He came back as often as he could, sometimes for only an hour or two; in a very short time they were engaged to be married. This roaring, swift romance was all extremely uncharacteristic of Charles, so uncharacteristic that it caught everyone by surprise, including my Uncle Jimmy. Apparently—although this was hard to believe, considering that shrewd man—he had suspected nothing: it may have been that he was too preoccupied with his own activities, which during the war involved enormous amounts of travel and were said by some to be invaluable. He had of course met Marie, but then he had met many of Charles's girls; when, suddenly, he had discovered that this was something different, he had been furious. First there had been the matter of James, to which he had only recently become reconciled; now there was Charles. He must have felt that his sons, one by one, were slipping away from his wishes, his plans, his control; he had raged at Charles (although as Charles told me, rather wryly, he could not threaten to cut him off entirely, as he had already settled a large sum on him on his twenty-first birthday); he had actually put detectives on Marie.

"And then when that didn't turn up anything juicy," she had said to me, much later, "he sent them out to my home town, to get a line on my pop. I think he was hoping for a blackmailer, or at least a thief. Instead all he got was a sleepy Polish butcher, who liked to drink and didn't like to work. So then all he could fall back on was the old wrong-side-of-the-tracks, but of course that didn't count much with Charles. And I don't think it really counted too much with Jimmy, either. He's pretty good on things like that. He's pretty good on a lot of things."

"He's just an old dear," I had said.

"No, he's not *that*. But he is pretty good. The only thing was, he didn't want his boy to be trapped by an adventuress. And then when he decided I wasn't one, he didn't make too much trouble. I think he might have liked me a little, even then. Anyway, he likes me now. So everything's turned out fine."

And it had. Jimmy had given in. Charles had been respectful but firm; unexpectedly he had received support from his mother, my Aunt Mary making one of her rare dissents from her husband. And Jimmy had capitulated, maybe out of sheer disgust; Charles and Marie had been married: a small wedding, a service wedding, but Jimmy had been there. And gradually he had come around. It may or may not have been true—as Marie had suggested—that Jimmy had liked her even then; I always thought that the turning point came sometime after my Aunt Mary's death, when my Uncle Jimmy began to spend more time with Charles and Marie. In any case, it was certain that she was a great favorite now. Charles had married well; Jimmy knew that and loudly gave praise where it was due.

"She's a sweetheart!" he had said to me, about five years ago. "And I had her pegged all wrong at first: I thought she was some kind of Hunky hustler. Well, why not? The woods are full of them. And Charles was a good-looking guy with plenty of dough: a perfect setup for some bimbo sharpshooter. When I first set eyes on this one I said to myself, 'She's got a great pair of legs: I'll bet they can run like hell after a million bucks!' Well, I was all wet. She's been the greatest thing in the world for him. When I think of some of the lemons he could have wound up with!"

For just a moment I had wondered if my Uncle Jimmy might not be turning obliquely to quite a different subject, one he had tried to discuss with me once or twice before—without much success, and with some unpleasantness. But then I had realized that he was not doing this, for he was not a delicate man: if he had decided to go after me again he would have done so head-on, not indirectly or by implication. So I had said nothing more, and neither had he.

Marie said now, "But you haven't even seen Charles yet!"

"I've tried, though. It's not that easy: everybody else has the same idea. But I'll make it."

"We were talking about you one night last week," she said. "Somebody—I guess it must have been your publisher—sent us your new book. We got in the house late one night—I forget where we'd been: campaigning somewhere—and there was your book, waiting for us. Charles picked it up and read it right through that night, all at once. He says it's the best one yet."

"Good for Charles. What did you think of it?"

She laughed. "That's a dirty trick," she said. "You know I haven't read it." Candidly she added, "And you know I won't. I always mean to, but I never do, do I? And everybody says they're wonderful. I always start them all right, but then I can't seem to pay attention to what's going on, and the first thing you know I'm lost. I think you have to have a special kind of mind to read mystery stories; anyway, I've never finished one. Not even yours, Jack. I feel terrible, but that's the way it is."

Ten years ago, I had written a suspense story. I had done this mainly out of uncertainty. I had written two books before this, both of them straight novels. The first had been ignored by all critics and had not sold; the second had been noticed by some, had won a mild respect—and had not sold. My situation had not been desperate, but neither had it been ideal. I was married, the income from the money my father had left me was constant but not large, in order to live comfortably I needed to earn more. There had been no shortage of available jobs, thanks to my Uncle Jimmy's influence, and he had several times urged me in one direction or another. But what I really wanted to do was write. I had no great dreams, I think I can honestly say I never overvalued myself as a writer, but what I did want to do was to write for myself, and to earn a living by that writing. I had discussed this with my publisher after the failure of my second book; he had not been helpful. He had dealt with the crisis in his usual manner: he had taken me to lunch. Here he drank a great deal and talked about his own problems and, toward the end of the lunch, he talked with a kind of mournful hopefulness about the possibility of my next book's achieving a "major breakthrough." I did not believe this, and I could see from his face that neither did he.

It was at this point that I had thought of writing a suspense story. Not a mystery, as Marie called it, not a thriller, not one of the newer *genre* in which the professional spy goes through his dirty business with disgust. I had thought of writing a book in quite another tradition—that of the ordinary unadventurous man accidentally caught up in the sinister world of international intrigue. *The Riddle of the Sands, A Coffin for Dimitrios;* I had often read and thoroughly enjoyed books like these, and now I thought I might try to write one. I did. I wrote it very quickly (for me): in less than four months *No Change for Connemara* was completed.

It was a success. It wasn't a best seller, but people bought it and read it, many more people than had ever bought anything I had written before. There was a fortunate sale to the moving pictures; my publisher began to ask me to lunch more often. I had found my niche at last. Or so he told me; I was not so sure. But when, a year later, I wrote another, and it also did well, then I was ready to believe. It was not the kind of writing I had intended to do in the beginning, but it was a kind of writing which apparently I did well, and—more important—it was a kind of writing I did not in the least look down on. I think they were all good books of their kind: they were honest, decently plotted, with believable characters, and were reasonably well written. I was proud of writing them, in fact; I knew that not everyone could have written them, and indeed that many writers who were better than I could not have written them, either. I was proud, then, of my particular competence. I wrote five more of these books, and by now I had a public: not vast, but steady. They were reliable buyers of my books, and these book sales, coupled with magazine and television rights, gave me an income which, although not handsome—it was miles short of Charles's or Phil's, for instance—still allowed me to live pleasantly and to travel as much as I wanted to.

The latest of these books, *The Zagreb Connection*, was shortly to be published. It was this which Charles had read and Marie, of course, had not.

"You're making a big mistake on this one," I said. "This one is great. It's about a Polish butcher's daughter who's torn between going into politics and becoming a private eye. It's based on real life."

"I'd *read* something like that," she said. "But you—"

She was interrupted suddenly by a roll of drums; we looked out of the alcove in the direction of the music and saw that the leader was standing in the foreground, motioning for silence. I had seen him often before: his name was Shep Nomad, and he was the current "society" orchestra leader, a prominent figure at the more splendid parties and receptions in the city. He was small and sleek and obsequious, and looked always as if he had recently been greased.

"Lovely ladies and your gentlemen!" he shouted. "May I have

your kind attention? May I? Please? If you will? Thank you. On this momentuous occasion, ladies and gentlemen, I would like to pay my own humble musical tribute, not only to our fine new Governor, but also to his very beautiful and very lovely First Lady. May we now play for your pleasure a song of my own composition, written specially for this great and joyous occasion? I call it 'It's Always Marie!' "

He turned with a great flourish of his baton; immediately the orchestra began to play a melody which sounded very much like several others they had previously played. The chunky blonde girl stepped up to the microphone and once more began to sing:

Who's the most beautiful?
It's always Marie!
Who's the most charming?
It's always Marie!

If anyone asks me
Who's fairest to see?
I tell them the truth
It's always Marie. . . .

The song went on for some time, through numberless mindless choruses; when it was over there was tremendous applause. Shep Nomad took the chunky blonde singer by the hand; they bowed together, acknowledging public tribute, and then they looked up and out over the crowd, possibly searching for Marie.

She was standing by my side; she hadn't moved since the beginning of the song. I hadn't looked at her, because I thought she must be dissolving in embarrassment. But now when I did I saw that I had been wrong, because she didn't seem embarrassed at all. The crowd had seen her by now and they were all looking toward us and applauding and shouting her name. She smiled and waved, and when she turned to me I saw that her eyes were truly shining.

"Oh, Jack!" she said. "It's so *cheap*. But isn't it wonderful!"

I suppose it would have been impossible for her to have been any happier than at that moment. She turned back to the crowd again and waved once more, and then, just before she went to meet them, she must have thought of something because she said to me, "Listen: I may not get another chance, but—have you heard from Jean? I mean, lately?"

"No," I said, a little stiffly, and a little untruthfully, too. Because I had heard from her, but this wasn't anything I talked about easily, not even with Marie.

"I wanted to tell you that I saw her a few months ago in Paris. We met on the street one day outside the Meurice. She was alone; I don't know where she was staying. She looked thin but very pretty and terribly chic. She came in for a minute and we had a cup of tea. She talked a lot about you."

"Yes, I know. She does that."

"Oh come on," she said impatiently. "Give her a break. What was so wrong about that? She knew I'd probably seen you and she just wanted to . . . I'll talk to you later," she said hastily, for the others had arrived and were thronging about her, and gradually she went through the crowd, away from me, shaking hands and smiling and accepting congratulations happily; I saw Shep Nomad moving steadily toward her, a sheet of music in his hand: the presentation copy.

For a few minutes after this I paid little attention to Charles's party; Marie's mention of Jean had for some reason troubled me much more than I would have expected. But I didn't think about this for long, because the party simply rode in over all private thoughts: it was too big, there was too much noise. And so once again I began to move around, wedging my way through the moving, shouting, munching surge of tuxedos, looking for Charles, who seemed to have vanished forever. Slowly it all began to seem like a tour of the past for me, because the longer I stayed, and the more I moved about, the more people I saw whom I hadn't seen for a long time, but whom I once had seen very often, some of them every day. One of these, the first I ran into, was a man I had been at school with when we were little boys. I hadn't spoken to him or seen him for thirty years, he was immensely altered—bald and very fat and every feature coarsened—with nothing of the little boy visible today, and I had even forgotten his name, but instantly, the moment I saw him, I knew him, in the way that you somehow do recognize some people who stay forever memorable, not because of themselves, but because of their connection with some early, unprecedented, even calamitous event—and in the case of this man shaking hands with me now, I could remember only that as a boy in the fourth grade he had been sent home to his mother time after time for the simple and appalling reason that he smelled bad.

And now he was greeting me and introducing me to his wife and announcing to me—somewhat disquietingly, in view of my one overwhelming memory of him—that he was my greatest fan. "I read them all," he said, "as soon as they come out. I read them all, and I like them all. They take my mind off myself at the end of a hard day's work. And that's saying something, because I work like a dog, day and night. Still, I can't complain. No man can that's done as well as I have."

"Kinsella," said his wife, looking at me. "Why, that's the Governor's name!"

"His brother," my fan said. "The Governor's his brother."

"His cousin," I said.

"Brother, cousin, what's the difference?" my fan said impatiently. "I'm not related to him at all, but did that stop me from giving him five grand for his campaign? You bet your sweet life it didn't. And there's plenty more where that came from. I may not write books, but I've done all right. I never like to talk about myself, but since you asked I don't mind telling you I've got it made. A good business, my wife here, a lovely home in the country, three wonderful kids, and in the sixty-three per cent tax bracket—how's that for a poor boy who had to make it on his own? And I did, Jack. I've cleaned up. But good!"

In more ways than one, apparently; I wondered if now he

sometimes remembered his old humiliations. I thought he probably did; they were usually the hardest to forget.

As I left him, still not able to recall his name, I saw Walshie coming toward me; I shifted course and got away. But the shift brought me smack up against another part of the past, for now I walked directly into a small, jam-packed circle of old acquaintances who were here rejoicing in the victory. I had known them all since college; fifteen years ago nothing could have brought them to a political gathering of any kind, but since that time there had been Adlai, there had been Jack, and now there was Charles. They had felt the touch, they had been spoken to, they had been awakened: for these correct candidates they had worked generously, hard, and sometimes with the arrogance of the freshly converted. In this they were assisted by their wives, who worked even more zealously, inspired by their belief that before the ADA and the League of Women Voters there had been Nothing.

We met, we talked, some of the wives asked me about Jean, but then we went back to politics and the victory which was theirs and the new regime in which it was assumed that they would all play some as-yet-undefined role. They were making their plans, they knew that Charles would call on them, they were very happy.

And still I hadn't done what I had come to do. I continued to walk and to stop and talk and to look around, but at no time did I so much as catch a glimpse of Charles; then, all at once, someone from behind gripped me by the elbow and held on, and when I turned around, there he was.

"Play your cards right," he said to me, "and I can get you an introduction to the Governor."

I hadn't seen him for months, apart from those television appearances; he looked fine. There were a few faint touches of fatigue around the eyes, but except for this he showed no signs of having been through a long and very difficult campaign. He looked the same as always: no sudden gray, no added lines. He seemed as self-contained as ever, he would never have been as openly rejoicing as Marie, yet I could tell that at this moment he was very pleased, and as I shook his hand and gave him my congratulations, I suddenly felt very happy for him and for Marie. And in a peculiar way I felt a satisfaction of my own, for this state, this city, was after all my home: I had had my childhood here, I had grown up here, I had spent most of my life here, and even though in recent years I had gone away often and sometimes stayed away a long time, I was a poor expatriate—I had never really felt at home anywhere else, and it had never occurred to me that this was not where I belonged. So I was bound here, it was a pleasant place to live, and yet it—and those of us who lived here—had been sold down the river time and time again. Politically it was a mess, and close to being a disaster. It had been this way for years, at least ever since I had begun to be interested in such matters. Someone once said of us that corruption here had a shoddy, penny ante quality it did not have in other states, that here everything was up for grabs and nothing was too small to steal. This probably was one of those facile overstatements much easier to make than to prove, but it's true that underneath everything in our politics there seemed to be a depthless cushion of street-corner cronyism, a special kind of tainted, small-time fellowship which sent out a complex of vines and shoots so interconnected that even the sleaziest poolroom bookie managed in some way, however obscure, to be in touch with the mayor's office or the governor's chair. (Three years ago, for instance, there had been an assistant attorney general who had conducted a series of investigations into fraud in the state. These investigations had been slow, expensive, and productive of nothing; they had been on the point of being abandoned when suddenly, through some slipup, it was revealed that two and perhaps three of those being investigated had hidden but firm business links with the assistant attorney general's mother. Further digging had revealed further facts: the governor had been in a quandary. It was a matter of some delicacy: not only was the assistant attorney general involved, but the mother had some time before been voted our state Mother of the Year. Reluctantly, and speaking feelingly of a mother's misplaced zeal, the governor had at last fired the assistant attorney general, who had then been tried, found guilty, given a suspended sentence, and had then, in penitence, purchased a rather pleasant property in Jamaica. The Mother of the Year, herself mysteriously at liberty, had never forgiven the persecutors of her son. "The bastards were out to get him," she said grimly, "and get him they did! I hope to God they all fry like sausages in hell!")

This was an accepted condition of our political life. It was given periodic official rebuke and constant unofficial encouragement. And now, with Charles in charge—what? Who knew? He was unquestionably honest, he was competent, he came from a different tradition and had inherited none of the usual obligations, so that he was certainly freer than most to make changes. And yet the question remained: could changes—anything other than token changes, that is—really be made? Given, for example, our legislature? Or given, for another example, our state? Or even, come to think of it, given Charles? Because as I stood here looking at him, congratulating him, and taking pleasure in his victory, I suddenly realized how little I knew him. The Charles I really knew was a fat little boy who fell off horses, who was a pest with his questions, who played catch with me on an Irish lawn, who was my junior by a year and who had always been that year behind me in school. And I suppose I still thought of him in that faintly patronizing way you do think of slightly smaller boys who are a year or a step behind, who always seem to be tagging along, when the truth was that he was a grown man, a rich man, and a powerful man, who must have changed no less than all of us change, who had had three children and all kinds of other experiences which I had not, and who, because he had a life of his own which was increasingly removed from mine, now had ideas and abilities and strengths or defects which I couldn't even begin to assess. So that it was probably presumptuous and even meaningless for me to be standing here, calculating his chances of success, especially when all the room was filled with an excitement, a positive hope that something new and good was about to happen. And despite my own pessimism I couldn't help, just at this moment, feeling at least some of that excitement myself, but all I said to him was, "I'll give you a compliment: you're a great improvement on your predecessor."

"Thanks a lot," he said dryly. "Don't say any more: effusiveness embarrasses me. How've you been?"

"Not bad." We stood, just for a second, looking at each other; I said curiously, "Charles, what does it feel like? Being elected Governor?"

"Oh," he said, "a little like being elected mayor. Only more so. You haven't met these two, have you?"

I hadn't. They were two men who had come up with him and were now standing slightly to his rear. They were slender, neat, unremarkable-looking—I could have seen either one of them a hundred times any day in this city—and young: I guess they were perhaps seven or eight years younger than Charles. And oddly, while they were not at all alike in their appearance, there was something about each one that suggested the other: a shared attitude, I think, more than anything else, an air which was pleasant but extremely alert; it was as if they were both enjoying themselves quietly but keeping their eyes peeled, too. When Charles introduced us I recognized the names as those I had heard again and again during the final weeks of the campaign: they were two of the inner circle of professional young politicians who had rallied to Charles from the beginning, who had served him while he was mayor, and who were now said to be closer to him than anyone with the exception of his brothers and my Uncle Jimmy.

"They know all about you," Charles said. "Jerry's read all your books, including the two early ones. Ray doesn't read much of anything but the voting lists, but then of course he went to Loyola, where the curriculum prepares you for that sort of thing."

The two men smiled; the smaller one—Ray—said to me, "We have one connection, though. I think you know my dad: Bill Keegan. He used to be a cop at City Hall; he was always assigned to Frank Skeffington."

I had known his father well: a slim, solemn-faced man fanatically tidy, impeccably honest—in short, a great curiosity in the force. Skeffington had been very fond of him, and I told his son this now.

He nodded. "It worked both ways. Dad always liked him a lot; he'd never hear a word against him." He smiled again and said, "Apparently the old man used to give him these Babe Ruth autographed baseballs to pass around to the kids. As souvenirs of the city. I always wondered who really did that autographing. Skeffington himself?"

It was a simple question which took me in an instant back across twenty years to a hot, dusty afternoon in summer—early summer, before everyone had left on vacation. The overhead fan was circling slowly in the mayor's office, the blinds were partly closed so that the light came in broken by thin slats of shadow, while the courtly old figure—looking, at this time of the year, like a Southern plantation owner in his ice cream suit—rose from behind the vast mahogany desk, slowly fingering a baseball which he had selected from the big box on the floor beside him.

"Magnificent game," he had said thoughtfully. "It has everything. A golden opportunity to throw deadly objects at the heads of all your friends and still claim it's all being done in the spirit of fun. I've always thought that a game like that had to be invented by the Irish. Come on, let's get these things signed. All these admiring youngsters have parents who vote."

I said now, "Sometimes, when he felt like it. But mostly I did."

The three men looked at each other; Charles said, "The good old days. You see how simple it was?"

"I'll tell my dad I saw you," Ray said. "He's retired now."

"Like Jack," Charles said. "Jack retired from politics years ago because of old age. He was twenty-five. He went out with Skeffington. The difference was that he went out voluntarily." He looked at me with amusement in his eyes. "Any time you want to make a comeback," he said.

And quite suddenly, as he was talking, I realized how odd all this was: standing here in Charles's house, talking to Charles about Frank Skeffington, with Charles himself now incredibly in the same position of powerful control that Skeffington once had held—and talking, moreover, as if we were having a private conversation, when I didn't have to look around or even lift my head to be reminded that it was very far from being private. All the while we had been talking we had been ringed by an audience which had kept the minimum respectful distance, and which seemed to be held back by invisible leashes. They were eager, not missing a word; obviously they were just waiting their chance to swoop in on Charles.

Jerry, who had said very little up to now, suddenly stepped forward and said something quietly to Charles, so quietly that I couldn't hear it. Charles frowned slightly, then looked at his watch and said, "All right. If you can stand it I guess I can." To me he said, "Jack, will you be around awhile? I have to see somcone."

"I think I might go along. It's a busy night, Charles; I just wanted to come in to say hello."

"No, stay," he urged. "We're all getting together up in the library. Pa's here, Aunt Gert: everybody. They'll want to see you, and I want to talk to you. Go on up to the library in about fifteen minutes; they'll all be there by then. Meanwhile," he said, glancing around, then coming back to me with the same amused look in his eyes, "I have a treat for you. Just to help you pass the time. And to remind you of those good old days."

He beckoned to the crowd and said, "Ben, come on over here a moment." Immediately a thin long-faced man in his late middle age shot out of the crowd and was by our side. Unlike the others in the room, he was not wearing formal clothes. He had on a military uniform, and in his hand he held an overseas cap. He said, in a voice which was like a salute, "Governor, at your service!"

"This is Commander Ben Bannigan, who's in charge of one the posts of the Veterans of Foreign Wars," Charles said, looking at me now with a complete absence of any kind of expression. "The Commander came to us several times during the campaign with a problem that's been bothering him, and I'm afraid we may have let him down. Knowing your deep interest in the veterans, Jack"—and here, privately, for me, there was just the flick of expression—"I thought you were probably just the man to help him out. Ben," he said, switching to the Commander, "this is my cousin, Jack Kinsella. He writes books, but more to the point, he used to be the confidential secretary of a great friend of yours, Frank Skeffington. So I know that your particular kind of problem is right up his street. Now, if I were you, I'd tell him all about it."

It was a dirty trick; I knew that even before I saw Charles's two aides exchange glances, I knew it as soon as I saw the Commander. He was a familiar type; he was on me even before Charles, with a little nod and just the faintest of smiles, left.

"Thank God you were a personal friend of Frank's!" the Commander said; he had me by the coat, grabbing me with a thick-veined little hand. "There's the man that could of settled all this with both hands tied behind his back. I don't say a word against your cousin the Governor, we're right behind him all the way, but there's a lot of young wise guys around him that tries to keep the veterans away from him. Wise little sons of bitches that never was near a trench. What the hell do they care about men that left their families and got gassed and died and . . ."

This went on for some time; after a few minutes he turned to a more particular grievance. A rival organization had been poaching on his preserve: on the previous Memorial Day, Legionnaires all over the state had been observed selling poppies. And not just selling poppies, but announcing them to be the genuine *Buddy Poppies*. The Commander was in a rage.

"What the hell right has the Legion got to sell Buddy Poppies? Buddy Poppies belong to the Veterans of Foreign Wars! We always had that name! There's only one veterans' organization in the country that's always had the right to sell Buddy Poppies on Memorial Day and that's the VFW! And this year what happens but all of a sudden those Legion bastards start showing up on street corners all along the whole parade, telling people that don't know any better that they were selling Buddy Poppies! All a damn lie, but who lifts a finger to stop it? Nobody! You might just as well live in Russia when men that gave up their jobs and their arms and their legs to fight for their country can't even come back and sell their own Buddy Poppies without somebody else that's got no right muscling in and . . ."

Charles had disappeared from the room. The Commander was his legacy to me, his little joke, and I couldn't decide whether he was paying me back for having said merely that he was an improvement over his awful predecessor—which was a fairly pale compliment—or whether he was showing me some of the slight contempt he undoubtedly felt for the older kind of politics and the simpler kind of problem which had been so conspicuous a feature of them—and showing me, moreover, by using (or slightly burlesquing?) a favored technique of Skeffington himself. In any case, I was saddled with the Commander, a survival from another day, and as he churned unhappily along, I heard him without really listening to him and without being particularly bothered or even bored. I had time to kill before I went up to the library, there was no one down here I especially wanted to see, and since more people seemed to have come in it would have been harder than ever to move around. So I stayed where I was, and while the Commander continued his aggrieved chatter, I found myself thinking once more of Skeffington, not only because this was his kind of trick, but because it was he who had taught me how to listen to all such sustained complaints.

"The thing to remember is that all pests are talkers," he had said to me one day. "The women are the worst, but the men are bad enough. There's no such thing as a pest who listens. A pest talks, and he talks all the time. Now, if one gets hold of you, there are a couple of ways of handling him. The first way is simply to stare at him while he talks to you. Just stare: don't answer back, don't say a word, don't make a sound: just keep looking right into his eyes. Sooner or later, this will get to him. Silence unnerves pests. They don't really want you to say anything, but they expect you to nod and make certain ritual sounds—'uh-huh' is highly acceptable—whenever they pause for breath. That proves you're there and listening. If you don't do that it throws them off; they start to stumble, pretty soon they stop talking, and then they go away. The only trouble is that they're apt to go away mad, and if you're in my profession it's necessary to remember that pests vote too. So I've settled for another way: matter of fact, I've become rather good at it. It requires the appearance of sympathetic understanding. It's not necessary to listen to anything they say—you can keep right on going with your private thoughts—but every once in awhile you have to cluck or shake your head and make little noises of commiseration. They won't pay any attention to *what* you say; it's the sound that counts. Once you get good enough at it you can say anything: you can spout Jabberwocky at them and they won't bat an eye. The secret is in using the proper tone. And then, when they're all done, you simply look at them, take them by the hand, and say, 'I thank you. You've done us all a great service.' Or words to that effect; I don't want to seem too rigid. You'll have to develop your own style. We've got a prize specimen coming in here in a few minutes; I may be able to give you a slight demonstration."

And when the man had come in he had come in talking; even while Skeffington was shaking his hand he was into his subject. A seedy little fanatic, he had come to talk about playgrounds. The city playgrounds were in poor shape; there were swings and dandles, yes, but where were the adult facilities; a cousin of his, an honor student at a well-known college for gymnasts, had been unable to secure summertime employment at any of these playgrounds; what was going to be done about the men's toilets? Skeffington had listened with courtesy, occasionally inclining his large head in grave agreement; whenever his visitor came up for air Skeffington murmured, indistinguishably and soothingly. This went on for a few minutes and then suddenly, during one of the pauses, Skeffington, using the same soothing tone, said very distinctly, "Abracadabra, dum dum dum!"

Startled, I had looked at his visitor, expecting indignation or at least bafflement. Instead the man had nodded vigorously and said, "Right! And another thing . . ." And he had gone on talking. Skeffington had not even glanced at me during this, but later, when the man had left, after first being thanked for being of service to the city, the old man had said to me, "I'm getting old: I'm showing off. Parlor tricks. But I wanted you to see that with people like that you never have to listen to a word because they never listen to you. And if you want to say anything it's perfectly all right, as long as you say it in the right way. The manner is everything. Now go on home and practice on a relative. Or the parish priest. First thing you know you'll be a virtuoso and you'll save yourself all kinds of trouble in later life."

I had not practiced, I had not become a virtuoso, but simply by being around Skeffington I had at least learned to listen the right way, and this is what I did now with the Commander. Finally he finished; at least there were no more sounds; I said that terrible things were on the increase and this was certainly one of them. We shook hands and the Commander left me, presumably to find another listener. Alone, I looked around, the room was as active and noisy as ever, the music was pounding away, Shep Nomad was now himself singing hoarsely a song of someone else's composition, and I looked at my watch and then I started for the front hall and the stairs which led to the library and the family—the more private division of Charles's great victory party.

six

THE library doors were closed; it was Phil who opened them. "Aha!" he said. "Writer, traveler, total stranger. Come in anyway. We're talking about politics. How's that for a surprise?"

I hadn't seen him since I had come home. Like Charles, he seemed completely unchanged, and for just that moment of meeting I got, once again, that sudden flash of confusion, the sense of jumbled identities. He said shrewdly and at once, "And the funny thing is I knew you right away."

I said, "Cut it out. Did either one of you ever think of wearing a moustache? Or a badge?"

"Speak to the candidate," he said. "Or correction: the Governor. As of yesterday. He's not here at the moment, but everybody else is, as you can see. We're all running away from that Elks picnic downstairs. How about that turkey-trot music, by the way? Isn't that the greatest? Were you moved?"

"Deeply. Every note an experience."

"I thought so," he said. "Especially that song to Marie. I tell you, Jack, the people who go around saying lovely melodies died with Jerry Kern just don't know Shep Nomad."

"Never mind that," Marie said, coming over to us. "Nobody's ever written a song to you, and nobody ever will."

"Positively not Shep Nomad," he said. "Or at least I hope not. Because for one thing he's queen bee in the local fag set. Just in case you've led a sheltered life."

"Who, the band leader?" my Uncle Jimmy said. He had been standing over by the television set talking to my Aunt Gert and Phil's wife, Flossie; they had all waved as I came in, and my Uncle Jimmy had left them and followed Marie over to us. Now sixty-seven or sixty-eight, he seemed to me the one who had changed least of all, because he looked exactly as I remembered him in Ireland thirty years ago and at all the stages in between. It wasn't that he had preserved his youth; it was simply that, to me, he had always looked just about the way he did now: never young, never old, but persistently ageless. He said to me, "Hello, Jack, how's the boy?" He made a fist and delivered a short mock-punch to my side. "What about that bandleader?" he said. "He's a nance, right?"

"The nanciest," Phil said.

"I thought so," my Uncle Jimmy said. "I can spot a nance a mile away. When I saw this chump with his greasy eyes waving his tail up there I said to myself, 'Oh oh: another one.' I'd get rid of him. Fast. I wouldn't have him around the house for five minutes."

"We thought it was safe enough," Marie said. "What can he do: seduce an alderman on the bandstand?"

From the beginning she had never been particularly deferential to my Uncle Jimmy. She had always spoken up to him, and although this had seldom been welcomed at first, in the end it had won her a position of privilege. It was a position not shared by everyone—Flossie, for example, although originally considered to be a far greater catch, had never quite managed to make the grade.

"Listen," my Uncle Jimmy said, taking me by the arm, "how about giving this subject the old heave-ho? Hah? Charles is Governor, here's Jack back again, and we stand around shooting the breeze about some fat-assed nance. Now if you and Charles want him in your house that's okay with me. Just so long as the kids are out of the way and asleep. For all I care he can shuck off his clothes and chase a monsignor around the piano."

"That ought to help out," I said, "with Charles as Governor. I imagine a thing like that could get into the papers."

My Uncle Jimmy gave me a derisive look. "What'll you bet?" he said. "For instance, what paper? Don't make me laugh. I hear you've got a new book."

"Brand-new," I said. "It comes out practically tomorrow."

My Uncle Jimmy nodded. He was greatly interested in my books. Not that he enjoyed reading them—I don't think he ever read one; in fact I never saw him read any fiction, let alone mine: he had little time for such frivolity—but his conception of family loyalty included more than support to his sons. Indirectly I learned that he bought, personally, a thousand copies of every book I wrote as soon as it was published; he distributed these books to friends and acquaintances everywhere. When, once, I had thanked him for this, and told him that it was far beyond ordinary kindness and, moreover, that it was not really necessary, he had denied the whole thing.

"I might buy a copy or so at an airport," he said, "to give to some lunkhead beside me on a plane. I figure it might keep him from getting airsick and heaving all over me. But that's all."

But I think he was really rather proud of having a writer in the family—even a writer of mysteries—and quite often I ran into people who told me that my Uncle Jimmy had been boasting about me. Quite often, too, I got little appreciative notes from people—sometimes people of surprising eminence—who had been on the receiving end of my Uncle Jimmy's largess. So that now when he nodded I knew that he was making a mental note for still another purchase order.

"I've seen it around the house," he said. "Charles has got it. He read it and liked it. Have you seen him yet?"

I said I had, and he said, "There's a sweetheart for you: he'll show them all how to do it before he's through. He ran a campaign that would knock your hat off."

I said, "I hear you helped."

"You're damn right I did," he said. "I hear you didn't."

I often wondered how long my immunity from my Uncle Jimmy's displeasure would continue. Like Charles, like Marie, like the rest of the family, he had always seemed to accept the fact that I just didn't get involved in Charles's campaigns, and this was curious, for although I think he understood the reason, I don't think he had any great sympathy with it, and he had always expressed himself frequently and loudly on the need for solidarity in family matters. Also, it was my guess that he privately thought that any contribution I might make would be negligible. I wasn't sure of this, though: he was a prickly man, and whenever he spoke sharply—as he had just now—I suspected that an explosion might be near. But I had always found directness the best tactic with him, and so I said, "That's right, I didn't. So I guess we both heard right."

Phil said easily, "Pa, are you getting set to wallop Jack?"

But it was all a false alarm; my Uncle Jimmy just laughed. "Listen," he said, in great good humor, "I feel too good tonight to wallop anybody. And can't you see an old poop like me trying to wallop this kiddo; he's got a build like a fullback!" It was a pleasant, if absurd, exaggeration: it was my Uncle Jimmy's high spirits. He swung another mock-punch at me and said, "And why should I want to wallop him? Hah? Whose beeswax is it if a sharp young guy with a lot on the ball wants to stay home horsing around with fairy stories when he could be out in the action and helping to run the show? All because he got mixed up with that old chromo twenty years ago and after that he got sour on the whole deal! Right?"

"You know that's the second time tonight somebody brought

Skeffington up," I said. "The first time it was Charles, about a half an hour ago. It's interesting the way he seems to stick in your mind."

"Don't try to give me the needle!" my Uncle Jimmy said, not quite so jovially. "He doesn't stick in my mind! I dropped that clown in the dead letter slot thirty years ago! All these mush-mouthed Micks around here thought he was God with that fake voice and the big hello! But I had him pegged from the start: a small-timer from the word go! Strictly a local con man: every time he left town to monkey with the big boys they had to loan him his carfare to get home!"

Even so long after Skeffington's death, my Uncle Jimmy spoke with a kind of growing fury; I never knew just what the quarrel between the two men had been. I had asked my Uncle Jimmy but he had refused to be pinned down to any definition; Skeffington had contented himself with ironic reference, calling him Mister Pazoosas, The Father of the Family, or The Kindly One. My father once told me that in his opinion there had never been any single quarrel, but that Skeffington had enjoyed baiting my Uncle Jimmy and had done so almost continually.

"He couldn't resist," my father said. "A man like your Uncle Jimmy, who was so full of the miracle of his own achievement, and who really had very little humor to go along with it, was a natural for Skeffington. The old man just kept on rolling off these elaborate compliments which always turned out to be rather mortifying taunts, and Jimmy kept on frothing at the mouth. It was foolish of both of them, of course. It was foolish of Skeffington because more than once Jimmy could have been of great help to him—and as it was, more than once he nearly ruined him. And it was downright silly of Jimmy, because by then he was operating nationally, he wasn't interested in purely local politics, and what Skeffington said shouldn't have bothered him at all. But it did. Oh my, how it did!"

And, apparently, still did. But it was a subject we left now, because my Aunt Gert and Flossie joined us—my Aunt Gert looking older now, her hair gray, but still laughing, still very fat, still going on her pilgrimages with her girl friends, and still keeping a very sharp eye on the things that mattered: AT&T, IBM, Standard Oil of New Jersey. She had never remarried; she was very rich. She greeted me now hugely and moistly with a great kiss on the cheek, and I said to her, "Aunt Gert, I've missed you more than I can say. I haven't had a word of sensible advice since I last saw you. Let's get together some day soon for lunch. I have a few questions I'd like to ask you about growth stocks."

"Growth stocks!" she said delightedly. "Listen to the boy, Jimmy: *growth stocks!* You might just as well ask me about Zulu cannibals or what it's like up there on the moon. Growth stocks: Mother of God, what would I know about a thing like that?"

And she gave her great laugh. It was a game she still loved to play: a bewildered woman, helpless in a male world run by skillful rascals. Phil said to me, "Aunt Gert's just back from Lourdes. How is it over there this year, Aunt Gert? They're still in the same line of work, are they?"

"Oh yes, they don't change. Well, they're like most of the rest of us, aren't they? I don't think we change much either. Of course," she said pleasantly, "some of us grow up a little."

"Pow!" Marie said. "Did anyone feel that, I wonder?"

"Hey, Aunt Gert," Phil said admiringly, "who taught you how to throw that right?"

Aunt Gert beamed at him. "God love you, dear," she said. "What right? Aren't we having just a little family chat?"

"Jack," Flossie said, in her clear and rather formal voice, "how long will you be back this time?" She was changing the subject and none too artfully, but she was never quite at her ease in the presence of this family badinage, even though by this time she had been exposed to it for a good many years. She was tall, as tall as Marie, but slimmer, dark-haired, and quite beautiful in a strange way: her eyes were a deep, extraordinary violet, really remarkable, and were long and faintly oblique. This gave her something of an exotic appearance which was entirely misleading, for Flossie was a great conservative: she was a good wife and an excellent mother, she did all the correct things instinctively and well. And yet in this family she remained a little bit of an outsider. She came from old, honored Yankee stock—she was the only non-Catholic in my Uncle Jimmy's family circle—and even her accent set her apart; Jean used to call her Little Girl Lost. This was too strong—in the family she was not a lonely or forlorn presence—but it's true that she failed to fit in as completely as the rest. The key to this was of course my Uncle Jimmy. He was neither cruel nor rude to her, but he was apt to pass her by, to pay her less attention than he paid others, and when, feeling this, she tried, with well-mannered little courtesies and well-intentioned behavior, to work herself into his particular good graces, she sometimes tried too hard.

"She presses," Phil had once said to me. It was the only time he had ever spoken to me about his wife and his father, but I knew that it bothered him. "She presses all the time with him, and you can't press too hard with a bulldozer like Pa: it just makes him worse. I've told her that, and she knows it, but she goes on pressing. She can't help it: she wants to be liked. Well, okay, I'm all for that, because he should like her: she's a great girl. But she doesn't understand Pa, and he sure enough doesn't understand her. He thinks she's la-di-da; as soon as she opens her mouth to offer him a hot dog he starts thinking of Episcopal bishops!"

I liked Flossie and felt a little sorry for her. Whenever I thought of her I thought of a well-tanned girl in a white tennis dress—she was a very good tennis player and had won local championships—walking with a brisk, long-legged stride off the court, to be joined by her four little children, who obediently and affectionately followed Mommy to the pool.

I talked with her now for a moment, and then my Uncle Jimmy came back. He had gone off to fix himself a drink; now he came back saying loudly, "Listen—"

But exactly what we were to listen to was not said, for just then James came into the room. He greeted me and explained that he had been off in one of the bedrooms, changing; he was leaving in a few minutes to catch a plane to Miami and then to South America; on the very next evening he would address some sort of ecumenical conference in Peru.

"Why Peru, for God's sake?" Phil said.

"Why not Peru?" James said. With a swift automatic deftness he folded a long white scarf, slipping it into a black attaché case and snapping the case shut. "The trouble is you can't hold all your meetings in Atlantic City if you claim to be a Universal Church. People eventually get suspicious. Besides, I like Peru. There's nothing I look forward to more than preaching in Cuzco. I'll be doing that next Sunday."

"It's your sense of continuity," I said. "The Incas, the Temple of the Sun, and now you."

"It's a matter of height, not history," he said. "You see, in Cuzco you're eleven thousand feet up. The plaza is packed with people, you begin preaching, and pretty soon they start dropping like flies, one by one. You never can be sure whether it's the altitude or the impact of your message. But it's very gratifying: I never come away from Cuzco without feeling slightly awed by my own powers."

Marie said, "James is right out of the Renaissance. A worldly cleric."

"A much-traveled cleric, anyway," Phil said. "This week Cuzco, next week Nome, then on to Barcelona. Have soutane, will travel. Has anyone ever done a paper on *Pan-Am and the Pastor*? James, whatever happened to all those good old country priests I used to read about?"

"They're right where they always were," James said. "In the country." He looked at me and smiled and said, "Actually."

He was not yet forty-five, but his hair was pure white; as slim and as elegant as ever, he was a handsome man: the best-looking of the three brothers. Twenty-five years ago he had surprised everyone by entering the seminary. Most of all, I remember, he had surprised my Uncle Jimmy, who had been furious: he had not raised his oldest boy to become a humble diocesan priest. He had been mollified, however, when James had not become one. Instead he had become famous. Or moderately so: he was certainly one of the best-known priests in the country, but owing to the imprecision which occasionally marks newspaper coverage of the clergy, he was not infrequently described as "the brilliant Jesuit preacher." This James had come to accept with an exasperated tolerance.

"The papers are wonderful," he had said. "And the magazines. You see, they have a simple gauge: any priest who can say 'nuclear' instead of 'nucular' is by definition a Jesuit. And any Jesuit is of course a brilliant Jesuit. Therefore . . ."

He was surely bright, probably brilliant; he was a remarkably good preacher; he was not a Jesuit. He was in fact a parish priest who had risen far above the limits of his parish. In this rise he was undoubtedly helped by my Uncle Jimmy, whose network of well-placed connections could hardly have been a handicap, but the greatest help of all had come from another quarter in the form of the winds inspired by Pope John and the *aggiornamento*. Extremely able, temperamentally suited to the new movement, James had ridden these winds; in the interest of Church Unity he traveled everywhere, an immaculate, persuasive apostle of peace, healing old wounds, addressing traditional enemies. His work was now almost entirely with what were called the Separated Brethren; so much so that Phil once said to me, "I saw James doing a funny thing this morning: he was talking to a Catholic!"

And now he was leaving the family, and the new Governor, on his way to Peru; my Uncle Jimmy said, "Watch out for those babies down there, boy. A handful of crooked Spics sticking the shiv into a mob of midget Indians: that's Peru. I know; I had a little business down there a couple of years ago. Everybody was on the take."

James said, "I've got protection: my host is Archbishop Segura."

"Forget it," my Uncle Jimmy said. "I know him, too. He's got a hand like a first baseman's mitt and it's always out. You'd be better off staying at the Y."

James nodded, seemed amused, but said no more. He got ready to leave, then drew my Uncle Jimmy to one side and they held a short private conversation while the rest of us talked together. In a few minutes they rejoined us; James said goodbye to us all, gave us his blessing, and then left to go looking for Charles. But this proved to be unnecessary, for just as he opened the door Charles came in. The two brothers stood there for perhaps thirty seconds, talking; James laughed at something Charles said. Then he turned and waved to us and was off on his way to Peru and still another conference.

Charles greeted us, kissed Marie, then dropped into a chair. "Does anybody here want to be Governor?" he said. "I've just finished a fifteen-minute talk with Dan Cogan."

I had known Cogan years ago, when he had been a young, primitive, and extremely ambitious politician. He had had great success and now ruled the state legislature with a firm and rather brutal hand. My Uncle Jimmy said, "What did that bum want?"

"He said he didn't want anything," Charles said. "Except to wish me well."

"For fifteen minutes?" Phil said.

"There did seem to be one thing more," Charles said. "He said he was eager to cooperate in every way. Jack, back in the golden days, what did it mean when a man like Dan Cogan, in Dan Cogan's position, said that he was eager to cooperate in every way?"

I said, "It meant that he wanted a piece of the action. Usually a rather big piece. And of all the action."

He nodded. "It's nice to know that the old customs still hang on. Because that's what Cogan wanted, of course. He reminded me of the help he'd given me during the past year. Then he talked a bit about legislatures and governors, and how one depended on the other. Nothing very specific: just good, general, reasonably offensive talk."

"He's bad news," my Uncle Jimmy said. "You're going to have trouble with that baby."

"I think we're all agreed on that," Charles said.

"He's horrible," Marie said, with a little shiver. "I mean, really horrible: of all the people in the campaign he's the only one I couldn't stand even being near. He's always *touching* you: even when he shakes hands he can't help hanging on for that extra second."

"He touches everyone," Charles said. "Except perhaps his wife; I don't think he cares much about shaking hands with her. He's had a succession of young secretaries; one of them was a pretty little Puerto Rican girl named Rodriguez. She's back in Puerto Rico now with nothing to remind her of Dan but a small income. And a five-year-old son who doesn't look particularly Puerto Rican."

"Can you tag him with that?" my Uncle Jimmy asked.

"No," Charles said. "That's always a chancy business. And in this case you just can't prove it. He's not a stupid man, you know. He's very clever. At least I think he is." He turned to my Aunt Gert and said, "How about you, Aunt Gert? You know about these things. Don't you think a man is clever who has a house in the country worth a hundred and fifty thousand dollars, an apartment in town which rents for thirteen and a half thousand a year, and tools around in a Cadillac Fleetwood—all on a declared income of twenty-two thousand seven hundred and fifty?"

"God love you, dear," my Aunt Gert said, "I only hope a clever man like that doesn't have any enemies. Because if he did I imagine one of them might put in a call to Charlie Halloran down at the Internal Revenue office. Charlie's a dreadful man for putting clever people in jail."

"I think those enemies have already called Charlie," Charles said. "He and some of his friends from Washington have had several talks with Cogan. It doesn't seem to have amounted to much."

"What about net worth?" my Uncle Jimmy said. "No soap?"

Charles shook his head. "No soap. He knows what he's doing; it's all covered up. Not a trace so far. By the way, how well do you know George Baxter?"

"Baxter Construction? I know him," my Uncle Jimmy said. "We used to play golf together once in a while at Shady Lawn." He said to me, "There was a hell of a golf course, Jack. Every green like a pool table. Your father used to play out there a lot; there was a dwarf caddie he liked. You ever been out there?"

I said I had, and he said, "I drove out a couple of weeks ago: you wouldn't know the place. All changed; it's not even a golf course any more. Some foundation's grabbed it and turned it into a joint where a mob of spongers live for free and tell each other how swell they are. Mostly writers and actors: your kind of racket. You know what I mean?"

"I know what you mean, Uncle Jimmy."

"I walked around for about half an hour," he said. "As far as I could see everybody out there was either a dope fiend or a dinge. Some foundation!"

"Fine," Charles said. "That's the kind of talk I like to hear. Let's get back to George Baxter: do you suppose you can get him in here to see me one day next week?"

"Why not?" my Uncle Jimmy said. "What for?"

"His company just got the contract on the new veterans' hospital," Charles said. "That's a Cogan project. I thought I'd talk to Baxter about a few of the details: there might just be something there. I doubt it, but you never know."

"You won't find out anything from Baxter," my Uncle Jimmy said, "because he's not running the show. The company's been reorganized; the real muscle there is the new treasurer: a sharp little Canuck called Allaire. From Quebec. Baxter's got nothing upstairs. He's a featherhead and he always was."

Charles said dryly, "That's all right with me. For this kind of talk I don't want Allaire; I want the featherhead. Maybe we'll get lucky. And maybe we won't. Maybe we'll just have to play along with the legislative leader a while longer." He looked across at Phil and said, "You haven't said much. No new thoughts?"

"No," Phil said, "but that's only because I'm pretty crazy about the old ones."

Charles said to me, "A behind-the-scenes glimpse of a crack in the solid Kinsella wall. Phil and I differ on the right way to handle people like Cogan."

Phil shrugged. "You're the Governor; you can handle it your way if you want to. That's obvious. And I'm not saying it won't work because I think it will. I *am* saying that in the long run it's dangerous, and dangerous to you. And you know what I mean because we've—"

And then Phil stopped in mid-sentence. He was now looking forward, talking directly to Charles as though the rest of us weren't here, and although he had started by talking casually, almost indifferently, he had suddenly begun to speak with intensity, even passion—which was startling, because no one in the room was prepared for it. Phil had probably realized this, because as he stopped so abruptly he glanced quickly around at all of us, and then he smiled and went back to Charles. He said in a quieter voice, and again as if only the two of them were talking together, "Just for a change, how would it be if I laid off crabbing tonight? And told you that I'm satisfied, that I'm glad, that I'm proud. And hopeful. Very hopeful. Because all that's true, you know. Believe it or not."

Charles looked back at him and smiled and said in the same personal, almost excluding way, "I think I'd like that."

My Uncle Jimmy broke in on this private conversation, sounding both annoyed and slightly baffled. "Hey hey hey!" he said. "What goes on here, anyway? You two going in business for yourself? Hah? What is all this bushwa?"

And for just a moment, in listening to Phil and Charles talk, I had shared my Uncle Jimmy's bafflement, because it seemed to me that I had caught a note I had not caught before—a somehow disturbing note—and when I looked at their wives I noticed that Marie seemed thoughtful and Flossie definitely apprehensive. My Uncle Jimmy stood facing them, his feet wide apart and his pose one of challenge. He was frowning, he was not fond of mysteries, and now, suddenly, and for the first time since I had known him, I found myself wondering whether my Uncle Jimmy was still on top of the family situation, or whether something might not now be going on which was beyond both his knowledge and control.

But this was a quick thought, a flash, an impression gained from no more than a look and two or three sentences, and it could have been all wrong. Certainly from what Phil now said it seemed to be, for he turned to his father with a quick gaiety and said, "Pa, you're right: it's bushwa all the way. Pure, homogenized, grade-A bushwa. The fact is that I've been nagging the Governor on a few minor points and now I've stopped. Anyway, for tonight. So what do you say, Pa? Do you want to lead us in a little family toast? To Charles, and to the greatest break this state has had for the last hundred years!"

"You're damn right I do!" my Uncle Jimmy said. "Only cut out that hundred years baloney. What happened a hundred years ago that was so hot? Hah? Why stop there? No, we'll all drink to Charles, and never mind any phony time limits. And I'll tell you something else: we're going to have *three* toasts, not just one. The first one is for Charles. My boy Charles," he said, looking fondly, almost burstingly, at his youngest son. "And then, when we've finished with that, we're all going to drink a toast to your Ma. Nobody ever lived for all of her family the way she did, and nobody, not even me, would have been happier here tonight. And last of all is another toast. This one I'm going to drink all by myself, and nobody else is going to join me. Because this one," he said, and his voice, which had trembled ever so slightly when he spoke of my Aunt Mary, now seemed for just an instant to become even more uncertain, "this one is for all my boys. For James, for Phil, for Charles. I wish James could be here right now, but he knows what I'm going to say because I told him just what I'm going to tell you. And that is that I'm a lucky man. The papers and the magazines have been saying that about me for forty years: Lucky Jimmy Kinsella. But they had it all wrong, because they never once put down where I was really lucky: with my family, all growing up and sticking together the way I always hoped it would, each one making it better for all the rest of us. I hear people telling me all the time how big a credit James and Phil and Charles are to me. But I never thought of it that way, and I never gave a damn what anybody else thought. Because I know what I know, and that is that nothing I ever did in all my life, except marry your Ma, gave me the right to have boys like you!"

It was an extraordinary speech—extraordinary because it was so completely unlike him. There had been no salty style, no picturesque touches: it had been straight and simple and towards the end it had shaken with emotion. I think it was this emotion which really took me by surprise, for I had never thought of my Uncle Jimmy as being an emotional man at all. Not only was he extremely hard-boiled—and his reputation for this was not merely familial or local: I can remember my sense of shock when, years ago, in a college lecture hall, I had suddenly realized that the man under discussion as the archetype of the newer, harder economic adventurer was in fact my uncle—but he did not have the weakness common to so many hard-boiled men: he did not have a soggy side. He did not weep cheap tears at sentimental movies; he did not weep at all. So that when he spoke as he had just now it took me completely off guard. I knew of course of his enormous pride in his sons, but this had come from more than pride—this had come from love. It had been a cry from the heart—the rarely observed precinct within my Uncle Jimmy—and I found it unexpectedly moving. Obviously, the others did too. The two boys were looking only at their father now, and their faces were not composed; I saw Marie look at Charles and then just touch the corner of her eye; my Aunt Gert made no bones about it: she was crying freely. It was a rare moment, a silent, almost breathless moment, a moment which I've never forgotten and which I know I never will forget.

And then, very quickly, this moment passed as we all drank our toasts and as my Uncle Jimmy, standing all by himself in the center of the room, looking solemn and proud and small and oddly touching, drank the final toast to his boys, his family. Then, suddenly, the atmosphere lifted, everyone began to talk at once, and slowly the emphasis began to shift away from Charles and the election and today back to my Uncle Jimmy and back to yesterday. It became now my Uncle Jimmy's evening, and it was Charles himself who led the way; assisted by Phil, he encouraged his father to reminisce. When my Uncle Jimmy was in good spirits, as he so clearly was tonight, he could do this very well, and over the years I had several times sat in on and been entertained by his memories of coups and deals and behind-the-scenes stratagems which were apt to embrace everyone from members of the hierarchy to Greek shipping magnates to Presidents. My Uncle Jimmy's view of history was that of the insider: he had been there. On the other hand, if he had *not* been there, he was not much interested; the result was that certain events of our time, normally considered as major or even critical by most observers, were in his personalized surveys severely diminished or simply ignored. So that it was a special kind of history, as fascinating as it was unbalanced, and made even more special by my Uncle Jimmy's unorthodox evaluations of the eminent men and women he had known. He was no respecter of reputations. He had few, perhaps no, heroes; he had worked with many of the great and ultimately he had quarreled with them; this intimacy had not bred awe. In my Uncle Jimmy's history the footprints on the sands of time were mostly made by feet of clay.

Tonight, probably in honor of Charles and the occasion, he talked largely about politics. He had never held elective or appointive office of any kind, but for many years he had contributed heavily to the Democratic party, he had ranged in and out of high Democratic councils, and although I don't suppose he had ever really been a kingmaker, he had undoubtedly had his moments of great influence. He had been called in by more than one President to help with specific financial problems, and when he mentioned this in passing now, Phil said, "I'll tell you what I heard: I heard they used to call you the Irish Baruch."

My Uncle Jimmy accepted this equably enough. "Okay," he said. "I don't get too mad at that. What was so wrong with Baruch? He knew what it was all about."

I said, "I guess he must have. Still, I remember reading somewhere that while everybody always said he gave advice to Presidents, nobody really said whether the Presidents ever took it."

It was an ungenerous comment; also, in view of the comparison that had just been established, it was an unwise one, and it did not go down well with my Uncle Jimmy. "Yeah?" he said belligerently. "Well, I can clear that one up for you right now. They took it. They didn't take all of it and they would have been nuts if they did. He wasn't as hot as he thought he was, not by a long shot. He always thought that after they made him they stopped making brains. All that magnolia bushwa. But he was okay. Mostly. And he had a hell of a lot more on the ball than those little left-wing wisenheimers that sat around picking their noses and making dirty cracks at him. Listen, Baruch gave away more in tips to cab drivers in a week than those babies earned in ten years." He stabbed a finger at Charles and said, "You've got a few of them around you, boy. Big liberals, right? They all bleed like hell for the poor Puerto Ricans and they boo hoo hoo all over the joint about civil liberties, but just say to them sometime you think you'll drop over to the Pavillon for chow and then see what happens. They'll kick each other to death trying to be first in line! Watch yourself with that gang or you'll all be out playing Pony Boy in the back yard, and guess who'll be the pony!"

"I'll bear it in mind," Charles said, smiling slightly. I had the feeling that this ground had been covered before; at any rate, he now gently changed the subject. "One question, Pa," he said. "Of them all—and I'm talking now just about the top men—which one did you like best?"

"Truman," my Uncle Jimmy said instantly. "A good little guy. And not a bad President. He did all right with what he had. And if you did him a favor he didn't forget it. He was never a double-crosser, and that was some switch in the White House in those days, because before Truman they had the world's champ!"

This was perhaps his favorite theme: I had heard him often on the subject of his old special hate. Charles said, "All right. But supposing you left all likes and dislikes to one side. I mean, supposing you had to pick one man of them all to be the President purely on the basis of capacity, of sheer ability—then what? It almost has to be Roosevelt, doesn't it?"

Surprisingly—or at least surprisingly to me—my Uncle Jimmy agreed at once. "Sure," he said. "And by miles. He had more soft spots than a banana, especially later on, but he ran the show. Not because he was smart or a genius or a great leader, but because he had what it took: he was a con man. It takes a con man to handle a country like this, and that's what Roosevelt was all the way. He had those chowderheads down in Washington sitting there with their traps open catching flies while he kept on smiling and blowing smoke at them and telling them to guess which shell the pea was under. I didn't like him for a minute and you could never believe a word he said, but he was good at his job. Pretty good. But don't ever hand me that Great Man malarky. '*My friends . . .*' " he said, derisively imitating the famous voice. "My friends my ass!"

"God bless us all," my Aunt Gert said. "There are ladies present!" And she laughed her great laugh.

Phil said, possibly maliciously, "We haven't heard about the General. What about him?"

"Don't make me laugh," my Uncle Jimmy said. "Amateur night!" Then, suddenly recalling something, he looked at me and said triumphantly, "But he showed all you birds something, right? With that book of his he didn't write? He got a capital gains deal out of it and made himself a bundle. Right after that they smartened up and locked the barn door and nobody else in your racket's made a buffalo nickel that way ever since!"

It was true enough, but since my own books were seldom in that category where any capital gains provision would have meant much, I couldn't feel deeply about it and I don't think I responded suitably. But this made no difference because my Uncle Jimmy, having delivered his thrust, saw no point in waiting for reaction, and simply moved on. His talk now took a different turn, for suddenly he left politics entirely and began to reminisce in a warmer, more personal way: he began to talk about the family, not as it was today, but as it had been when he and my father and my Aunt Gert were children together, growing up in the city and living in one of the many three-tenement houses which his father—unknown to them all—owned. I've said that my Uncle Jimmy was not an emotional man, but now as I listened to him talking about those early days I was not so confident. Because I had been over substantially this same ground before, not with my Uncle Jimmy but with my father, and while my father had been in every way kinder and gentler, an infinitely more appreciative and sympathetic man than his brother, his memories of this early family life had been much harsher, particularly when these memories had centered about his father. Whenever I thought of my grandfather I pictured him either as the tight, tough, essentially tyrannical man of my father's stories, or as the old, curiously mottled, largely silent little wisp of a man I had seen in my Uncle Jimmy's castle in Ireland. It was hard to square the one picture with the other; it was harder to square either with my Uncle Jimmy's present and on the whole rather proud portrayal of the returned sailor who had settled down in the city of his birth to build a home, a fortune, a dynasty.

"A hard nut," he conceded. "But he came around in the end. We all got what was coming to us and a little more besides. He was rough in the clinches, but I learned a hell of a lot from him, and not just about do-re-mi, either. I learned about the family and how important it was. You boys know what I've always said to you about the family: all for one, one for all. Right? Well, I learned it from him: he was the original stick-together guy. And if you didn't want to stick together he beat it into you. Even from the time we were little kids with the ring of the pot still on our seats, if he ever caught you going outside saying anything about the rest of us, he gave it to you good. He wouldn't say a word; he'd just shoot you one of those looks and reach for the razor strap. I had a sore tail for ten years, but I wound up knowing what you could do if you all stuck together!"

My father must have had a sorer tail and for a much longer period of time, but with him the lesson, so fruitful and unforgettable for my Uncle Jimmy, simply had not taken. My Uncle Jimmy made no reference to this now; he went on filling in the picture of my grandfather, not entirely ignoring the warts—every once in a while a peculiarly sharp memory seemed to prod him and then he departed momentarily from benignity—but on the whole touching them up here and there, so that while there were glimpses of harshness and silent violence, what finally emerged was a hard but reasonably picturesque figure, whose stern example had taught his children the value of a dollar, and whose extraordinary concealment of his wealth from his own family for so long a time now seemed in retrospect an antic gesture, more eccentric than anything else, arising no doubt from a basic love of that family, and in any case more than atoned for by the healthy settlements made on each of his children. And as I listened I wondered whether there was any kind of truth in this at all—whether, that is, my Uncle Jimmy, so much closer to my grandfather in his temperament and aims, could have caught qualities that my father had ignored or simply had not seen—or whether perhaps it might not be a matter of age, that as my Uncle Jimmy had grown older his memories had mellowed, and that indeed something of the sort might have happened to my father if he had lived, so that their separate accounts of their father might by now have come closer together. But somehow I didn't really think so, and when I looked over at my Aunt Gert for some possible clue—for she was the only other member of the family who had memories of those early days, and certainly by the end she had come to know my grandfather better than had either of her brothers—she was no help at all. She was listening and seemed to be listening intently, but her large white poker face was set in its perpetual and rather pleasant mask of potential laughter.

And so my Uncle Jimmy went on talking, leaving his father after a while and starting to rove at random through the past, and as he continued to do so with a kind of special gusto, and with smiles and laughter from us all—because, tonight, he seemed in really great form—I found myself unexpectedly feeling faintly regretful and sad, as you sometimes do on joyful occasions when there apparently is no reasonable excuse for sadness at all. I sat there for a few moments, not really knowing why I felt this way, still watching and listening to my Uncle Jimmy, but beginning to drift back over the evening, thinking of all the different and rather surprising things that had happened to me since I had arrived, thinking of Walshie and Edso and the extraordinary coalition of forces which had been brought together to celebrate Charles's triumph in the room below, thinking of old memories of other and quite different political nights that had risen to the surface in me, thinking of Charles and Marie standing hand in hand together as though in the first of a series of official portraits, thinking just of Charles—Charles as *Governor!*—but thinking particularly, and for no special reason, of that one brief instant when Phil and Charles had been talking together, so openly but so privately, too. Once again, as I thought back over this, I had the feeling that something had changed, that something was different, that something was going on I didn't understand—and once again I had the feeling that in this I was not alone, that unlikely as it might seem, especially since this was so obviously a family matter, my Uncle Jimmy was in the dark as well.

Was he? I didn't know, of course, but the feeling persisted, it was unavoidable, and yet at the same time the evidence right before my eyes pointed in just the opposite direction. For if he had even suspected that there were family secrets which were being kept from him, he would have been furious and deeply troubled, but now, certainly, no one seemed freer from troubles of any kind—so free, in fact, that suddenly and unexpectedly he began to dance. Or rather, to go into the beginning of a little clog step—it turned out that he was illustrating a point in a story about a small-time vaudevillian who had lived in the tenement above them more than sixty years before. He went through this performance with a heavy-footed exuberance—although a small man, he was not a natural dancer—and as he danced he sang in a jaunty nasal voice:

She's the daughter of Rosie O'Grady
A dear little old-fashioned girl. . . .

He was not a natural singer, either, but sheer energy carried him through: it was impossible to pull away from this vitality, this challenging bounciness. And so here he was, at the moment of my conviction that the focus was somehow slipping away from him, as happy as I had ever seen him, clogging his way through memories, the undisputed center of family doings. Charles was sitting, completely relaxed now, next to Marie; one hand rested lightly on her knee. Phil was standing, half-smiling, behind Flossie, who seemed to have shed for the moment the faint overlay of distress she always brought with her to these family gatherings; my Aunt Gert was as expressionless as ever, but she was humming and tapping the floor with one fat little foot; I saw Phil and Charles suddenly glance at each other in quick delighted recognition of some gesture or piece of business on the part of their father that I failed to catch. It was a complete, unified, strong family scene, all pulled together and made what it was by the same powerful little presence who had always been able to do this, and under the impact of this cohesiveness, this visible shared enjoyment, my own strange feeling of disquiet began to disappear.

Soon after this Charles and Marie left to return to their party downstairs—it was an indication of the strength of the family atmosphere that for the past few minutes I had forgotten completely the real reason for our being all together tonight. As she was leaving Marie came over to me and said, "Back to the lions. Jack, are we going to see you?"

"I hope so. I'll be around, at least for a while."

"Well, so will we. After the first, that is; we're going off tomorrow for about three weeks. Charles hasn't had a break for ages, so we're going to all the places *I* love. Paris for a week, then down to Rome for two. This late it'll probably rain every day in Rome, but I couldn't care less. We'll have Bill and Pony Brady's house, and you can't do much better than that. Want to come along?"

"Not this year," I said. "It's not fashionable enough: everybody's going to Greece."

"I know: all that good clear light," she said. "We were there last year, in the islands. It was beautiful, all right, but I don't know, I'm not mad about beautiful places where I can't speak the language and I don't like the food. And of course I fool people: they all think I want to put on a bathing suit and go skin-diving or water-skiing, and I don't. My idea of heaven is to be absolutely comfortable in an elegant apartment in a nice big city. . . . Anyway," she said, "listen, Jack: you wouldn't do yourself a favor, would you? And give Jean a call?"

It was one of her quick blunt shifts to the personal which I'd never handled very well and which, instinctively, I tried to duck; I shook my head slightly and said, "Come on, Marie. . . ."

"MYOB?" she said. "When I was in grade school that was the hot slang for Mind Your Own Business. Come on yourself, Jack: don't be so stuffy. She's a good girl. And don't try to tell me that old one about not knowing where she is, because *I* know where she is, and if I do, you do. . . ."

"If I do you do what?" Charles said, coming up and putting his hands on her smooth shoulders.

"Jack's getting in a stew," she said, "because I'm interfering in his domestic affairs."

"I have a pretty good idea," Charles said. "Why don't you stop interfering in his domestic affairs and start interfering in mine? To the extent of going downstairs and acting like a Radiant First Lady."

"That's what the newspapers call me now," she said, turning to me. "Don't you love it?"

"And while you're radiating," Charles said, "tell them I'll be down in a minute. Also, you might tell Jerry I want to see him in the study before I go down."

She made a face at him, kissed his cheek, and said, "All right." As she left she said to me, "Anyway, think it over. What can you lose by being nice?"

Charles watched her go and said to me, not at all as any kind of an apology, but as a plain statement of fact, "She's always liked

Jean. And they keep in touch, I think. She likes to strike a blow for the cause now and then."

I said, "Your wife's a romantic girl."

"I know," he said. "But why not? She's had good luck that way: all the best things that have happened to her have been what I suppose you'd call romantic. Tonight, for example." With one hand he made a large, all-inclusive gesture, taking in the room, the family, the party downstairs, the entire occasion. "This is pretty heady stuff," he said.

I said curiously, "For you, too, Charles?"

He nodded at once. "Sure," he said. "I'm not that blasé." He gave me a quick amused smile and said, "I find it easy to be dazzled by my own achievement. By the way, how did you make out with the Commander? Did you have a pleasant chat?"

"Fascinating. Thanks a lot."

"I thought it might be useful for an old-timer like you to see that even in the new politics some things haven't changed."

"Including techniques," I said, and I told him now what I had suspected at the time: that in diverting the Commander to me he had deliberately been using an old Skeffington ploy.

"Oh," he said, "I'm not above borrowing techniques. Especially if they work. Incidentally, I don't share Pa's feeling about your old boss. I don't buy the legend, either, but he was better than Pa thinks. He knew how to get elected most of the time, and he knew how to maneuver all of the time. I'd say a man who could do that was a pretty fair politician."

I said, "That isn't exactly the same thing as saying that he was a pretty fair governor, is it? Or mayor?"

"I guess it isn't," he said pleasantly, "but then, I guess he wasn't." He looked at me again with the same slightly amused expression and said, "Do you really think he was, Jack?"

I said, "That's the old argument, isn't it? I've heard it ever since the first day I met him. I don't know how good he was. I do know that he's the only one who ever did anything. And I know that if I just look around this city today, about every major improvement I can see—buildings, tunnels, roads, playgrounds—was started or finished or helped along by one man. So I guess that's a kind of answer, isn't it?"

"For someone who quit politics in disgust," he said, "you're surprisingly loyal to old politicians. Or at least to one old politician. Although I wouldn't mind betting that hasn't much to do with politics." He added shrewdly, "It's probably all personal. Anyway, I know those major improvements. Or those of them you can see: half of them have fallen down. Your old friend's contractor pals didn't always use the best materials. By the way, you never happened to look at the city's books for the years all this improving was going on, did you?"

I said defensively, "Crooked books, I imagine?"

"No," he said, "not crooked. You're behind the times, Jack: you believe in the legend. I don't want to strip this picturesque old figure of even a shred of his glamour, but he wasn't the great quixotic crook people still think he was. The awful fact is he wasn't a crook at all. Or not much of a one. By the standards of his time, that is: remember that those were the days of 'honest graft.' But the books weren't crooked. They were worse: they were incredible."

"I'm not too surprised. I don't think bookkeeping was his strongest point."

"I'd agree with that," he said dryly. "You know, when I first went to City Hall I thought I'd better have a look at the records, just to see what had been going on. Well, to begin with, I had to find them. It wasn't easy, as you can imagine, but they finally turned up in some side room as dark as a closet, full of old newspapers and sneakers and underwear and, naturally, the official records of the city. All this was presided over by a little old Irishman who'd been there forever and who—again naturally—couldn't read. I got the books out, I had the city's accountants go over them, and then I put Pa's people to work. It all added up to one thing: Skeffington had no financial sense at all. None. He couldn't have known the first thing about money. Except that you took it in and you paid it out, from anyone and to anyone, and of course it became a matter of policy to pay out more than you took in. That was the way he ran the city, and that was the way he ran the state. And it never hurt him for a minute. Not many people knew about it, and most of those who knew didn't care. That's the way things were then. He was very popular, and that's what elections were around here in those days: popularity contests."

I thought of his own enormous margin of victory; I said, "And you don't think they are today?"

"Sure they are, but there's a difference, isn't there?" he said. "It's not that simple any more. Look at it this way: yesterday I got eighty-five thousand votes more than Skeffington did on his best run. Of course we have more voters now, but there are a few things left you can't blame on the population explosion. My percentage of the total vote was still way ahead of his. And why? Because I'm more popular now than he was then?" He smiled again and said, "Nobody is. We both know that. Nobody's got that kind of popularity any more. It was a personal thing that depended on tribal loyalties, immigrants on the way up, racial spokesmen, Communion Breakfasts—there's some of that still around, of course, but in Skeffington's campaigns it was the big thing. You could do very well for yourself if you could get up and tell a few funny stories, quote Robert Emmet, and shout 'Ireland must be free!' for a finish. Today it's slightly more complicated."

"You need a whole new set of quotations," I said.

"That's right. Among other things."

"Which ones? Who are you quoting these days, Charles?"

"Roosevelt, George Washington Carver, Ben-Gurion," he said imperturbably. "And, just occasionally, Robert Emmet. So as not to slight a minority group. And then on another level, and because I have an extremely well-read staff—you've heard about my support from the intellectuals—Eliot, Unamuno, Aquinas, and Alexander

Pope. We try to box the compass, you see." He gave me the look he had given me twice before, and said, "Quotation-wise."

It was to me a curious and a fascinating conversation—curious because although the room was still full of family, Charles and I were talking in unbroken privacy: none of the others had even come our way. And yet I had no feeling that we were deliberately being "let alone"; it was rather as if the general family atmosphere had relaxed with the finish of my Uncle Jimmy's centralizing performance, and the party had split up into little groups, each one returning for a moment to its own habitual concerns. Phil and Flossie had gone over by the fireplace where Phil was talking in a low voice, and Flossie was listening and slowly pulling on her gloves. Directly above their heads on the rear wall hung a large painting which I had noticed earlier, but which I looked at more carefully now. I knew that I had seen it somewhere before, that it had some special significance for me, but just for the moment I couldn't place it, pin it down. Then, suddenly, I remembered: it was the painting of my Uncle Jimmy in his Knight of Malta costume that I had last seen so many years ago in his Irish castle—had it now been permanently transferred to Charles's house? My Uncle Jimmy himself had moved from the center of the room and had joined my Aunt Gert who, having been silent for most of the evening, was now talking emphatically to him; I gathered that this might be business, for she did not at this time seem to be on the point of any merriment. What she was telling him must have been of some importance, for he was listening without his customary impatience, but even so, every once in a while I saw him shift his head just slightly and flick a fast inquisitive look in our direction. It was not his habit to be left out of anything, not even for a moment, and while it was now clear that whatever my Aunt Gert was saying was significant enough to keep him with her, I knew that he ached to be over here with us, listening to his son.

He might have been surprised by what he heard—although, come to think of it, perhaps not. I was. Not by anything Charles had said—for by now I didn't really care whether Skeffington had been a great governor or a good mayor or even a financial responsible; it was all in the past, and whatever he had been couldn't modify my affection for someone who had been unfailingly kind to me, and with whom it had been such great fun and so exciting for a young man to be, day after day—but by the authority, the easy confidence with which he said it. The same man who, twenty years ago, had known nothing about politics and who could hardly bear to sit through my stories about Skeffington and City Hall and local politicians, was now calmly setting me straight on the facts of my old scene and of political life in general. It was a queer reversal, more than a little incongruous, and yet as I listened to him talk, so easily, so surely, so peculiarly impressively, I didn't think of this at all. What I did think of was that Charles seemed to have changed far more than I had suspected, and I think it was only now, in these few moments of talk, that I began to realize what I suppose I should have realized long before: that Charles was *in fact* the Governor, and that as Governor, and as the man who had worked to become Governor, he was a different and indeed a far more formidable figure than the Charles I had always known.

But all this came from a manner, an attitude, a presence, for there was certainly nothing formidable in anything he said. He talked on casually, apparently in no hurry at all—although of course he knew very well that everyone downstairs was waiting for his reappearance. Just as, of course, he knew very well that they would continue to wait: in this gathering no one was likely to go home imprudently. He said to me, "It's all changed, in every way. It's a matter of style as much as anything else. Frank Dooley is a good example. Do you remember him?"

"Vaguely. I remember the family, of course." The Dooleys had been a conspicuous political family: Frank Dooley's grandfather had been a ward boss, his father had run the state senate, his uncle had been a Superior Court judge for decades. But Frank himself . . . I said, "He hasn't done well, has he? Wasn't he supposed to be a comer? It seems to me they used to talk about him that way."

"He's old hat," Charles said. "He's actually younger than we are, but people think of him as an old-fashioned pol, and that's the kiss of death these days. He had all sorts of possibilities. He's not bad-looking, he dresses well, he's a good talker, and his father sensed which way the wind was blowing in time to send him to a non-Catholic college. The first Ivy Leaguer in his family. The New Breed. But it didn't work. He got to the City Council and that's as far as he'll ever get. He wants to be attorney general and he wouldn't be a bad one. He's reasonably bright, he's not bad on civil liberties—that's the big thing today, by the way—and he doesn't steal. But the minute he leaves the ward he's done. As soon as he gets in a campaign he starts talking like his father. He starts out on the rights of the Negro to equal employment opportunity and then, before he can stop himself, a bit of a brogue creeps in, a 'God love you!' slips out, and that kills him. He just reminds people of yesterday. Thirty years ago he would have been a shoo-in. Today he's a born loser. In a way it's a pity, because he could be useful to someone."

"But not to you, I gather."

He shook his head. "No, not to me. There's too much going against him. Too many drawbacks. Including the fact that in the primary he nearly killed himself trying to stop me from getting the nomination. I guess I think of that as a drawback."

"No magnanimity, Charles?"

"I know the word," he said. "It's sometimes pronounced 'folly.' " He smiled again and said, "It's too bad you can't talk to your old friend. He could tell you all about that."

"How about Skeffington?" I said. "How does he fit the changing-style theory? You don't think he'd do well if he ran today?"

"You used to be a vaudeville buff," he said. "Remember a thing called *Change Your Act or Go Back to the Woods?* Well, I think he'd have had to change his act. And I don't think he would have, and I don't think he could have. So I think he'd probably have had a very hard time. That's the diplomatic answer. If you want to know what I really think, I think that today he wouldn't last five minutes."

I felt one more surge of old loyalty; I said, "Work it the other way. I mean, let's suppose you'd been running in his day: how long would you have lasted?"

"Oh," he said, "that's a different story. In my case . . . say three minutes." He looked at me and laughed and said, "So it's lucky for both of us we came along when we did, isn't it?" And now for the first time he looked at his watch; the conversation was over. He said, "Feeding time. I've got to see a lot of people. Marie probably told you we're going to Rome for a couple of weeks?"

"Yes. Rest period . . ."

His eyebrows went up just a little. "Is that what Marie said?" he said. "She must have thought you were a spy. Did you ever try to rest in Rome? And at Pony Brady's? That's wild and woolly country, Jack."

I remembered that years ago, in his more hectic days, Charles had not been unknown in that wild and woolly country; I said, "You think you can handle yourself?"

"I'll try," he said dryly. "In fact I can hardly wait to try. I've spent most of the past couple of months in the western part of the state: La Dolce Vita out there is a bean supper at the Epworth League. Have you ever been to a bean supper, Jack? I've been to lots of them lately. I don't know of a better reason for going to Rome. Anyway, we'll be back before long, and when we do let's get together."

"Good, fine." And then, not really meaning anything by it, but just making casual small talk in a half-joking way, I added, "Socially? Or professionally?"

And for some reason this seemed to catch him by surprise, and

I saw just a momentary change of expression before he answered. "Any way you want to play it," he said. "Socially by all means. I'll even guarantee to keep Marie out of those domestic affairs. Professionally—well, that's up to you, isn't it? You call it. I'm agreeable. I've told you that before and it still goes. You can come along any time you want to. The trouble is that you don't really want to, do you?"

By now I was embarrassed at my own clumsiness in having brought it up; it was something we had talked about now and then over the years, and never to anyone's satisfaction. I said, "No, I guess I don't. Apart from everything else, I like what I do now, and I couldn't do both. Besides, I don't see where anything like that would be very useful—to use a word of yours—for either of us. Especially for you. I'd always have the out that everything's grist to the mill, new material and so on, but I don't see what you'd have to gain at all."

"Oh," he said, "I'd think you could almost leave that to me. I've been known to think of myself occasionally." And then, although his face didn't change, remaining as quietly pleasant as ever, his voice became more sober, more reflective. "It's a funny job," he said. "No complaints, you know, because I wanted it, and I worked like a dog for it. We talked about popularity. All comparisons aside, I had at least a measure of that in my favor, and I had a lot of other things going for me too. If your name is Kinsella around here, that's not a bad head start in itself. We've both always known that, and Pa still packs enormous weight. And then there's Marie and all the peculiar snobberies of the whole family situation: all those little Irish secretaries daydreaming away. A kind of glamour, I suppose. I got the Catholic vote because everybody knows I am one. I got the non-Catholic vote because the others don't think I'm a very good one. Or, as they'd put it, I'm not 'typical.' "

"That matters still, doesn't it? I keep hearing that it doesn't, that bloc voting is all gone, or mostly gone. I've never believed it."

"James sometimes talks like that," he said. "He's very bright and he knows a lot, but he makes one mistake: he thinks ecumenicism has reached Ward Five. No, it still matters. There's a surface civility, and it's not as obvious as that old magic scream, 'He's one of our own!' but it's there, all right. And it's respected: just look at the careful assortment of trash at the head table of the average interfaith dinner. Jack got to be President, but by a hair: he was almost licked by it. Oddly enough, in this situation, it benefited me. And then of course I was lucky in my opponent. He could have won, but first he got clumsy and then he panicked. And finally, I had another advantage. I know I won't shock you when I tell you that to win cost money. Fortunately I had it. And I used it."

I had heard, from the time I had come back to the city, that this had been the most expensive campaign in the history of the state, and now I couldn't resist going to authority. I said, "How much money, Charles?"

"A lot," he said. "I won't tell you more than that because I really don't want to shock you." Again there was the slight smile and he said, "I want you to preserve your illusions. Anyway, I won—and I know why I won. And having won, I think the idea is that I'm supposed to run the state. I can do that all right, but it won't be easy. I told you earlier tonight that being Governor was a little like being mayor, only more so. It's the 'more so' that counts. I used to deal with the City Council; now I'm going to have to deal with the legislature—which is bigger, tougher, smarter, more complicated, and impossible as it may seem, more corrupt. So it's no cinch. But I have a certain amount of experience, and I'm not exactly unarmed. Although I could use a few helping hands."

"I thought you had plenty of those," I said. "What everyone seems to be talking about is your organization, and how strong it is."

"They're very good," he said. "They're all competent. Some of them are more than that. And a few of them I can even trust. You can't reasonably ask for more than that. What I wouldn't mind having around is someone closer, someone I can not only trust, but whom I've known—and who's known me—for a long time. I have a feeling there are times when that's important. Even indispensable." He smiled again and said, "Maybe I'm getting like Pa: the sense of family."

I said, "You couldn't do better in that department: you've got Phil."

He nodded. "I've got Phil. But Phil is one man, and one man, even if he's as good as Phil, can't be everywhere, and can't do everything. Besides, Phil is . . . my conscience, I suppose. Or so it appears." He hesitated just a bit in the middle of saying this, and after he had said it he hesitated again, as if he were going to say something more along the same line. But he didn't; he said only, "If you ever change your mind, or if you feel like talking about it again, let me know. You can't tell, you might get something out of it at that. Something you could use in a book. If worse came to worst, you could even use me. I understand," he said, the dryness coming into his voice once more, "others are planning something of the sort. The difference is that I might not sue you. Anyway, think it over."

I said I would—although I knew that thinking was unlikely to change anything: probably he knew this, too—and he left, slipping quickly out of the room with just a wave at the others. As he did, my Uncle Jimmy came over beside me and for just a moment didn't say anything but stood looking at the door which Charles had closed behind him. I didn't know when he had left my Aunt Gert—during the last few minutes I had been too interested in what Charles was saying to look around at anyone else—but now I saw that she had joined Flossie underneath the Knight of Malta painting, and that Phil seemed to have disappeared. There was another way out of the library; I wondered if he had left by it, to be with Charles downstairs.

My Uncle Jimmy pointed to the door and said proudly, "Some kiddo, right?"

I agreed, and he said, "It's his night to howl and that's jake with me. He's earned it. He's a great boy. Well, they all are. Every one of them." He seemed to be back in his mood of earlier this evening, when he had spoken so emotionally of his satisfaction in his family. He said, "You talk to James at all?"

"Just long enough to say hello. He was on his way out when I came in."

"A funny kiddo," he said. "He could have been anything. Doctor, lawyer, businessman, politician: you name it. And he double-crossed me and became a priest. Well, who wanted that? Hah? He was my oldest boy and he had a hell of a lot on the ball. You think I wanted to see him planked down on his can in some rectory in the sticks, playing Parcheesi every night and watching the ball games on TV? I tell you, I raised hell when it happened. I went to the bishop and asked him if he thought we were some kind of Shanty Mick family that had to hand over a boy a year to the Church!"

I said, "He must have enjoyed that."

"He got thick," my Uncle Jimmy said. "Well, what could you expect? He's a Shanty Mick himself. And that's the way it happened with him: I know the whole story. I would have belted him right in the puss, bishop or no bishop, but he yanked out that cross he wears and started waving it around. Anyway, it all wound up okay. Look at James: today he's all over the world and everybody knows him. Who else in his racket can do what he does? One minute he's up in Alaska singing 'Holy God, We Praise Thy Name' with a crowd of Eskimos that never did anything but swap reindeer bones until he came along. The next he's in Kansas City glad-handing a convention of Presbyterian chumps. The next he's in Rome listening to the Pope asking him, 'What's new?' I tell you, if those Guineas over there have got anything besides Jello in their heads they'll shoot that baby to the top. And fast!"

First Charles, then James; idly, almost automatically, I said, "And then there's Phil. . . ."

But my Uncle Jimmy snapped this up the instant it was said. "What about Phil?" he said truculently. It was possible that he saw in the question an attempt to hurry him along in a family narrative; more probably, though, he suspected what certainly had not been intended: an implied criticism of one of his boys. For it was Phil with whom my Uncle Jimmy felt least secure—or so it had always seemed to me. He was more complex, less clear of outline, harder to figure out: also, by any popular standard, he had not done as well as the others. This was curious, because I had always thought that of the three boys it was Phil who was the most naturally gifted. Whatever he had done, he had done with the appearance of ease; in school, growing up, he had never seemed to study and he had always done well; teachers—even those who had not been eager to placate my Uncle Jimmy—had praised him and spoken of his extraordinary promise. He had gone through college and law school in the same effortless way; like Charles, who had followed him a year later, he had gone on to practice law, but unlike Charles he had at once made his mark as a remarkably good lawyer. He was at his best in a courtroom, preferably caught up in the midst of some incredibly complicated trial, preferably questioning some hostile, positive, slightly pompous and supposedly unshakable expert: two or three times, years ago, I had gone to court just to watch him in such circumstances. He had given a fine performance on each occasion, with his fresh vivid intelligence vibrating through every sentence he spoke, with his old gift for mimicry now and then flashing out to disconcert the witness and delight the rest, and with a kind of swooping sardonic good humor overriding everything so completely that it seemed to fill the court so that, in watching the trial, you were aware of very little else but Phil. It seemed to me in those days that he went to his work with a special feeling for what he did: not merely pride but a positive *joy*. He was popular and respected;

his fellow lawyers, like his early teachers, had predicted the arrival of great things for him. And yet—the great things had not arrived. They had not arrived—I think—mainly because Phil had stopped pursuing them. He had been in great demand, but gradually he had given up responding to this demand: he took fewer and fewer cases. There were those who said that he had grown lazy; there were others who said that, thanks to his father, he was already a rich man and therefore had no need to work; and there was Phil himself who, one day, about a year before Charles decided to try his luck in politics, had given me a somewhat different explanation.

"I got bored," he had said. "It's as simple as that. I got bored with a job that a couple of years ago suddenly began to seem silly and then with the passage of time got even sillier. Who was it who said, 'The law is a ass'? Someone in Dickens, I know, but who? Pumblechook? You ought to know, you're the literary man. Anyway, he was dead right, and it gets assier by the second. You wouldn't, you *couldn't*, believe how absolutely trivial it is unless you were mixed up in it every day. And it's all the same. Take the case I wound up last week, the one I got saddled with thanks to Charlie Murphy's very convenient double hernia. My client turned out to be a Mafia hood: the real article, a doughy little olive-eyed thug, a genuine melt-the-man-down-and-stick-him-in-the-highway type. He'd probably knocked off twenty or so of the usual business competitors on his own. Eventually the government decided to go after him, and on what charge? What else? Income tax evasion. The same old comedy. It's like getting McCarthy for disrespect to the Senate. So off we started, playing charades, with this IBM clown from the Feds licking his chops over missing fifty-dollar vouchers and improperly kept expense accounts, with my client's pleasant associates slipping in every now and then to tell him the good news that in spite of all the hard luck the 'stuff' was still moving, with my little killer himself whining to me that if he got sent up even for a day it would probably kill his little

Angela who was making her First Communion at Saint Anthony's next month, and with the presiding justice on the bench nobody else but Breezy Willie Magee: seventy-nine years old, an alcoholic, a party hack all his life, and who in those rare intervals when he's fully awake suspects—God knows why!—that the case has something to do with dirty books!"

I had said, "How'd you make out?"

He had shrugged. "Acquittal. Why, I don't know. I didn't really care. By that time it all seemed so absurd that I wouldn't have been surprised if that old imbecile Magee had stood up and announced that he was going to reach his decision by picking the petals off a daisy. In one way there was a certain beauty to it, though. The hood was grateful: he cried. I was invited to watch little Angela receive. And I imagine from now any time I need a trigger man. . . ." He sighed and said, "No, I think the old Romans played it right: they had no lawyers. It was every man for himself, and not a bad idea."

"Then why not leave the hoods alone? Switch around, go in for something else: civil liberties cases, that sort of thing. . . ."

"I told you, they're all the same," he had said wearily. "I've had a few respectable clients in my time. Including Pa. But the *process* is the same. The ritual, the bogus dignity, the words words words, the appeals: it all adds up to nothing—or almost nothing—and what's more important is that it bores the bejesus out of me. I used to get a charge out of it, but either it's changed or I have. It's probably me. Anyway, now whenever I see two lawyers in a court—and especially when I'm one of them—all I can think of is two little men standing on the seashore, taking turns peeing into the Atlantic. They're having a contest: the judge is an old man somewhere on the coast of Japan who decides the winner by measuring the mean high tides in the Pacific. It's all about as meaningful as that. No, I'll keep my hand in—or I expect I will: it's what I know best, and it's a bit late to break new tracks—but it's not for me. It's not really what I want."

And with something of our old intimacy—for suddenly I had become aware that he had changed very much, that the old merriness was not much in evidence now, and I didn't know why and I was genuinely concerned—I had said, "What is for you, Phil? What do you want?"

"Oh," he said, slowly, "I don't know. Something I haven't got, I guess. And I *have* got a good wife and kids I love, so it has to be something else, doesn't it? Something I can get interested in enough to get lost in occasionally. Not that I want to get lost, particularly, but it would be nice to have something worthwhile losing yourself in, wouldn't it? I expect that's all I want." And then his face had suddenly lightened, there was a return of the old high spirits, and he laughed and said, "In other words, something unreasonable. . . ."

I had known him for most of my life, and for a long time during those years he had been my closest friend, yet he had often puzzled me: there had been those times when I felt that as well as I knew him I had never really, entirely, grasped him. I'm sure that my Uncle Jimmy, while at moments enormously proud of him, must often have found him maddening and all but incomprehensible. Publicly of course he would never have said a word, but I knew that he and Phil had frequently had their explosions, and once he had expressed his baffled exasperation to me.

"What drives me nuts," he had said, "is that he's as good as the best, and better than that if he wanted to be. But who knows what he wants? Hah? What the hell is all this mumbo jumbo about wanting something but he doesn't know what? Who's he trying to kid, anyway? For the love of Pete, he's not some teen-age kid on a bicycle: he's nearly forty years old!" And then he had looked at me and I had seen the anger in his face, but also another expression which was much rarer for him: one of puzzlement, of troubled inquiry; he had said, "You think he *is* kidding?"

From all this I gathered that for some reason of his own Phil had told his father approximately what he had told me, although why he had done this was a mystery—perhaps he had been tired or irritated or caught off guard. For no one understood my Uncle Jimmy more completely than Phil, and of course no one knew better how unlikely he was to sympathize with hesitations or self-questioning. My Uncle Jimmy had stood there, waiting impatiently for me to say something—it was one of the few times when he had asked me a question and really wanted an answer—and so I had said, "No, I don't think he's kidding at all. I think he's probably just looking around and wondering a little. That's not so wrong, is it?"

I could have said nothing worse. "Not so wrong!" he had howled. "At his age? What's up with you: have you gone bats, too? Listen, by the time you're as old as he is anybody that doesn't know what he wants is halfway home to the booby hatch, and you can put that in your pipe and smoke it! It burns me up! Here's a kiddo as sharp as a tack and as nifty a lawyer as ever walked into this burg, and what does he do? He shoves himself up off his can and down into court maybe once a month, and the rest of the time he stays home playing beanbag with Flossie and waiting for some half-assed Good Fairy to tell him what he really wants! Well, that kind of baloney goes over with me like a lead balloon! He'd better wise up in a hurry, that's all I've got to say. I'll tell you one thing: I didn't raise anybody to be a second-rater!"

This was an unusual—in fact, an unprecedented—diatribe; it had not been repeated. I doubt that it would have been in any case—my Uncle Jimmy, I think, must have had sharp regrets at having so impulsively blasted one of his boys, even if he had done so only to me—but now Phil had suddenly made his move: he had astonished everyone and delighted my Uncle Jimmy by doing a complete turnabout. It had happened in this way. Shortly after my talk with my Uncle Jimmy, Charles had decided to run for mayor. It had been a family decision rather than a purely personal one, and in this decision Phil had participated. He had of course been asked to help in the campaign, and he had of course agreed. Then had come the surprise. Almost at once what had started as a dutiful fraternal service, a matter of family obligation, evolved into something much more than that. Phil, whose interest in local matters had been greater than Charles's but still not much more than casual, now had found himself fascinated by the whole intricate business of our politics and by the possibilities of political control and reform, and although—as he had said to me on that hot night years ago, when we had driven home from the beach together and had stopped for supper in the awful cafeteria—he had no ambition for himself in office, his vision of what could be done if the right person was in power was an overwhelming one. There was no question in his mind but that Charles was the right person. The fact that he was Charles's older brother could not have mattered less to him. He was not an envious man, and he was extremely clear-sighted; he was sure of his own gifts and knew very well what he could do and what he could not do; he knew that although he was a far better lawyer than his brother, Charles in his turn had talents which he did not possess: he was in fact the first member of his family—perhaps even before Charles himself—to correctly assess those talents and to see where they might lead. Accordingly he had gone into action, not only joining Charles's campaign but taking over its direction. He was acute, energetic, not easily fooled; he was an excellent organizer, able to cut with quick decision into the fat and the flab that always bulks and swells behind a candidate; his work at the bar had given him varied connections which now proved most valuable. He had become not merely Charles's second in command but the ideal complement to him, and more than anyone else—more than my Uncle Jimmy and, some said, at this stage of the candidate's career, more even than Charles—he had been responsible for that first victory. Ever since that time, although he had continued to maintain a token law practice, he had been with Charles. He believed in him; he was as close to being indispensable as one man can be to another. This was a fact acknowledged by many, and among those who had always acknowledged it was Charles.

It was also acknowledged by my Uncle Jimmy, and so now, after his first quick automatic flash of belligerency, he realized of course that of all people I was not likely to talk Phil down, and all he said was, "Why should I tell you about Phil? You know as much about him as I do. You know what he does. I tell you, those two make a great team. They're going places together." Then, without breaking stride or changing his tone, he said, "I saw you gabbing with Charles just now. For a long time. He offer you a job?"

And from his expression I couldn't tell whether he knew this, that it was something he and Charles had talked over beforehand, or whether it was merely a shrewd guess. I said, "Not exactly. We sparred around the edges a little, but there was nothing definite."

"Don't give me that 'nothing definite' crap," he said. "Who cares about that, hah? He asked you to get on board, right? And what did you say? No soap?"

"More or less, I guess. You're not too surprised at that, are you, Uncle Jimmy?"

"Listen," he said, "I gave up being surprised when I was still wearing knickers. I knew then that there were some people you could hit in the mouth with a sack full of gold and they'd spit it all out into the gutter because it didn't taste good. You can't change people like that any more than you can teach a pig to pick cherries. Your old man was one of them and so are you. But I don't get sore at that any more. I just wish for once in your life you'd wise up and latch on to something when it's handed to you. What's the percentage in staying a boob?"

"You want me to hitch my wagon to a star, Uncle Jimmy?"

But he had said his piece; he was not now interested in persuading me further. I was his nephew, not his son; it was late at night and I'm sure he was tired. It was not often that I thought of my Uncle Jimmy as getting along in years, but now I noticed signs of fatigue in his little, ageless, combative face. He said only, "I want you to use the squash God gave you. But if you want to be stubborn it's up to you, Buster. It's no skin off my tail." And absentmindedly, he had done something I had never known him to do before: he had called me by the nickname he had always called my father. He looked at his watch and said, "I don't know about you but I'm going downstairs with Charles while he spouts his piece to all those free-loaders. Then I'm going to come back up and hit the hay. I've got to get out of here early in the morning; I'm going to Ireland."

And of course that was where I had my first real memory of him; I said, "Have you still got the castle, Uncle Jimmy?"

He nodded. "God knows why. It's a dump. There's nothing to do over there but go out in the rain and get wet. But Mary—your aunt—liked it so I go back now and then. Then I get the hell out. Fast. Thank God for the jets." He looked at me inquiringly and said, "You do a little traveling: you ever get over that way?"

"No, only to touch down at Shannon now and then. And once I stayed in Dublin a couple of weeks, but that was years ago." It had been in fact on our honeymoon: Jean and I had gone there, just as my father and mother had a generation before. We had had a wonderful time; we had been very happy. I said, "I haven't been in Ireland now for a long time."

"You're not as dumb as I thought you were," he said. "Well, I keep the place open all the time. A Mick farmer and his wife look after it for me. God knows what they do with themselves when I'm not around. Throw potatoes at each other, I guess. And sleep: everybody in that damned country sleeps fifteen hours a day. At least!"

And suddenly, for no reason, the name Teddy came leaping into my mind, and instantly I remembered the long-faced Irish chauffeur who used to drive James and Charles and Phil and me all around the country on rainy days, and whom my Uncle Jimmy had fired in one of his rages. I said, "Whatever happened to Teddy, Uncle Jimmy? Remember him?"

"Sad Sam," he said promptly. "I tied the can to that baby in a hurry, but I had to hire him back. He was strictly n.g. but he was better than the others. The clown I got in his place lost the carburetor. How the hell you can do that I don't know but he did! The next one drove the car right into the ocean. With me in it! So I got Sad Sam back. Your aunt liked him okay. He's dead now. TB. They've all got it over there, it's in the milk. But anyway," he said, "if you get over, look me up. I might be there."

I promised I would, and once again he swung his fist in a mock-punch at my arm; this time it was in farewell. "Keep the faith," he said, and his tone was sardonic. "That's always the Big Goodbye in this burg, right?"

He went off, stepping peppily across the room, going down to share the final big moment of the night with his son. It was his night as well as Charles's, he was obviously on top of the world, and yet on this night when he was so happy—when one of his great dreams had come true for him—it was curious that for much of the time he had been talking to me, and now as I watched him walk away so jauntily, I found myself thinking of him not as I usually did, as I had always done, but instead wondering if in fact my Uncle Jimmy, in spite of his family and all his activities and his dreams beginning to come true, was not quite often a fairly lonely man. . . .

But it was late, and in a few minutes I left too, saying goodbye to Flossie and my Aunt Gert, who by now were the only members of the family remaining in the library. As I went down the stairs I could see immediately that it was now no trick to either enter or leave the house: the front hall which had been bursting with people an hour earlier was now completely empty. Not that the party had grown smaller; it was now larger than ever, but the cargo had shifted: all those who had been out on the fringes, eating and drinking and talking together out on the lawn or in the hall or up and down the staircase, had now pushed their way into the ballroom, aware that the moment was at hand when the new Governor would tell them what they had come to hear: that he had won because of them. They were jammed so tight in the big room that it seemed, literally, that if anyone had dared to lift a hand or twitch a shoulder everyone in the room would have shivered in pain. Nothing was clearer than that if only some of the guests had chosen to stay here in the hall they would have been far better off: they would have heard more, they would have seen more, they would have done both in some degree of comfort. But this did not matter: what *did* matter was the feeling, apparently common to all such gatherings at all such climactic moments, that it was enormously important to be physically as close as possible to the man who was shortly to say precisely what everyone present knew was to be said.

Standing on the bottom step of the stairs, I could see over all heads to the bandstand, where the musicians had now been pushed back into a little clump against the wall. Separated from them by the distance due his leadership was Shep Nomad: plump, ever-smiling, watchful, he seemed frozen into a posture of anticipation and delight at a point just halfway between "the boys in the band" and the handful of men who occupied the foreground. There was no music, there was no talk: there was just plain bedlam. Charles had stepped forward and was waving to the crowd; if at that point he had said anything it could not have been heard over the shouts, the whistles, the great explosive spasms of applause. Suddenly, as if on a cue perceived by no one else, Shep Nomad dipped a plump hand, and from their cramped positions the musicians somehow managed to swing into "Happy Days Are Here Again," followed by Charles's campaign song. Impossibly, the noise from the crowd grew louder; the music itself was now barely audible; Charles, still standing in the exact center of the bandstand before the slim upright microphone, continued to smile and to wave. On the platform with him were Marie, my Uncle Jimmy, the new Lieutenant Governor, a monsignor whom I did not know, and three or four others—presumably figures of greater than usual significance in the campaign. The group was joyous but incomplete: someone was missing and all at once I realized that of course it was Phil. He was nowhere to be seen, and I wondered where he could have gone at such a moment, and why? But just then Charles turned to Marie, took her hand, and brought her forward; she waved; they stood arm in arm; the band played the terrible song their leader had written for her; there was more bedlam. Then she stepped to one side and my Uncle Jimmy came up, holding his hands clasped over his head like a victorious boxer. He stood between Charles and Marie, shorter than both of them, smiling happily; suddenly he reached out with his arms and pulled his son and daughter-in-law up close to him, hugging them hard: the crowd stamped and cheered and screamed. Clearly this gesture of togetherness, made by the tough and famous little father of the family, was the high point of the evening so far. And down on the floor, right next to the bandstand, almost brushing Charles's feet, one bright blue arm was raised in the air and waved about wildly: Edso, that experienced and well-nourished veteran of a hundred such occasions, had made it to the front and now was aching for his reward: a nod, a wink, a flick of a finger—any sign would do, as long as it came from the bandstand.

The noise continued; Marie and my Uncle Jimmy soon stepped back, leaving Charles alone before the microphone. He began, several times, to speak; the crowd would not let him. He waited, smiling, never once putting up his hand, until gradually, very gradually, the cheers and cries and whistles began to die, and then there was only an occasional diehard shout and an isolated spurt of applause, and then, at last, a silence which was deep, respectful, waiting, total.

Out of this silence Charles began to speak, and as he did so I left—there would be no more surprises from now on. The big front door was open and I walked out into the cool night air. The state policeman on guard at the door nodded and said, "A great night."

I said, "A great night." I walked out to the edge of the terrace and stood there for a moment. There was no moon: in the dark night that part of the lawn which stretched away to my left seemed black rather than green, fading off into the even blacker and barely visible bordering trees. To my right all was brighter, lit by the still gay but dying fires of the Japanese lanterns. Even though it was much cooler now the breeze was pleasant, the sharpness of full fall was not yet here, and so I stood there on the terrace, looking out into the night, listening to the sounds coming out of the house, hearing Charles's voice but not really getting what he was saying, and hearing too the applause that broke in on virtually every phrase. Out on the lawn half a dozen men moved silently and systematically about, clearing the tables, folding them up and carting them away, spearing the debris from the littered grass: the party was very nearly over. I watched for a few seconds more, and then I turned to go off across the lawn to my car when someone standing just behind me said, "It's no fair to eat and run. You're supposed to stay for the speeches."

It was Phil. Apparently he had been standing in the dark on the far side of the terrace when I had come out; quietly he had come over to me. I wondered again why he was not where it seemed he should be at this moment; I said, "You're not in on the finale: how come?"

He said just what my Uncle Jimmy had said earlier, except that his meaning may have been a little different. "It's Charles's night. There's a good reason for Pa and Marie to be up there with him. Not so for me, unless we're out to establish our family solidarity, and I don't think that's required by now, do you?"

I said, "You're selling yourself short: that's new, isn't it? My guess is that they want to see you up there with the others, that they even expect to see you."

"They've seen me," he said. "And they'll see me again, don't worry about that. They're all good party workers and sooner or later they'll all come around to find out what goodies are in the basket. And when they do, I'll be the one they'll have to see. So

I'm in no danger of being overlooked. Besides, there's another thing: it's a matter of tactics. Do you know that right from the beginning I've never gone up on a platform with Charles—never, that is, when it was at all important or when he had something he wanted to get across? That's something we both agreed on—matter of fact, it was my idea. Know why?"

I didn't; he said, "It's obvious: we look too much alike. Or we remind people of each other, which comes to the same thing. Charles alone is fine; Charles with me is vaudeville. Comedy stuff: all we'd need is straw hats and ice cream pants. Charles could talk all he wanted to about Consolo or Corruption or Higher Minimum Wages or Lower Hospitalization Costs, but half of the crowd would simply be looking at us and saying to each other, 'Isn't it wonderful, Agnes: do you think they're really twins?' You can't lick that; it's inevitable. So Charles appears alone. With pretty fair results."

I was suddenly curious to know what he had thought of the whole campaign; I said, "Now that it's over, did you think he'd win all along?"

He nodded. "Sure."

"No doubts?"

"Doubts, yes, but only because you're foolish if you don't realize that accidents can happen. And probably will. But I knew that if we got our share of the breaks we were in, and in big. It wasn't by any means as hard as the mayoralty fight, no matter what you may have heard. And neither one of us ever thought for a minute that it would be. Surprised?"

"Yes, a little. I would have figured Consolo as much tougher than that on past performance alone."

"The trouble with past performance is that it's in the past. Everyone is over the hill sooner or later, and we thought Consolo had just about had it. He'd lost a lot of support where he'd always been strongest—with the Italians. When he first ran I don't think there was an Italian in the state who didn't vote for him: he was their boy. But everything changes, including Italians. We had polls taken, and every one of them showed that by now the Italians were getting tired. They didn't want just another Italian in there, they wanted a good Italian. Well, there just wasn't one around—at least, not one who could run for governor. So they voted for Charles—I don't suppose the 'Kinsella' hurt there, by the way. It was the old confusion all over again. Remember: 'Hey, are you Irish or Eyetalian?' "

I remembered: it was a family joke. When I was a boy in school I had often bitterly regretted having one of those names—Costello was another—which was subject to mortifying misinterpretation. In a way proud of the name because it was my father's, my mother's, I nevertheless longed for something clearcut: Sullivan, Murphy. But now, years later, ambiguity apparently had paid off. . . .

"Whatever the reason," he said, "when they ditched him he was dead. He had to be: without them he just didn't have the horses. Anyway, for my money he was always overrated. He had this reputation for almost supernal cunning: well, I had a couple of long sessions with him and I couldn't see it. What I could see was a rather stupid man who'd had almost supernal luck. And now the luck had run out and he had nothing—or very little—left. So that's why I figured it would be easy. On top of which we got a few breaks, we had the organization, we had drive, we had the money. And we had Charles."

First things last? I said, "In short, a breeze?"

"No," he said. "Not a breeze. Damned hard work all the way."

"No fun?"

"Well, you know: a funny thing happened to me on my way to the State House. Funny things are always happening around here: the whole state's a joke machine. But overall it didn't add up to much fun: as I say, it was mainly hard work. Not fighting Consolo; just keeping our own crowd in line. Which was no cinch, believe me. "

"The celebrated coalition?"

"That's right. Labor for Kinsella, Small Business for Kinsella, Ministers for Kinsella, Negroes for Kinsella, Professors for Kinsella, Conservatives for Kinsella, Liberals for Kinsella. And—inevitably—Independents for Kinsella. You name it, we had it. It took a little doing to get them all in under the same tent, but we did it. We put them all together and then we found out we had to do something more: we had to keep them all together. And the one way, the *only* way, we could keep them together was to keep them apart: as far away from each other as possible. A slight paradox. You follow?"

"Yes, sure." It wasn't hard to follow: the rivalries, the potential clashes, the hurt feelings and the jealousies inherent in this reluctant combination were easily imagined. And now, again, I remembered the talk we had had on that night five years ago; I said, "But isn't that more or less what you wanted? You were out to take control away from the stumblebums by broadening your base: wasn't that the whole idea?"

"That's right. And we did. Of course we've still got the stumblebums—you don't get rid of an army of hacks and grafters overnight, and they're still important: look at Cogan, for one—but the point is they don't have control any more. *We* have that."

"You and the coalition."

"Yes, but we run the coalition. With some difficulty, but we do. The real trouble is that each group wants Charles all for itself. Just by the way, nobody's any worse there than the Professors. They don't want their piece of flesh, they want the whole body. One hundred per cent: they want him for their very own, they want to serve him up for dinner, they want to eat him up. And failing him, I'll do. Fortunately Charles is just about tooth-proof and I'm not so soft myself, so we survive. But it's not easy." He sighed and said, "They all want something different: well, okay, you expect that. The Negroes, of course. They're catching up and they're shooting for everything now: fine. Maybe not fine, but understandable. The poor bastards haven't had a fair shake for so long that all they want to do is grab the dice and run. But you can deal with them—at least you can deal with whichever spokesman you're talking to at the moment. And with them it all means something, it's exciting, it's real, and at least you feel you're in the land of the living. Whereas with some of the others . . ."

He shrugged, and I said, "The Professors? You don't love the eggheads any more, Phil?"

"There's a certain kind of arrogance that puts me off," he said. "I suppose we're arrogant enough in our way, but it's not *that* way. I talked to a couple of them here tonight: they have a rather peculiar idea of their own contribution to the campaign. The fact is that it wasn't all that great. Do you know Kurt Vogelschmidt, for instance? Have you met him?" Switching to mimicry, he said, "Haff you as yet had zat disdigdt blesshure?"

"No. I know who he is, of course." This owl-faced, mountainous refugee from savage European oppressions had come to America at the outbreak of World War II. Weighing close to three hundred pounds, paralyzingly articulate, he had bullied a succession of Midwestern political science faculties into helplessness until finally, ten years or so ago, he had wound up here in the city for emergency abdominal surgery. He had remained to teach and to talk. There were rumors that he had been on the point of beginning a distinguished political career in Vienna when the war had unhappily intervened; these rumors remained rumors, but it was a fact that he was now one of the most vocal of academic political activists, and I remembered seeing his name heading a list of professors who had vigorously supported Charles. I said, "He's . . . what? To the campaign, I mean. The Brains Trust? The big theory man?"

"I'll tell you just what he is," Phil said. "He's a waste of time. He's my mistake. I got him in; I thought he packed a little weight with the others. Well, he does. But not enough. Not enough, for example, to justify calling me every other night around one in the morning to tell me what he expects of Charles on the basis of his own keen analysis of Austria before Dollfuss. The hours I've spent listening to that chucklehead outline a strategy which would be just swell if only Consolo were Franz Josef! At first I thought he was kidding; by the time I caught on it was too late. And all the while, chirping away in the background—because she's an intellectual type too, you see—is his charming wife Elli, who weighs a cool thirty-five pounds, has bangs, wears knee socks, lives in the past, loves Bartók, hates supermarkets, and serves a special kind of iron strudel she bakes herself! It's ghastly beyond belief. It drives you right back to the stumblebums: I'd a lot rather spend my time chewing the fat with One-Eyed Danny Geegan of the Police Athletic League. At least I'm sure we got his vote. For all I know charming Elli wrote in one for Leopold Figl."

I said, "He's dead, I think."

"That's all right with me," he said. Then he smiled quickly and said, "That shows you how parochial I've become. Do you think this state is getting to me?"

"What about Charles?" I said. "How does he get along with them?"

"Better than I do. That's partly because I'm with them more. But also he's more patient and he's developed this great self-control. And that marvelous way of looking gravely attentive, as if he were really listening hard to what you were saying. That's big magic in the academic league: they're all talkers. And then they also misread Charles rather seriously. They know he's not really one of them, but they think that in a way he is, they think he values them especially, and they think that now he's the Governor they'll all do very well."

"And they won't?"

"No," he said soberly. "They can't: it's not in the cards. Oh, they'll do all right, but that's not what they want. They want a little power. They want to be right up there with Charles, running the show. They haven't got a prayer: Charles is much too smart to let that happen. He knows exactly what they've given him, and he'll make some sort of equivalent return: equivalent, but no more. Well, some of them will accept that, and others won't. But if they don't, what are they going to do about it? Support somebody else? Who? You see in a funny way they're a little like the party hacks: they may not much like what's happening to them, but where else are they going to go? And nobody knows that better than Charles."

And suddenly it occurred to me to wonder what my Uncle Jimmy had been doing while all this had been going on. He must have known of this wing of Charles's support: did he ever meet with them, talk with them, discuss the details of an overall strategy? It was a picture impossible to envision, and when I mentioned it to Phil now he agreed.

"He didn't see much of them; I kept them away from him as much as I could. You know: what could come out of that? And as it turned out, Pa had a great time in the campaign: a ball all the way." He added reflectively, "I don't know, I guess you might say Pa in politics today is a mixed blessing. On the one hand you have all his energy, his savvy, the funds, the people who get behind you: old pals of his you couldn't get near otherwise, and who really can make a difference. On the other hand, he's not quite used to the little delicacies that now have to be observed: he was born in a tougher age. So that sometimes, when he's angry, he just lashes out and to hell with the consequences. And then you have to persuade him that the NAACP doesn't look kindly on their members being called 'jigs.' Plus the fact that he's been in the saddle so long it's a little hard for him to move over. Even when it's Charles who's supposed to be driving the horse."

I said, "Pitched battles?"

He nodded. "Now and then. Well, you know: inevitable. When Pa wants his way he leans hard. But in a more subtle way Charles is quite a leaner, too. So we had our moments. As you can guess."

"As everybody could guess, apparently. The papers were always full of the real inside dope about what happened at those high-level policy meetings between the Boys and Pa."

"I know, I know. I read them all. Nothing was ever right. Where do you suppose the papers get their political writers, anyway? They used to ship them over from the sports page in carload lots: where do they come from today? The classified ads? It's pathetic. All that imaginary expertise. . . . If I read once," he said, "I read a thousand times that old chestnut about Charles and me standing up to Pa, trying to beat him down on those old reactionary ideas he kept insisting on. Of course it didn't happen that way at all. He had plenty of reactionary ideas, but the point is that he's also very skillful; it's only when you're working with him on an operation like this you realize how quick and how smart he is. The truth is that he was right half the time. It was when he was wrong that we had trouble, because he was always more stubborn then. But it all worked out in the end. Probably because Pa wanted Charles Governor even more than he wanted his own way. And probably because on the things that really count Charles and Pa aren't as far apart as you might imagine."

And there was something in his voice as he said this—or rather, something *missing* from his voice—that brought me right back again to that night years ago when he had been filled with buoyant prophecy, and had spoken with such excitement about Charles and politics and the future. Now the future had arrived, but the excitement and the buoyancy seemed to have gone: on this night of triumph Phil was strangely muted, and I had no idea why. It may have been simply that he was tired, that this was the natural letdown after the long campaign. Or it may have been that as he became more deeply involved in the endless local political tangles and quarrels he saw no great reason for excitement, perhaps discovering that no matter what he and Charles and my Uncle Jimmy might accomplish, they could hardly work the miracles he had hoped for in the beginning. Or it may have been merely that he was five years older now—or it may have been something entirely different, something I hadn't even thought about at all. But in any case it bothered me, because once again, as he was talking, I felt again that same sense of disquiet that I had felt throughout all the family party: a faint uneasiness, a troubled conviction that something in some way had gone wrong with Uncle Jimmy and his family, and now I think that perhaps I may have showed something of what I felt, because I saw Phil suddenly give me a quick and curious look. But he said nothing, instead turning away so that he had his back to the house and to me; he flipped his cigarette and it sailed in a long high curve out into the night, the little red spot of light landing somewhere on the dark lawn. He stood for a moment, looking out in that direction, and then he said slowly, "So there we are. Or rather, here we are. 'Around and around she goes, and where she stops, nobody knows.'" He turned around again to me and said, "Who used to say that all the time? Someone on the radio, wasn't it?"

"Major Bowes," I said. "The old Amateur Hour." But it was a strange quote to dig out of the past, especially now, tonight; I said, "How'd you happen to remember that? I mean, the quote."

He shrugged. "I don't know. It just came out of the blue. Bits and pieces from the past: you know the way they do." With a quick grin he added, "Although I grant you that this was an odd one. Considering the moment. Winners aren't supposed to talk like that, are they? Whatever happened to positive thinking?"

"Maybe it got used up in the campaign."

"Maybe. But to tell you the truth I wasn't thinking about the campaign. Or politics. I guess I was thinking more in personal terms."

He seemed about to say something more, then stopped, and turned away again to look out across the lawn. I didn't say anything. It would have been difficult to know just what to say, but I had the feeling that he neither wanted nor expected me to. So I stood there, looking at the tall slim back, and thinking, oddly enough, of Phil not as he was now, but as he had been as a boy, and of how he had always been the most exuberant and the happiest one of all the family, and thinking too that we were both now . . . what? Middle-aged? And by one of those queer tricks of association I found myself thinking not only of Phil or Charles or my Uncle Jimmy, but of Jean and myself, and of how we had all and so unexpectedly changed. . . .

Gloomy thoughts in the silence. The silence out here on the terrace, that is; inside the house Charles had finished his talk, the music had come up again, there were cheers and roars and a great burst of loud applause. I heard cries of "Speech! Speech!" and I wondered from whom this speech was demanded. My Uncle Jimmy? Marie? Anyone who would speak? Nothing happened immediately; then, gradually, the noise died down, and someone began to speak. Not Marie, not my Uncle Jimmy, but someone I could not remember having heard before. The voice was heavy, the articulation was none too clear, and although I could hear words I couldn't understand what was being said. Phil had turned back to me again and was watching me as I listened; after a moment he said, "The voice of the turtle. Cogan. Recognize it?"

I didn't, but that wasn't surprising, because I hadn't heard it in years, and I had hardly expected to hear it tonight—in this house, that is, and in this way. For Charles, I knew, despised Cogan, and while it may have been logical to invite him here—to a gathering that was, after all, political rather than personal—it was not quite so logical to serve him up in this position of preference. Puzzled, I said, "What's that in aid of?"

"Class. We always like to lend the program class." In the same dry voice he said, "It's what's technically known as a master stroke." He paused, and for just a moment I thought he had decided not to say anything more, but then he said, "It was an idea Charles had. All in the interest of party solidarity. He seemed to think it would be wise."

"And you?"

"Oh," he said, "I guess I seemed to think it wouldn't."

I suddenly thought of Charles, earlier this evening, saying—lightly—that there were "cracks in the solid family wall," and now, not because I was merely curious, but also because I think I was still troubled, I said, "More pitched battles?"

"Of a different sort," he said. "Well, not really battles, because there are one or two areas where Charles isn't . . . persuadable." Then he said, "It's late, isn't it? I've got to go in and get Flossie. Jack, you'll be around for a while? Back here, I mean?"

"I think so, yes." I wanted to learn more about those one or two areas, but I knew that I wouldn't—at least, not tonight. I said, "I can work here as well as anywhere else, and also the house needs touching up here and there. I'd like to see to that before I go off again. So I'll be around."

"We'll get together," he promised. He reached out and tapped me lightly with a forefinger on the upper part of my arm; it was the way he had signaled his departure to me ever since we were boys. "See you soon," he said.

I said goodbye to him, and he walked with his long steps back across the terrace toward the house. He had nearly reached the door when I called out to him, and as soon as I did he stopped and stood, waiting. I had called because suddenly it seemed to me that there was something more to be said, but now that he stood waiting for me to say it, all I could think of was a clumsy, even rather foolish, "It's all right, isn't it? I mean, with you?"

"You ought to get together with Charles," he said. "That's more or less what he asked me a couple of hours ago. I must be radiating cheer. Anyway, the answer is yes: it's all right. It's even better than that: it's fine." He gave a little wave of his hand and said, "Thanks."

Then he went quickly into the house, and I was left alone on the terrace. It was darker now: the last of the Japanese lanterns had gone. Even in the darkness, though, I could see that the swiftly moving men had done their work, for all the tables had been taken away and of the great spreading quilt of debris only an occasional scrap of paper remained, blown by the wind in and out of sight. The lawn looked dim and deserted. The air was sharper, more seasonal, now, and in the moonless fall night there was a clear pale splattering of stars. Out in front, toward the street, there were now no shouts, no songs, no signs of activity: presumably the students and other sightseers had gone home. The only action came from within the house where, with Cogan, the speaking seemed to have come to an end, and the music was once more pounding out through the still open windows. A door at the far end of the terrace opened, and I saw a small group of people come out, the first sign that it was now permissible for the party to begin breaking up—although I knew it would be a long time yet before everyone called it a day. I waited until this first group had gone down the drive away from the house, and then I left the terrace and cut across the lawn to the side where I had put my car. There were now other cars there, parked in a long row; to get to mine I had to detour around them. As I did so I heard, suddenly and very loudly, the sound of someone shouting, and almost immediately I saw a man come crawling on his hands and knees out from between two of the parked cars. He was about fifty feet away and he was not alone; following him slowly, and looking down at him, was a uniformed state trooper. He said soothingly, "Okay now, sir, okay. Everything's going to be okay. Just try to stand on your feet. That's the boy now!"

"Don't tell me what to do!" the man on the ground cried belligerently. I was nearer now, and when he turned his head I at once recognized the thin foxy face: it was Walshie. I don't think he saw me, and it would have made no difference if he had: clearly the party with its abundant free drink had been too much for him, and he was very drunk. He pushed himself up onto his knees and said to the trooper with surprising distinctness, "By God, if you want to hold on to that badge, buddy, just you don't tell me what to do!"

And then he collapsed on the ground and lay there on his back, one hand raised and making a small and threatening fist, his face tilted to the stars. The trooper saw me; he shrugged and smiled. "Par for the course," he said. To Walshie he said, "Come on now. On your feet, sir."

From his back Walshie howled, "One more word outa you and you'll be back pounding a beat where you belong. I'm a personal friend of Governor Charles Kinsella! You just ask the Governor if he don't know Leo J. Walsh!"

"Okay, Mr. Walsh," the trooper said patiently. He bent forward, reaching down as if to put a supporting arm under Walshie, but suddenly Walshie sat bolt upright.

"Leo J. Walsh!" he cried. "Remember that name if you know what's good for you, buddy. I'm a man that's got a million personal friends! Governor Charles Kinsella! Rudy Vallee the Vagabond Lover! And more! And I got up off my ass to lick cancer of the bowels and I can get up off my ass to lick you!"

And then, as sometimes happens with drunks, lucidity deserted him and so did consciousness: abruptly he collapsed once more, this time falling face down on the ground, where he lay absolutely motionless. Walshie had passed out. The state trooper, who had been bending forward all this time, now merely reached down and picked him up easily, as if he had been a pillow; he said to me casually, "Out like a light. It's funny, it's always a poor little bag of bones like this that tells you he's going to murder you."

I said, "Want any help?"

He shook his head. "No sir. I'll just take him back into the kitchen. We're all set up for this in there. We'll sober him up some and then we'll see he gets home all right. Don't worry, sir."

He freed one of his arms long enough to give me a quick salute, and then he walked off toward the rear of the house, cradling little Walshie in his arms. And this was the last thing I saw at Charles's victory party; in a sense, perhaps, it was not inappropriate: I had begun the evening with Edso and Walshie, and now I had closed it with one of them.

I drove home slowly, of course thinking of nothing but this

strange celebration which had turned out to be so different from what I had expected. The night had been full of the usual bounce and euphoria and laughter and noisy self-congratulation common to all such nights, but it had also been full of queer undercurrents and surprises, none of which I had anticipated, and none of which I found reassuring. . . .

And the surprises were not over: I found this out shortly after I got home. I lived, now, in the house in which I had always lived—the house where I had been born, and where I had had my extraordinarily happy childhood with my mother and father and Tom and Ellen and Arthur. My father, who in his later years almost certainly could have used extra money, had persistently refused to sell the house, but after his death the question naturally came up again. Jean, who was besides myself the one most intimately involved, had not seemed to care much one way or the other, and it had been my Uncle Jimmy, that sentimental family man who was also a practical man, who had advised immediate sale.

"It's an ark: why hang on to a place you could raise buffalo in? Who lives like that any more?"

"You do."

"Cut it out," he had said, briefly—and correctly—indicating the difference in our circumstances. "Listen, you can't afford to run a shebang like this. The taxes alone will put you in the booby hatch in ten years. Right? Wise up. Sell it to the developers: you'll never get a better price than right now. All those halfwits with that loose dough falling out of their pockets. Sell, get yourself a nice piece of change, pick yourself up an apartment. Down on the waterfront, the new ones. What's wrong with that, hah? There's just the two of you: why stick around here?"

"Because this is where I want to stick around. This is where I want to live."

"Bushwa!" he had exploded, but then he had let it drop and pushed it no farther. Instead he had said only, "You're just like your old man. They'll be running tag days for you before they're through!"

But so far, at least, he had been a poor prophet. I had been able to swing it—not easily, but it had been done. And somehow it had seemed enormously important to me that it be done, that I hold on tight to this house which was the only place, really, that I had ever thought of as my home, so that no matter where I traveled or how often I went away I never felt that I *totally* belonged anywhere but right here: in this city, this house, this specific setting which had been so familiar to me for so long.

Except that of course it was not quite so familiar now: changes had been made and some of them were great changes. The open land which had stretched out from our house on all sides was open no longer: ranch houses blanketed the former fields, and not far away the noise of the new divided highway could be heard. Our own land remained intact, but to the rear of the house the barn, or garage—or, for a brief period, the hangar—had long ago been torn down, and there was, in its place, a great square patch of new grass, darker than the rest. The house itself I kept in decent repair, but it was hardly the spick-and-span and shining white house of my childhood, and Arthur, who was still alive—Ellen had died twenty years before—and who, at the age of eighty-four, came over once a week from the rest home where he now lived to putter around and to lend a not-quite-steady but unrefusable hand to small maintenance, mourned its appearance, thought of better days, and regularly commiserated with me.

"It'll be better, Mister Jack," he said, "when your dad gets back and takes things over, the way he used to. There's no one can get things going like your dad!"

For most of his moments this white-haired, good old man—as red-faced as ever, and still astonishingly unlined—lived in a world where my father was always about to return. In the beginning I had tried to tell him the truth, but this was no kindness: it bothered him, his eyes grew cloudy and his manner agitated and uncertain, and so in the end I let well enough alone and he was happy in his dreams of the old splendor which was soon to come again.

And the changes had reached inside the house as well: here there was a great mixture of old and new, a strange blending of objects which seemed to date from five minutes ago with those which were as familiar as my bones. When Jean and I had moved in after my father's death, she had been anxious to begin renovation at once. Naturally enough: it was now *her* house, and certainly I had no plan to treat it as a kind of museum of childhood memories, to foolishly try to preserve something which in any case could never be preserved. So the house had been cleaned, rearranged, and in large part refurnished, with some of the best and the oldest and the well-remembered pieces kept, and others stored, sold, or discarded. Automatically, the house became smaller. We closed off the top floor entirely; two of the third-floor bedrooms we kept open and ready for use, but they were in fact never used: it was a childless house, and the help we had—two cleaning women, each of whom worked part-time—came in the morning, left at night, and had no need for accommodation. There were other rooms which had been transformed in their purpose: the long bedroom where Tom and I had slept now became my study—a silent, pleasant, sunny room where I could write undisturbed whenever I was at home. The big rooms, the main rooms—the dining room, the library, the music room—were the least altered, or so it seemed to me. Many changes had been made here too, but curiously, even though surrounded by chairs and mirrors and tables and lamps which had been here for no more than a few years, I often felt that something about the rooms themselves seemed to come through, and to come through so strongly that it would seem to me that everything that was now here had always been here, and that nothing really had changed at all. This was especially true of the big master bedroom which had been my father's and mother's room, which had become

Jean's and mine, and which was now . . . well, which was now mine. Here, where the only things to connect the present with the past were my mother's dressing table and a small writing desk my father had been fond of, I have found myself suddenly overcome by an absolute conviction that this room was in some mysterious way identical to the room I had known as a little boy, and in spite of the evidence so clearly here before my eye, I nevertheless seemed physically to *see* this down to the very last detail. It was an odd hallucination which didn't happen very often and when it did it was gone as quickly as it came, but I think as a result of it I came to feel that in this room there was some persisting, abiding quality that all the other rooms—even those in which the sense of the past was strongest—seemed to lack.

It was in this room tonight that I received the last surprise of this surprising day.

The telephone rang just as I had thrown my dinner jacket on the big bed; I answered with a feeling of certainty that it was either Phil or my Uncle Jimmy with a final post-party word. Instead Jean said, "I've been calling for hours! Where've you been: out on the town?"

Her voice was warm and friendly and interested, sounding exactly as it always had, as if she couldn't wait to hear just where I had been and what I had done—and sounding too as if we had seen each other last when I had left the house this morning, when the truth was that I hadn't been near her or seen her for seven months next Tuesday. For just a moment I didn't—and couldn't—say a word; it was a kind of paralysis which was not new to me at these times. She was likely to call me—not often, but occasionally—usually late at night, certainly when she was alone, and probably when she was lonely. Sometimes I didn't even know where she was calling from—once, a couple of months ago, the voice of an overseas operator had come floating maddeningly in and out—but in any case, although I had come to know that she might call at any time and that perhaps it might even be necessary for her to call, when the call did come it never failed to take me by surprise and to leave me, always, momentarily voiceless and seized with the same quick unexpected ache.

She said, "Jack?"

And then, as always, I came to and answered her and we talked. For a while we talked as we usually did during these calls, which means that she was almost incomprehensibly at ease and composed and even gay, as if we were apart only through some comic accident or temporary circumstance, while for my part I was only too aware that I was formal and stilted and strained, and that the tone of my voice must have surely shown her that in a way I wished she hadn't called at all, but that in another way I wished the call would last forever. Tonight, moreover, it was one of those rare, mechanically perfect calls in which the voices come through so marvelously clear and undistorted and *near* that it seems impossible that a telephone is even being used, that the two speakers are not seated five feet apart and looking at each other as they speak. And in fact she was not very far away; uncharacteristically, she mentioned at once that she was in New York, having arrived only the day before—from where, she didn't say, and I didn't ask. These talks seemed to have sprouted rules of their own—that is, she clearly, for whatever reason, wanted to talk to me from time to time, but only on the subjects of her choosing. Anything else—evasion. Pleasant evasion, but evasion all the same. And about what was most important to us, from the moment she went away she simply had not said a word; for some time now, I had felt that she was, in some peculiar way, waiting—but for what, I didn't know.

Tonight she wanted to know more about the party. "Good old Charles," she said, although in fact he was not, somehow, a great favorite of hers. "He couldn't miss, could he? That's what all the papers said. Or anyway what they're saying now it's over. There's a difference, isn't there? Listen, Jack, who was there tonight?"

"A lot of people you know. A lot more you don't." I went into some particulars on both, and she said reflectively, "Well, I hope they enjoyed themselves. Because that's the last time most of them will see the inside of that house, wouldn't you think?"

It was true, certainly—at least until another election. She said, "Tell me about Marie: how did she look? Marvelous?"

Marie, on the other hand, was a great favorite; they had hit it off from the first. I agreed that she had looked marvelous.

"What was she wearing? Well, no, you wouldn't be any good on that, would you? But I'll bet she was all in white."

"She was: good guess."

"No guess at all. White's her color; nobody looks better. . . . You know she's going to have a baby? In April."

I didn't know, of course; I think I was even a little annoyed that she did—it was almost as if, having gone away, she had no right to know. I said, "Are you sure?"

"Yes, she told me. Well, she wrote: I haven't really seen her since this summer. In Paris." Then she said, "It was funny: I saw a lot of the family there in just a couple of days, but you probably know that. I saw James the day after I saw Marie. He was very nice and gave me lunch. He spent a long time talking to me; I seem to be one of his special targets, although I'm not really sure I qualify. Having been baptized and confirmed and everything. Also, one night I saw Uncle Jimmy. He didn't see me—at least he didn't *seem* to see me, but I think he did, all right. I think he cut me. Not that I minded so much, but it was something that had never happened to me before."

She was silent; so was I. It was a new note for these talks; it was as though she had struck it in spite of herself, expressing not self-pity but a little surprise at what had happened. Surprise, and a slight hurt. And suddenly I found myself getting angry at my Uncle Jimmy for what he had done, but then I realized, of course, that this was an absurdity, because I didn't know just what it was that he *had* done. I knew none of the circumstances: whether he had really seen her, and if he had, whether she had been alone at the time, or whom she had been with. My Uncle Jimmy was not ordinarily a delicate man, but he might not have behaved tactlessly here.

I continued to say nothing. The silence lengthened, stretching out until I began to feel, very strongly, what I had not felt before: that something had happened that made this talk different from all the others. It seemed to me that this time the awkwardness, the embarrassment, was not all mine, and as this gap, this emptiness between our words grew, I became suddenly apprehensive, and all at once I knew that the time had come: that at last, after all the months, something was about to happen. And then Jean broke the silence. She said, in a voice which was not the voice she had earlier used, "Jack, I want to say something to you."

And then I knew it was coming, and I knew *what* was coming. It was what I hoped with all my heart would not come, ever, and now I felt as if everything inside me had crushed together into a small, dry, airless ball that kept getting smaller and smaller and more withered with each breath I took. Suddenly, all over, I *hurt*, and I wanted to shout out, "No!" Don't!" But I didn't because—because I couldn't. I couldn't make a sound, I couldn't even move. I could only sit, curiously hunched forward as if this would in some way protect me, on the edge of the bed, squeezing the telephone in my hand, and waiting for the words I wanted so desperately not to hear.

Jean said, "I . . ." Then she started again and said, "I think . . ." And to know that she was finding it difficult to say what she had to say didn't help—it didn't help at all. She tried again, and this time, finally, she said it, and when she did I felt . . . I felt, simply, what I had never felt before in all my life, and what I never, never, never will feel again.

Because, speaking quickly, in a voice which was much lower than usual but which was quite distinct, quite clear, she said, "I think—if you'd like to have me, that is—I think I'd like to come home."

And at first I don't think I heard her. I mean, really heard her, or remotely took in what she was saying, because it was so far from everything I had been so sure was coming, so far from what the long dull months of separation had increasingly prepared me for, so far from the appalling, numbing finality of someone you love with all your heart telling you that the part of your life which has been so totally hers is now at last all gone—it was so far from all this, I say, that in that first split second there was only a dazed blankness, a stunned suspension of the senses. Then, carefully, slowly, the words came in, one by one, and I reached for them cautiously, like a child who sees bright toys before him and can't yet believe they're truly his. And then at last, suddenly and blindingly it all came together and came bursting through, blasting me, smothering me with a great wild spreading joy, and I had all I could do to keep from crying out into the telephone, "Come now, Jean! Come quickly, as fast as you can!"

Instead I must have taken too long a time, for before I spoke she said again, this time I thought a little anxiously, "Jack?"

And I said, all too palely, all too flatly, holding myself in because at this point I didn't trust myself to say any more, "Come on home, Jean. I'd like you to. I want you to." And then I added, "Very much."

I thought I heard a slight gasp, although I wasn't sure; she said, "All right. I'll be there."

I said, "How soon? When?"

"Oh," she said, "I can come about any time."

I said, "Tomorrow?"

There may have been the faintest hesitation at this; maybe not. I don't know: at this point I was reading meanings into every silence as well as every word. She said, "Tomorrow, yes. If that's all right with you."

"I'll meet you at the airport."

"No, I'll come to the house." She stopped, and then said, "I guess I've got lots of things to tell you, Jack. Not now, though."

"No, not now. When you're home."

"It may take me a little time even then." With a little embarrassed laugh she said, "I'm not too experienced at this sort of thing. As you know."

But I didn't answer this; I just said, "Come home, Jean."

"All right." Then she said, "Well . . . tomorrow, then. Good night, Jack."

"Good night. Good night, Jean." And before I heard the click in my ear I thought I heard her whisper something else to me, but again, this could have been imagining too.

And so I undressed and went to bed. I didn't sleep. I lay there wide awake, all through the blue-black star-struck night, thinking only of Jean and Jean and me. And of Charles and Phil and my Uncle Jimmy and Marie and all the rest, who up until the telephone call had filled my mind and memory, and whose world had once more seemed so interwoven with my own, I now thought not at all.

III

seven

About three weeks before Christmas, we went down to Georgia to visit Phil and Flossie. It was a good time of the year to go, it was convenient for Phil, who was relaxing before all the business of the inauguration, but more than this it was the time to celebrate Flossie's birthday. There was no more appropriate place in which to celebrate this day, for this Georgia house had been Phil's birthday gift to her, ten years ago. Jean and I had been at that birthday party too, and I can still remember Flossie's lovely face as it changed from disbelief to doubt to a kind of trembling ecstasy: after years of marriage to Phil she still felt some alarm over the fact that money should be used in such delightful ways. Unlike Marie—who, although not obsessed by money, was certainly pleased by it and frankly rejoiced in all the good things it could buy—Flossie had not been a poor girl. Her family had had money for generations, but they had been "careful" for generations, too; they had the traditional Yankee distrust of expenditure for ease and comfort and the strong belief that most of the abrasions encountered in life were not only necessary, they were also desirable.

"It all goes back to Big Daddy Calvin," Phil had said to me, when one day we had been talking about his in-laws. "They don't know it, but it does. Ooop oop oop: watch it! Don't have too much fun! You can see it in everything they do—even the way they eat. You ever notice that, by the way? You ought to: it's very revealing. They start out fine. They put everything on their plates very tidily: meat, boiled potatoes, stewed tomatoes. Not too much of anything, and maybe instead of the meat there'll be a small portion of fish with some sort of awful white sauce dumped all over it. Then do you know what they do? They mix it all up. Before they put a fork to their mouths they mash everything all together on their plates. One big central ungodly mess, just so nothing will look too good or taste too good. Then they eat. Yum yum. Well, Flossie went through all this but somehow she escaped. She got it all but she really didn't buy it, and all I can say is thank God for that!"

And it was true: conditioned by it, she nevertheless had not bought it. In her mild way she hated all the harsher aspects of life which she had always been assured were good for her health and even better for her soul. She loved comfort and pleasant living: even in the simple matter of our climate she had found herself at odds with her elders, disliking our long and severe winters and often rather wistfully complaining about them. Sometimes Jean used to talk about her in terms of the weather.

"She's a summertime girl, our Flossie. That's what she adores: soft breezes and plenty of sunshine and tennis and all the kids beside her on the beach. It's too bad hammocks went out of style: wouldn't she be perfect in one? And when you think, when you just *think* of all the years she spent with those frozen-faced relatives at Crabapple Acres, it nearly breaks your heart!"

I had said, "You sound like Phil."

"That's not bad, is it?" she had answered. "After all, who knows Flossie better?"

And certainly she was a summertime girl. This was her season: she mourned its late arrival and its early passing, and now, with his astonishing birthday gift, Phil had extended that season—not forever, but for weeks and weeks, now and for all the years to come. Watching her face at this birthday party ten years ago, I could almost see the last of the old "not-quite-right" spirit struggling weakly, gaspingly, losingly against the all-too-evidently Wonderful.

And in its way the house was wonderful: I thought so more than ever when Jean and I went down this year. It was located on the Georgia shore, not far from Sea Island: an old, spacious, and rather sprawling house, not remarkably designed, not particularly handsome. It was simply the most comfortable house I have ever been in in my life. The country around it was as purely *agreeable* as anything I could have imagined: soft and green and gentle, with pine woods beginning a bit inland from the ocean and rising slowly into a series of low hills. The smell of the sea—somehow different here than in the north—was always in the air, and even when the full complement of children were on hand it was quite possible to spend one restful day after another doing nothing but reading or walking or swimming or sunning—and never once be disturbed. Flossie ran the house well, she had good help, the food was excellent. Everything seemed to move smoothly and without effort: it was of course an effect that can only be achieved with the help of a great deal of money. And yet, while this was a rich man's house, perhaps the greatest merit of it was that while you were there, you never thought of it as being that at all.

Phil and Flossie made the trip often, never in the summer months—when, Phil said, it was pure hell on wheels because of the heat—but in the fall and winter and early spring they frequently flew down, sometimes staying for weeks, sometimes only for as little as two or three days. The children loved it as these flying visits to their Southern home gradually became a part of their lives—their necessary removal from school for some of these visits seemed to worry no one; a tutor went along from time to time, and of course I remembered that Phil, as well as his brothers, had not attended any regular school until well past the usual age—

and Flossie, for her part, could have wished for nothing better. But as time went on, it seemed to me that Phil's feelings had begun to shift, and now, although he appeared to enjoy the house itself and the surrounding country as much as ever, his pleasure in his neighbors—as well as a certain amusement at their manners, their general behavior—obviously had lessened, and his view of them had become increasingly sardonic.

"All this pecan-pie charm loses a lot in the translation," he said to me on this last visit. "Sooner or later you catch on to the fact that what you're really listening to is the voice of the swamp. Nine out of ten of them are still right up there with the Stars and Bars, and when they talk about the Enemy they don't mean Mao; they mean the Supreme Court. The approach has changed, of course. Oh, you still meet two or three of the old Cunnel Beauregard V. Culpepper buffs, but mostly they're younger: about our age. The new-style honeysuckle gasbags. They all talk in a smooth and civilized way about the orderly processes and about their 'very genuine fear' that the time-honored protection of States' Rights is going down the drain, but every so often something breaks through and then you can see that what they're really afraid of—and all they're really talking about—is good old Black Sambo, seven feet tall, running naked and drooling through Dixieland, moaning, 'I's gwine to git yo' sistah!' Well, you know, enough is enough. When I come down here now I stick pretty close to the house and I horse around with Flossie and the kids and I swim in the ocean and I talk to the people who come down to see us, and that's that. I've just about had it with the homegrown product!"

It was disenchantment, but it did not affect his guests: we had a marvelous time. We came for four or five days; we stayed for eleven. They were long, easy, languorous days: a great smooth stretch of time in which we seemed to move gently through the soft and unresisting Southern air, sometimes active, more often idle, sometimes with Flossie and Phil, more often by ourselves.

None of the children—all of whom would be here for Christmas—had as yet arrived, and the four of us met mainly at dinner every night, where we ate and sat and talked for hours, mostly about other days when we had first been married and had regularly gone out together, often with Marie and Charles. There was something about this house, this place, which seemed to keep us in the past, like old people reminiscing about their days of vigor and delight; about recent events and developments—the campaign, Charles's prospects as Governor, politics in general—we did not talk at all: although this, I think, was due less to the setting than to the general feeling that Phil, after his long and steady immersion in political talk, at least down here deserved a rest. There was a common if unspoken agreement that if anyone introduced the subject, it would have to be he. But he didn't, and so—neither did we.

One day in particular was memorable, and for a reason that had no connection with either Flossie or Phil. It was the day on which, at last, Jean and I talked freely and completely to each other.

This talk we had been on the point of having ever since her return. She had come to the house from the airport and she had come quickly: I knew that because, unexpectedly nervous now that the time was here, sure that something would go wrong, I had called—twice—to check on the plane; I knew the exact time of its arrival. And, astonishingly, here she was, minutes before I had thought possible. Watching from the window, I saw the cab stop, I saw her get out, and then, as soon as she was clear of the cab, I saw her turn and look down at her right leg in quick exasperation: a run? I opened the door as she began to hurry up the front walk, and for just a moment I saw her before she saw me: small, stylish, pale gray suit so clear and simple it must have cost the moon—she had money of her own, her clothes were her own province—tiny deep blue hat, small dark rich-mouthed face, looking as beautiful as ever and as if she had never been away.

She was almost running, and then she saw me looking at her and one small elegant foot stopped for the barest fraction of an instant, uncertain in midair; then she came forward again, running now, and at the door she was in my arms. We said something to each other—what, I don't know: I don't think either one of us paid attention to the other's words—and then immediately in the house we came together eagerly after the long months of apartness and deprivation, and for a time—an hour, maybe more—it was as though nothing bad had ever happened to either of us, as if the weeks and months just past were a mercifully annihilated dream. Eventually, however, she pushed herself up, and I saw the doubt and anxiety come into her eyes; she suddenly said, "Jack, I—" and then just as suddenly she broke off and continued with words which we both knew had nothing to do with what she had been about to say. At exactly that point we remembered and knew that everything was not as it once had been, and that it had no hope of being so until what had to be said between us was . . . well, was *said*, and we could begin to face it and each other and make what had certainly once been there come alive again.

So then, she would have to tell me: I knew that and so did she. I thought at first that she would do it soon, very soon, because as long as I had known her she had always faced her problems immediately and courageously; she did not like procrastination. But now a curious process of postponement set in. Often I saw her ready herself and even actually begin—by now I could recognize all preliminary signs—but she never finished or really got into her story, and I never pushed or pressed her. I thought it best to let her take her own time, to make her own occasion, although to be really truthful there was something else at work as well: this wasn't the purely generous act it seemed to be. The fact is that I willingly collaborated in each postponement, because in a way I was as reluctant to listen as she was to speak: I knew that whatever she told me, it would mean not only pain for both of us, but humiliation for me as well—and no man hurries to that. We waited, then: a week passed by, then two, then three, and on the one all-important subject we kept our silence. We went to Georgia; the silence continued. And while it did we lived very pleasantly, laughing a lot and never quarreling, remembering all the better parts of all the earlier days, being—in a sense—happy. Certainly I was far happier than at any time since she had left, and I think—I know—she was happy, too. But it was in the end an unsatisfactory happiness, a happiness without depth, it wasn't a *married* happiness: we were like two people playing house, doing all the things that real-life married people do, except of course the one important thing: we did not share each other fully, we did not *shake* each other with our lives. We were living agreeably in a kind of truce, together but apart, never quite unaware that beneath the smooth and placid surface ran a thin uneasy current.

This all came to an end on that one day in Georgia. I remember that it was a rainy day: the only rainy day we had. The morning had been fine, like all the other mornings we had seen down here: clear blue and gold, with a gentle steady onshore breeze, and a handful of small and very white clouds, no bigger than puffballs, scattered out across the length of the ocean horizon. It promised to be the best day yet, and as a bonus over the radio came that news which always warms the heart of the wintertime vacationer in the South: there had been a snowstorm up north, a blizzard, the first of the season. We congratulated ourselves and all drank a toast to absent and snowbound friends; then, shortly after lunch, Phil and Flossie rode off on their horses, to be gone for the rest of the day. An hour after they had left the rain started. It came down with a sudden tearing violence, streaking in from the sea through the pines and across the lawn, the wind sweeping it along so powerfully that it seemed to come in great driving sheets almost parallel to the ground. For perhaps twenty minutes this furious storm slashed against the house: there was no thunder, no lightning, but the noise of the battering rain itself was so loud that we had to shout to each other to be heard. Then it was over. As quickly as it had struck the storm settled down into a soft and decorous rain, becomingly seeping from light gray skies onto the soaked green hills. We were alone in the house: the cook and the maid had left as soon as the heavy rain had stopped, going out to their own small cottage in the rear; we saw them plodding off across the sodden lawn, barefooted and side by side, their shoes tucked under their arms. For a while we sat in the long living room, watching the rain, and talking about Phil and Flossie, wondering if they had been caught in the storm, wondering what we could do that might help. Nothing; we didn't even know the direction they had ridden off in, it would have been impossible to find them. But they knew the country well, and Phil was extremely resourceful; we agreed there was no reason to worry.

Jean, in bright canary slacks, suddenly plumped down on the floor, kicking off her sandals, stretching out on her stomach before the fireplace. During the storm we had lit the fire, more for cheer than for warmth; it was welcome now on the softly gloomy afternoon, and as she faced directly into this fire I sat on the side, just watching her face: it was alert and mobile, always changing, and yet there were times, such as now, in this light, when it seemed to rest, to brood, when it seemed to have about it a queer kind of dark, deep, almost gypsy beauty—although this was a reflection which would have killed her father had he been alive to be killed. He had been an irascible ignoramus who had made a fortune in junk; he had been married to an extremely handsome woman—more intelligent, equally irascible, still alive—whose Irish antecedents were as unmixed as his own; before his death this had come to be her one remaining merit in his eyes. Out of their turbulent, quarrelsome, parochial union had come Jean: the only child, convent-trained, willful, as vaguely unsatisfactory to both of them as they were precisely unsatisfactory to her.

"Growing up," she had said to me, shortly before our marriage, "I heard only two sounds in our house: screams and prayers. I got a little tired of both."

Her own voice was soft; she never screamed. In the observance of her religious duties she was quite likely to be casual.

Now she said, still looking into the fire, "This is a great fireplace: do you know it's the first fire we've had in it since we've been down? How's that for a crying shame?"

"It's been too warm, even at night. I might speak to Phil: maybe he could put in air-conditioning to give us a little fake cold. That's what they used to do in Havana, remember? In that nightclub the Detroit thug owned? At midnight the temperature outside was an even seventy-five; inside on the dance floor you could freeze to death. They did it so all the Cuban ladies could show off their furs. Made weather: that extra little touch that marks the truly superb host. What do you think: could we get Phil to spring for something like that?"

She smiled, but didn't answer; she kept looking into the fire, and for a little while neither one of us said anything. Outside, the rain was still falling at the same easy pace. I was getting drowsy; normally I ate very little at noon, but today, because we had all been together for lunch and it had been more of an occasion, I had eaten heavily, and I was on the point of falling asleep in my chair when I heard Jean say, in the same tone she had been using, as if she were still talking about room temperatures and open fires, "It's funny—I must have rehearsed this a hundred times, and now what good does it do me?"

And suddenly I was no longer near sleep; I knew from the first word what was about to happen. She said, "I knew I'd tell everything to you some day, and I thought it would help—help *me*, I guess I mean—if I knew exactly what to say, step by step, and then when the time came I'd say it in such a way that you couldn't help seeing that whatever I did I might have had a little something—not much, but just a little—on my side, and anyway I'd say it as fast as I could, and then it would at least all be over. Except of course for what you'd say to me, and I couldn't very well rehearse that part of it, could I? But it didn't do any good, because I'm not going to say it at all the way I planned. I can't; I've been lying here trying to remember just how I'd decided to do it, but I can't. So my fine plan's all gone: that's fairly silly, isn't it?"

All through this she had remained looking steadily at the fire, but now she turned and looked at me, and there was in her eyes an expression of . . . what? I don't know; something I couldn't read. I said, "It doesn't make any difference, does it? You've never had to work from a blueprint with me before: why start now? I've got one question, that's all. If you want to answer it, okay. If you don't, okay too. I just—"

"I know," she said, breaking in quickly. "I know I know: *why?* And why Tony White, of all people? That's it, isn't it?"

I nodded. Because that was it: the great question which had remained absolutely incomprehensible to me after all these months. I still had no clue at all: none for her leaving, and certainly none for Tony White. . . .

She looked at me and then took a long breath, swallowing air like someone about to go down underwater. Then, quickly, she exhaled, she was ready to talk, and it seemed to me there was a touch of sadness, even of pain, in her face. She said simply, "Because he bowled me over, Jack. It won't make any sense to you, I know. It doesn't even to me now. But he did. He knocked me right off my feet."

And looking back on it now I don't know what I had expected her to say—but not this. I just stared at her, stupefied, disbelieving; she said, "You see, it's no good: I told you it wouldn't make sense. You can't believe it: you're looking at me as if I'd just said down was up or that I'd just seen a herd of buffalo in the back yard. But it's true, Jack. I'm not proud of it, but it is!"

Suddenly, for the first time since she had started talking, for the first time since she had come back, I got angry, really angry, for I had known Tony White very well for a very long time. I pushed back, as if I were trying to get away from her; I said sharply, "I don't believe it, not for a minute! Tony White, for God's sake! You, bowled over by *that!*"

"By that," she said, unhappily but calmly. "By cheap little Tony White. The kind of man you make jokes about, don't you? If you talk about him at all, that is. He's a coward, he's a dreadful liar, he's a sponge, he's lived off at least two women I know of, and I think he's probably mixed up in some very shady deals here and there. Oh, I didn't know all that at the time, I picked most of it up—very quickly—along the way, but all the same I knew enough to keep clear of him. Only I didn't keep clear. Not this time. And now I'm looking at you, Jack, and I know what you're thinking, but it can't be that big a surprise, can it? After all, I *did* go away with him: there had to be a reason. Did you think he kidnapped me? Or hypnotized me? So it must have been something, mustn't it?"

She was talking rapidly now, but very quietly: it was no panicky waterfall of words. All the time she talked she looked straight at me, keeping her eyes steadily on mine, not as if she were watching for any reaction I might have, but more as if this deep and reaching regard were a part of what she had to say, that without it the words themselves might not get through. And I listened: angry, but baffled and badly confused. Because obviously what she was saying was true, everything about her told me that, and yet there was no *reason*. . . . I said, "Why? Or no, not why: *how?* How could it even be possible? Can you tell me that?"

"All right," she said, "I'll tell you. And do you know what it's going to sound like, Jack? What you're going to think? You're going to think I'm out to excuse everything, that I'm trying to . . . what? Cop a plea? Well, I guess maybe I am, but whether I am or not it's the only answer I know how to give. I fell for Tony White because for two weeks, while you were off on one of your trips, a man who was reasonably young and reasonably attractive and had reasonably good manners looked at me and talked to me and complimented me in a way that I hadn't been looked at or talked to or complimented since I was a pretty girl around town with a list of beaus. Do you know something, Jack: I'd almost forgotten there were men who could actually talk to women and say something more than 'How are you today?' or 'Are you through with that part of the paper yet?' It's silly, it's foolish, it's much worse than that, I know, but Jack, that's the way it all began: *Tony White paid attention to me*. You see, you're wrong if you think he's just five feet nine of nothing. He isn't; he's even charming when he wants to be. At least he is to women. All right, he's contemptible and all that, but contemptible people can have charm, they can have appeal, and they can be clever enough to know when to use it. And on *whom:* I don't imagine they waste their ammunition much. Men like Tony are very very good with lonely married ladies."

And I stared at her with a curious feeling of hallucination: it was as if I'd never heard her talk before, as if this woman I had been married to for so many years had suddenly begun to be someone I hadn't known at all. I said, "Which means what, as far as you're concerned? I don't get it: are you a lonely lady? With me?"

"Yes I am, Jack," she said quietly. "Don't you know that? Or haven't you ever thought about it? I don't think you have. Well, you can think about it now if you want to. A little." Her voice changed and she said, "You see, I know you love me, Jack. I've always known that. I don't know how I've known because you really aren't very good at showing it, are you? You haven't been for a long time. You're my husband and everybody would call you a good husband. You don't cheat on me, you don't get drunk on me, you don't hit me and you don't abuse me. But Jack, you *neglect* me. You do, you really do. I've tried to tell you this before, but it's hard: no girl wants to say over and over again—even to herself—that she's being ignored. But I am ignored, Jack. I'm loved, but I'm ignored. And that's not what I want, it's not good enough, it just isn't!"

I said, "That's not true. . . ."

"It is true. Just because you don't wake up in the morning and say to yourself, 'Today I'm going to ignore my wife!' doesn't mean you don't do it. You do; you've been doing it for years. I don't mean just the most obvious thing, but that too in a way, weren't you? Lately? I'm a married woman, I haven't any children, and I'm not blaming anybody for that: you, me. I don't know. But anyway I haven't got them, I'd like to have them, but I haven't. And that's that. So what I had was you, and you had me. The trouble was that I seemed to have you part-time, and you had me in pretty much the same way you had your car or your books or some college buddy. I was an old pal, Jack. You got used to having me around: I was as comfortable as an old shoe. You read about these people who've been married so long and know each other so well that they know every moment what the other one is thinking and so they don't need to talk at all—well, that's not my idea of marriage! I don't want to be a buddy, I don't want to slip through the years sitting beside you and gradually beginning to knit and to watch TV and look up at the clock at nine every night and think that pretty soon it'll be time to hit the hay. And then one day you'll look at me and I'll look at you and we'll both say, 'You know what's happened? We've grown old!' And that can happen, Jack. It's easy, easier than you think. Time goes by so fast and the next thing you know, that's it, you've had it, everything's done, finished, all over!"

I said, "More excitement? More bubbles? More kicks? Is that what you wanted?"

"No," she said. "All I wanted was *you*. But I couldn't have you, because half the time you were a married man living by yourself. In a way you've always been a married bachelor: sometimes I've thought you lived exactly the way you would have lived if I hadn't ever come along. You do your work and that takes most of your time. We live in your house, the house which is all yours—don't think, by the way, that because the furniture and a few touches here and there are my idea that it's now my house as well: I know the way you think of it, I can see that all the time. You're still thinking of the boyhood here with Tom and Ellen and Arthur and everybody and that's fine, that's great, except—well, now I'm here, too! You've told me all about your mother and father and I loved your father, I think he was marvelous right up to the end. But maybe you ought to remember, just once in a while, the way he lived with your mother and the way he talked to her and behaved with her and spent his time with her—I know all that because you've told me. I've often wondered why a little of that didn't stick. For instance, I know that whenever he went away he took her with him. Of course I know one reason why he did and I know that doesn't apply to me, but after all it wasn't the only reason, was it? I always had the idea that they went off together partly because they loved each other and wanted to be with each other and so . . . and so there they were. But you, Jack, if you go off on a trip to get material for a book or to do a magazine piece, I don't go with you any more—or not often—and to tell you the truth I don't know how that happened. It just happened, it just somehow seemed easier that way, it seemed that you could work better and do whatever you had to do without me around and so I stopped going. And then I stayed at home and every other night or so you'd call and say 'How's everything?' and I'd say that it was fine. And then we'd talk a few minutes and that would be it until the next phone call or until you got home. Meanwhile I'd go out with my 'girlfriends' or have them in—although not too often, because they're married, you know, and they have their own homes and their husbands—and we'd gossip and talk girl talk, and when I wasn't doing that and even when I was I'd be waiting for you. Until this last time when, suddenly, I just didn't wait any more. I don't know why, I just didn't. I couldn't seem to help myself. All of a sudden I pulled up stakes and got out. One day, without even planning to do it, almost without even thinking about it, I said, 'All right, I will.' And I did. And that's how I left you, Jack."

For the first time now she stopped—though only to get her breath, I think, not to invite any comment or sign of sympathy or understanding from me. And this was just as well, because I couldn't have given her one: right then I couldn't have given her anything. I sat staring down at her—for she was still on the floor in front of the fire, but sitting now, steadied by one hand on the rug, her knees pulled up before her, and her eyes still watching me with the same unchanging expression—and I sat blank and frozen-faced and speechless, as if I'd been paralyzed by very hard and unexpected blows.

She said, "I ran away. I ran away with Tony White and that was insult to injury, wasn't it, because I don't know a living soul who really likes Tony—even I don't any more. But I went off with him, I hurt you, I might have made a kind of fool of you—although *that* I never intended, I never thought about that at all—and I made, maybe not a fool, but something else of myself. I went off with him like some cheap little two-dollar girl—if that's what they cost these days. In fact he got quite a bargain; I didn't cost that much. I even paid for my own plane fare: Tony isn't really much of a spender. But I went. I went at five o'clock in the afternoon on BOAC, first stop London; I went with one suitcase, a hatbox, and Tony by my side—he kept looking around for detectives. Detectives! And it was a Saturday afternoon, it was April seventh, you were in Chicago, and I knew you wouldn't know a thing until Monday when you got home. I even had the good manners to leave a note, but I couldn't think of what to say except, 'Don't worry: am all right.' And so far as I know that's all you knew until I called from London and told you what I'd done. I think I even asked you to forgive me. I hope I didn't, but I think I did: it's the sort of cheap theatrical touch that would have fit right in. I keep on saying 'cheap,' don't I? For want of a better word, which I don't happen to be able to find—although I've looked hard enough, I can promise you that. Anyway, here you were and there I was. With Tony. For a time. For a very short time, as a matter of fact, but there I was and that's what counts, isn't it? And the next time you heard from me was two weeks later and the whole thing was over and I was alone in Edinburgh, of all places. But you didn't know that—about it being over, I mean—and I didn't tell you because . . . well, how would you tell a thing like that? 'Surprise surprise, Jack: guess what? I've had my fling and now I've just kicked Tony out'? Besides, I didn't want to tell you. Not then. I don't know what I wanted then. I just knew it was better to be alone. With what remained of my pride—not that that was much. But at the moment it was all I happened to have."

Vaguely I was aware that something in her story was beginning to shift, that the emphasis, the *tone*, had become slightly different, yet I didn't fully take this in because all I could think about was what she had just been saying before this. I don't think, now, that I was angry at all; I was stunned, bewildered, and memories had begun to rush in on me, one after another and then all together—memories which I had often had before, but which now seemed oddly unfamiliar and disturbing, as if they had been completely changed, and suddenly I felt shaken and queer and full of a deep and spreading pain.

She said, almost dreamily, "Were you ever alone in Edinburgh, Jack? On a weekend? Of course you're not a girl and of course you wouldn't have been there in exactly my circumstances, would you? But anyway . . . I've had better times. And then after I left there, I didn't have any place special in mind, so I just traveled. To places I'd been and places I hadn't. Sometimes I looked up people we knew. They were glad to see me, I think. When they asked about you I always told them you were finishing some work, that you'd be along in a week or two. Well, of course you never were, but by that time I'd moved on so it never did any harm. And then I used to meet other people, lots of them: strangers, in trains, on planes, in hotels. The usual places. And the usual people. Some of them were even rather nice: you know, to pass the time with. Of course there were always others who wanted to do a little more than pass the time. I suppose that after a while they develop a nose for the natural pushover: wouldn't you think that was it? Only it didn't turn out to be quite like that. I don't know that it matters now but my 'adventure'—I think that's the polite word for it, isn't it?—wasn't repeated. Ever. With Tony or anyone. I'm not after a merit badge for that but . . . I just thought I'd tell you. I was alone and I stayed alone. Unbelievable as it may seem."

And now it seemed to me that her eyes did change, just a little, as if at last she wanted some sort of response from me. But still I didn't say a word, and for the same reason—I couldn't. Her eyes changed back again and she said, "You see, I thought you might say something. I don't know what: something appropriate, I guess. Like 'Congratulations!' For being such a good girl. Of course if you were James you could give me your blessing, couldn't you? I mean, as a kind of reward for exceptional chastity—"

And suddenly and loudly I said, "Don't!" Because what she was saying—and the way she was saying it—finally came crashing through my own private numbness and confusion: it was as if some special narcotic had worn off in a split second, leaving me sharply and freshly aware of everything that was going on around me, and I realized all at once that it was *herself* she was talking about with this harshness, this contempt, and suddenly this seemed to me unbearable and the only thing that mattered at all. I reached out and grabbed her arms and yanked her over to me. She half slid, half fell across the rug against my knees, and I saw her look up at me, startled and uncertain and I think even afraid, and she said very quickly, "Jack, *please* . . ."

And somehow this was the worst of all and almost broke my heart, because I couldn't bear the thought that she might think, even for the smallest flash of a thought, that I could hurt her. I pulled her close against me as I slipped down onto the floor beside her, and there on the floor I held her in my arms. I said again, but softly now, "Don't. Don't say any more. You don't have to. You shouldn't."

She said, in a kind of wondering way, "Shouldn't I, Jack?"

"No. Not for me. Ever."

She gave a strange, quivering motion and put her head down

against my chest, staying there for a moment, still shivering lightly, and because I'd never seen her do it before, it was actually a little time before I realized that she was crying. I held her more tightly and she continued to cry silently, and after a while she said, "I'm sorry. I don't cry very much, and I didn't think I would now. It's only that . . ." She didn't finish; she raised her head and looked at me and I could see no more than the faintest traces of her tears.

I said, "You ought to cry more often. You look great."

"I'll bet," she said, and with the back of one hand she brushed hurriedly and automatically across her eyes. Then she sat straighter and said, "Isn't this the place where they always say, 'She managed a wan smile'?"

"I guess so, but it's not compulsory. Either to say it or do it. You can even cry a little more if you want to. It's permitted."

"Ah, Jack," she said, and she sounded, not joyous, certainly, but easier, happier. Casually, almost unconsciously, she slipped her arm around mine, the way she once did rather often, and we sat there together like two children on the floor.

After a moment I said, "I don't know what to say, Jeannie. Except that I'm sorry. For everything. And that's not much of an apology, is it? A little thin and a little late—you get short change even there. But anyway, I mean it. And if you'll buy it—or even if you don't—I'll do better for you from now on. But I hope you're buying."

"Oh, I'm buying," she said. She reached up with one hand and stroked my cheek; she said, "Besides, I'm the one who's sorry: I bitched you up good, remember? The trouble is I'm also sorry for myself, and half the time I don't know which is which. I've been floating around in pools of self-pity for so long I swear that if I saw a man knocked fifty feet by a passing truck I'd feel sorrier for myself than for the man. Simply because I'd seen the accident."

I said, "This is a new game you've got, isn't it? What do you call it: Pick Yourself Apart? You want me to get in on it?"

"No, I play all by myself. I'm the only one who knows the rules. You see, there I was, having this perfectly crummy time and trying to make believe I wasn't, and most of the time I just wound up feeling sorry. For me. You know how that can be? I was always lonely and I could never seem to do much about it; I guess I don't have any talent for that kind of life. I couldn't even drink enough to get drunk because I always get sick first, remember? So I'd do different things. Sometimes I'd call you and talk to you and put on my party hat and play gay as if I'd just come in from another marvelous time, and nothing like that was happening at all. I was just plain miserable and I suppose I kind of hoped you were, too. That cheered me up a little: I don't know why, but it did. Once when I was in the South of France, staying in this horrible hotel that was full of German pansies and jazzy South American sports, I was so low one night I got on the phone and called Marie here at home and talked to her for an hour and a half. That one phone call cost more than my whole hotel bill! So it was crazy. But I'd seen her a couple of times in Paris the week before and we'd had fun together, and then she had to go back home because Charles was campaigning like mad and he wanted her there. So that made me feel lonelier than ever—are you beginning to see what I mean by the self-pity? Anyway, on this one night I felt like calling someone up, someone from home, someone I could let my hair down with, and so I called Marie and just talked and talked and talked. I couldn't stop talking and I didn't want her to stop, either. It was quite a phone call. Didn't Marie ever say anything to you about it?"

"Not a word. But she wouldn't, would she? She's not a talker."

"Come on," she said. "She talks all the time."

"Yes, but gossip, chitchat: that kind of thing. She's always been pretty good on secrets. Charles trusts her and he doesn't trust anybody. And she's always been in your corner."

"I know that, but all the same I don't—of course she probably figured that if she did tell you you'd start wondering what was up, why I'd suddenly talked to her all night and not called you."

"Why didn't you call? I mean, if you were that low. I wouldn't have eaten you. I even used to be able to give you a little lift, didn't I? Now and then in the good old days?"

"You did, but who was in the good old days? This was only a couple of months ago: do you think I could have picked up a phone in France and said, 'Jack, your runaway wife is down in the mouth tonight: tell her a story and make it all better'? No, I used to call you when I did because I missed you—you probably guessed that—but the only way I could talk to you at all was with that awful small talk that didn't mean anything. I couldn't talk to you about anything that mattered; I just couldn't. Once I started to and then . . . well, you know. It was no good: I didn't know how to say it. I was ashamed, I felt guilty . . . and of course I still do. You know that, don't you?"

I just held her closer to me, and we sat silent again; it seemed better not to be saying anything. Pretty soon she said, "It was funny the way the family kept popping up during one stretch. I know they're great travelers and all that, but still, I don't think it was all by accident. Phil and Flossie weren't over at all last summer, so I couldn't see them, but I know that Marie came to Paris really to see me, to see how I was. All those lovely shops didn't hurt, but I know the main reason was me. She's pure gold, that girl."

"You didn't see Charles at all."

"Just once: he flew over for a weekend, and I saw him for a few minutes the day he went back. I wouldn't say *he* came to Paris to see me. He was charming and agreeable, but cautiously so: it wasn't exactly open arms towards the Scarlet Woman."

I said protestingly, "Hey, hey, hey . . ."

"Well, you know what I mean. Charles is careful: he likes to have everything all buttoned up before he commits himself. And I was still dangerous. For all he knew I could have kicked up a scandal, and this was an election year. I don't know, whenever I see Charles I always feel that he's looking at me with that cool eye and wondering whether I'm going to get myself into a mess—and wondering whether any of it will rub off on him. Is that unfair? Well, anyway, then he went off, and after that of course there was Uncle Jimmy. I told you about him: he pretended not to see me, but I think he did, all right. I also think he had me watched."

"Watched?"

"You know," she said. "Shadowed. Tailed. Isn't that what you write about, Jack?"

I stared at her. "*You* were shadowed? And by Uncle Jimmy? Cut it out!"

"I don't mean *he* was following me," she said. "Not personally, that is. But somebody was. All the time I was in Paris. Of course I can't prove that he was being paid, but he wouldn't do it for fun, would he? And he was always there, Jack: a thin, sick-looking man who needed a shave—I saw him one day by accident and then I began seeing him every day, wherever I went. He was following me all right, and he wasn't on the make, either. He was just following. Well, of course I'd never been followed before and at first I was frightened, but then when nothing happened it wasn't so bad. I even began to try to give him the slip—going into powder rooms that had a back door out, and so on. You'd have been proud of me. Sometimes I'd lose him for a couple of hours before he'd catch up again. But the thing was, I couldn't figure out why anybody would be following *me*. And then it was just about that time that I saw Uncle Jimmy, and all of a sudden I put two and two together and I'll bet I got the right answer! Because who else would do a thing like that? Who else would *bother*? Doesn't it make sense, Jack?"

It was preposterous—also, annoyingly, it made sense. Suddenly I was sure that this was exactly what my Uncle Jimmy would have done. He was protecting me—and the Family, of course—against my wife. I said grimly, "I'll have a little talk with Uncle Jimmy. He carries this business of family obligations a bit too far."

"Oh, don't do that. Not for me, anyway. It's all over now, and it even seems sort of funny, doesn't it? And even a little flattering, in a screwball way. How many people get all that attention from Uncle Jimmy? I never did before."

But I did not want to linger over my Uncle Jimmy; I said, "What about James? Didn't you say he turned up, too?"

"Yes. And in a way," she said reflectively, "he was the best of all. I suppose because I didn't expect him to be. He was so considerate and tactful and just plain nice. After all, he was only there for the day, and I'm sure he must have had a million things to do, but he found out from Marie where I was and the next thing you know he came whizzing by to take me out for lunch. It was a great lunch, too. You know how elegant he can be: nothing but the best and everything done in exquisite style. We had all this marvelous food, and James kept talking his beautiful French to the captains and the waiters and they kept jumping through hoops for him. But with me he was just simple and gay and all the time I kept waiting for him to stop and get solemn and say that he wanted to 'talk' to me. But he didn't. He didn't once tell me what a terrible thing I'd donc or scold me or warn me that I'd have to mend my ways—you know, the kind of thing you'd think a priest would be supposed to tell you. Even if he was James and I was the kind of fallaway I am. But instead all he did was to tell me about a trip he'd just made to India, which sounded wonderful, and then some very funny stories about an Italian cardinal who's always being embarrassed because he has a brother who's a midget. So we had a fine time. And then, just after he'd taken me back to the hotel and was saying goodbye, I almost spoiled it by saying something bright and flip. I suddenly felt embarrassed, you know, because of everything, and because he'd been so careful not even to mention it, so I said, 'You took your reputation in your hands, James, coming in to see me like this. You never know what you might have walked in on: you might have been surprised.' It was a silly thing to say, wasn't it? As if I was trying to prove that I wasn't a bit nervous or unsophisticated or on the defensive. But he didn't bat an eye. He just smiled and said, 'Oh, I didn't think much about that. All I thought about was how nice it would be for me. It was purely a question of the alternatives. On the one hand I could lunch with a rather saintly old Lutheran ascetic who talks marvelously about the efficacy of grace and who dines horribly on something called Vita-Crisp and cottage cheese. And on the other I could lunch with someone who's an old friend, who's my favorite cousin's wife, and who's a very lovely girl who may sometimes mistakenly imagine that some of her old friends don't love her just as much as they used to. So you see, I had no choice, did I?' Well of course it was all a fib, but he said it in such a way that I knew he really meant it, too, and I thought it was the nicest thing I'd ever heard. I almost broke down and bawled like a baby right there in the lobby!"

"Oh well, it never does to sell James short. He's an extraordinary man."

"I know. Well, the whole family is extraordinary, if it comes to that. Isn't that so? It's just that some of them are a little nicer than others." Then she said, "Jack?"

"Um?"

"It's going to be all right now. Isn't it?"

It was a statement and a question, certainty and . . . what? Doubt? I think a little; what she wanted from me was support, backing up, the assurance that I wanted, as badly as she did, to do what we had so sadly and mysteriously failed to do before. I looked down at her face, and in this curious, trusting, and touching moment she seemed, not like a woman who had been married for nearly twenty years, or a wife who on a spring day had suddenly left her husband and her home, but almost like a little girl. And when I thought of my own carelessness, my own culpability in what had happened, I felt the stab of pain again, and I knew that from now on I would have to walk with care and a new tenderness. And I hoped with all my heart that we could make it; I said, partly exhorting myself, partly answering her, "We *will*. It's going to be all right. We'll see to that."

"Ah, good," she sighed. "That's good, Jack. Because I don't want anything else. Just that now."

"Same here," I said. "Same here all the way."

And so we sat for a long time, silent once more, before the fire on a darkening Southern afternoon. We sat there, thinking and hoping and now and then reaching out to touch and hold each other, until Phil and Flossie came home.

eight

RIGHT after the Christmas season, following so closely that it seemed almost a part of the holidays, came Charles's inauguration. We had been invited to the State House for the swearing-in and had decided to go; on the morning of Inauguration Day the weather changed our plans. It was the worst kind of winter day: no snow, but gray and dismal, with the city drowning in a heavy drizzle that seemed to freeze the instant it hit the highways and through which it was almost impossible to see. We thought of the city traffic, the crowds in and near the State House, the probable length of the proceedings, the badly overheated and acoustically doubtful legislative hall where, by tradition, inaugurations were always held. We balanced all this against the fact that it was Charles, my cousin, who was being inaugurated. We stayed at home.

We watched the ceremonies on television, and it seemed to me that in doing so we had advantages which the spectators on the spot had not—advantages, I mean, beyond the apparent one of comfort. For one thing, all along Charles had been at his best on television, and I thought now that his inaugural address—which was good, but not remarkable: I had heard him better, sharper—had a peculiar directness and intimacy which would have been lost in the hall but was most effective in the home; once again

I was struck by how *believable* he was when seen in this way, and I remembered how often during the campaign I had overheard people, strangers, speak of "personally trusting" him—it had always seemed to me a curious compliment to pay to a man who could be so impersonal. But it was the sort of response evoked by the extraordinary quality which came across so powerfully on television, and I was never more aware than on this Inauguration Day that to see and hear Charles other than on television was to somehow miss a beat—was in fact to see and hear him as considerably less impressive than he really was.

There was another advantage to watching the televised ceremonies, and this one had nothing to do with Charles at all. It was the advantage of watching a comedy, a special kind of comedy, a comedy of contrasts intermittently and unwittingly provided by the television personnel. For in addition to covering the speakers, the cameras played slowly back and forth across the floor of the hall, pausing now and then to focus on individual legislators in the audience; as they did so an invisible announcer supplied a running commentary: it was richly hyperbolic, mindless, totally irrelevant. To have only heard the words and to have seen nothing would have been to imagine perhaps the Athenian senate: grave, dignified, concerned. But here there were the pictures, and so with each reverential, preposterous phrase: ". . . distinguished deliberative body in its wisdom . . ." ". . . the Honorable Daniel E. Cogan in solemn consultation with his distinguished colleague, the Honorable F. Peter McGee . . ." the camera cruelly halted on still another huddle of guffawing figures, yawning faces, and open flies. It was Phil who once said of our legislature, "I look at them and it makes me think that someone's invented a club for disbarred lawyers. They get together every day to swap dirty stories, drink, get down a few bets with the bookies, and give each other the hotfoot. And naturally, with all that going on, who's got time for laws?"

This bizarre scene continued on and off until that part of the program when Charles was introduced and began his address; from this point on we could no longer follow the antics on the floor, as the cameras now were fixed on the new Governor. As he talked we saw other members of the family on the platform with him: Marie seated just to his right, my Uncle Jimmy next to her, and Phil and Flossie not far away on the left. I did not see either James or my Aunt Gert, and I wondered whether they were elsewhere in the hall or whether, like ourselves, they had remained away because of the weather. I thought this most unlikely.

That night we went to the Inaugural Ball. By now the weather had improved surprisingly; the skies were clear, the streets were dry; for some reason traffic was light and we arrived in good time. As soon as I entered the hall—the ball was in the state armory this year: a huge and echoing all-purpose auditorium, possible for dancing, perfection for parade drill—I had the feeling, before anything else, that I had been through all this before. And in a sense I had—and very recently—for it was the victory party all over again. Larger, and less crowded because of the great size of the armory, it seemed to me otherwise almost identical with the earlier gathering: the same strange, expectant, boisterous, multilayered, multicolored mixture that had astonished me two months ago, the improbable coalition held together by such bonds as hope and loyalty and selfishness and force and fear and money and dreams and—of course—Charles. A precise count was impossible, but I was certain that just about everyone who had been at the victory party was also here tonight, although in slightly different costume. White tie and tails had replaced the tuxedo: the effect was at once more formal and more comic, for all too often the figures of today wore the tailcoats of yesterday, and from these hastily altered garments rose the pervasive smell of camphor.

"The mothball fleet," said Phil, dancing by with Flossie. He paused to gaze out across the floor at some of his elderly coworkers, resolutely accommodating the dance steps of their youth to the bold rhythms of Shep Nomad and his men. "Anyone for the Maxixe?"

Labor, the military, businessmen, professors, wealthy friends of my Uncle Jimmy, wealthy friends of Charles, civil servants, party hacks, Negroes, young Irish with smooth anonymous faces, older Irish who were pinker and porkier and faintly disheveled, bleached Greek merchants, an Italian spectrum, a few Chinese, a mahogany-colored man in a turban, students: all were here, all were dancing. Unannounced, the Bishop suddenly appeared, striding down through the center of the hall, waving indiscriminately as the people parted so that he might pass: a walking granite pillar in full episcopal robes. He reached Charles and Marie; he posed with them, then with my Uncle Jimmy, then with all three; he roared an incomprehensible greeting—a blessing?—into a microphone; he disappeared as suddenly as he had come. The dancing was resumed, spirits soared; a touch of raffishness set in. A retired admiral, socially impeccable, alcoholically vulnerable, suddenly pitched forward and lay rigid and face down, his pinched patrician nostrils hard against the floor; his much younger wife giggled, pushed at him tentatively with a toe, and shouted, "Let's Spin the Bottle with old Sid!" At the far end of the hall, Hollywood was here: a small group of entertainers, two of them famous, friends of friends of Charles, who had helped in shrewdly selected spots during the campaign. Now they stood, ostentatiously apart and uproarious. Once I saw Charles glance over at them but he did not approach them: I had the feeling that he now considered them a mistake, not to be repeated.

And Walshie was here. He had come up to us, walking with but slightly behind a tall angular woman who looked as if she had been put together out of clothespins. This was Mrs. Walshie. She said severely to Jean and me, "This is a pleasure, I'm sure. Leo J. has often spoke of the Governor and all his lovely big family."

"The wife comes to all the dances," Walshie said. "By God

I'll tell you why I think she comes: I think she comes to see I don't get tanked up! Ha ha ha!"

"That's enough of that, Leo J.," Mrs. Walshie said unsmilingly. "Not everybody's got your sense of humor. Not everybody knows when you're joking." To us she said, "The fact of the matter is Leo J. doesn't touch alcohol of any kind. Ever since his sickness."

I had a vivid memory of the belligerent, staggering little figure collapsing on Charles's back lawn, being carried, insensible, back into the house by the state trooper. Did Walshie share this memory? Apparently not; he nodded in vigorous agreement and said, "By God, that's the truth. Not a single drop since the time I was at death's door. You all know what I had and you all know what I licked. I'll say no more because there's ladies present!"

But something—or someone—was missing from this scene; I said suddenly, "Edso: where is he?"

"*Edso,*" Mrs. Walshie said. "That one!"

"The sister's dying," Walshie said. "A lovely woman with a bum ticker. And rotten with TB as well. They say she won't last the night. Edso was always the favorite there. Only this afternoon, they tell me, she opened her eyes and said, 'I want Edso with me when I go.' So things being the way they are I guess he won't get over here tonight." Thoughtfully he said, "Unless he's lucky, of course: she could go faster than they think. Still, you can't count on that. Well," he said, beginning to back away, "it's been grand to see you again, Ralph, you and the lovely wife both. Say hello to the Governor for me, just in case we miss each other in the crowd. Tell him Leo J. Walsh was here and wishes him the very best all the way. That's the kind of thing he likes to know. Isn't that a waltz I hear?"

"Leo J. is a beautiful dancer," Mrs. Walshie said to us.

"Waltzing Walshie!" Walshie cried. "Come on, love, pick up your heels with the old champ, and we'll show them all a thing or two!"

He winked at me, Mrs. Walshie bobbed her head primly, and

they were off, waltzing away to a melody which I did not recognize, but which was most certainly not a waltz. All during this exchange Jean had merely stared without saying a word; now she said, "What was *that?*"

"You've led a sheltered life," I said, and I told her about Walshie and about Edso. She had of course not been at the victory party, her interest in politics had never been great, and although I had occasionally told her stories of my own brief involvement with Skeffington and his court, I knew that she looked upon these as reminiscences of some inconceivably remote past, having little if any connection with the present. So that now, tonight, everything was pure revelation: she was startled, appalled, interested, fascinated. We stayed until very late, and when we left I knew that she had enjoyed it all, that it had been for her—as well as for me—one of those rich and rare evenings where almost every minute contributes to success.

Strangely enough, one of the reasons for this success (and by no means the smallest) was the family—and who could have predicted this? Not I; certainly not Jean. For even though she had agreed to go to the ball, and even though it had been she who first suggested that we go, as the day came nearer she grew apprehensive: it would be the first time since her return that she had faced all the members of the family gathered together. During the past several weeks she had seen them all singly; the results had been uneven and perhaps foreseeable.

"Marie was fine, of course," she had said, reviewing the situation with me before the ball. "And Phil and Flossie: there's no sweat there. Well, there wouldn't be: not after Georgia. But with the others I felt . . . awkward. I didn't expect to feel like the Queen of the May, but I didn't expect to feel quite the way I did, either. Oh, they were all right, very pleasant, except possibly for Uncle Jimmy, and even he wasn't too bad. But I don't know . . . take James, for example. He was just as nice as he could be, urbane and marvelously courteous, and of course I can't ever forget how kind he was to me over there, but somehow I feel there's a difference in him. Toward me, I mean. Maybe it's just because he's a priest, maybe I'm just imagining things—anyway, it's not quite the same as he used to be. And Charles was very agreeable, he always is, unperturbed and even charming in that cool way of his, but I thought he seemed just a tiny bit knowing and *amused*. I didn't much care for that, because he was being amused at me."

I said, protesting, "I would doubt that. I would doubt that very much."

"Would you? Well, maybe. And of course I'm not the best witness in the world where Charles is concerned, am I? And then there was Aunt Gert, who pretended that absolutely nothing had happened, and that I might have been away taking sulphur baths or something like that. She didn't go quite so far as to suggest that I might have been off making pilgrimages to shrines the way she does—I suppose you can push farce too far, can't you?—but she was being terribly delicate all over the place. In a nice way. You see, it's turned out to be a kind of game. They all know, and they pretend they don't know, and then I pretend I don't know that they're pretending. So that for the time being we're all stuck. And of course I can't talk about it with them, and of course I don't want to. Which leaves us with a certain constraint all around."

"Yes, but that's not so bad: it's the sort of thing that wears off, and in not too long a time, either. It's uncomfortable, not fatal. It'll go, you'll see." And then I said, "But tell me about Uncle Jimmy. You said he was different from the rest: how? Rude?"

"No, not that. He didn't actually have much to say. He was gruff but cordial enough. Still, I got the picture, all right: he wasn't having any too much of me. I'm sure he thinks of it all in terms of an insult to the family, and he's not about to forget it. So now, instead of jumping and roaring around the way he usually does with people he likes, he's very guarded and neutral and quiet with me. Not hostile, you know—he wouldn't be that, because of you—but sort of noncommittal, strictly hands off. And of course, regardless of Charles's being the big man now, it's still Uncle Jimmy who sets the tone at these family get-togethers, which is why I'm not really panting for tonight. But," she said, "it's something I've got to do sooner or later, I know that, so it might as well be now. Anyway, from what you say it'll be big enough so that we won't be in each other's laps, and if the going gets too rough we can always break away, can't we?"

But we didn't break away, we didn't even try, for the going proved unexpectedly smooth. Very early in the evening, shortly after we arrived, we fell in with the complete family group. By pure chance, all of us—with the exception of James, who, it appeared, had left on another of his far-flung ecumenical journeys early this morning—met in the same corner of the dance floor at the same time. The music had stopped for the moment; we congratulated Charles; we all greeted each other. My Uncle Jimmy, who had been dancing dutifully but laboriously with my Aunt Gert, was polite but muted: I saw immediately what Jean had meant. I think everyone else did, too, because an uneasiness settled over us all, one of those awful foot-shifting pauses which seem endless and unfillable. There were efforts at talk which were worse than no talk at all; at every second the strain seemed to mount for everyone except, possibly, for my Uncle Jimmy, the author of it all. And then the music began again, and as it did Marie said suddenly, "Don't you think the father of the Governor deserves a break? Like dancing with the prettiest girl in the room?"

And as she said this she pushed, really *pushed* Jean so that she faced my Uncle Jimmy and was practically in his arms—it was like a magician forcing a card on an unwilling victim. It happened so quickly that neither of them could do anything about it; Jean shot a desperate look back at me, and I saw my Uncle Jimmy scowl, but it was too late. Marie grabbed Charles and danced away, Phil and Flossie were already moving, and I put my arm around the great bulk of my Aunt Gert. This left Jean and my Uncle Jimmy alone, either to dance or to sit it out. I watched, we all did: they hesitated, they danced. Jean was a miraculous dancer, one of the best I had ever seen; my Uncle Jimmy must have found her a staggering relief after my Aunt Gert, whose heavy-footed companionship I was enjoying now. And "enjoying" was not altogether the wrong word, for while she danced dreadfully, she was an amusing woman, with her sharp mind and her pretended helplessness, and I had always gotten along well with her. As we trudged our way around the outskirts of the floor she talked contentedly about the family and about the events of the day. "We're all tickled pink, of course, aren't we? Well, who wouldn't be after a day like this? This lovely dance tonight, and then the big inauguration this morning. I heard you weren't there, dear."

She missed very little. I said, "No, we were set to go, but then the weather got in the way."

"The weather," she said, and clucked solicitously. "Oh my my. Well, I can't blame you for that. Rain can do terrible things to a man. They say it stunts the growth."

It was the kind of gentle infighting at which she was extremely good. I said, "I hear you weren't there yourself, Aunt Gert."

She gave her great laugh. "God bless us all," she said, "I never get up before noon. Except to go to Mass on Sunday, and they tell me I don't even have to do that nowadays, what with Masses every ten minutes or so all day long and all night, too. But I don't know, I wouldn't feel right going to Mass when everybody else was having his supper. I like the old way best. So I get up on Sundays, but the rest of the time I'm under the covers till noon. God knows I should be at my age. I'm an old woman now, you know. I'm all slowed down to nothing."

"It must be hard for you, Aunt Gert: a little more feeble every day, the mind just about gone . . ."

She flicked just the beginning of a glance at me; I think she was always amused whenever I tried her game. "Very hard, dear," she said. "But that's the way it is with me nowadays. I manage to crawl around and say a few prayers now and then, and that's about all."

"It's a shame," I said. "Still, while you're crawling around and saying those prayers, I wouldn't be surprised if maybe you didn't do one or two other little things along the way. That weren't too strenuous for a frail old lady, you know. For example, there was a report a couple of weeks ago that there was a pretty bitter proxy fight at Brill Oil, and that when it was all over, who came out with the controlling interest but you! I thought I heard that from someone."

She gave me a delighted look. "Is that what you heard?" she said. "God bless us all, but this is a noisy town! Well, you know, an old woman like me who's got a few dollars that the government hasn't taken away from her yet has got to put them someplace, hasn't she? Of course I could always give them to Con Hagerty to take care of for me. He's a nice safe man who has a couple of nice little banks he does business with. They pay four and a half per cent."

"I imagine that Brill Oil does a little better than that, doesn't it?"

"That's right, dear," she said composedly.

We danced on—or moved on—and after a moment she sighed comfortably and said, "Aren't you the good boy, though, to be pushing an old Mack truck like me around? Well, I was always a bum dancer. Big as a house, you know, and two left feet. When I was a girl I used to pray at night that God would come down and show me how to do the two-step. Well, He never did, but I don't complain. He taught me how to do a few other things as

I went along. Things that might have been even better." She added thoughtfully, "I don't know that we have many good two-steppers in Brill Oil today."

She fell silent, and I saw that she was looking out toward the center of the floor where Jean was coping with my Uncle Jimmy. He had by now overcome his original reluctance and was stamping away in the vigorous foxtrot that appeared to be his Universal Step. She said, "It's a kind of a family thing, I suppose. Your pa was a little different—God bless us all, I guess you could say that about him in most ways. But what I mean here is, he was a good dancer and the only one of us who was. Jimmy was just like me, but that didn't stop him from trying. He was always out on some dance floor, torturing poor girls; they used to call him the Water Buffalo." She continued to watch him, then said, "He hasn't changed much. Still, isn't your wife a living wonder at keeping out of his way? And he seems to be having the time of his life!"

He did indeed; a moment later the music stopped and he and Jean came over to where we were standing. The others did too; I thought they might not have returned so willingly to a group which only a few minutes before had been fairly strained and uncomfortable, but they did—I suppose out of curiosity as much as anything else. Phil and Flossie joined us first, reaching us at the same time as Jean and my Uncle Jimmy; I saw Marie making for us, looking slightly apprehensive, but being held back by the people who had ringed themselves around Charles, trying to shake his hand. I looked at Jean, but her face was without any particular expression; my Uncle Jimmy, on the other hand, was beaming; it must have been one of the Water Buffalo's greatest moments on the dance floor.

"Say, that band is the cat's pajamas!" he said. "I don't give two hoots if that baby's a fag or not, he plays music a white man can dance to!" He was exuberant; his earlier reserve was at least for the moment abandoned; he turned to his partner and said, "I've got to hand it to you: you're pretty nifty with the footwork. You followed me all the way!"

And then Jean, without any warning, without preparing any of us—not even me—in any way, threw the bomb. She said quietly, "Well, that was fair, wasn't it, Uncle Jimmy? Because after all, in Paris, didn't you follow me?"

And for one extraordinary instant it was as if all of us in this little group had suddenly been stripped of the power to speak or to move or even to *breathe*. Or to hear: the band had once more begun to play, something heavy and pounding and familiar, and yet we could pay no attention; all we could do was stand and stare. From the shocked stillness I knew that no one had missed the allusion, that everyone here must have known about the shadowing in Paris, yet certainly no one could have anticipated or even imagined that any one of us—let alone Jean—would have flung this so boldly right in my Uncle Jimmy's face. For just that moment I think I was literally stunned (and so, as she later told me, was Jean: she had not intended to say this, she had not in fact intended to say anything, but the "follow" had apparently served as a kind of irresistible trigger, and before she knew it the words had simply come leaping out).

Gradually, heads began to turn toward my Uncle Jimmy; I couldn't see Marie or Phil, both of whom were slightly behind me, but the others wore expressions which ranged from the inscrutable (my Aunt Gert) to the watchful (Charles) to the simply horrified (Flossie). My Uncle Jimmy stood with his feet wide apart and his mouth wide open, looking as if he had been poleaxed. I'd never seen him like this before; it's probable that no one in the family—and very few outside—had ever dared to challenge him so directly. And if we had all felt uneasy and taut a few minutes ago, before the dance, we now felt an almost impossible tension as we simply stood and waited . . . for what? The explosion? Suddenly my Uncle Jimmy looked up and his mouth snapped shut—really *snapped,* so that you could actually hear it. He glared at all of us, one by one: a small, fierce, oddly frightening figure who seemed mysteriously to *swell* in his anger, right before our eyes. And then, to the astonishment of everyone, he began to laugh! It was a strange sight: while my Uncle Jimmy had his moments of good humor, he was not a man who laughed a lot, and certainly I had never seen him laugh like this. He was laughing so hard that his eyes were shut, his little body was bouncing up and down, and he couldn't speak, and as we looked at him in amazement—I think we were all too flabbergasted to feel as yet the relief that came in a moment—he continued to laugh and laugh and laugh.

"How do you like that?" he cried finally. "How's that for nerve, hah? Pow: right in the kisser! And I didn't even see it coming!" He looked at Jean and said admiringly, "I would have laid fifty to one you didn't have it in you!" Then he turned to me and said, "And as for you, you're one lucky stiff: that's a real sweetheart you've got there!"

And he started to laugh again. Suddenly he leaned forward toward Jean; startled, not knowing what to expect next, she stepped back, but he caught her and gave her a great proud hug.

"You're all right!" he said. "I wish I had a hundred more just like you! Listen, if there's one thing I go for, it's a kiddo with spunk!"

It was a marvelous and, I suppose, even a ludicrous scene—because here we were, in this huge hall, with music pounding down on us from all sides, with a thousand people dancing all around us, with everyone here to pay honor and homage to the newly inaugurated Governor, and that Governor was with us in a little oasis of family, completely ignoring—at least for the moment—his own celebration, and instead sharing with us the glow that came from Jean's unexpected triumph! As for Jean, I could see that she was still bewildered, but I could see that she was pleased, too. It was a rare moment for her; before going away she had been on reasonably good terms with my Uncle Jimmy, but she had never enjoyed anything like this accolade. My Uncle Jimmy stood beside her, one arm around her, smiling a wide watermelon smile, as if he had just made a discovery and was now entering into permanent possession. I was reminded of what Jean had said earlier that day, that no matter how far Charles had risen, or what shifts of emphasis had taken place within the family, it was still my Uncle Jimmy who set the tone of any gathering. It was true: he had a remarkable effect on the family weather. It was a great part of his success, I suppose, that in any mood he was impossible to ignore. He was one of those rare men who could make himself felt, and when, as now, he was in top form, he was peculiarly irresistible: his good spirits were powerfully contagious and affected everyone around him almost instantly. I was no exception—nor was anyone else. In the last few moments all the earlier sense of strain had vanished: it was as though we had all exhaled vastly and in unison and had come together happily on the old free terms. Jean was smiling; I knew she was delighted. Marie was the same, happy because her long shot had paid off. And as for my Uncle Jimmy, I think that at this point he was ready to dance again, but just as he turned to Jean, Charles stepped in and said, "You see, I don't get the point of being Governor if you're not allowed any privileges!"

And so he danced away with Jean, and my Uncle Jimmy, still in the residue of his good spirits, shouted, "Come on, Flossie, and I'll give you the dance of a lifetime!" This was true, but Flossie responded eagerly. Phil gallantly now chose my Aunt Gert; on his way to her he said to me, "See how the plants grow when the sun shines!"

"Am I wrong," I said, "or could this have gone either way?"

"Easily," he said. "One thing you get to know about Pa is that you never know. Good old Jeannie was playing in beginner's luck. Still, she won, didn't she? And that's what usually counts."

And Marie, with whom I now danced, put it another way.

"Well," she said happily, "I guess now she's back."

I guess this was true: that Charles's Inaugural Ball, which must have been so many things to so many different people, was to Jean the night that officially she came back: back to the family, back home. And for the rest of the long and happy night we were for the most part together, relaxed and easy and even joyous with each other, and in the midst of all the hullabaloo and party turmoil, we still managed to enjoy the kind of warm and unified and totally memorable family night which, I think, we had not often had before, and—as it turned out—we were not often to have again.

IV

nine

I REMEMBER that when we left the Inaugural Ball that night, it was with the feeling that we had been to a vastly successful family party rather than a state occasion, and when we said good night to the other members of the family, it was commonly agreed that from now on we would—and must—meet more frequently, that the ties which had been allowed to loosen would now be pulled up tight. In fact, nothing of the sort occurred. As the weeks and months went by we saw each other no more often than we had before—indeed, I think we saw each other less. There was nothing conscious or determined about this: it simply happened and I suppose it had to happen. The euphoria of that night could not last, we all had our separate routines to which we had grown accustomed and which were not to be changed with a wish or by magic, and there was also the plain fact that we were all somewhat less available than before.

Charles, of course, was busy: busier than he had ever been. His new duties left him—and Marie—with much less free time for purely social engagements, and all those people who had so confidently expected that the new Governor and his wife—so young, so rich, so handsome, so widely traveled—would set in motion a train of glamorous and even slightly madcap evenings were quickly disappointed. Charles, as Governor, ran a taut ship from the start.

He entertained often, to be sure; there seemed to be innumerable parties and dinners, but into none of them—as far as I could gather—came the faintest whiff of Rome or Acapulco: Pony Brady and other high-flying friends were, if not forgotten, at least temporarily shelved. We went to two of these dinners in this period. The food was good, the wine was good, the tone of the evening on both occasions was semi-official: clearly, several of the guests were present only for political reasons. Charles and Marie presided impressively and with charm, but the evenings were not—at least, so I thought—a great success.

"I liked the old way better," Jean said, riding home after the second of these. "A little more fun and a little less of the Commissioner of Public Works. And Marie feels the same way: I know she does. Once when she saw me looking at her tonight, she winked. But she knows that Charles is out for bear, and she'd shoot all of us including herself before she'd do anything to slow him down. And I guess you can't blame her for that, can you?"

Apart from these two dinners I think we saw Charles only once, although Marie and Jean continued to meet occasionally for lunch. It was from these meetings that I learned all family news and gossip, because all other sources had suddenly become unreachable. Phil was as busy as Charles and seemed to have disappeared in his work; since Inauguration Day I had seen him once, and that was for a quick lunch. My Uncle Jimmy was no longer in the country, having left a few days after the inauguration for Europe, where he planned to remain for some months. He told me before he left that it was mainly a business trip, and he added, chortling in a queer and semibelligerent way, that this was one time when nothing could get him to go near Ireland. Yet a month or six weeks later he sent us a postcard—or, more accurately, he sent Jean a postcard: it was evidence that his enthusiasm of inauguration night still lingered, for in all his life he had never sent me a card or a letter or a message of any kind—on the front of which was a picture of broad green Irish fields, bisected by a stream, and on the back was a scrawled message which read, "They ought to fence this whole place in and give it back to the rabbits." And from the postmark I knew that he had gone back to his castle.

James we saw fairly often, but not in person. He came rarely to the city now, but he was regularly on television, usually on panel or forum programs, engaged in urbane and low-pressure dialogue with ministers, rabbis, and champion atheists. Once, when he did visit the city and gave us a call, we complimented him on these television performances, and he said, "I'm getting fan mail, an incredible number of letters. They're mostly from teen-agers who want me to help them escape military service. So you see I'm speaking to Youth. I don't suppose I have a really vast audience: no one on television has that unless he's a doctor, a cowboy, or a spy. Still, in my kind of television I'm making all sorts of progress: they tell me my rating is slightly above that of *Teach Yourself Spanish* and that there's just the chance I may catch up with *The Crazy Chef*. I live in hopes. Don't you think that would make a wonderful epitaph for a priest: HE CAUGHT UP WITH THE CRAZY CHEF. It's all there, isn't it?"

My Aunt Gert, like my Uncle Jimmy, was traveling. She drove—or rather, was driven—over to our house to say goodbye: a vast, spreading woman in a vast, spreading car. She was fond of luxury automobiles, had owned all kinds, changed them every year, and loved nothing better than to ride along great superhighways at breakneck speed. She had a chauffeur named Ernie who had been with her ever since I could remember. He was a small and now rather elderly Filipino who always seemed to be smiling ("Why wouldn't he smile?" my Uncle Jimmy had once demanded truculently. "Listen, with what that baby hauls down from Gert every week he ought to be laughing out loud!"); he drove expertly, shepherded my Aunt Gert tactfully through all the tangles of travel, and in a pinch could produce a splendid improvised meal. My Aunt Gert went nowhere without him, and now, she told us, she was driving with her old friend Alice Leary cross-country to

California, where she planned to follow the old Spanish Mission trail.

"I'm tired of the big cathedrals," she said. "The older I get, the smaller I like my churches. And they're all small out there, they tell me, and there are plenty of them to see. God bless us all, I don't know how poor Alice will like that. She's not as religious as she used to be since she lost all her money and got put out of the Plaza. And she's got a little peculiar in the last year or so: she keeps on telling me she's not the little girl she used to be. Well," said my Aunt Gert practically, "who is? But she'll have a nice long ride, she likes the car, and she'll be out of the cold winter; she goes mad at the sight of a snowflake. So I wouldn't imagine we'd be back for a long time."

So that, with all these departures and increased activities, we now saw very little of the family. Yet somehow this didn't seem to matter at all, mostly because we were so busy with our own lives. I was writing again, having begun a new book; Jean, who several years before had been sought after by some of the women's specialty shops to help them with their dress designs, now spent a part of each day among the materials and colors which she loved, and for which she had so sure and inventive an eye. Neither one of us of course had been able to forget anything of what had happened, but I think we genuinely tried to put it out of our minds as much as we could, and we tried, too, to avoid or correct the steady, erosive mistakes of the past. We went out more often at night now, to dinner, the theater, maybe just a movie; sometimes we went by ourselves, sometimes with other couples. We took trips to places we had gone in the first years of our marriage, places we had been fond of, but to which, for some reason neither of us quite understood, we had slowly stopped returning. These were not long trips; they took place mostly over weekends and served mainly to vary the pace of our daily life. In short, we began to work out a pattern of living which in some respects must have seemed not so different from the old, and yet in which, when we were together, we were together in a way we hadn't been for a very long time. I'm sure that at first we were both extremely aware of what we were doing, or trying to do—after all, we weren't children, and we knew that old habits, fixed ways, were not smoothly and instantly changed—and we had our moments of great self-consciousness and doubt. And difficulty: it wasn't altogether easy. Not for me, anyway, and I know it couldn't have been for her. But we tried and kept trying, and gradually these moments became fewer, gradually everything was done more naturally and without thinking first about it, gradually we realized that what we both had hoped for was at least beginning to work. And this was all right: at this stage, I don't think we could have reasonably expected more than that. It was a start. . . .

Curiously, in the midst of all this, while I almost never talked to Charles and rarely caught so much as a glimpse of him, I was aware of him as I had never been before. There were days when, in one way or another, he seemed to creep into every hour. A good part of this I had expected; the newspaper coverage, for example, was no surprise. Charles was good with newspapermen. This had not always been so, but the early stiffness on the one side and the suspicion on the other had pretty much dissolved by the end of his first year as mayor, and since then the two had gotten along well. Charles was not a newspaperman's delight in the way that, say, Skeffington had been, but he was active and interesting and he had style: he was good copy. Moreover, he had a sense of what was really news and what was not, and he did not waste the reporters'—or his own—time. At his press conferences, which he took care to schedule frequently and at convenient hours, he handled himself with skill and humor, being candid whenever it was possible, and at least seeming to be when it was not. As a result he was given great space in all the papers, far greater than had ever been given his predecessor, and while there were quibbles and criticisms they were for the most part minor; in general—and so far—he had led a charmed life: his press was as favorable as it was enormous. In addition to this he did not neglect his main strength: he introduced a series of biweekly television reports to the people. In contrast to most political broadcasts these seemed to be watched and listened to faithfully; according to the surveys which Charles had ordered, his audience was both constant and surprisingly large.

So that I saw Charles often—if indirectly—and I read about him every day, and this, as I say, I had expected. What I hadn't expected was that I would suddenly be engulfed by Charles in a hundred small, personal ways with the most unlikely people—and this now happened all the time. I was invited to parties, receptions, by women I did not know and of whom I had not previously heard; strangers introduced themselves to me as fans: they had read all my books and could hardly wait for the next one to appear; I saw faces which had been familiar enough to me in school or in college, but which I hadn't seen for decades: they now came looming up out of prehistory, all close to unrecognizable, but all smiling, all delighted to see me, all mystified that so many years had passed so quickly. And even with friends, with people I had known for years on more or less the same unchanging footing, there were now queer twists and turns: a conversation would begin as usual and then suddenly break away and arrive, inevitably, at the single point where all these meetings and invitations and reunions and letters and telephone calls ultimately arrived: at Charles.

It was new to me. Not the process itself; I'd seen this funneling operation a hundred times over—no one could have worked for Skeffington a day and not known all about the role of the middleman—but I'd never been a part of it before. Oddly enough, not even while Charles was mayor. It had just not come up—why, I don't know. It was almost as if the public, wise in such matters, had been holding off, waiting to see if Charles was here to stay or if he was only a bright but disappearing flash across a local sky; then, when he had won the governorship, a signal had been given and they had all leaped at once, scrambling desperately to become a part of this young man who was now so clearly on the rise. It was of course this scramble that gave me my new value: I was an obvious conduit to Authority. I quickly found that it was useless to suggest—as I always did—that I could be of no help, that I was not an aide or adviser, that Charles's plans were made entirely without reference to me. I was simply not believed. Almost without exception, all those who approached me in one way or another were convinced that with one magic word of intercession I could, at the very least, get them in to plead their case in person. They refused to be put off; they clung; I even noticed this: that with every refusal, everything I failed to do, I seemed to be more in demand than ever. At first this puzzled me; then, one night, an explanation came. We were at a party, one of those strange, mixed, half-political parties that friends now gave to prove that they were in the swim. It was very late and we were about to leave. I was standing alone in an alcove off the main hall waiting for Jean when suddenly I heard a woman's voice mentioning my name.

"I make it a practice not to say anything bad about anybody, as you well know," she said, "but there's a mean bastard for you!"

Concealed in the alcove, I could not be seen, but neither could I see; fortunately, this was not necessary as the voice was unmistakable: it belonged to a woman with the unlikely name of Margaret Lucille Elderberry. She was by profession a schoolteacher: a great grotesque woman with a huge marshmallow face and a tiny bright red mouth; she was invariably seen in the company of her husband, a diminutive and silent man who looked like a very old son. She had come to marriage and motherhood late in life, but she was proud of both, and she displayed this pride most visibly every Sunday in the cathedral when, shortly before the ten o'clock Mass began, she would move massively down the center aisle with her little husband, trailed by four pale little boys who might have been her grandchildren. She now taught very little, spending most of her time around the state legislature, where she lobbied ceaselessly for higher salaries for married teachers, and just as ceaselessly against the penny milk program for children. For years she had repeated, over and over again, her two slogans: "The teacher was not meant to be a waitress in a Howard Johnson's" and "My one concern is for the child." She was a ludicrous and not entirely ineffective figure. Earlier this evening she had come up to me with a new proposal for Charles. I had responded as usual; the tiny red lips had parted in a tiny patient smile and she said, "You know, I really don't think you understand our program. I really don't think you appreciate what's behind it all."

"I think I do. Your one concern is for the child."

This time the smile had grown even tinier, tighter; she had turned and gone away. And now I heard her saying, "Oh yes, mean as the day is long. I never pass along gossip and I don't like people who do, but they tell me those books he writes can't get into lots of libraries."

"Loaded with filth, are they?" a man's voice asked.

"I imagine so," Mrs. Elderberry said. "I wouldn't be a bit surprised. In fact I'm sure they are. I wouldn't soil myself even going near him to talk to him except that he's got the Governor's ear. That's well known."

"And won't talk into it," the man said. "That's well known, too. What good is it to have the Governor's ear when you won't say a single word into it for a pal? And with jobs going begging all over the state: big jobs, good jobs, jobs with swell pay!"

"But when he *does* say a word," Mrs. Elderberry said. "He's the Governor's cousin: you don't want to forget that. You know how close that family is. And he's just the kind of a man the Governor will listen to: someone that isn't always asking him for favors morning, noon and night. So that if you can just get to him and get him to ask one for you—well then, JoJo, it's as good as done. Positively. That's why I talk to him every chance I get. Not for myself but for the wonderful people I represent. And for the child as well, of course. You know how it is in politics: it's a sad thing, but you've got to play all the angles. Otherwise," sighed this motherly educator, "you wind up with your ass in a sling!"

Were there, I wondered, many Margaret Lucille Elderberrys? Or, more to the point, were there many who reasoned as she did? I think so; it was the only explanation for the fact that, although I continued to do nothing, the requests continued to come. I had found a popularity I had not sought, did not want, and could not escape.

There was one day when I talked about this to Charles. I had gone in to the center of the city for lunch; coming back, I had decided to walk. It was a beautiful day in February, clear and cold and windless, with a foot of snow on the ground, so freshly fallen that none of it had yet turned to ice or slush. I walked along by myself. There were few people on the street, traffic was sparse, and I was perhaps halfway back to the house when the long limousine pulled up beside me and in the back, and alone, was Charles. He waved, the window slid down, and he said, "Come along: you may never get another chance like this."

"I can't, thanks. What's happening?"

"Your government in action," he said. "There's a national convention of urologists out at Belmore Hall; apparently I'm supposed to welcome them, make them feel at home. We statesmen operate on many levels."

"I know. How do you welcome urologists, by the way?"

"Just the same way your old friend used to welcome meat-packers. Or florists. Or urologists. There doesn't seem to be much new in the ritual. You thank them for coming, you congratulate them on their recent spectacular advances, you suggest that the state is honored by their presence, and then you mingle a bit and listen to small talk about the prostate. Then, with luck, you leave. Speaking of luck, I hear that you've been seeing something of Margaret Lucille Elderberry lately."

It was a quick, surprising shift; I said, "I have, yes. Not very often and not very willingly, but I've seen her, all right. Or she's seen me. How did you hear about that?"

"I hear about everything these days," he said, "whether I want to or not. Someone once told me that life in the State House was a daisy chain of confidential whispers. I'll buy that."

I said, "Regrets?"

He smiled slightly. "No. But I'm interested in Elderberry. I would have thought she was a little rich for your blood, even for short takes. What's up?"

"You, mainly." And then I told him about Mrs. Elderberry and the others: all the sudden interest in me, all attributable to him. He listened and smiled again; he said only, "It's the old story, isn't it? Everybody's got an embarrassing relative; it looks like you've got me." He reached forward and opened the door. "Get in and I'll drive you home," he said. "It's too cold standing here and I want to talk to you." I still wanted to walk and I must have showed some hesitation, for he said, "Come on, you'll be doing me a favor; at least you don't whisper."

I got in and we drove off; I said, "I'm pulling you out of your way: what about your urologists?"

"One good thing about being Governor," he said, "is that doctors wait for you. For a change." We drove on; after a moment he said, "I'm sorry I'm complicating your life. The worst thing is that I can't do much about it. As long as I'm Governor you're going to get more of the same. How does Jean react to all this?"

"With growing impatience."

"Well, why not?" he said. "It's an unnerving experience to find yourself suddenly taken up by this tattered Society they have around here. All these fake hostesses latching on to the Heart Fund or the Cancer Crusade and having Musical Evenings with the Swedish vice-consul as the Honored Guest. Or else presenting some shabby baronet who's promoting a new Scotch. High Life. I'm afraid I can't help you there, but I can help you with the pols. As soon as they get in your hair just send them along to Ray Keegan. You remember him: you met him at the party. Young, quiet: his father was the cop with Skeffington. The minute they start in on you, just tell them I would like them to see Ray Keegan at the State House at the first possible moment. Just stress that 'first possible moment.' That'll get rid of them. It won't solve your problem completely, but it'll take some of the curse off. Meanwhile," he said, "look on the bright side. You may be increasing your public. Conceivably I may be putting you in touch with hundreds of new book buyers. Your sales may soar."

"Yes. Somehow I doubt it, though."

"So do I." And then he said, "For example, I don't suppose Margaret Lucille reads many books, and I know she doesn't buy any. Just in case you're interested, she doesn't buy anything. Including the clothes she wears: she gets them at Jack Grumman's shop. He came in to see me the other day; he told me she owes him about five thousand."

"Five thousand! Mrs. *Elderberry?*" On several counts, this wouldn't have seemed even possible; I said, "Has she that kind of money for clothes?"

"And as Marie says, for *those* clothes? No. She hasn't. But then she doesn't need it if she doesn't pay it, does she?"

"What's the matter with Grumman? Why doesn't he collect? Can't he sue?"

"He can. As a matter of fact, that's more or less what he wanted to see me about: whether he should or shouldn't. You see," he said, "to some extent it's a question of tact."

"Tact?" And then, suddenly, it dawned on me, it was the old pattern repeating itself once more, and I understood. I said, "He's afraid of her."

"Not entirely. But he's thinking about being afraid. He's in business, he has his store, he's vulnerable in the usual ways: tax hikes, sudden building inspections, fire law violations. Jack's a polite man who doesn't like to antagonize lovely ladies. Especially when one day they might be in a position to pull the string on him."

It seemed unnecessary, unlikely; I said, "She's misleading: I've never taken her for the pure farce some people think she is. But she doesn't pack anything like that punch, surely?"

"No. Not yet, anyway."

"But Grumman thinks she might?" I looked at him; he looked back at me, still smiling slightly. I said, "What does the Governor think?"

He said, "He thinks that this is a funny city. Do you know anything about Margaret Lucille's family?"

I shook my head, and he said, "Her maiden name was Margaret Lucille Hennessey. Her grandfather Hennessey was a fireman and a ward runner: in his later years he won a limited fame as a multiple voter. His son, Margaret Lucille's father, was a lawyer. Unsuccessful: he took the bar examinations three times before he passed, then some friends of his father's hid him away in the city solicitor's office and he stayed there for the rest of his life. Her older brother Tom finished high school, went a year to the Jesuits, became a part-time bootlegger, supported Father Coughlin, and finally, because some money had to come from somewhere, got a job with the state in the Department of Agriculture. They put him in the Division of Plant Pest Control. It was the theory that he couldn't do much harm there; the theory was wrong. He died in 1943. The younger brother Dave is very much alive, and I know it will surprise you to learn that he also works for the state. He's employed by the Highway Authority, and his job is an interesting one. It's called Consultant on Highway Facilities. This means that he sits in a parked car outside the different restaurants that have a franchise to operate on the state highways and clocks the number of customers who go in during meal hours. For this he gets an annual salary of twelve thousand, seven hundred dollars. Then there's also Margaret Lucille's husband, who has married into the fine old family tradition of public service. Dr.

Elderberry is a dentist who's never had much of a private practice. For years he handled nothing but state welfare patients, but recently he's begun to branch out; I'm told that he's worked himself—or he's been worked—into the school system's dental program. And finally, there's Margaret Lucille herself."

"That's quite a dossier. Have you got one like that on everybody?"

"Oh," he said, "people in the office draw these things up. And I like to read. Besides, I find Margaret Lucille interesting. At a distance. I keep her away from me: she has to get at me through intermediaries." He added dryly, "As you've noticed. But I like to watch her. She's clumsy, but she's not stupid. You remember that the biggest compliment people used to pay a politician around here was to say that he was 'cute.' Well, that's what she is; she can shoot around corners. Pure poison. And while she's never done very much so far, I just have the feeling that all the ingredients are there if she ever got hold of the right—or the wrong stick."

I said curiously, "You take her seriously, don't you? Why? I wouldn't have guessed that she was worth that kind of attention. From you, that is."

"Who knows?" he said. "She's nothing now, or close to nothing. For all I know she may stay that. On the other hand I keep on hearing that she may be getting ready to move. Well, all right: half the politicians in the city are always getting ready to move. But I have a hunch she's slightly different."

"Because her one concern is for the child?"

"That's a matter of definition," he said. "A month ago, at an adult education meeting in the East End, she said, 'What is an adult? Why, we all know that: an adult is nothing but a grown-up child.' That gives her a little more room, wouldn't you say? I think that given the right circumstances, Margaret Lucille might come full-blown out of the woodwork. And that's why she's worth attention."

"The right circumstances being what?"

He shrugged faintly. "Some sort of crisis. Not just the usual thing: redistricting Ward Four, another penny on the sales tax. But something that might get the city emotionally stirred up. A gut issue: maybe the Negro thing. Or No More Puerto Ricans. Or The Child in relation to both. She might ride something like that all the way home. It's the sort of thing she could do well with. She's tricky and she comes from the right stock to have a following. And she's a fanatic. I'd say bigot but I don't use that word any more: my liberal speech-writers keep slipping it to me to describe anyone who goes to church and who doesn't agree with them. No," he said, "I think that if something like that came along you'd hear a good deal more about Margaret Lucille. As I said, this is a funny city, and in many ways she's oddly suited to it."

"I thought all that was supposed to have changed with you?"

"Is that what you thought, Jack?" he said. We had reached the house by now; the car had stopped, but I made no move to leave because I was caught up in this strange discussion. For a moment Charles grew silent and stared, not at me, but straight ahead, and as he did, something in the way he held his head, in the peculiar suspended *considering* expression—as if he were deciding just how much to reveal—reminded me of Phil, and once more I was struck by the extraordinarily strong and yet not really definable resemblance that existed between the two. And by an odd coincidence, when he began to talk again, to my surprise it was his brother, not Mrs. Elderberry, about whom he spoke. He said, "Have you been in touch with Phil lately?"

I said, "Not for weeks, no. He's even harder to get at than you."

"I've noticed that," he said dryly. "Well, he's managing twice as many people. Himself, and me. Or so it seems."

He said this lightly enough, and yet as if it were something about which he wasn't altogether pleased, and also as if he were on the point of saying something more about it. But if so he must have changed his mind quickly, for now he looked down at his watch and indicated pleasantly and rather wryly that there were limits beyond which even urologists could not be pushed. And so we said goodbye as usual—that is, promising to see each other very soon—and then the long car drove away; through the rear window I could see that Charles, presumably back in affairs of state, had already picked up the telephone. It had been a strange meeting, and as I went into the house I couldn't help feeling that it had been an unsatisfactory one as well. For one thing, the matter of Mrs. Elderberry had been dropped too early, but more than that I had the strong impression that Mrs. Elderberry, despite all the time he had given her, was really not what Charles had wanted to talk about to me at all. As I say, this was an impression: guesswork, nothing more. All the same, it stuck with me, even though now, of course, it was too late to do anything about it: the meeting was over.

During the next few weeks and months, my new popularity continued unchanged; Charles's suggestion helped, but not much. Only the greedier and less sophisticated of the petitioners trotted off obediently to Ray Keegan at the State House; others, canny veterans of many a similar siege in the past, recognized the diversion for what it was and preferred to take their chances with me. And so they kept on coming—or most of them did—and they kept on telephoning, along with the hostesses and the old schoolboy friends and the new acquaintances and the total strangers, and along, too, with the merely curious, who wanted no job or favors or help of any kind: what they wanted was inside information. They belonged to that peculiar band of people who are sustained by gossip—and not necessarily scandalous gossip—about the great or the prominent. They rarely interrupted us while we were inside the house but often, as we were leaving or returning, one or two or more of them would be on the walk waiting—teenagers, some of them, but others quite elderly women—for us to answer their questions: Do the Governor and Marie get a chance to get off by themselves on weekends, Where does Marie get all her lovely clothes, Is it true that the Governor is a weekly communicant, Was the Governor smart in school as a boy, How do the children like their schools, Is it true that the Governor's favorite song is really "The Isle of Capri"? This was Charles's fan club: it was exactly as if he were a screen star or a television idol.

All this, in one way or another, now dripped steadily into our lives, and while I suppose it seemed worse than it actually was, and while it never really took up an enormous amount of our time, and while in fact days often went by without our being bothered at all, still it was always there, we were always aware of it in the background, and we knew that to all of those who troubled us we represented merely a way station on the highroad to Charles. It was this, I think, that particularly exasperated Jean. She was not at her best with strangers, and she did not enjoy these calls which were neither for her nor for me.

"Oh, I don't know," she sighed one night. "It's like these people who used to open their doors on Christmas Eve and find an abandoned baby in a basket on the top doorstep. Only if we ever find a basket on our doorstep I'll tell you what will be in it: a fifty-five-year-old baby smoking a cigar and asking us if we'll give his regards to the Governor! No, but isn't it dreadful, Jack? I mean, half the time it's almost not our house any more. It's all right for Charles and Marie, or Phil and Flossie: they're in it, they asked for it. But not us: we didn't ask for anything. And especially not this. I don't want to be stuffy about it, but don't you think it's even a little *humiliating* . . . ?"

And in a way I suppose it was, and yet at the same time it was comic, too. For one thing, there was Edso and there was Walshie: I had apparently inherited them, and now saw them constantly. Unlike the others, they never came to the house, but obviously they had taken pains to learn when and where I could usually be found in the city, and now, with a heavy-footed transparent craftiness they maneuvered themselves—sometimes together, sometimes not—into frequent meetings with me. At each of these meetings they betrayed stage astonishment at seeing me ("Well well well, Walshie, will you look at who's here!") and then there followed, always, an invariable ritual: expressed concern for my health and my wife's, a summary of their own doings on behalf of the Governor since we had last met, elaborate instructions on precisely how they were to be remembered to the Governor when next I saw him. After the first few meetings I gave up explaining that in fact I saw the Governor very rarely, and now I simply listened and said nothing: it was somewhat like being the silent member of a rowdy vaudeville act. I saw them often, as I say, and yet one day after I left them I suddenly realized that after all these encounters I still had no notion of what either one did for a living, or if either one did anything at all. I think probably not, although Edso sometimes spoke elliptically of "the office," but I suspected that it did not exist, and that the two men, like others I had met in this city over the years, mysteriously survived within the framework of "the Party," their long experience and their knowledge of "the ropes" serving somehow as a substitute for work.

In this comedy my publisher also played a part. His name was Andrew Pout, and if it was a strange name, he was also a strange man. Strictly speaking I suppose he was not really my publisher at all, since he neither owned nor controlled—nor, in fact, influenced to any great extent—the firm which published my books. Although I think he may have owned some small amount of stock, he was essentially but one of several senior editorial employees; still, almost from the beginning, in his heavy dogged way, he had managed to suggest, rather successfully and to a great many people, that he was not a representative of the firm but, instead, was the firm itself. I had known him for many years, during which time he had changed very little except in his appearance. In his younger days he had dressed soberly, wearing dark Victorian suits which lent him age, weight, dignity; now in his middle age he no longer felt the need of such props and indeed was heading in the opposite direction: he patronized a well-known undergraduates' tailor, and draped his heavy, spongy body in the clothes of a collegian. Phil, who had known him as long as I had, always called him the Man in the Putty Mask.

"And you know what's behind the mask?" he had asked me, more than once. "More putty! And if you dig down deep enough, you'll find a putty core. Answer one question for me: why did Andrew become a publisher? He doesn't know anything about books. He doesn't read them. He doesn't like them. So why does he publish them? More important, why do people let him publish them? What's he got, anyway? Besides putty, I mean?"

In fact, it was not an easy question to answer.

I went to his office one morning to talk business. I wanted to talk, first, about the sales of my last book, and second, about the possible delivery date of the book I was working on now. He listened as I talked about both; then he said slowly, "I had a digestive upset last night."

It was not an unusual response for him: with writers he had known for some time his talk was almost exclusively autobiographical. It was only with young writers whom he was meeting for the first time that he discussed books, waving vaguely and solemnly at the well-filled shelves behind him ("The fruits of a century, *a hundred years* . . .") and reciting, once again, and with an animation rare in him, the story of Dan Papageno (". . . sensitive young writer, almost a poet, but he never made a dime; he slept in doorways and walked around, *literally*, without a crotch to his trousers . . ."), whose enormous first novel had been published by the firm and had proved to be one of the great fiction best sellers of the last thirty years. It was the firm's big rags-to-riches story; Andrew always told it, then produced the photograph of Papageno with its totally illegible inscription (". . . as you can see, the beginning of a friendship of which I'm proud. *Very* proud . . ."). Then, after telling this story, Andrew would simply fall silent and stare at his listener, and the young writer, caught by those heavy worried eyes looking out of the heavy, worried, mottled face would invariably wonder, a little awed, which book, which author, was the cause of such obvious perturbation. He need not have wondered. Writers and their books seldom caused Andrew a moment's concern; he worried about himself.

Now he said to me, "You see, there wasn't any *reason* for it: that's what's got me . . . thinking. I had a very bland dinner: broiled chicken, a little rice, a dish of caramel custard. And no salad. So . . . although I guess everybody has a touch of it now and then, don't they? I mean, that . . . defies explanation."

"I guess they do. Andrew, I—"

"All the same," he said, "it bothers me. The doctors say there's nothing wrong, and they should know, shouldn't they? But sometimes I lie awake most of the night. I just lie there. On my back. Without sleeping. It could be all sorts of things, of course. It could be my heart, although I don't think so. I've even wondered if it might not be partly . . . sexual."

"You think you've contracted a disease?"

It was perhaps the first thing that I had said that he really heard, and he was instantly offended. "Of course not! Why would I think that? Why would you say a thing like that? Why would *anybody* say a thing like that?"

"I don't know, Andrew. I thought of it more as a joke than anything else."

"Joke," he said disapprovingly. He was not fond of jokes; he had been their victim too often. But I knew that he was not really angry now; his immediate sense of outrage had quickly disappeared, and I knew that, as usual, he was rather flattered by any suggestion of prowess in this dark department. He said, "I'm not saying I don't have strong . . . appetites. I do. Of course since I got married it's been quite different, but before that, Jack, I was quite . . . adventurous."

His heavy eyes did not gleam, exactly, but they seemed to undergo a slight and curious change of color, and in this I recognized the prelude to one of his elephantine confessions of a mild and long-ago libertinism, the outgrowth of his "appetites" (". . . at times, almost . . . *ungovernable* . . ."). He told these stories often to old friends, I had heard them all before, and now I said firmly, "Andrew: listen to me. I have to leave in a few minutes. Before I go I want to talk about *The Zagreb Connection.* Then I want to talk about the new book. That's really why I'm here."

"What? Oh. Well: go ahead." He added, as if he were using for the first time a daring and scarcely known word, "*Shoot.*"

I talked; we talked. In his way I think he liked my books well enough. He did not read them—I knew that—but by now they had become familiar, part of his surroundings. They came in regularly, they had their following, and each produced a modest profit for the firm—sometimes, in the case of a good sale to a paperback house, a slightly more than modest profit. Especially, I think, he liked the fact that I was an author who caused him relatively little trouble. He did not have to write long letters to me, he did not have to explain royalty statements, he did not have to sit with me at luncheon and listen to talk about writing or about my hopes for my career, he did not even have to see me more than once or twice a year. And on these occasions I usually said what I had to say in a few brief sentences, and then he could go on to topics of some interest, importance. When I finished talking now he said, "Well: good. That's good news that the new one is coming along so well. We're all pleased about that. And I don't mind telling you that we're all pleased at the sale of *The Zagreb Connection.* Pleased and . . . gratified."

It was his publisher-talk; I said, "I'm glad you are. I think I might be even gladder if you put a few more dollars into the advertising budget for it. How about running a few more ads?"

"We only wish we could," he said swiftly. It was only at such moments that he approached glibness. "We only wish we could. But you know what the fiction market is today." He gave me his heavy worried stare and said, "It's . . . down."

From the stare I was sure that he had left me and was thinking again about his digestion, but apparently not, because almost immediately he said, "It's a great coincidence, your coming in like this today. I wanted to see you. On another matter. You see, the other night I met your cousin. The Governor."

"Charles? You'd met him before, hadn't you?"

He shook his head. "No. Only his brother. I've known his brother for a long time. Phil." And as he said the name his face darkened; I knew that Phil's assessment of his capacities had undoubtedly got back to him. He said, "He makes . . . wisecracks. I never liked him. I never liked him at all. It's very hard for me to like people who are . . . superficial. But the Governor seems quite different. Much more . . . more . . ."

He was groping, visibly: one plump hand reached up, clutching for *le mot juste*. I said, "Gubernatorial?"

"No," he said seriously. "No, that's not quite . . . *Impressive*," he said suddenly. "I thought he was impressive, Jack. Most impressive."

"Oh, he's that all right."

He said, flatly and solemnly, "I think he's got a book in him."

This had become his special, perhaps his one, interest in publishing: the squeezing of autobiographies out of the eminent. Top-ranking actors, industrialists, politicians, retired generals and bishops: all "had books in them"; to them all, slowly, methodically, he wrote his elaborate form letter (". . . we wonder if, in the midst of your most distinguished career, you have ever thought of putting down on paper what would surely be . . ."). Most replied, in one way or another; some, flattered, replied personally; a few eventually and with much help even produced books. For the most part these books were not good books and for the most part they failed; Andrew did not care. He had his letters, the most cordial of which he had framed, and he had enjoyed the association, however brief. Usually it did not endure past publication day, but that was all right: there would be other autobiographies, other publication days. He greatly preferred the company of these high-level, well-heeled amateurs who, in the main, could be counted upon to write—or have written for them—only the one book, to that of the professional writers he published, who were not only grubbier, more troublesome, and much less pleasant in the face of editorial suggestion, but who never knew when enough was enough, and instead kept writing: book after book after book. It was not for this that he had become a publisher.

He said now, "There's a story there. A real . . . romance."

I was curious about one thing; I said, "I'm surprised that you never tried my Uncle Jimmy. The Governor's father. I would think that there's the real story."

He hesitated, then said, "As a matter of fact I did write to him. Once. Some years ago."

He did not seem to want to go on, but I pushed. "What happened? No answer?"

"Oh, he answered," he said. He hesitated once more and then said reluctantly, "He's very rich, of course. And very successful. I find that men on that level sometimes express themselves a little . . . crudely. They don't mean anything by it, of course, but . . ."

"Well, what did he say? Come on, Andrew: tell all."

"Oh," he said, "I don't think there's any point in repeating it now. It wasn't much, anyway. Actually it was quite . . . brief." The memory seemed to depress him, but in a moment he said more cheerfully, "But the Governor seemed very pleasant. Quite polished. And of course any book by him would have to have quite a lot about his father in it, wouldn't it?"

"Did you speak to Charles about this?"

"No. Well, for one thing the setting wasn't really . . . favorable. You see, we met at this charity bazaar my wife helped to organize. For Rumanian Relief. At first I wasn't even going to go because there didn't seem to be a great deal . . . in common. But at last I did and it was there that I met the Governor. We didn't really get a chance to chat because he had to spend most of his time talking to other people. Rumanians, I think. From their appearance. Naturally I didn't want to break in. They're quite a touchy people. As you know. So I thought I might write to him. And then of course I thought . . ."

He hesitated again and stared at me; I said, "You thought I might be of some help?"

"Well, yes. Yes, I did. After all, we've had a very pleasant relationship over the years, haven't we? You've written your books, and we've published them. We've always published them. We've *enjoyed* publishing them. I know that by now all of us here think of you as one of the . . . family. And naturally we know how close you are to the Governor. So," he said, "we thought that under the circumstances you might be willing to be our . . . good will ambassador."

He smiled a small dumpy smile, as if he had just said something irresistibly pleasant. I said, "Look, Andrew, I haven't any objection to saying a good word for you. But it won't do any good. To begin with, I'm sure he's not interested in writing his story, or having it written. Not yet, anyway: it's a little early for that. And second, you're wrong if you think I'm that close to him. We're cousins, we're friends, but I haven't a bit of influence with him. And I don't advise him. On anything."

I knew it would be a futile protest; it was. He replaced his smile with a look of heavy cunning: it implied that we both knew better than that. We quit the subject, and soon afterward I left his office; as I said goodbye to him I saw one slow and fleshy eyelid dip in a wink of cumbersome complicity, and I knew that I had added one more name to the long and determined list of those who were convinced that merely to speak to me was somehow to have one hand on Charles's sleeve.

And so the weeks went by in this way until, one day, I decided that it was time for us to leave the city for a while. Partly, this was for selfish reasons. I was growing restless here: I suppose because my work, which had begun so well, had now slowed down badly. I found that I was working and reworking the same paragraphs over and over again without much happening; I was conscious of far too many words and far too little action: defects perhaps endurable in more leisurely, more introspective fiction, but fatal to the pace of my stories of suspense. Whenever this had happened in the past I had invariably pulled out of it by moving about from one place to another—I was fond of traveling, and oddly enough I'd always been able to work well in transit—and lately I had begun to think longingly of this proved remedy. Also, I thought it would be good for Jean: a vacation from what she had come to call the Charles-hunters. This nuisance still persisted; it seemed to me now that to break away from it for a few months or so might be the best thing in the world for both of us. I suggested it; Jean was delighted (her design work was such that it could be dropped and picked up again at any time); we began to make our plans: a long slow trip by boat to Naples, the remainder of the spring in Italy, then north to Sweden and Norway—where neither of us had ever been before—then back down to London, where we would spend the final weeks of our stay.

"With maybe a week in Ireland," Jean said, "just for old times' sake. How do you feel about that?"

Second honeymoon? I think we both thought this, although we said nothing about it. And now and then—not often, but every once in a while—as we talked about these plans, going over them with almost a first-time pleasure and excitement, as if neither of us had ever been anywhere before, I saw a different look pass over her face—a faint, troubled, dusting shadow—and whenever this suddenly came and went I knew that she was remembering the circumstances of her last trip to Europe. Inevitably, I suppose.

But she didn't speak about it and, of course, neither did I. There was no need to. We had made our start and it was a good one: we both knew that. I think it was far better than either one of us had expected. And now we were in a sense like invalids who were getting well slowly: each week brought us new strength, and I think that now we felt a steadiness, a confidence in each other—and in ourselves—that we hadn't felt even as recently as a few weeks ago. At this stage we both felt reasonably sure—without being foolish, or overconfident—that it was going to work for us.

We did not delay: two weeks after we made our decision, we sailed. Before we left we tried to have an evening together with the family, but this turned out to be impossible. Charles was not even in the state for most of this period; he had joined a group of governors who were making a tour of state capitals: our capital was not one of these. Flossie was unavailable, having left for Georgia the week before. But Marie came over one day and spent most of the afternoon with Jean; they went out shopping, they came back to the house, and I saw her just before she left. Jean had gone upstairs to get something for her and had called me out; I stood for a few minutes with Marie in the front hall.

"I love this house, Jack," she said. "I always have. I think in some ways it's the nicest house I've ever been in, and I don't know why."

She looked lovely and golden, as always, but bigger now—and I suddenly realized that of course she was going to have her baby in the next month or so. I said, "Boy or girl?"

"Girl," she said instantly. This question over the years had become a kind of family game—that is, it was always asked, and Marie always answered in the same unhesitating way, never treating the certain, positive answer as being in the least unusual. At first I thought she did this as a joke, but then I came to suspect that this fashionable, sophisticated, extremely contemporary woman had a stubborn, almost a peasant's, belief in her intuition in these matters. And certainly she had results on her side: the fact was that she had accurately predicted the sex of all her children some time before their birth. "Well," she said, looking down with a wonderful unconcealed satisfaction at her now heavy body, "I'm getting a little old for this sort of thing, don't you think? But I don't care: it seems like a hundred years since we've had a baby around the place, and I can hardly wait!"

She took great joy in her children, but now, very quickly, she began to talk about something else. I had seen her do this before with me, and also with Jean; I think it was that, as someone both sensitive and tactful, she did not want to talk too much about her pleasure in her own children before people who had none. She said, "I've heard all about your trip: it'll be marvelous." She added, "Especially now."

"Yes." I looked at her and said, "Everything's fine."

"I know. She told me. Well, not that she needed to: I could see that miles off. Anyway, I'm glad. And not just for Jean." Impulsively she grabbed my hand and pressed it against her cheek. "You're not the worst man in the world," she said. "Did you know that, Jack?"

She was a handsome, kind woman who embarrassed me; I said, "I know: I'm a charmer. Listen, before you go: what's life in the palace like?"

"A little bit of everything," she said. "Part Versailles, part pad. The French consul and that crowd to dinner one night, Beaver O'Brien and Chubby DiAngelis the next. I don't know which I like better. Neither very much, I guess."

"Boring?"

"No, not that. I know it's supposed to be, but it isn't. Oh, I miss seeing some of our friends as much as we used to, and I'm not that mad about most of the people we do see—does that sound terribly snobbish?"

"I don't know. It could be just a reaction from seeing too much of Cogan and friends."

"Cogan," she said, and made a face. "Anyway, we're not all

that elegant any more, but it's never boring. Well, you know me, Jack: I love the good life and all the nice things money can buy, but I'm still sort of a simple tough girl who can't really believe that the Governor's house is *my* house. Half the time at these parties I'm just looking around and saying, 'Good for me!' And it's exciting—that's what keeps it from being boring. I love all this business of watching them all jockey for position with Charles, and then watching the way he handles them. He's gotten terribly good at it. And it's what he really wants to do: anyone can see that. He's doing a great job, don't you think?"

I nodded. "It's a great job just to get everybody in your corner the way he has. It's a love affair: so far, no dissenting votes. Or none that count."

"Yes, that's nice. Still," she said shrewdly, "it's the honeymoon, isn't it? I imagine they'll start to hack away at him when it's over, don't you?"

"Probably; they always have. Nobody gets away from that. On the other hand, Charles is pretty good with hackers; I'd say he's just about hack-proof."

"Isn't he?" she said happily. "They'll find out. Because Charles just doesn't chip: the tougher it is, the better he gets." And then she looked at me, radiant and happy, and at the same time with just a touch of reproach, as if she were blaming me for not being able to share this delight as fully as she'd like. She said, "If you weren't such a stick-in-the-mud, you'd be in there with him."

To Marie, from the beginning, Charles had been so clearly marked apart from all the rest in his abilities that I think she found it genuinely puzzling, perhaps incomprehensible, when someone whom she ordinarily respected and of whom she was fond—in this case, me—decided, for whatever reason, not to go along on Charles's ride. She had a stubborn and rather marvelous belief in her husband, and while I knew that now she wasn't angry with me, I also knew that she privately considered I had let, not Charles, but myself, down.

Jean joined us, we all said goodbye, and Marie was the only

member of the family we did say goodbye to until almost the last minute: then, the night before we sailed, Phil dropped in at the house unexpectedly at dinnertime. The three of us sat and ate in the kitchen; supplies were low, we were eating up what we had: a mountain of scrambled eggs and sausages, toast and coffee. It was more a breakfast than a dinner, but we had a long, pleasant, gossipy meal. Phil seemed in great spirits, we had good talk, and in fact it was only after some time had gone by that I realized it was also peculiarly limited talk. For Phil, who after Charles was the most important man in this new and presumably exciting administration, said not a word about his job or about politics; instead he talked reminiscently and entertainingly about old times, and about our recent stay in Georgia, and also—because of our coming trip—he talked about Norway and Sweden which, it developed, he had once visited a few years ago. He supplied us with a swift and characteristic review of his impressions. . . .

". . . you'll love it. I can't imagine anyone not flipping over Sweden. Still, it's surprising to find the number of people who just can't take it at all: I can't think why. You'll probably stay in one of those hotels they've got over there that are on the third floor of a department store. Or up over a garage. The one I was in had all sorts of de luxe amenities: a shoeshine machine in the lobby, room service nearly every other day. The food, by the way, may take a little getting used to. And then when you do get used to it you may not especially care for it. Not everybody does. Well, you know: whale, reindeer, that sort of thing. I suppose I must have eaten my way through the greater part of a herd of deer while I was in Sweden. Incidentally, I'd bring warm clothing if I were you. It can get unpleasantly cold at any time of year. Of course you're not likely to mind that in view of the warmth of the human companionship you'll run into. I tell you, for sheer geniality you just can't beat those cheerless Swedish boozers who go around knocking themselves off one after another!"

"Good for you, Phil," Jean said. "That's just what we needed to cheer us up: a useful corrective to all those travel folders we've been reading. How about the scenery? You didn't say anything about that; you probably didn't want to discourage us. Because I imagine it's all pretty awful, isn't it? Drab? Ugly? Maybe like Kansas with trees?"

"Well now, there you've got me," he said. "The difficulty seemed to be that I never actually *saw* any scenery. You see, I went there in winter, and in winter they've got something over there called daylight. It's not very bright and it's on for only about twenty minutes a day, as I remember it. But while it *is* on you can perceive dim shapes around you; otherwise you can't see anything. That's why accurate information about Sweden is so hard to come by: very few foreigners have ever seen anything of the country. They have to rely on what the natives tell them. Strangely enough, Norway is something else entirely."

I said, "Not necessarily better, I imagine?"

"Not necessarily, no. Although some people seem to like it better. On the other hand, some don't. It's purely a matter of taste. A taste for fish, really. That's what it comes down to. You both like fish, don't you? I hope so. Because that's what Norway has to offer: a superfluity of fish and fjords. . . ."

He went on in this way for some time, amusing himself, amusing us, and then he moved on to talk about Flossie, and about the children and the peculiarly bland and boneless education they were receiving in their various private schools. But until the time he left he still said nothing about politics or Charles. Only when I walked out to the car with him did he say, "Well, you're well out of this rat race for a few months. The only thing better would be a few years. Or just possibly forever."

And this wasn't said in the sardonic, disparaging tone with which he had disposed of Scandinavia; clearly, he came closer to meaning this. I said, "Why so down?"

"It's a matter of balance," he said. "Everybody else is up. Way up and riding high. You must have noticed that, Jack: you read the papers."

"I do, yes. I thought everything was going smoothly enough. Isn't it?"

"Smooth as glass," he said. "Not a wave, not a ripple, not a motion."

"Well then . . . ?"

"Well then," he said, "it all depends on how you feel about smoothness, doesn't it? I have a question for you, Mr. Bones: if we really got into the ball game to make a change or two around here, then why should everyone be so contented? And why should everything stay so smooth?"

"You want a few shakes and trembles?"

"I guess I do," he said. "I guess I really do."

"And Charles?"

"Charles is a man of peace," he said, a little dryly. "I'm all for that, except that we differ on how you get it. However . . ." He broke off and said, "Anyway, you're well out of it. The whole place is a morass. Well, we always knew that, didn't we? The only think is, I thought it might be fun to sink a few pilings. Somehow, and here and there." He got in the car and said, "So long. Have a good trip. And tell Jean I was only kidding. Sweden's all right."

"She knows." And then I said, "Phil?"

He looked at me, almost as if he had been waiting for a question; he said, "What?"

"Do you remember one night, years ago, when we drove back to town together from the island? It was a hot night; we stopped somewhere to eat . . ."

"Sure," he said. "In that bum cafeteria. Horrible. I remember."

"It was the night you told me Charles was going to run for mayor."

"That's right," he said.

"Do you remember what you said to me? About Charles?"

"Roughly. I told you that you'd be surprised, and that he was going to get in. I told you that he was going to surprise a good many people. And I told you that in my opinion he might be the answer to a lot of things around here. Isn't that about it?"

"Yes, that's it."

He kept looking at me and after a moment he said, "And you want to know if I've changed that opinion?"

I didn't deny it; I said, "Have you, Phil?"

He still looked at me, with a little smile on his face. He said, "I think what I said still goes."

"That Charles might be the answer."

"That's right."

"Might be."

He nodded and said, "I guess that's what I said."

I said carefully, "You wouldn't want to make that a little more positive? Now?"

"Oh," he said slowly, "that takes us into another question entirely, doesn't it? And there's not a living soul who can answer that one, Jack. Certainly not your old friend Phil." And now he reached out through the open window and tapped me on the arm with his finger in the old gesture; he said, "Bon voyage: bring me back a herring. Take care of yourself. And Jean. And come back soon."

He waved a hand, and quickly he was gone. I stood on the front walk for a few minutes, thinking about him, and feeling the same apprehension and disquiet I had felt at the victory party, but feeling it more strongly now. Because now I knew that whatever had happened between Phil and Charles, it was not merely a trivial and temporary disagreement over political tactics. In these last few minutes with Phil, when he had talked briefly about Charles, I had heard a quality in his voice I had never heard there before. It was sadness, even pain, and the moment I heard it I knew, just as strongly as if he had told me so explicitly, that something was now different between Charles and himself, and that something which had been a special part of both of them as long as they had lived was now, at last, gone—and was gone forever.

It was a gloomy and deeply depressing thought—perhaps unreasonably so, since it came from nothing more than a few words, a tone of voice. Yet the instant it occurred to me I believed it, and I believed it now. I knew that something, somehow, had gone very wrong, and just as I knew that, I knew too that I could do nothing about it at all.

And so I went back toward the house, but instead of going directly in I walked around by the side out into the back yard. The lawn was heavy and moist, but slightly springy under my feet. Winter had stayed late this year, but now we were into April, and there was the deep rich spring smell of recently thawed ground. The night air was heavy and still fairly cold: the kind of night that in autumn would be full of woodsmoke. I could see a few stars; everything was very still around me: there wasn't a sound. This was a change: years ago there had been a small pond nearby and at night, around this time of year, the peepers would go mad in a thin soprano frenzy. I stood where the barn had been and looked back across the grass to the big shadowy house. For some reason I always did this, every time I went away, on the night before leaving; the last time I had done it the lights had been on, just as they were now, but there had been a great difference: the house had been empty. And that had been the bad time for me. And now . . .

And now it was Phil and Charles—and probably, eventually, inevitably, my Uncle Jimmy as well. I wondered what would happen next. A light went on upstairs in our bedroom; it was Jean, with the last-minute packing. And as I went in to help her, I kept on wondering, but of course I came no closer to an answer.

ten

WE sailed the following day; we were gone for half a year. We went first to London, and this was a change of plan: almost literally at the last moment we both had decided —on no firmer ground than a sudden whim—that instead of beginning with Italy and then moving slowly and sensibly with the season to the north, it would be good, it would be great fun, to be in London right away. We had scrambled hastily—reservations had to be canceled, accommodations secured—but in spite of the short notice all went well: within a week from the time of our whim, we were in London for the start of our long stay abroad.

It was a busy start: our life here proved to be dramatically different from that at home. Far less political, it was much more social: we had many friends in London, and to these were added a few old friends from home who had suddenly arrived in London at about the same time as ourselves; the unexpected convergence bred an unexpected activity. At first we had intended to strike out often into the country; instead, caught up in the group, we found ourselves sticking very close to London. We left it only for occasional picnics, four or five of us going off in the early afternoon, never very far from the city, to spend a few recuperative hours on the green banks of a slow stream, and coming back early to get ready for the night. We all went out to dinner together; we went to the theater every night; afterward we went on to the supper and gambling clubs, playing *chemin de fer* too much and drinking far too much until all hours amid the opulent surroundings of another day. We went to bed late each night, we rose late each morning. It was a routine which was alternately exhilarating and exhausting, and one morning when we woke up—it was nearly noon—Jean said to me, "Love, I know I'm having a marvelous time, but the strangest thing is this: I'm beginning to feel like the end of the world. How do you feel?"

"Old. Very old."

"The trouble with us is that we're out of practice and I'm not so sure how we get back in." She was wearing a very short, very sheer white nightgown; she looked rumpled, sleepy and lovely. She stood in front of the full-length mirror and turned slowly, examining her reflection with great care; she said untruthfully, "I'm about to run to fat. I think I'm too pooped to care. How did you sleep?"

"Not very well. I had a weird dream. I dreamed I was alone on this island—how, I don't know: shipwrecked, I guess. There weren't any people at all: just coconut palms and parakeets and huge red and yellow flowers and little brown wild pigs that I hunted with a spear. After a month of this I was nearly stir-crazy. Somehow I accepted the fact that I was never going to be rescued, but I kept on hoping I could have someone, anyone, to talk to. Then, the very next morning, I saw someone in a small boat, just off the island. Suddenly the boat tipped over and he—somehow I knew it was a man—began swimming for the shore. I saw that he was going to make it and I rushed down to help him or meet him, and I remember saying to myself that this was terribly important, because I would have to spend the rest of my life with this man. Just as I got down to the beach he came out of the sea and flopped, face down, unconscious, in the sand. I ran over to him and was just about to give him artificial respiration when all of a sudden he turned over and sat straight up and who was it but Andrew Pout! He was dressed in that junior varsity costume he wears these days—hopsack trousers, Shetland jacket, button-down shirt, knit tie—and the funny thing was that even though he'd just come out of the sea everything was perfectly creased. 'Hello, Jack,' he said. 'That digestive upset I was telling you about apparently has spread. Now I'm having great difficulty in . . . passing water. I'll tell you all about it later. We'll have lots of time to talk from now on!' And then he flopped down again and went to sleep, and I stood over him, looking down at him and thinking that from now on I'd be sharing every waking minute with Andrew Pout. I tell you, there was a great moment. And then I remember thinking that if I just left him there, right where he was, there was a good possibility that the tide would get him while he was asleep and wash him back out to sea. And then," I said, "while I was thinking this over, I woke up."

After a moment she said, "Poor Jack. You're not working at all, are you?"

"Very little. Well, you know, a little here, a little there, but nothing any good." It was all too true. Our schedule had not encouraged work; my book was not a page farther along than when we had left home.

She said thoughtfully, "Well then, what's so sacred about England? I mean, about staying here? We've been here three weeks: how about a change of pace? This is killing us, and what's more it's costing the moon. What do you say, love: let's go!"

And so I agreed: willingly, even hurriedly, as if the stay in England which in one way had been so enjoyable had come to be a penitential experience. We left the very next morning for Rome.

We stayed here for only a week, then moved on to Florence: it was here that we planned to establish our base. We stayed pleasantly, even luxuriously, in a handsome and surprisingly inexpensive old hotel where we had once stayed before. We were given two enormous, immaculate, rather sedate rooms from whose windows we could look out across the Arno to the Tuscan Hills:

the food was good, the service was exuberant if slow. We didn't care; we were in no hurry; day after day we soaked in an atmosphere of politeness and kindness. In no time we developed a schedule which was agreeable to both of us. In the morning, after breakfast, I worked; Jean sometimes drew, sometimes went out to the gallery or shopped. When she came back to the hotel to meet me for lunch I was usually downstairs, talking with Signor Barbettura. He was a newcomer to the hotel since last we had been here, but was now a permanent resident: a dapper little twig of a man, frail, elderly, with a pale muddy face and theatrical white hair. He wore, always, an ice cream suit with a cornflower-blue boutonniere; he liked talking to me about the United States where he had spent some time years ago, and he liked to talk in English.

"A pleasant country," he said. "A rich country: not like our poor Italy. And always so exciting, no? Babe Ruth, Jack Dempsey, Lucky Lindy: who can ever forget them?"

His period had been the 'Twenties; he had come back home after that and had never returned, but his memories were green.

"Coolidge," he said reverently. "*President* Coolidge. Your great President, Good Old Cal. That is what he was called?"

"Yes. By some."

"A humorous man," he said surprisingly. "What a one for jokes was Good Old Cal!"

"Jokes?"

"Oh yes. Jokes, good jokes. Pretending to be serious and silent, you know. Keeping the straight face while inside you are a volcano of laughter. He fooled many people but he could not fool me. He could not fool an Italian so easily. He was a profound humorist. We have no one like him today. When he died," he said simply, "I cried."

"Ah . . ."

"The whole world cried," he said, "and Barbettura cried too. Out loud. Boo hoo. Well, we are an emotional people. Our hearts are on our sleeves. But I cried perhaps more than most. For Good

Old Cal and for his country. *Your* country. A fine and happy country which at one time in my life was very good to me. Very *very* good!"

A certain mystery surrounded this fragile old man. He was treated with great deference by all the hotel staff, but they did not talk about him much, and I had noticed from the first that although he was a willing, even a greedy, talker, he did not often talk about himself. He had once gone so far as to tell me that he was "retired," but from what he did not say. Certainly, now, he did not appear to be a busy man. He sat all day, every day, in the same spot in the hotel lobby, his small white-clad figure swallowed up in a vast baroque chair. He had few visitors, and he seemed to look forward to my arrival downstairs late every morning: he was always there, he always greeted me immediately and cordially, he was always ready to reminisce. During our conversation he would remain seated until Jean came in through the doorway, returning from her morning in the city; then at once he would spring to his feet and step—one, two, three—toward her, his hands clasped far out in front of him as if he were holding a presentation bouquet of flowers. It was a gallant gesture but it was not appreciated, for Jean did not much like Signor Barbettura.

"There's something cold and lizardy about him," she said. "He's creepy: it's in his eyes. Can't you see it?"

I shrugged this off and said, "Come on: he's an old old man."

"Well, every old old man was once a young young man. And when this one was young I'll bet he was something special. What, do you suppose? A big-shot Fascist? That could be, couldn't it? I mean, look at the way they handle him around the hotel. Talk about kid gloves!"

It was a measure of the soft and peaceful flow of our lives here that we discussed Signor Barbettura in this way every day.

In Florence we picked up our first mail from home. We had left no forwarding address for England; content to cut our communications for a time, we had given this hotel as our only address, and now our letters were beginning to catch up with us. My mail, while not heavy, was varied. There were letters from readers, some pro, some con—one, in reading *The Zagreb Connection*, had discovered a minor discrepancy in the arrival and departure times of trains and had hurried to write me a sharp reprimand; I had heard from him before. Often. There were the usual letters appealing for funds, differing only in degrees of ingenuity; one was from a missionary priest from whom I had heard for years. His letters were always very long and began like novels ("The rains have come again to our remote corner of the world. As I write to you, dear friend, I am once more out on the river, seated in the dugout canoe which is my only means of getting from place to place. In the stern my native catechumen, Paul, paddles slowly but steadily . . ."). There was a letter from an old friend, enthusiastically suggesting that we visit him on a small Caribbean island which some months before had been laid waste by a savage hurricane (". . . contrary to reports, there is no—repeat, *no*—epidemic; everything is coming back very nicely, although of course accommodations are still on the primitive side . . ."). There was a letter from my agent, cautiously hinting that there was some unexpected if as yet indefinite motion picture interest in one of my earlier books. And there was a letter from Andrew Pout. It expressed the conviction that I was making great progress on ". . . the new one, for which we all entertain our customary high hopes"; the inevitable "Yours ever" had been replaced by a preposterous "*Erin go bragh!*" It was like a nudge in the ribs, a touch of leaden waggishness which identified the writer even more unmistakably than did his signature.

The real news came to Jean. In among all the invitations to parties, concerts, dances, benefits—all of which had been held weeks ago by now, and all of which had been sponsored by Jean's Charles-hunters—there were two letters from Marie. They arrived some weeks apart, the first coming shortly after we got to Florence. It was short: merely a happy announcement that the baby had been born. A boy: Frank. The second came much later—when, in fact, we had been in Florence for nearly two months. It was, I saw, a very long letter; Jean settled down on the chaise to read it slowly, pleasurably. I was at the desk, writing; suddenly I heard her gasp, and when I turned I saw that she was sitting straight up, holding the letter out in one hand and looking, not at it, but at me. I said quickly, "What's wrong: the baby?"

"No." She hesitated, then said, "It's Phil. . . ."

And in that second it was as if all my earlier apprehensions, those faint and never-quite-defined misgivings I had known on and off for some time whenever I saw Phil or even thought of him, now came smashing together into something acute and perilous; I said, "What's happened? Is he all right?"

"It's not like that," she said. "I mean, no sickness, no accident: nothing like that. It's something else: he's split with Charles!"

It was bad news, it was shocking news, and yet as soon as I heard it I think what I felt most of all was an almost overpowering relief! Because as soon as Phil's name was mentioned I was suddenly sure, absolutely sure, that something awful had happened to him: something vague and dark and cataclysmic, some personal catastrophe in which he was totally helpless and from which there was no hope of recovery. All this was unfounded, reasonless, I suppose, and yet I did feel it most strongly, and so when I learned what actually had happened, it was so much less than what I feared that for just a few seconds it seemed almost trivial. It was of course far from that, and as Jean handed me the letter I began to realize something of its seriousness; I said, "When? Why?"

"About three weeks ago, as near as I can make out. And why—I don't know. I don't think Marie does, either. Read what she says."

And so I read the letter through. Jean was right: Marie seemed genuinely mystified. There had been a meeting between the brothers one night in Charles's house: apparently a routine meeting. There had been a disagreement—over what, Marie did not know. There had been disagreements before; she could not believe that this one had been anything new; she had come in toward the end of it and neither brother had seemed angry. They had stopped talking; Phil had got to his feet. He greeted her and then had said quietly to Charles, "Well . . . that's it, then."

Charles had said, just as quietly, "I guess it is."

"All right," Phil had said. Then he had smiled a little, first at Marie, then at Charles, and then he had said, "But who could ever have figured it out this way?" Then he had left the room and the house; it was only later, in talking to her husband, that Marie had learned with a shock that he had left Charles as well. It was clear from her letter that she was hurt, extremely hurt, that she was angry with Phil, but it was also clear that this anger was all mixed up with other feelings, for she had always felt a great affection for Phil, and now she simply could not imagine how anyone like him could ever have broken—just like that or in fact in any other way—with Charles.

"Because you know how much they mean to each other," she wrote. "And now it's all different, Charles doesn't want to talk about it, and we don't see Phil at all any more. I haven't the foggiest notion of what's wrong. Do you—either of you—have a clue? There's another trouble now which makes it all worse, and that is that right now of all times Charles needs someone around he can trust, and who can take Phil's place for that? So I don't know what will happen; I wish I did. Maybe it will work itself out, although it doesn't look like that right now. Anyway, I'll let you know whatever happens. Meantime, when are you coming home . . . ?"

She went on like this, mentioning that she had talked to Flossie, who seemed worried and baffled and who also seemed to understand no more than Marie about the cause of the split. She did not talk about my Uncle Jimmy, beyond saying that as yet he did not know anything about this, that the boys had so far kept it from him, that she dreaded the complications when he did find out. She closed offering some hope, but not much. I handed the letter back to Jean, who stared down at it, bewilderment still on her face. "I don't get it," she said. "Did you have any idea this might happen? Any at all?"

"No. Not really."

She looked up quickly. "What does that mean: not really?"

"Just another way of saying no, I guess. Because I didn't I mean, I certainly knew that Phil wasn't satisfied with the way things were moving, that he was unhappy. . . ."

"Unhappy with Charles?"

"Well, sure. It would have to be that, wouldn't it? Charles is the one responsible for the moving. So I was convinced that there might be a storm or two along the way. What I didn't expect was an outright break. I didn't even imagine that."

And I didn't. Even now, when it had happened, it seemed to me unimaginable. Not merely that there was now for the first time a split in the solid family front—I suppose that mattered, but not so much to me, because now I wasn't thinking of the family at all. I was thinking of Charles and Phil, my oldest friends, who as far back as I could remember had been as close together as two brothers could possibly be, and whose closeness had really been part of my life as well as of their own. And now, apparently, this closeness was over. I say "apparently" because Marie's letter was vague: for all I knew the rift might have been alarming but temporary, by now everyone might well be friends again. It was a consoling possibility, but one in which I didn't believe. I was not optimistic; I had sensed trouble in the air for too long; now, even with only the letter as evidence, I felt that there was a finality here, that something had now changed for all of us, and for good.

Jean said, "What now? What do we do?"

"I don't think we do much of anything. You can write to Marie,

I'll write to Phil; it's possible that by now things may have jelled and we can find out something a bit more definite. But if you mean what can we do to help, then I'm stuck."

She said, "You could do something if you were there, couldn't you?"

"What? And I'm not there; I'm here . . ."

"I know, but that doesn't *have* to be, does it? We could always leave early. It's lovely here, but if you wanted to go home now I'd be game. Maybe if you were on the spot and could talk to them . . ."

I said, "There's no point to it. I haven't heard that we're needed. Or wanted, for that matter. Have you? Remember what the nuns used to tell you in that deportment school you went to: 'Always wait until you're asked.' Well, we haven't been asked. For anything. By anybody."

"Oh come on!" she said impatiently. "I don't believe in that and neither do you. That's all right for just plain manners, but when people are in trouble and they're friends and you think you can help, who waits for an engraved invitation? Do you? Since when? All I can think of is what Uncle Jimmy would say: bushwa to that!"

"Okay, I'm all for that, but you have to at least think you *can* help before you start anything. And that's the difference between us here: you think I can, and I don't."

"But how do you know? You sound so sure: why?"

"Because I know Phil and Charles. I've known them all my life. And I can tell you that if there's anything really wrong between them, you're not going to help and neither am I. Nobody is, and includes Flossie and Marie and my Uncle Jimmy too, whether he knows it or not. Whatever is going on now, it's a very private affair. It's all—*all*—between themselves. And if they want anybody else is on it, they'll ask."

"But you don't think they will?"

"No. No, I don't."

"Well . . ." she said doubtfully, and I could see that she was unconvinced. After a moment she said stubbornly, "But if they do? What if they do?"

"Then we'll go, and we'll go right away. I promise you that. In the meantime, we're not going to be of the slightest help at all, so let's sit tight and keep right on doing what we're doing. Right here in sunny Italy."

We talked a bit more about it, but in the end she gave in, and we continued to stay in Florence. Our days were calm, uneventful, wonderful. After the morning work, after Signor Barbettura at noon, after lunch, we usually went up to our rooms to rest: we had fallen easily into the habit of the short afternoon nap. When we rose we often went downstairs and out into the streets and walked about this extraordinary city for hours. On other days we took a car and drove off into the country, going up through rows of cypresses and vineyards and olive groves to the old hill towns, or else turned off and made the longer but straighter journey down to the sea. It was marvelous, all of it: we were lucky in everything. The weather held for us and was glorious, week after week. We swam at Viareggio; we spent unhurried afternoons in Pisa, Luca, Fiesole; we ate everywhere, alternating between the simplest meals and elaborate feasts, and I remember especially one night driving back to Florence after a long day at the sea and in the sun. We had stopped somewhere along the road—I forget exactly where—for dinner: we ate on a terrace high over the sea, the stars were bright in the blue-black sky, the air was soft and smelled of pine, a three-quarter moon was low over the water, we dined on scampi, spitted larks, and bottles of Soave. We drove home lightheaded, light-hearted and singing. The car radio was on, and at some point I pulled off the road at a wide turnout, parked the car, and to the music of the radio—and I remember that oddly it was an American song: an old tinny recording of *Whispering*—we had a dance. Then we got back in the car, and there in the open air, in the soft deserted night we came together, and I thought that nowhere and at no time could anyone have been happier or luckier or more deeply in love than I was that night. And Jean, beside me, gave a great sigh and said, "Oh boy: it's even better than Buffalo!"

(A family joke: an uncle of hers, raised in northern New York and never away from home for a day until the First World War, had found himself stationed in Paris for a month before he came back. The family had asked him how he liked it. "I'll tell you this much," he said. "It's lots better than Oswego, and *maybe* it's even better than Buffalo!")

So then, I suppose we were having a second honeymoon after all, and as such it was a great success. In fact everything about our stay here was a great success: Jean was happily occupied, day after day, and I was working well: my book was now more than halfway to the finish. Only the weather reminded us that a change was due. It got steadily hotter, and we both realized that soon it would be time for us to leave on our trip to the north. We talked about this often, although in no conclusive way, and finally one day, we decided to change our plans once more: neither of us, it appeared, now had the faintest wish to go to Scandinavia.

"And I don't know why," Jean said, "because it sounded like such a good idea in the beginning. Maybe Phil did his dirty work after all, do you think? Anyway, I don't want to go and you don't want to go, and that's great: I couldn't be happier. The only thing is: what do we do now?"

I said tentatively, "We could always stay here. Give it a try . . ."

"I'm for that," she said, promptly, decisively. "I'm all for that. Oh, let's do, Jack!"

And so we did. We stayed on and did not regret it. The weather grew hotter but never unbearable. Our activities were somewhat curtailed, but not much: we continued to work, to travel around, to enjoy ourselves. Even the greater crowds were in a peculiar way enjoyable: we viewed them with the occasional snobbish tolerance possible to old hands. Now and then friends passed through: we saw them, we had good times with them, we did not regret it when they went away. It was I suppose a selfish life; we were happiest by ourselves, and somehow this seemed right, just as it should be.

It was during this time that, finally, the riddle of Signor Barbettura was solved.

The waiter who brought our breakfast up to us each morning was a handsome, bright-faced Italian named Rinaldo: he seemed scarcely more than a boy, but he was married and the father of two. Early in our stay he had asked us to speak only English to him; he spoke it badly but was eager to improve: the tourist season was at hand, he needed every weapon. We had obliged, falling into a pidgin English for the most part. This went on every morning for a long time; then, one morning, as Rinaldo was arranging the cups and dishes, Jean said, "Rinaldo: you know Signor Barbettura?"

"Ah Signor Barbettura! Si, Signora!" Bright eyes gleamed, bright teeth flashed; he said, "Yais, oh yais!"

"A nice man?"

"Oh yais, Signora. 'E'sa nice man. Vairy nice. Vairy old."

"And very rich?"

A cautious, guarded look dropped over Rinaldo's face, obscuring the brightness: it was the look common to all the hotel employees whenever this subject was pursued too far. He said, a little reluctantly, "Si, Signora. Motch money."

Jean persisted, moving on to the second step. "Rinaldo, you know Signor Kinsella and I leave one day soon?"

"Ahhh!" he said, the guarded look succeeded by one of open woe. It was exaggerated but, I think, genuine: he liked me, he adored Jean.

"You know when we go we may not be back for a very long time?"

"Ahhh! Bad, vairy bad!"

"Yes, very bad. But that means we will probably never see Signor Barbettura again. You understand? We will go away, and then we will never talk to him again." She paused; he looked at her impassively; she said, "Rinaldo, Signor Barbettura has much money. The money: he made it in America, yes?" For she had abandoned the theory of Barbettura the Fascist Leader; her new theory, based on the dates of his stay in America, turned about Prohibition. She said sharply, "Signor Barbettura!" She held up her hands and pointed them like pistols at the stupefied Rinaldo. "Bang bang!" she said. "Gangster! Al Capone!"

He stared at her and at this extraordinary pantomime; then, suddenly, he broke into great laughter. We stared back at him; he continued to laugh. Then he threw up his hands apologetically; he said, " 'Scusa, Signora. Signor Barbettura, 'e'sa no gangster in America. No no!" He laughed again. "No no!" he said. He looked all around him, as if fearful of being overheard; lowering his voice he said, "In America, Signor Barbettura, 'e'sa do *this*." And, bending forward, he went into a pantomime of his own: with his two hands out and close together, as if gripping a cloth between them, he pretended to polish my shoes.

I said incredulously, "Signor *Barbettura*?"

"Si si! Shoeshine boy!" He laughed again, but immediately became more circumspect; he said, "You don't tell?"

I shook my head; Jean said, "But the *money* . . ."

Rinaldo explained. " 'E'sa 'ave *zia*. Aunt. In Positano. Vairy rich. Vairy vairy rich. But . . . nobody know. When she'sa die, they know. Motch money. She's not marry, no *bambini*. Only Signor Barbettura. So," he said, with a great shrug and a brilliant smile, "Signor Barbettura, 'e'sa come home. Long time ago. Vairy poor. Now," he said, gesturing dramatically downward toward the lobby in the manner of an impresario, "*ecco!* Signor Barbettura!"

He smiled again, placed one finger on his lips, and left the room. I looked at Jean; she was frowning slightly; she seemed baffled, a little annoyed. She looked up suddenly and saw me watching her; for a second the frown remained, then she shrugged, pointed her hands at me, and said, "Bang bang!" Then she laughed and so did I: it was the end of Signor Barbettura as a subject of daily discussion.

Both of us, as the weeks had passed, had written home—I wrote to Phil, while she wrote to Marie—but we had received no answer. And, with this silence, and as time went by, some of our sense of urgency vanished, and only at odd moments did the split between Charles and Phil seem quite as important as it had on that first day. Then, suddenly, one day more than two months after those first letters, another came, and this one, surprisingly, was from neither Phil nor Marie: it was from Flossie, and it was addressed to me. We read it together: it was a touching letter but also a maddening one, because it was as vague and uninformative in its way as Marie's had been. We learned only that the situation had worsened, not improved; that my Uncle Jimmy now knew; that Phil was obviously troubled and at home was quite apt to be silent and withdrawn as he had never been before. We learned no more about the cause of the break; atmosphere was conveyed instead of information. Still, the letter closed with an appeal which was definite enough. . . .

"I hate to ask you this, Jack, but do you and Jean plan to come home soon? I wouldn't want you to feel that I was pressing you, and I surely wouldn't want you to think I was asking you this to make things easier for myself, but if you *were* to come back fairly soon, if you could just see your way clear to doing this, I think it would help Phil so much just to be able to talk to you. I know he doesn't want me to get mixed up in it, so he doesn't really talk to me very much about it, but I know he would talk to you. It would really help him, I think. And not that this matters enormously, but I'd be terribly terribly grateful. . . ."

I don't think Flossie had ever written anything remotely like this to anyone before; when we finished reading Jean said, "Poor Flossie. In a way it may be harder on her than on anyone else. She's not very tough. . . ." Then she looked at me and said, "So . . . ?"

I nodded. "So. There's not much choice, is there? No, we'll go, all right. I'll shoot Flossie a wire and tell her we'll be home within a week. We shouldn't have much trouble with plane reservations now; the hotel will take care of that for us. . . ."

We went on talking, about our plans for departure, about Charles and Phil and what we could expect to find when we got home. We talked until it was time for bed; Jean, standing in the middle of the room, threw off her robe and plopped easily down to the floor where she lay, face up and still, preparing for the nightly round of calisthenics which she had begun, almost in a panic, a week ago. I lay there and watched while the slim, beautiful body twisted lithely through the impossible contortions; finished, gasping slightly, she said with dissatisfaction, "Ten pounds at least; I'll never get . . . but," she said, turning to me, "it's all right, isn't it? It's what you want to do?"

"Go home? Well, I'm not exactly champing at the bit, but we're in a little bit of a box, aren't we? And it's Phil, so . . . but I wouldn't be furious if we had another month of this."

"I know." She disappeared for a moment, then came back and came into bed, curling up against me. "Ah, Jack," she said, half asleep already, I think, "but didn't we have the loveliest time?"

And then, almost before I could answer, I heard her soft breathing: she could fall asleep in an instant. I lay awake awhile, thinking, and then I too went to sleep. For how long I don't know, but suddenly I woke: it must have been two or three o'clock in the morning, but even before I looked I knew that Jean was awake too. She sometimes woke in the middle of the night, and when she did she was wide-awake: wide-awake and startled. Once I had asked her if anything was wrong; she had said simply, "I'm scared." So I had held her, and slowly she had gone back to sleep. And once, months ago, at just this hour, I woke and knew that she was crying softly. Troubled, I hesitated, then I reached out and placed my hand lightly on her, and she said immediately, "It's nothing: I sometimes do this. It's just that everything is so good." And now, tonight, I knew she was awake again, and when I opened my eyes in the dim, moon-washed light, I saw that she had propped herself up on one elbow, and was looking down at me, her eyes large and deep and about an inch from mine. They were smiling; I said, "What?"

But all she said was, "My dearest love." And then she pressed her mouth on mine and kept it there for a long while; then she turned and, pressing herself close to me, she went back to her sleep. But I stayed awake now for some time, thinking of what had happened and what it meant, thinking that I was very lucky, and thinking too that I had never been so happy in all my life. . . .

We left three mornings later. We drove away from the hotel door, the manager and two of his staff standing inside, bowing slightly in our direction, while outside, on the steps, stood the man who in this final moment had assumed the role of the *patrone*. It was Signor Barbettura; he had presented Jean, on this last morning, with a genuine bouquet; he had bade us the most profuse goodbyes. We left him standing there, and as we looked back now for the last time at this hotel where we had been so happy, we saw that he was still standing, a small and isolated figure in his immaculate ice cream suit, one arm still upraised in a gesture of courtly benediction.

V

eleven

We got home late on a Sunday night, in the last week of September. No one knew exactly when we were coming; the wire to Flossie had not been that specific. And yet when we reached the house and as soon as I opened the front door the first thing I saw, lying on the floor just inside, was a telegram. It read, "Call me at hotel soon as you get in." It was signed by my Uncle Jimmy, and it had been delivered less than two hours before. This shrewd man had his own sources of information.

The hotel, I knew, was the hotel at which he always stayed, and which I believe he partly owned. In any case he kept a suite of rooms there on a year-round basis, and apart from his sons' houses it was now his only residence in the city. I had gone to see him there half a dozen times in the past, and I had called him there often—he had a private line which bypassed the hotel switchboard—but tonight I ignored his request: really, I suppose, his command. It was late, I was tired after the trip, I was in no mood for my Uncle Jimmy, but most of all, before I talked to him or to anyone else, I wanted first to talk to Phil. I was so anxious to do this that I had almost called him from the airport, but Jean wanted to get directly home; now, here at last, after six months away, when logically I should have at least taken one quick look around the house before doing anything else, I went to the telephone and called Phil. I heard the ringing, but there was no answer. On the chance that I might have dialed incorrectly, I tried again: still no answer. So they were out—but where? Had they gone down to Georgia? Because of my cable to Flossie, I thought this unlikely; still, I didn't know. . . .

I joined Jean now and together we unpacked a few things, looked over the house very superficially, just to be sure everything seemed to be in reasonable order, and then, because we were both dead tired, we went to bed. Before we went to sleep I rang Phil again, but once more there was no answer, and so I gave it up for the night, and went to sleep almost immediately.

The next morning my telephone rang, sharply and early; it woke us and I answered.

"What's the deal here?" my Uncle Jimmy said abruptly. "Why didn't you call, hah? And don't say you didn't get the wire because you did. I checked: it was delivered at nine-seventeen. You think I send telegrams for fun?"

"Hello, Uncle Jimmy. I didn't call you because it was late." I added, "Just as, right now, it's early."

"It's eight o'clock, what's so early about that?" he said combatively. "And don't hand me any of that bushwa about 'still being on European time.' I do more flying back and forth than anybody you know and you don't catch me drooping around with my can scraping the floor a week later!"

I said, "Well, we had a grand trip, Uncle Jimmy. Good weather all the way, good food for the most part. Both of us came home feeling fine. I mention that just in case you thought of asking."

It was an approach that sometimes worked with him, and it did now. He gave his little barking laugh and said, "Okay, okay. Well, why wouldn't you feel fine? You're young. If you feel fine when you're as old as I am you can shoot your mouth off. Say hello to your wife for me: she's a great girl. Now listen," he said, in a so-much-for-small-talk voice, "I want you to do me a favor. There's a dinner I have to go to tonight; I want you to come with me. Black tie, be here at seven. Right?"

No: not right. I said quickly, "Thanks, Uncle Jimmy, but I don't think I can. We just got back a few hours ago, remember; we haven't been near the place in six months; we have a million things to do." All excuses, frail enough, to postpone seeing him until after Phil; I said, "So if it's all the same to you—"

"Banana oil!" he shouted. "What the hell have you turned out to be: a smoothie? 'If it's all the same to you!' Don't pull that on me, Buster! The minute anybody pulls that he knows damn well it's *not* all the same! So why say it? Save that for your classy pals. Now look," he said, quieting down a bit, "I said I wanted you to do me a favor. Okay, that's the favor: come to chow. Is that so tough? And how many favors have I ever asked you for? Any? Hah? Think that over while you're at it! Now, what about it?"

It was bulldozer supplication; once again it seemed to me that I was in a position where I had little choice. And so I agreed, saying finally, "It's about Charles and Phil, isn't it?"

"Just be there at seven," he said shortly. I was now aware that he could not have been alone, for I heard another voice in the background; then I heard my Uncle Jimmy say very clearly, but not to me, "You tell that sawed-off greaseball bastard he's got until three o'clock this afternoon to sell or I'll kick his Spanish ass all the way back to that Madrid bucket shop!"

In this way I knew that my uncle's business day had begun. He said suddenly, "Jack?"

"Right here, Uncle Jimmy."

"Seven sharp!" he said, and with that he hung up. It was not until later, when I was telling Jean about the call, and explaining —with some difficulty, because I didn't entirely understand the reason myself—just why I had to go, that I began to realize just how unusual the invitation had been. For as my Uncle Jimmy had said, he did not habitually ask for favors; I felt that, whatever his reason, he very badly wanted me at the dinner tonight.

I felt also that it was important that I get in touch with Phil before I went. I telephoned his house again, not really expecting to get him, but to my surprise he answered at once.

"I just got up," he said. "We came in late last night: we were up seeing the kids at school. Football stuff: Charlie's a halfback now. Or whatever they call halfbacks these days. He's not bad, either. How are you? Good trip?"

"In great shape. And a fine trip. In the end we skipped both Norway and Sweden."

"No man who can say that can be all bad," he said. "You're back early, aren't you? How come?"

I said quickly, "No, not early: we planned to come back about now. There wasn't any definite schedule . . ."

I heard a low chuckle; he said, "I had a moment of ego: you know what I thought? I thought you might have come back to see me. To have a sobering word. In response to the distress signals."

I protested, guiltily, but I heard the chuckle again and he said, "Cut it out, Jack: they've been shooting up flares all over the place, and you know it. I know Flossie wrote you: she told me. So when are you going to come calling? You can get the lowdown on the Great Betrayal from the lips of the Great Betrayer himself."

It wasn't the way I wanted to begin, it was all wrong; I said, "Supposing I said I'd like to see you anyway, and no questions asked? Any chance you'd buy that?"

"Any time," he said promptly. "Come on over this morning, the sooner the better. You can even bring the questions." But then, in a voice which was crisper, more serious, he said, "No kidding, do come. Because I've been wanting to talk this over with you. I'm glad you're back."

And so I agreed to go over within the next hour or so. When

I hung up, Jean said thoughtfully, "So here it is. You don't want me along? I don't mean for the talk, but I might be useful with Flossie."

"No, it's better alone, I think. And I'm a little bit counting on Flossie's not being there: I think they both might see to that."

I was right: when I got to the house I found that Flossie had gone off on some shopping errand—or so Phil told me. He met me at the door, opening it before I even rang the bell. All the way over I'd felt a peculiar growing apprehension, the sort of thing I'd never felt with Phil before: it was unpleasant to feel it now. I suppose I'd heard so much, or inferred so much, about the change in his behavior that I now half expected to see something in his face or body—loss of weight? furrows? a trace of a tic?—to indicate the altered Phil. But of course there was nothing of the kind, he was just the same as he had been for years, and so obviously the same that I must have been obvious in my relief, because he said at once, "What did you expect: leprous sores? Come on in. Watch out for the boxes: they're all over the hall. The kids went out West in August on some sort of dig, and the results are just coming in. Boxes of bones. I don't know what the hell they found: it must have been at least a mastodon!"

We went back in through the cluttered hall. The house belonged to the same period as Charles's, but it had been built in a different and more joyous spirit. Though large, it was much less formal and dark: rose-colored brick, great bay windows, an air of sweeping and slightly haphazard space comfortably used—it was not in any of its details like the house in Georgia, yet the one somehow suggested the other: it was totally a matter of atmosphere, of feeling. We went into his study: a long room with a somewhat lower ceiling than the rest of the rooms on the floor, but loaded with books and, at the moment, full of sunlight. There was the huge leather couch against one wall; several old, oversized, well-sprung chairs waited to be sat in; at the far end of the room was a massive and magnificent desk, all mahogany and brass and mysterious, silently sliding drawers—I remembered that my Uncle Jimmy had bought it in London a long time ago and had given it to Phil the day he'd gotten out of law school. The vast smooth surface of this desk was kept perfectly clear except for two objects which were always there: a small, silver-framed portrait of Flossie, and the huge table lamp which had been made some years ago by young Jackie—the oldest of the children: named, in fact, for me—in a manual training class at school: it was somewhat lopsided and did not work.

I had been in this room many times and yet each time I came in I looked around with pleasure and a kind of envy, because it had always seemed to me a marvelous study, the ideal room in which to work—although exactly why I didn't know. I'd often said this to Phil and I said it to him now.

"It's not bad, is it?" he said. "I don't know why, either: just a good room, I guess. Flossie gets itchy about it now and then and starts feeling it's a little too tacky, but we always end up by leaving it alone. I'm used to it for one thing. And then," he said, "it's got a certain historical interest. On these chairs have perched some of the most corrupt behinds in this part of the world."

I thought of the years when he had been a criminal lawyer; I thought it quite likely that what he said was true. I said, "But ancient historical interest. All long long ago."

"Oh, I don't know about that," he said. "Not so long ago at all. You're probably thinking of my old associates: the hoods. I think of my new ones as well. The pols."

I said, "No difference?"

He didn't answer directly; instead, he went back to the furniture. "For example," he said, "that chair you're sitting in now. Just about fifteen years ago Augie Benedictis sat right there most of one night telling me his troubles. You remember Augie?"

It was a name heard somewhere, at some time, but I couldn't place it more precisely. He said, "No reason you should. I do, because I defended him once on a murder charge. To this day

I don't know who he really was or what he was or where he came from, but by the time I got to know him he was pretty well established in the rackets around here. A big man in the numbers, owned a night club, had a fighter or two—that kind of thing. He was one of the syndicate—although a hidden one—that built the dog track. One night in his club he killed a man: he shot him once, right through the heart. Then he ran out, got in his car, and came to me. He sat in here the rest of the night, talking. He wasn't a particularly lovely sight: a fat, slobbery, warty brute who had a reputation for beating up women and for going after his friends with broken bottles. Not that night, though. That night he was scared; he even began to cry. He cried quite a lot. In between the tears he told me about himself, including the fact that he'd once done time in California for criminal assault and had once crippled a man for life in St. Louis: he had knocked him down and then backed a car over his legs. His behavior here seems to have been milder, but he told me a lot about his local business associates and how they operated. I don't know that you'd call it an altogether wholesome story. I think he may have been a little crazy along with everything else. In the end I got him to surrender, he was tried, I got the charge reduced to murder in the second degree—which it should have been in the first place—and instead of going to the chair he went to the pen where he died of paresis within the year. Unmourned, I should say: certainly by me." He looked at me and said, "A vignette of local life."

"All right," I said, and waited. In a moment he said, "We skip now: about ten months ago I had a small group of party bigwigs in here, discussing various matters of strategy. Charles was here that night, and seated in your chair—in Augie's chair—was Judge Charles E. Kilrane. Now, how's your memory on that name?"

"Better." I had met the Judge, and his name was one of those names which no one who read the papers could possibly avoid, a name inseparable from head tables, fund-raising campaigns, anti-tuberculosis drives, Holy Name parades, political rallies, group photographs of dignitaries welcoming other dignitaries at the airport (under these photographs the captions always seemed to run *Standing from left to right: Probate Court Justice Charles E. Kilrane . . .*).

"Good for you," he said. "I'd seen the Judge often during the campaign, of course, but on that night there was an odd, almost an *eerie*, coincidence in his choosing that particular chair to sit in. It was a coincidence apparent to no one but me, although I told Charles about it later on. You see, as soon as I saw him sit in that chair I suddenly remembered Augie—and I remembered that the Judge and Augie had once had an interesting connection. For years Augie had maneuvered very well around here without much trouble from the police; he should have been arrested every day, but in fact nothing like that ever happened. In other words, the fix was in. The fixer was the Judge. I don't think many people know about this. I gathered from Augie that while the service was excellent, the price was heavy. It was through Augie that the Judge was declared in as a director of the dog track, but it didn't stop there. For all those years the Judge was, for all practical purposes, a silent partner of Augie's: he literally got a percentage of the take from everything Augie did. And, as Augie was a fairly busy man, the Judge did quite well. He must be a very rich man today. And the beauty of it is that nothing, absolutely nothing, can be proved. I've seen documents which would be embarrassing, to say the least, but Augie took them back and God knows where they are now. Probably gone, like Augie. Whereas the Judge is still with us, riding high, never higher, very respected in certain quarters, so much so that I hear he's shortly to be made a Knight of Malta. The poor Maltese: they've never done a thing to us and look what we've given them over the years. And why not the Judge? Why not, when you come to think of it, Jack? A heart of gold, a grand family man, generous to a fault, and as I'm constantly being told, 'Who's been more loyal to the party?' "

It was a story I'd never heard before: I found it strange and awful. I barely knew Judge Kilrane, I didn't care much about him one way or the other, but to be told suddenly that this small, spruce, omnipresent man with the shy face and the gently obliging manner, who had been for so long a pleasant, harmless, and even slightly foolish figure in the community, was in fact something far more formidable than this, that all along he had been both serious and corrupt, left me shaken and repelled. Phil was watching me; I said, "Is that an answer to my question about hoods and politicians?"

"In part," he said. "It's also a kind of introduction to what both of us really want to talk about." He sat down on the couch, half reclining, with one long leg stretched out on the worn leather, the other still touching the floor. "What do you want to know, Mr. Bones?" he said.

I said, "I want to know what happened. And I want to know why. Is that all right?"

He nodded slowly. "Who knows about these things?" he said. "Somewhere along the line, Charles and I began to think in different ways. For months before I pulled out—before the election, even—we were arguing every day. Nobody knew it. Pa guessed some, but not too much: there wasn't any point in distressing him. But we were arguing. Not bitterly; Charles was usually calm—calmer than I was. And he was always reassuring: everything would be handled in good time, I wanted too much too soon, I couldn't reasonably ask for what couldn't reasonably be done. When you see him, he'll tell you I was a perfectionist—it's a pejorative term." He shrugged and said, "Perfectionism be damned. I never cared about that. I just wanted him to keep a few promises. Promises that we'd made to the voters, promises we'd made to ourselves. I didn't expect all of them to be kept; I'm pretty good at making allowances for campaign oratory. I was ready to settle for a good bit less than everything; my trouble was that I wasn't really ready to settle for nothing. And that's just what I saw happening every day whenever I looked around: nothing. A good big round cool nothing. You don't believe it, do you?"

"I'll believe it if you say so. I've been away; what do I know about it? But I do know Charles a little bit; it's not easy to think of him as a do-nothing. . . ."

"And then too," he said shrewdly, "you've probably seen a newspaper or two since you got home. And you've probably seen where a new old-age assistance bill was passed last week. And where the poor are still going to be poor only not quite so poor because now we're going to do something about it—we're going to hold meetings with them to tell them they're poor. And where those hundred and fifty-six Negro families who used to have outhouses can now go to the john indoors practically any time they want. You've seen—or read—that these things are happening right here in our own state and you strongly suspect Charles might have had something to do with them. Right?"

And he was right; I said, "Just about."

"Well, okay," he said. "He *did* have something to do with them. That's true: he's the Governor. On the other hand it's equally true that all these valuable and praiseworthy developments would have occurred whether the Governor was Charles or Aunt Gert's chauffeur Ernie. They all look great on the record, Jack, but they're Federal shows from the very beginning: all the Governor has to do is go along. Still, the fact remains that Charles has gone along very well. It's also a fact that he's done a few things on his own; he hasn't been merely a pipeline for Uncle Sam. He's inaugurated a tax reform program: it's not bad and I think he'll be able to get it through without much trouble. The state Waterways Division is a mess: he's reorganizing that. He's begun to do something about the state police, another project that's long overdue. So don't misunderstand me: I'm not suggesting that he's been rocking away on the front porch with his thumb in his mouth. He's been busy; he's done a few things."

"Or perhaps even a lot of things?"

"Perhaps even that," he said.

"Well then . . . you don't see a contradiction here? In what you're saying?"

"None at all. You mean because a minute ago I said that nothing was happening and now I admit he's been active? So what? Activity's no good unless you're active with something that counts."

"And civil rights, old age assistance, fixing up the state police: they don't count? You're a hard man to please."

"No I'm not and of course they do. What's that supposed to be: a pointed rebuke? Look, all these reforms and reorganizations are fairly easy to arrange these days: the time is right, they're in the air, everybody's doing it. The trouble is they don't solve anything. Or not much, not around here. They're so many Bandaids, Jack—and this patient is dying of a carcinoma!"

I said, "All right: and what do you want Charles to do?"

"I want him to stop playing doctor and running around with his first aid kit. I want him to do the one thing, the *only* thing, that matters. Look, nothing, absolutely nothing, of the slightest permanent value can be done for this state unless you first get rid of the grubs who've been munching it to death for years. I know that and Charles knows that. I told you we made promises to ourselves—well, what do you think those promises were about? Every last one of them was about the one great central problem: the state, the party, how to clean it up; how to strip down the machinery, how to get rid, one by one or in wholesale lots, of this fantastic load of parasites who've been around so long they're part of the building, they're way down deep in the subsoil. Did you ever go into the State House at night, Jack? Alone?"

I hadn't; he said, "I have. Often. It's quite an experience. Nobody's there except the night watchman, who doesn't count because he's off sleeping in the first floor toilet—that's his privilege because his first cousin is the senate president's uncle. There's a complete silence at first, and then, if I listen closely, I think I can hear them, way down deep, munching away. And I *know* I can smell them. Do you know the State House smell, Jack? No matter what you do, it's always there: an Airwick as big as a palm tree couldn't take it away. A thick soiled smell: grease and garlic and old cigars. It's great sometimes just to stand inside the front doors and watch the old pols come in from all over the state. The first thing they do is breathe deep and smile: they know they've come home!"

I had heard this, or something like it, years ago: I remembered Skeffington speaking with a kind of weary resignation of the "regiment of slugs" up at the State House. I said, "Maybe you're asking for miracles. Charles is a governor, not a rainmaker. What you want is hard; maybe even impossible. I know a little something about that. . . ."

But this apparently was the wrong thing to say, or it may have struck him as presumptuous, for he said immediately and sharply, "Correction: you damn well don't!" I was startled; he saw it; he said quickly, even contritely, "Don't get sore. Bear with me a minute. You see I'm trying to do something that's not easy. I'm trying to figure out a pleasant way of telling you that when it comes to politics around here today, especially as they relate to Charles, you just don't know your ass from your elbow!"

I said, "Well, you can't get much more pleasant than that, can you?"

"No, come on, come on. You know me, Jack: this is Phil. Since when have I ever tried to whittle you down? I know you're tired of hearing hotshots like Charles and me telling you the world has changed since old Pop Skeffington ran his corner store, but it has, it has! What I want you to do is *understand:* about Charles, about Charles and me, about how and why everything happened. And you're not going to do that unless you just sit there and listen. Because only two people know the whole story, Charles and me, and you might just as well listen to me first, because I'm right here in front of you, and Charles isn't. So what do you say: agreed?"

And as I sat there, not so much listening to him as watching his face, and seeing on it the familiar half-smile but also something else which was not so familiar—an expression of eagerness, of urgency—my brief irritation passed, because I knew that he was simply driving ahead, wanting more than anything else at that moment to put me in the picture, to have me understand just why he had done what he had done. So of course I agreed, and he said, "Good. Let's start simply by telling you why we won, why Charles is Governor today. Any ideas?"

"Only the obvious ones: a good candidate, good people behind him, plenty of money, dissatisfaction with Consolo."

He nodded. "All factors, but not the big one. Not even the money, although that may be harder to believe, because so much of it was needed. Have you any idea how much the campaign cost?"

I hadn't; I said, "A million? They tell me it takes that to elect a Governor today."

"They tell you low. It took two million to elect this one and a little more besides. That's a lot of money to lay on the line for a thirty-thousand-a-year job, right? But that isn't why we won. We really won because we *knew* more. The simple fact is that Charles is Governor today because he took the enormous trouble to know more about this state than anyone else who's ever been near the State House. That was our secret, Jack: information, knowledge. All sorts of information that the others never bothered with because it was too small or too unimportant or too hard to get at. The minutiae of politics. I'll show you what I mean: name a city. Any one: big, small, so long as it's in the state."

I hesitated, then said at random, "Deerford?"

"Fair enough. Now any candidate would know that Deerford has a population of forty thousand, mostly French-Canadian.

Charles would know this, but he would also know that the population has been slowly but steadily dropping and is now approximately thirty-five thousand, that of the eighty per cent French-Canadian majority only five per cent who get away to school ever return to stay, that fifty-five per cent of those who remain are over forty, and most of them read and write English with difficulty if at all. Any candidate would know that the mayor of Deerford is J. Albert Doucette, in his fourth term, boss of the city, and one of the most popular politicians in that part of the state. Charles would know that J. Albert is also a slight alcoholic and has been for some time under the deepest obligation to Monsignor Cuthbert Dupre, the pastor of Saint Anne's Church and the real boss of the town, who owns a half interest in the radio station and who, through his brother-in-law, Amedée Piette, controls every newsstand and magazine rack in the city. Any candidate would know that Ray Calamart, a delegate to the convention from Deerford, suddenly switched his vote at the last primary. Charles would know that before he switched Calamart left the convention floor very suddenly the day he voted, that he immediately moved from the Sheraton to the Chester, and Charles would also know why he moved and who paid the bill in both places. Any candidate . . . well," he said, breaking off, "had enough? I can go on; there's more?"

"No no, I get it. And I'm impressed."

"You should be," he said. "Although your mentioning Deerford was a lucky break: I just happen to have done a lot of work in that area myself. But either Charles or myself could do substantially the same thing with any city or any of the key towns. It's all in the files. As I say, the minutiae of politics. We've got among other things the most complete dossier you'll ever see outside the FBI on every politician, every delegate in this state. We spent a small fortune, we worked like dogs, we dug it all out piece by piece, and then we put the pieces together. And then," he said simply, "we used whatever we had. Whenever the occasion arose."

"A little arm-twisting now and then?"

"A little. And sometimes more than a little. And sometimes more than now and then."

"Dirty pool? If you don't mind my asking?"

"Occasionally," he said. "And I don't mind your asking because that's what it was. Only we called it 'fighting fire with fire.' Same thing, but more class. Not very pretty under any name, but we weren't playing with very pretty people. I don't say that some of our supporters would be too proud of that if they knew; I don't even say I'm too proud of it myself. But I guess it was necessary, or so we thought: there was so much to be done, and we had to get on with it. That's the classical justification, isn't it? Anyway, there it is. It just kind of worked out like that. From rather different beginnings, I must say." He stopped and said, "But you don't know how it did begin, do you?"

"No. I've wondered, but I never knew. I guess because nobody ever told me."

"Nobody ever told anybody," he said. "So I'll tell you now: it's a First." A sardonic look flashed across his face and was gone; he said, "You know very well that about seven years ago Charles and I never even thought about going into politics: we'd just as soon have become beekeepers, spacemen, anything. But then one night, after dinner at Charles's, Pa called us into one of his family conferences and announced that he thought that one of us—he didn't really care which one—ought to go into politics. He said that the city and the state were going to hell in a handbasket, that everything political in this neck of the woods was in the hands of crooks or absolute fools, and that it was high time the family stepped in and began to straighten out the mess. He said that we'd never gone in for politics before, but he now thought the time had come, that we were the only ones around here who had the ability and the resources to crack things wide open, and that for some time he'd been thinking we had an obligation to make our move. Well, you know Pa. This high-minded approach was a little unusual, but you can't tell, it may very well have been true: he's got this great pride in the family, he thinks that together we can do anything. On the other hand it's just as possible—again, knowing Pa—that it was somewhat less high-minded, that all this really happened that night because that afternoon some cop may very well have handed him a traffic ticket and a little lip on the side. I wouldn't be surprised. It doesn't matter now, of course, but just suppose it did happen that way: wouldn't it be marvelous, Jack? The accidental forces in history all over again, wouldn't you say? Remember that crack old Bewley used to pull to get laughs: 'Constantius Chlorus's foot slipped and the result was Constantine'? Well, a flatfoot gets sullen on a summer afternoon and Charles is in the State House today!"

I said, "Think of this: it could have been you."

"It could at that. As a matter of fact Pa asked me first out of courtesy—I was the older. But I told you once I never wanted it and I told him the same thing that night. So that left Charles and he wasn't wild about it either. Not at first. But Pa kept on driving and finally Charles said all right, he'd give it a try. I remember that the next morning he called me up, asking me if we were both crazy and if I thought there was any way he could get out of what he then called 'this God-damned mess,' without driving Pa right up the wall. I told him I didn't think there was, and he said glumly that neither did he. And that's how it happened, Jack. Just like that. Which is why I love these magazine stories about Charles now: *From Boyhood Reared for Leadership!* Isn't it great? Right out of the opium pipe to the printed page and You, Dear Reader!"

And to me all this was completely fascinating, completely in character, with my Uncle Jimmy and his slightly startled, slightly unwilling sons, all of a sudden one hot summer night sitting in a room and arranging for the future of the city and the state. I said, "Why mayor, in particular? Instead of something else for a start? Was this your Pa's idea too?"

"At that point everything was his idea: we just sat and listened. He went right down the line, ticking off the possibilities. He turned thumbs down right away on the School Board and the City Council: small potatoes, waste of time. The State Legislature was a swamp in which you could get lost and a rotten platform for anything else. To go for Congress would take Charles out of the state: a mistake at this time. To go for Governor, equally a mistake: too early, too uncertain. On the other hand, according to Pa, the mayor's office was wide open: the city situation was primed for blasting; even more important, it was here in the city that Pa packed really tremendous power. It was logical, it was convincing; by the time we broke up that night a fairly halfhearted candidate for mayor and his equally halfhearted brother were on their way!"

I couldn't help remembering once more the night when he had first told me of Charles's plans: certainly there had been nothing halfhearted about him then. I reminded him of this now, and he was nodding impatiently even before I finished.

"Well, by then we'd begun to catch fire. Up until then it had all been Pa. Well, who else? What did we know about it? Charles knew how to vote, and I wasn't much better. So it was Pa who hired a staff, brought in the pros, set up the press interviews, had polls taken, laid it on the line with the district leaders, and put a little frosting on the cake by importing some muscle from Washington, just to show the local boys he meant business, that he was going for all the marbles. He did everything: it was the first stage and it was *his* stage. Frankly, we were bored; we would rather have been any place else. But then, suddenly the damnedest thing happened: *it got interesting.* It did. More than that, it even got exciting. For a lot of reasons, but the biggest of all was Pa. The funny thing is that with all the time we'd spent with him, we'd never really seen him in what you could call *action* before. He was fantastic. He's got more pure *charge* than anyone I've ever seen: running around, jumping, screaming, on the phone all the time, shooting off sparks, and the first thing you know some of the sparks fall on you and you're running and jumping and screaming too! And remember we were used to him, we'd seen all the tricks before—or thought we had. We were a couple of grown men who knew all about Pa, who were a little blasé, who'd always laughed about the politics around here as something strictly for the birds or for out-of-work Irish comics or for a few old thin-faced Yankee farts who carried Cal Coolidge's hair clippings around in their wallets—and all of a sudden here we were like two kids in the Gee-Whiz Academy, holding hands with everybody and everybody was running! I don't think any of us except Pa knew what we were doing, but we were moving, it was exciting, and we were having ourselves a ball! And more than once, Jack, *much* more than once, I looked around and said to Charles, "My God, where the hell is Jack? He's missing it *all!*"

And now, listening to him, as the words spilled out of him, I found myself almost regretting that I had missed it all, and thinking that it must have been a great time, maybe a unique time. Certainly Phil seemed to think so, because as he talked with this strange spilling energy there was actually a glow on his face and suddenly he looked very young, like a boy at a party, or taking a first peek into the tent to see the greatest circus in the world. I said, "You're making me sad; I wish I had been there."

"It was great while it lasted," he said. "Amateur night all the way, I suppose, but who cared? It was fun and we won. Later we realized—when we got to know a little more—how lucky we'd been, and afterward we never did anything like that again. As the going got tougher, so did we: much more organized, more professional. We figured out finally what amounted to a new style of campaign—well, it's essentially the one I told you about a minute ago. It wasn't as much fun as the first, but it had its moments. It was exciting."

I was curious about my Uncle Jimmy's role in the new campaign; I asked about this and he said, "Well, he was still there, and we were always ready to listen. Although I suppose somewhat less ready to obey. No, we began to control it pretty much ourselves. And sometimes he grumbled, but not much. He was surprisingly good about that: he knew we were all going for the same thing and that sooner or later it had to be our show."

"What about now? Today, I mean: is he still an influence on Charles?"

"Not really. Well, nobody's much of an influence on Charles today. Except Marie, and she's not in politics. No, Charles calls his own shots."

"And you think not well?"

"That's right. I think not well."

I said, "I don't want to be the village idiot asking silly questions, but can he really do much better? I'm not talking about capacity, now. I mean, let's grant that he wanted to do everything you wanted him to. Has he really got all that power. In this state, with this legislature?"

"Yes, he has the power. No governor in the history of the state has had the power Charles has right now. He came in with a tremendous plurality, he has no party debts, if anyone wants anything done, they have to come to him—he doesn't go to them. As much as any candidate can ever be, he's his own man. And he does nothing."

"But *why?* You see, I keep coming back to that. There has to be some sort of explanation; at least I assume there has."

"There is," he said. And paused.

I said, "Well . . . ?"

"Politics," he said tersely. "With a capital P. It's got him. Charles's eye is on the sparrow."

"Which means what? That he's got ambitions?"

"That's about it," he said. "Not a very fraternal thing to say, is it? But it's true. Once you accept it as the premise, everything adds up."

I found this puzzling; I said, "Maybe to you, but not to me. Why would someone like Charles—if he is ambitious—put up with this seamy, old-hack setup? It could only embarrass him, do him harm!"

"You think so?" he said. "Try this on for size: suppose they don't embarrass him? Suppose they—and by 'they' I mean all of them, from Cogan on down—are really very careful not to embarrass him. Suppose they all agree to help him rather than harm him? What then?"

"And you think that's likely?"

"Oh, I think it's much more than likely. I think it's exactly what's happening. Right now. Every day."

I stared at him; clearly, he meant it. I said, "I don't get it: why would a gang like that do anything to help anybody like Charles?"

"Look at them," he said. "Think about them: who they are, what they're like. They're not a band of heroes; they don't attack with flashing sword and flaming eye. Oh, there are a few of them at the top who slash around and cut people up now and then, but by and large the rest of them form a big slow inert mass: a huge fleshy puddle that doesn't so much move as it oozes or spreads. The older parts of this puddle play pinochle, the younger, gin—that's the principal difference. They all respond to simple stimuli; when you want reaction of any sort you say things like 'Thirty-hour week!' or 'Double time for overtime!' or 'There's a snap job for your brother-in-law over in Sanitation.' At this a greasy look comes into their eyes and they start to munch a bit faster. A group like this isn't a battle force. They don't want to fight, ever: they simply want to *survive*. They know that if they started to get tough, Charles would get tough too. They know that if it came to a fight they might get damaged; they might never be able to get back to their nice warm cushy world where nobody ever bothers them; they might find themselves out in the cold where people use unfeeling words like 'work.' Well, why risk that? Isn't it much better to go along quietly and do what the man says? If you leave him alone, he'll leave you alone. It's as simple as that."

"I can't argue with you because you have all the answers. The only trouble is that the answers raise questions. For example: why would Charles leave them alone in the first place? Are you saying he's in love with the *status quo?*"

"It's a question of tactics, not love—and tactics depend mainly on what you want, ultimately, to do. If, as Governor, Charles wanted to clean up this state, the first thing he'd do would be to walk right into the middle of our big fleshy mass and rip it apart into so many chunks and pieces that nobody could ever put it together again. But if, instead, Charles wanted mainly to keep the state running smoothly, with no trouble from anyone, and with one bill after another feeding smoothly through the hopper, with an extremely impressive list of accomplishments piling up for his administration, then he might be very careful to keep hands off. Because don't you see, Jack, it's easier and safer that way? It's always a great deal of trouble to tear up an existing order, to put in fresh new parts where the old ones used to be; not only that, you can't always be sure the new parts will be entirely amenable. Or that they'll do enough things fast enough to do you any good—always supposing, of course, that you've made certain immediate plans. This is known to all parties concerned. Charles, who's an extremely capable administrator, knows that he can administer the state very well with the old crowd. The old crowd, for its part, knows that they will be somewhat restricted under Charles, but not too much. And they have the consolation of knowing it won't last forever. They know he wants a good record so that he can move up; they want him to have it so that he can move up as quickly as possible. Then, after he goes, with a little luck they'll have it all back again. So everybody's happy—except possibly the other people in the state. After a while they may feel that somehow they've been short-changed, but by then it will be too late. And a kind of inertia will set in. Until the next bright and shining new hope comes along. Just as, once, we did."

He spoke as if this had happened in the dim and barely remembered past, and as he spoke I could almost feel the immense surge of sadness which must have been there all along but which only now, for just a moment, had risen to the surface. In this instant he looked desolated and alone and completely different, as if he'd been struck by lightning, and for the first time I think I saw what his split with Charles—and his disappointment in Charles—had cost him. I said, "He's going to the Senate, then?"

He nodded slowly. "Not right away. Timing's important: you have to avoid the appearance of being too greedy. One more term as Governor should do it; he'll run for re-election next fall. Then, after that, hello Washington. And the old gang here will yawn and stretch and smile and get ready for business again. And the state can look back on Charles's four-year reign and say to itself, 'You know what we are as a result of that? We're just four years older! And that's all!' "

It was a bleak account. Too bleak? Possibly, and yet . . . I said awkwardly, and not very helpfully, "It's the damnedest mess . . ."

"It's all of that," he said. "It gets even more so when you remember that we all got into it in the first place because we were going to clean up the original mess. Remember Pa and his getting us together and telling us about that 'family obligation'? As I say, I'm not very sure that he really believed that himself; probably not. The funny thing was that I did. After I got to thinking about it. And us. Do you ever think much about the family, Jack: what we are around here, what we've done?"

"Sometimes. Not very much, though. And probably not from quite the same angle as you."

"I suppose not. Well, of course your old man was no help there: he was always the one who played hooky from the family picnics, wasn't he? I used to talk to him about it; he was marvelous." Then, as if he needed to offer an explanation of the circumstances, "I saw him a couple of times out at the hospital the year he died."

"I remember." And I did, for my father, who in the last year of his life had spent a long time in the hospital, dying slowly and—mercifully—without pain from cancer of the stomach, had been visited, not a couple of times, but every week by Phil. He told me once that these were the visits he liked most.

"He took a poor view of the family," Phil said. "Well, no one knows that better than you. I think he started out by being sore at it, and ended by being amused. I remember one afternoon he said to me, 'Never forget for an instant that you belong to a proud and ancient house which was discovered thirty years ago by your father. It was a Saturday afternoon, it was raining, and he was smoking a cheap cigar at the time.' Well, he had something there, and I knew it, but all the same one day I started thinking. About the family, and about how we've all done pretty well around here since Grampa came back from being a pirate or a slaver or whatever he was and started fiddling around with that double set of books he used to keep. Since then we've gone a long way and a lot of the time we haven't been around, but this has always been our base, and it just began to occur to me that we've always taken plenty out of it without ever putting too much back. So it seemed to me that maybe we ought to start, that maybe it was our turn to begin . . . what? A fine old hallowed tradition of family public service? Isn't that what your Pa would have called it?"

"Probably." It was not hard to imagine.

"Fair enough. Still, I began to think that maybe it really *was* high time, as Pa said. Purely in terms of myself, if nothing else. I have all the money we'll ever need: I suppose you'd call me a rich man. Well, I've never particularly done anything about it. I've amused myself, I've worked with some fairly exciting if repellent people, I haven't done too much since I quit that. And I've never gone in for remarkable private exercises in virtue: I don't go secretly to the chapel at midnight, I don't read the latest novels to the blind. And, you know, occasionally you question yourself—I guess everybody does. Don't you?"

"Yes."

"So it just seemed to me that maybe this was something I could do. And should do."

"Did you ever talk about this with Charles?"

"Sure. I think we agreed that we both should do it. That we should step in and make things shine. Or at least rub some of the crud off. Well, it didn't work out. Too bad, isn't it?"

It was the saddest talk I had ever had with Phil; I said, "I'm sorry . . ."

"So am I," he said. "Because he could have done it; *we* could have done it. He had all the strength that he needed, there was only a slight risk, but he decided to play it cautious. A few minutes ago I told you that Politics had got him. Well, it's true. He's very good at it: far better than I ever imagined he'd be. Far better than *he* ever imagined he'd be. He's an odd political natural, but that's what he is. He's happier now than I've ever seen him; he loves every day of it. He loved being mayor, he loves being governor, he'll love being senator even more. It's not just the power—although being top banana isn't exactly painful to him; it's the excitement, the challenge, the cheers, the intrigue—everything that goes with it. It's *politics,* Jack: that's what he loves. Politics itself: every high-minded, low-minded, statesman-like, ward-heeling second of it—he's crazy about it! He's found his natural habitat and he won't run the slightest risk of giving it up. Nobody who feels like that ever does. And that's why he's safe and cautious now, that's why he keeps to all the rules of the game, and that's why, Jack, that's why I don't want to play in his yard any more!"

And once again I was aware of the surfacing sadness, the quick bleak look which crossed his face. I would have done anything to help him at that moment, and yet I didn't know anything I could do. It was difficult even to find anything to say which he wouldn't have already said a hundred times over to himself. I said, "Well . . . what now? What happens next? What are you going to do?"

"Oh," he said, "I'm going to do something I don't very much like to do, Jack." Then, quietly, very quietly, he said, "I'm going to stop Charles."

And I simply stared at him. I didn't say a word because I couldn't. I stared, and he stared back. I think he must have known exactly what was going through my mind, because he began to nod very slowly, as if with his head he were acknowledging my thoughts, and silently saying to each of them: *I know.* And then suddenly, out loud, he did say, "I know. But I haven't got much choice, Jack. He won't do it himself, so it has to be me."

He said this very calmly, very reasonably, as if it were the most natural thing in the world; I finally said flatly, dumbly, as if I were merely repeating. "Stop him. How?"

"That depends to some extent on what Charles does. I could oppose him in the primary. I could, if it became necessary, go on television. I could simply give a list of Charles's campaign promises, one by one. I could even give them just as he did: we sound alike. I could then take those promises, one by one, and show what's happened to them. I could go over in detail every featherbedding operation in this state. I could go over all the minor appointments that have been made; I could just spell out the qualifications of each appointee. I could point out, if I had to, the network that connects them. I could give all the facts and figures because I happen to know them. And believe me, Jack, they would be damaging. They would be so damaging that they would defeat Charles. I know that."

I looked at him for a long time. Then I said, "*Would* you do this?"

He nodded. "I would. And more. I would even actively run against him, if it came to that. Although I don't think it will." Then he said, still calmly, still reasonably, patiently explaining, "You see, there's only me. Nobody else in the family can do it. Can Aunt Gert do it? She's two thousand miles away, she's an old woman now, she leads her own life: she really doesn't care. It has nothing to do with her. Can Pa do it? It's not Pa's show any more. And even if it was, he wouldn't help because he couldn't. I've talked with him; he just gets mad. He thinks I'm crazy: and why not? Charles now is his great dream of the family come true—and I'm the Serpent Son, sabotaging his own brother. No, he's with Charles. He has to be; his whole life says he has to be. Well, who can blame him for that? I'd love him to understand, I'd love him to help, but there's not a prayer. I know that."

I said, as if by supplying one overlooked name I could suddenly bring him up short or change his course, "There's James. . . ."

"There's James," he agreed. "And if I wanted anyone to divert me for an afternoon, or distract me from my problems with an hour of witty and agreeable chat, there's no one I'd rather have than James. But for something like this he's hopeless, because as the years go by, Jack, James slips farther and farther away, and when you want to talk to him about a little problem of your own you'd like to have some help with, he looks at you but he really isn't listening, because with the back part of his mind, the serious part, he's four thousand miles away in Uppsala where the day after tomorrow he gives the soft sell on prevenient grace to a gymnasium full of Swedish Lutherans. That's his life, groups of souls: he's marvelous at it. The only trouble is that it can't do me much good."

Still slightly stunned, still really repeating words I had heard, I said, "So you're going to do it? All by yourself?"

"That's right."

"And Charles: what will he do? When he finds out?"

"Oh, he's found out," he said simply. "I told him."

It was incredible; I said, "And . . . ?"

"He was perfectly calm. As usual. And at first faintly ironic. The strange thing was that at first I don't think he quite believed me. So I impressed it upon him, and then he did: I could see that easily enough. He was still calm but the irony noticeably diminished. I knew that he was disturbed."

"And now what? You don't think he's going to sit still?"

"No. Whatever he does, it won't be that. He might just conceivably back off and behave himself. Rather than force this kind of fight he might make a compromise here and there, and at least begin to run things the way he should."

Another unreal element; I said, "I see. And knowing Charles, you think that's likely?"

"Not very. Still, it's possible. And at this stage I'm considering all the possibilities. And if he doesn't do that . . . well, I'm not sure what he will do. One of several things, which I won't bother to go into now. But I *am* sure that he'll never let it go down to the wire. That's the one way he can be beaten, and he knows it."

"And if he is beaten, Phil?" I said. "If he is beaten, if in fact you beat him or help to beat him, what will you have gained? A new governor? You think he'll be a better governor?"

"No," he said, "but that's not the point, is it?"

And suddenly I became exasperated. It was as if very gradually I had been emerging from some queer narcosis and only now saw the full implications of what we were saying, saw that under all the reasonable discussion was really a situation so bizarre and explosive and dangerous that it could destroy them all. And at that moment I lost my patience and my self-control; I no longer cared who was in the right and who was in the wrong; I wanted only to stop a course of action which seemed to me senseless and worse, suicidal; I said to Phil sharply, angrily, "Then what *is* the point? Don't be an idiot: you talk about stopping Charles as if you were going to do a turn around the maypole! The truth is that if you do this, if you even try, there'll be one big loser and that will be you! You'll knock yourself down so hard you'll never get back! You say you'll defeat Charles: why? To what end? Will Flossie be better off if you do? Will Marie? Will Pa? Will Charles? Or will you? In any way? All right, you're the political hotshot, as you said, but if you do this you're finished, and not just in politics. Beat him or not, you'll wind up laughed at or despised.

Despised as a family turncoat, laughed at as some kind of fool, a nut! You'll give everybody in the state a fine big first-class field day at your expense, and then you'll go down the drain. And what good will come out of it? Nothing except your own satisfaction at having been a spoiler, and one sweet consolation that's going to be! If Charles is doing whatever he's doing that you're sore about, that's tough, it's too bad, but it's not catastrophic. What you're proposing is: to Charles, to your Pa, to the family and most of all to you. Because by the time you're through you'll have split the family forever, and that will be all you'll have done. So for the love of Christ come out of your Dostoevsky dream and use your head: you used to have a good one!"

It was too much, it was uncalled for, it was in fact appalling: even before I finished I had begun to realize this, but even so the words kept rushing on—I couldn't seem to help myself. I saw Phil straighten slowly in his chair, as if at first he couldn't quite believe what he heard; then his face got pale and freezing cold. He started to get up and for one split second I was sure he was going to come toward me, but I still kept talking, shouting, and suddenly he seemed to stop before he was fully on his feet, and slowly he sat down again. His body gradually lost its tension, and by the time I finally stopped he was simply sitting there looking at me, his face still very pale. There was a short silence; then, to my surprise, he laughed. It wasn't the happiest laugh I'd ever heard, but it was a laugh—and a relief.

"Whatever happened to that grand old custom of your best friends never telling you?" he said. "I was very fond of that one."

I said, "I'm sorry, Phil. I talked too much. . . ."

"That's all right. It was a change. Not necessarily a refreshing one, but a change. And I know why you did it; I even thank you, in a funny way. But it's no good, Jack. I know everything you say: I've played the course before. I know that a lot of it's right—not all of it, but a lot. And it matters. But it doesn't matter enough. Not to me. Not any more. Because I've had it up to here, Jack, and now I'm going to do something about it. I can't stand by now. I just can't."

He had said all this very quietly, but now he leaned toward me as if he were pointing himself at me, his head thrust forward insistingly, and now quicker, louder, with much more force. "You talk about splitting the family. It's split already—"

I interrupted. "But not for good. Not irrevocably . . ."

"Yes. For good, irrevocably. As a family we're done, Jack. That's just a simple fact. Because the family, or the *spirit* of the family, the thing that kept us glued so close together, was all Pa. Well, Pa's old now. He's still got plenty of spark, but he no longer rules the roost, and I'm not so sure there's any roost to rule. James is gone, Charles and I are apart, our kids haven't been brought up to believe in My Family: Right or Wrong, and no matter what I do or what anybody does about it, we're not going to come together again. No, it was Pa all the way: the family as we all knew it was his idea. Well, okay: I don't quarrel with that. It was a good idea. I grew up with it, I cared about it, I care about it now. I care about it enough so that I got in all this really because of the family: I knew that it was going, that it had to go with Pa, and I thought that while we were still all working together we might just do one thing that would be good for everybody, and that might even be remembered. Well, I think we'll be remembered all right, but not quite in the way I'd hoped for. Because this state's going down the river, it's going down more each year, and when the history of the journey is finally written, we'll get our lumps for having helped to push it along. We may get no more than a footnote, but it'll be there: that in spite of all our noble pretensions, we weren't a bit better than the rest of them, and perhaps because of what we had to start with, we were even a whole lot worse. That's what I think they'll say in the end, Jack. And they'll be right. And it sickens me, it sickens me right to my soul!"

As he had talked he had risen and walked rapidly across the

room, very tall, very tense; he stopped behind the great desk and turned so that he faced me. Both hands gripped the edge of the desk and held it very tight. He seemed to be holding himself back, and with some difficulty; even his voice, when it came again, now sounded as if it were being *wrenched* out of him.

"But what sickens me even more is what's happening to Charles. You remember Charles, Jack? The way he used to be? You look at him now and he seems the same, he sounds the same, he looks the same: not a hair less, not a wrinkle added! And yet the change is there, and oh my God, Jack, what a change! And it hurts, it hurts, it hurts! You know the way we were: I don't have to tell you that. All my life Charles meant more to me than anyone else. When he was small, still a child, I protected him; when he grew up and didn't need that any more, I was always glad to be with him, not because I had to be, but because I liked to be, just as he liked to be with me. And when he grew up even more, in college, in the war, and later, we were always close because we both wanted it that way. I was proud of him, I *loved* him, Jack. And I thought at one point—and this wasn't too long ago, you remember—that he was going to become a big man, and that he could even become a great one! I was sure of that. And then, after a time, I stopped being quite so sure. And then, after some time more, I stopped being sure at all. And now," he said, "now all I know is that I don't want any more of it. I don't want any more of it at all. I don't want any more of these sweet silent sessions where Charles is closeted with Dan Cogan! I don't want any more of friendship lunches with Margaret Lucille Elderberry and that crowd! I don't want any more of Charles walking arm in arm day by day with that sleazy parade of pork-barreling grifters that five years ago neither one of us would have spit on! I don't want any more of my brother slowly selling himself off piece by piece to some of the worst infesting bastards around, and laughing laughing *laughing* while he does it because he knows it can't happen to him!"

His voice had been rising while he talked, he was shouting now, and suddenly he leaned forward and screamed at me, "*No more! I can't take any more!*"

And his eyes blazed, they really blazed, with a queer light; his whole body was shaking; I was startled, even frightened; I didn't know what to do. But then, gradually, the shaking stopped, the light left his eyes and for one quick moment he seemed vague and unsettled, as if he weren't sure where he was or what he was doing. Then he looked at me, almost surprised; he blinked and then, slowly, he grinned.

"Wow!" he said. "That must have been quite a performance. You get it all? You don't want a replay?"

"No. Listen, Phil: just one more—"

"No," he said, quietly but very firmly. "Nothing more. Not a word. I don't want to talk any more about it; we've wasted too much time already. What I want to talk about now is you and Jean and Italy. So talk."

So I talked and he talked. Not easily; we both knew we were going through the motions, that we were caught up in something else entirely. But we didn't mention it again, not once, and pretty soon, because there seemed to be no more to say, I left, and for the first time in my life, standing on Phil's doorstep, I found I didn't know how to say goodbye to him.

And all he said was, "As they used to say on the radio, thanks for listening. Do you understand at all, Jack?"

"Yes, I think so. But—"

He shook his head. "No buts. And no more, not today. Maybe we'll try it again some other time. Meanwhile, *ciao*. Isn't that what you Eyeties say?"

And so I left him. I drove away from his house, and when I looked back I saw that he had already gone inside. I drove home very slowly. I now knew the story I had not known before—the knowledge did not help. I was much more troubled than before, and all the way all I could think of was Phil, my oldest friend, screaming, and then standing, so quietly, behind his desk, with that strange unsettled look in his eyes.

twelve

I SPENT the rest of the day thinking about Phil, and doing no work of my own. I had told Jean most of what had happened; she was as worried as I was. It seemed to both of us that if Phil went ahead with his plan there could be only the most serious consequences; on the other hand, if my impressions were right, there was almost no chance of persuading him to stop. Jean held out for another visit by me, for one more try. I agreed, but privately I had not the slightest hope of success. For I had an advantage—or a disadvantage—that she had not: I had heard Phil's voice and had seen his face; I had the disturbing feeling that perhaps arguments no longer mattered at all. . . .

"And then of course there's Charles," she said. "Will you be seeing him tonight?"

"Probably. Uncle Jimmy didn't say, but I expect that's really what it's all about."

"You might be able to do something there," she said doubtfully.

"Well, we can't lose much by trying." It was a flabby cliché of evasion rather than of optimism; she knew it and nodded in instant agreement. She had never had a high opinion of Charles's capacity for the generous response.

That night when I arrived at the hotel—on the dot of seven—

my Uncle Jimmy was already downstairs and waiting for me in the lobby.

"How goes it?" he said, plunging his hand at me. "You look okay. Good trip, right?"

"A fine trip, Uncle Jimmy."

"Tell me about it sometime," he said vaguely. "Come on, come on, we don't want to be late. I know these babies: you keep them away from the feedbag too long and half of them get at the booze and start talking lobbo. And if there's one thing I hate it's to make a speech to a room full of tanked-up clowns!"

We got in the car and drove off. He did not further identify "these babies," but in any case it was the rest of what he had said that interested me. I said, "Are you making a speech tonight, Uncle Jimmy?"

"Sure," he said. "I can't get out of it. That's what the whole damn thing's about: I'm the big cheese tonight. They're giving me a dinner. It's a surprise."

He seemed remarkably unsurprised; I said, "There must have been a news leak somewhere."

"Well, you know how these things are. They all start out to be surprises, but how the hell can you have a surprise when there aren't five people in the whole burg that can keep their mouths shut for more than ten minutes? In this town everybody knows all about everything a month before it happens. At a dinner like this it doesn't make any difference; everybody's too lit up to notice. Speed it up, speed it up!" he suddenly yelled to his chauffeur. "What are you doing: taking time out for a smoke? I'll let you in on a little secret: the green light means Go!"

His manner with his drivers, I saw, had remained unchanged. This driver I had not seen before: he sat, staring hard, straight ahead, while the car accelerated sharply. After a moment I said, "Well, anyway, congratulations. What are they honoring you for?"

He shrugged. "You figure it out," he said. "Who the hell knows these days. It's the same old baloney. There are six guys in this town who hate to eat at home: they spend all their time getting together dinners to honor other phonies just so they can eat out and on the cuff. They have a hell of a time now because they've run out of people; they go half nuts trying to figure out who to honor next. And for what. It's got so now they'll throw a feed for you for being a Jew. Or a Catholic. Or a garbage man. Who cares, so long as they get a free lamb chop out of the deal? Small-time stuff," he said, "like everything else around here. A bunch of half-assed fakers that have been sucking around me all my life. I wouldn't give them the time of day before, but now I do. On account of Charles."

This gave me an opportunity to ask him about Charles, but suddenly he was no longer communicative. A man of swiftly alternating moods at any time, he grumbled a short answer and fell into a glum silence for the rest of the ride. It was possible that he was merely contemplating the distasteful evening before him. On the other hand it was equally possible that the mention of Charles's name had reminded him of a more serious vexation, one which we had so far avoided but which was sure to come up before the evening was over.

We stopped in front of the city's biggest hotel. Inside, we went upstairs and into a long large room where, I instantly remembered, I had been before: it was in this very room that we had given Phil a bachelor dinner, the night before his marriage to Flossie. It was the strangest of coincidences, but one over which I had no time to linger, because at that moment the applause began; everyone in the room—there were perhaps two hundred of them—had turned to face the door and the solid little entering figure of my Uncle Jimmy. They now began to cheer and sing, very loudly, "For He's a Jolly Good Fellow!" My Uncle Jimmy stood stock-still in the doorway, a vaudevillian's mask of surprise on his face; then, as the song continued, he grinned widely and raised his hands over his head in his boxer's gesture of victory.

At this they all laughed and crowded around him, slapping him on the back, while he shook his head in rueful wonderment and kept on repeating, "You birds sure put one over on me: I thought this was going to be for Dan Leahy!"

I was introduced all around. It was an all-male gathering: some of them I had known for years, others I had seen or heard of, most were strangers. It was in no sense a mixed group. With a rare exception, all—like my Uncle Jimmy—had sprung from one stock, all were men of means. They were businessmen, bankers, lawyers, doctors, judges; they were the leaders of what older and not necessarily friendly voices used to call ". . . our Irish-Catholic community." They were all of a certain age, my Uncle Jimmy's age, and as I looked around me at the crowd of stout, bald, tuxedo-clad figures, I thought it was like nothing so much as a reunion of World War One veterans, all of whom had done well for themselves, and all of whom were now gathered together in celebration of that fact.

We sat down to eat. My Uncle Jimmy and I were separated: he, at the center of the head table, I, several tables away. I knew no one at this table, they all knew one another; only the fact that I was apparently a switch-head for the condiments made me any part of this uproarious circle. I ate rapidly and in silence and finally, blessedly, the toastmaster, with a rapping of his knife against his glass, signaled that the meal was over and the ceremonies would begin.

For me it was a voyage into the past. Years ago with Skeffington I had gone to dinners the perfect duplicate of this in ritual and spirit: the songs, the speeches, even the people seemed the same. The songs were the highlights: they were parodies, original lyrics fitted to tunes which had been written and sung when all the guests were young. It was in the tradition of such get-togethers that these songs were not especially flattering to the guest at whom they were directed; they were conceived in the spirit of the "rib," the "roast." And now a piano played, a trio sang, and

I watched my Uncle Jimmy as he listened to a song my mother used to sing. I remembered the title—"Every Little Movement Has a Meaning All Its Own"—and now I heard it for the first time in more than thirty years, much modified to apply to my uncle:

Every little dollar has a meaning all its own
Every little nickel is just all I want to own . . .

This went on for some time; there was occasional laughter and applause; I watched my Uncle Jimmy's face grow darker. Those who had imagined that he would enjoy—or at least accept—such "kidding," that he would be a "good sport," had severely miscalculated. He did not appreciate fun, particularly clumsy fun, at his own expense. Looking at him now I could sense all the possibilities of an explosion, and apparently others could too, for abruptly the toastmaster rapped his glass again and announced that it was now time for the speeches, that several of the members had a few words for their honored guest.

There were a number of speeches. They were long, tiring, somewhat fanciful tributes to my Uncle Jimmy: each began facetiously, each ended solemnly as the speaker pounded home his "moral." As one speech succeeded another, my Uncle Jimmy's face lost its fractiousness and became weary; my attention wandered. Suddenly the voice stopped, there was applause, everyone began to rise, and looking up, I saw that Charles had come into the room and was now walking quickly toward the head table. My Uncle Jimmy was standing and applauding more vigorously than anyone else; Charles went directly to him, put one hand on his shoulder, smiled, and said something; my Uncle Jimmy beamed. Everyone now sat, Charles slipping into the chair next to his father; the toastmaster announced that with no further delay we would now hear from our Governor. "Who, I hear," he said, "is not altogether a stranger to our guest of honor tonight!"

The archness drew applause; when it subsided Charles began

to speak. His talk was swift, graceful, and witty; it was not, properly speaking, a talk at all so much as it was an introduction to his father; it was not at all emotional, yet it was perfectly clear to everyone what lay beneath the calm surface of his words. When he finished there were shouts and cheers and cries of "Jimmy! Jimmy!" until at last Charles moved over and my Uncle Jimmy got up to make his speech.

It was a strange speech—by which I suppose I mean it was my Uncle Jimmy talking in a way I had never heard him talk before. For a few minutes I couldn't quite place the difference—it was a scrappy, slangy, reminiscent speech, but not reminiscent in the same warm way that his speech at Charles's victory party had been, and full of touches which completely eluded me (references to people I had never heard of, to parts of the city I didn't know, to organizations and groups with improbable names) but which obviously did not elude his audience. They were attentive, delighted and even occasionally moved by what, to me, was for the most part an almost incomprehensible monologue. And then of course I realized that all this was as it should be, that my Uncle Jimmy was not talking to me; he was speaking strictly to his own contemporaries: they knew it and they loved it. It was his crowd, not Charles's; they had welcomed Charles warmly enough, but he could never have drawn from them what Jimmy did now. The bond that held these men to Charles was clearly my Uncle Jimmy; I saw now that his single purpose here this evening was the reinforcing of that bond.

We left soon after his speech. Charles must have seen me from the head table because he came straight for me, and we met for the first time in months. As usual, he was not effusive, but he was obviously pleased to see me; we talked briefly and as best we could—people came and went, paying their respects to Charles on their way to my Uncle Jimmy; Charles asked me about Jean and the trip and my book, I asked him about Marie and his first year in office. Neither of us mentioned Phil.

Finally Charles looked quickly around. "All right, let's go. We've done all we can here. We'll go in my car; as soon as we make a move Pa will break away."

It seemed unlikely, for my Uncle Jimmy was now surrounded at the far end of the room and showed no sign of wanting to leave. Nevertheless, when we got outside and into the official car, he joined us almost immediately, slightly out of breath and grumbling.

"You say hello to those babies and half of them think you want to marry them!" he said. "Al Cahill followed me to the door; he practically had his duke in my pocket. He wanted me to go into some phony stock deal you could smell from here to Pittsburgh! I wouldn't go into a handful of jelly beans with that crook; he's been a nickel phone call away from the pen all his life! Come on, let's get out of here!"

As we drove away Charles said, "Well, it was a thing that needed doing. They're not uninfluential. Thanks."

"Forget it," my Uncle Jimmy said. As we rode along he seemed to be in fairly good spirits, and I suspected he may have enjoyed the evening more than he would have admitted. Almost as if to defeat such suspicions he now said to me derisively, "Swell time, right? Real live wires?"

"Just great. I wouldn't have missed it for worlds."

He gave me a fierce smile but said no more, and Charles and I talked until we reached the house. When we went in, Marie was waiting for us in the front hall; to my surprise Jean was with her.

"Last minute addition," she said. "Marie knew I was alone so she asked me over. We've just been sitting here, talking. And I've seen the baby—Jack, it's beautiful!"

"Hey hey hey!" my Uncle Jimmy said. "What's all this 'beautiful' baloney? It's a *boy!*" He walked over to Jean and kissed her. "You look swell," he said. "How about a dance?"

Charles joined them; he and my Uncle Jimmy and Jean talked, and Marie and I were left together, a few steps away. Marie said, "Hello, Jack: it's good to have you back."

I said, "Tell me all about yourself. You can even start with the baby if you want."

"Oh," she said, "he's a great baby. Just the greatest, that's all." She looked across at Jean and said, "She's in marvelous shape, isn't she?"

"I think so. Everything's fine." And then I said, "What about yourself?"

"I could be worse." She said soberly, "And I could be better, too. I really could, Jack."

I said, "Phil?"

"I don't even like to talk about it," she said. "Because when I do I just get mad. Maybe because none of it makes any sense to me. I just don't get it!"

I said, "You get it enough to be sore at Phil."

"Sure I do. And sure I'm sore at him. What do you expect me to be? He turned on Charles: I don't send people fan letters for doing that!" She was angry just thinking about it, but then she sighed and said in a calmer voice, "Oh, I don't know, it's not just being sore. It's a lot more than that. You know me: I've been sore a million times in my life; before I married Charles I think I was sore most of the time. But then at least I knew what I was sore *about*. This thing is just . . . fantastic. If you want to know what I think, I think he's behaving like a lunatic. I mean it. The whole thing's nuts and so is Phil!"

I wondered just how much Charles had told her, just how much she knew. I was about to try to find out, but at that point Charles came over and suggested that we go up to the library. Marie and Jean remained downstairs; clearly, this was to be men-talk. And as I went up with my Uncle Jimmy and Charles, I could see that Jean was keeping her eyes on me; I turned and tried to read whether she now knew anything more, whether she had some message for me, but in this I was completely unsuccessful.

The last time I had been in the library with both Charles and my Uncle Jimmy had been on the night of the victory party, and when Charles handed us our drinks I mentioned this to him. He said, "Yes. A good night, wasn't it? Nearly a year ago now."

There was a silence as the three of us sat down. We formed, roughly, a triangle, all able to see each other full face with only the slightest movement of our heads, but now Charles shifted about in his chair—I think so that he could more directly face me—and as he did so I said, "What's going to happen, Charles?"

"I don't know," he said. "Have you talked with Phil yet?"

"Yes, this morning."

"And what did he say to you?"

And so I told him substantially what Phil had said to me, diplomatically softening a few of the harsher touches. Not many, however: it was on the whole fairly complete and even included the fact of his possible political opposition to Charles. I did all this because I was reasonably sure that it could do no harm—after all, according to Phil, anything I now said would have already been said to Charles by Phil himself—and also because I thought it just barely conceivable that it might do some good. The chances of this were not great, I knew, but it was at least possible that an account of Phil's side of the story, as well as of his present mood, might be helpful if given to Charles by a third party, someone who hadn't been directly in on the battle. In any case I talked and Charles listened—without comment and, as far as I could tell, without any particular surprise. Because of the seating arrangement—and because it had been Charles who had asked the question—I found myself talking mainly to him, and becoming less aware of my Uncle Jimmy. Occasionally from his corner there came a restless motion, nothing more, but when I came to mention Phil's possible outright opposition, I heard an angry grunt, a peculiar snort-like sound, and when I turned I saw an expression I couldn't quite identify—bewilderment? rage? frustration?—on his homely little face. He was quite clearly holding himself back with difficulty; his body was straining forward as if secured by invisible ropes; he was aching to speak but, astonishingly, he had not interrupted, and even more astonishingly, he had so far said not a single word. I realized now that this had probably been agreed upon beforehand, that my Uncle Jimmy must have consented, possibly for this one occasion only, to let Charles do all the talking. And this in itself was interesting, because it reflected the changing balance of the family situation that Phil had touched upon. . . .

When I finished Charles said, "These things are always like the description of the elephant, aren't they? It all depends on the way you look at it. And this is Phil's way. Jack, you used to see eye to eye with him on most things: how about this one? You find it pretty convincing?"

It was a little of the challenge, a little of the needle; I said, "I've always found Phil pretty convincing. I remember that you used to find him that way yourself."

"You've got a great memory," he said. "Well, maybe I will again. I hope so. If we ever can cement ourselves together . . . did Phil tell you, by the way, the reason he left that night? The specific issue, I mean? The straw that broke the camel's back?"

He hadn't, I was sure of that; I said carefully, "I don't think he mentioned any one thing . . ."

"There was one," he said. "Let me tell you about it; I think it'll be interesting to you. As a writer," he added dryly. He went on. "On that night I was in here, sitting just where I am now, when Phil came in. When he came, literally, bursting in, demanding—not suggesting, you know—that I fire Arthur Toomey. Now, I'd bet you don't know who Arthur Toomey is."

I said, "You'd win."

"It was a sure thing," he said. "Because *I* didn't know who he was. When Phil mentioned the name I couldn't remember ever having heard it in my life. Then it turned out that a couple of weeks before I'd given him a job, over in Public Works. There were several vacancies, all of them unimportant, and I'd filled one with Arthur Toomey. And then I forgot it—and him. Until Phil came in that night and told me I had to get rid of him."

I said, "But not just like that. There was some reason: what had he done?"

"Not much of anything. I don't think he ever had. That seemed to be the trouble. I've checked him out pretty well since then: the record would seem to show that Arthur isn't much of a doer. He's a typical hack: fifty-three, married, four children, in and out of political jobs all his life. No particular qualifications. Not a very good record."

"Not a very good appointment."

"No. But one of a thousand: you live in a dream world if you think you can fill the donkey jobs with dedicated public servants. You know that."

I said, "But Phil knows it, too. It's a little hard to believe that he'd go to the mat with you on anything as trivial as that."

"Isn't it?" he said. "Still, I want to be fair. There *was* one more factor which—according to Phil—made it slightly more than trivial. Arthur Toomey is Dan Cogan's first cousin."

I looked at him; he looked back at me steadily. "That's right," he said. "Now the truth is that I didn't know that when I appointed him. I should have known—as a matter of fact I'm a little annoyed that I didn't; somebody slipped up there—but I didn't. Phil has some difficulty believing that but, as I say, it's the truth. On the other hand, it's also the truth that if I had known it, the chances are that I would have appointed him anyway. It simply wouldn't have struck me as important enough to raise a fuss about."

I said, "Just important enough to break with Phil about."

"Apparently." Then he smiled and said, "No. That wasn't it: you know that. Toomey's nothing: a name, a symbol. Do you think I wouldn't have fired Arthur Toomey in five seconds if Phil really wanted me to? I know I've suddenly become an unprincipled politician in the last few weeks, but even we men without principle need to keep track of our obligations. And the fact is that I'm obligated to Phil. I owe him a lot, especially for what he's done in the last couple of years. Things that no one else could have done. Including me. Of course if anybody should ask me if I could have been elected Governor without Phil, I'd say yes. But just between ourselves, I wouldn't mean it."

Humility? Or objectivity? The second was far more likely, but I said, "You're in danger of talking yourself down, Charles."

"It's a failing of mine," he said. "No, I was merely trying to point out that I was obligated to Phil. And to suggest that he had certain rather special qualities: qualities that I haven't got. If so much modesty disturbs you, I'll go on to say that I've got qualities that *he* hasn't got. I suppose we're all fitted for different things. I wouldn't think, for example, that Phil would make a very good governor."

I said, genuinely curious, "Off the record, Charles—and just for me—how do you rate yourself? A good Governor?"

He looked at me; he seemed to be amused. "That's right," he said. And then: "But we were talking about Phil. And Arthur Toomey. Do you seriously think that for someone like Phil I wouldn't have got rid of fifty Arthur Toomeys if he asked me to and if, as I say, that was what he really wanted? But of course that wasn't what he really wanted at all. What he really wanted was to have me do something I can't possibly do. He wanted me to turn this administration into something it can't possibly be: a moral crusade. *His* kind of moral crusade. In case you're in any doubt, that's slightly more moral than most."

I said, "But that's an idea I don't find so outrageous, do you?

After all, wasn't that one of your campaign themes: the new broom, sweeping the old corrupters out? Didn't you put yourself down rather firmly on the side of the angels?"

"That's right. That other side's not much good, by the way. But when you're elected, Jack, you find there's one trouble with angels: there just aren't many of them around. You may be all for them, but you have to work without them. All you've got is living, breathing men. Our trouble came when Phil suddenly decided that it was our duty to work only with *good* men. No more bums, second-rates, or citizens who didn't meet our high standards. Sounds fine, doesn't it?"

"You don't think it does?"

"I think it sounds magnificent. In fact if all I had to do was listen to it sound I'd be all for it. But unfortunately I have to make it work. And unfortunately I have to work with what's available to me, I have to work with what I've got."

I said, "But that's what everyone has to do; we're not in the Communion of Saints. What you're saying is that you can't get good men."

"You sound like Phil," he said. "He was always telling me what I was saying; the trouble was that when he said it, it wasn't at all what I said. Now look: I'm saying that the men with whom I *must* work are sometimes good men, sometimes indifferent men, and sometimes, I'm afraid, fairly bad men. Well, I'm not an evangelist; I'm the Governor. My job is to run this state, to make it work. You've been to school, Jack: who was it who said that piety doesn't dispense with technique? If I've got a highway program to push through, and in my judgment it's essential to the welfare of this state, then I don't and I can't go to old Monsignor McGrath who doesn't know a thing about building roads but has never said a swearword in his life. No, I go to men whose job it is to see that roads are built, that they go from point A to point B, that they don't bulge or buckle with the first frost, and that they're built within a reasonable period of time at a reasonable cost. And in the process of doing this, Jack, I do what every other elected official in the country finds it necessary to do: I deal, directly or indirectly, with some very worthy men and also with some whose virtue is very much in doubt. And I do that because that's just the way the ball game happens to be!"

I said, "And you don't think Phil knows that?"

"Of course he knows it. He's not in the least naïve."

"Well then . . . ?"

"Well then," he said, "knowing the way it happens to be, he went one step farther and pointed out the way it should be. So far, so good: no argument. But then he took one more step: he announced that from now on we should play the game this way. As it should be. In other words, we would break completely with the existing operation, and it would be up to us—or, in effect, to me—to change it all for the better and without delay. At this point it seemed to me that a slight element of unreality was creeping into the picture, and since that just happens to be one of the things I can't afford right now, I said no. He was firm; so was I. So we parted. Firmly."

The story troubled me. I was on Phil's side, and yet as Charles talked on, gradually the story of the conflict began to seem slightly absurd. I knew of course that I was getting only the bare bones of it, that he was simplifying vastly, and also I knew that Charles was a very clever man; nevertheless, what was emerging was a picture rather different and far less dramatic than Phil's, a picture which was even a rather ordinary one: the public servant trying to do a job in the middle of difficult circumstances, and being pressed and perhaps goaded by a lieutenant who was asking only for the moon. And as he told this story, Charles's manner had its moments of wry and occasionally baffled exasperation, as if he even now failed to understand how something which was almost a caricature of the old high school debate—*The Realist Versus the Idealist in the World of Politics Today*—could really have provoked so severe a schism between two such experienced and practical men. And this was what troubled me, because now I began to wonder about this too. There did seem to me to be something preposterous here, something not quite rational; I thought suddenly of Phil looking at me as he had in the last moments of our talk together, and as I thought of this Charles went on talking, quietly, reasonably, persuasively.

"It's a problem of reality. Well, you know at least some of the realities around here. Looking at it coldly, I suppose that we're just about the worst state in the country. Considering our resources, our potential, our opportunities. We're a laughingstock, a national joke. It's true that the others don't laugh at us all the time—they can't afford to, they're not all that well-off themselves—but they do laugh because we seem to have that extra little dimension of clownishness, of shabby corruption. It's been that way for a long time. Not to speak ill of the dead, but your old friend did his part in making it that way. Anyway, here it is, and I'm stuck with it. So, Jack, what do you think I ought to do?"

"I think you ought to stop the laughter."

He shook his head. "That's another Phil answer. I *can't* stop the laughter: it's gone on too long. All I can do is reduce it somewhat—and that's what I'm going to to. Or going to try to do. I'll make changes: *some* changes. I've made a few already. I will improve—slightly—the level of political operation in the state. But that's about all I will do because that's all I can do, and even that I'll have to do gradually. If I try to speed it up even slightly I find that something gets in the way. It's called the state government. I think I'm supposed to keep it running. Well, I'm going to—at least I'm going to if I don't get stopped. And it's my opinion, Jack, that the one thing that could stop me cold would be Phil's little scheme of Good Men Only Need Apply."

I said, "I didn't realize that was the way reformers talked."

Once again he seemed amused. "It isn't. But then I'm not a reformer. Jack, you've spent most of your life in the state: do you think most of the people who elected me really want reform?"

I said, "I think they want a lot of things—"

"So they do, but reform isn't one of them. They'll take small changes, changes around the edges, but they want the basic setup let alone. I sit and listen to that small army of sociologists and their translators that I have around me, and I learn that the old antagonisms and prejudices are melting away in the face of a growing tolerance, that ethnic voting is on its way out. Well, that's heady stuff for the graduate students: the kind of thing they like to hear. I think I probably won't pass it along to the Greek who tried to run for the City Council from Ward Three, though; it's too much like the kind of news he heard before he ran."

He finished his drink slowly and placed the glass on the table beside him; he said, "The great fact of political life around here is simply this: we have an enormous number of people in this state who seem to have changed in a great many ways, but the more you know them, and the closer you get to bedrock, the more you find that they still think and feel—and vote—precisely as their fathers and grandfathers did, and for pretty much the same reason. Or lack of reason. The difference is that they haven't their fathers' and grandfathers' excuse: they aren't poor, they've gone to college, by and large they've got it made. And yet in spite of all the A.B. and LL.B. degrees, they're still the same old gang at heart. With the same old aspirations. Half of them are in the legislature or in key places in the different cities. You have to watch them every minute, and whether you believe it or not, Jack, you have to work within the limitations they place upon you."

I said, "Do you? A minute ago you were hinting around about Skeffington. He used to say quite a bit about something called 'leadership.' Whatever happened to that?"

"Let me tell you about leadership," he said. "A good leader is one who recognizes what cán be done, and does it. If he sees something which he knows would be good to do, and which he would like to do, but which he knows simply cannot be done, then he forgets about it—at least for the time being. Because to do anything else would be merely to waste his time and his energy—and there's never a surplus of either. Now this is what I battled with Phil over for so long. He says that once upon a time we used to want the same things, but now we no longer do. And his reason is simple: I've changed. Well, it's not that simple. And it's not true. What is true is that I now know that a great many of the things I wanted I just can't have. Well, that's hard on a greedy man like me, but there it is and I can't do anything about it. But whenever I tell that to Phil I don't get to first base. A strange look comes into his eyes—and I mean strange: this is something new, you haven't seen it yet—as if he's listening to voices I can't hear, and suddenly I become The Enemy, reneging on all my promises. And all the while, all I'm really saying, over and over again, is that if I'm going to do my job—if in fact I'm going to do any job at all—I have to stay somewhere within the realm of the possible. Well now, it's conceivable that a few people might regard that as a fairly reasonable proposition. What do you think?"

And put this way of course it was reasonable. I now found myself greatly disturbed. I knew—I had known Charles too long not to know—that he was now deliberately trying to win me over to his side; what was so disturbing was that even though I knew this he was making some headway. I found that I was listening to him without much of my first skepticism; I found that I was telling myself that much of what he said made perfect sense. And it did, of course, yet I think it was his manner rather than anything he said that was so effective. I don't think I'd ever sat down with Charles—at least, not in recent years—when he had really set out to convince me of a point; now, for the first time, I grasped something of that quality which had served him so well on television: his sheer *believability*. Face to face with it, in the same room, I saw how really formidable it was, how strongly it came through. I've said earlier that Charles was no spellbinder, and certainly he wasn't in the old, traditional sense, but there was something about this easy convinced delivery, with its occasional sharp edge, with its air of absolute candor and assurance, which made it enormously compelling, and I listened without missing a word. And, I had been struck by—and bothered by—that one quick reference to strangeness; he had merely mentioned it and gone on, but still I wondered. . . .

He said again, "Reasonable? Or not?"

I said, reluctantly, as if I had no business admitting even this much, "Yes. It's reasonable, Charles."

He gave just the briefest forward movement of his head. "I thought so, too. But I haven't been able to get that through." He went on now to talk about Phil. "Ordinarily he's completely flexible; recently, no. He's got a bee in his bonnet. People have noticed it; one of them came up to me and said, 'Phil's got religion.' " He shrugged and said, "I don't know what he's got, but he's got something. As a result he's holed up over there, I haven't seen him in weeks, I can't reach him by phone, we have no connection at all. Meanwhile he has his story. It's a good story. Vivid. Full of detail. There's a hero and there's a villain. It probably makes fascinating listening. Since I happen to be the villain, I wouldn't know."

He smiled, it was a completely friendly smile, but then I seemed to see something else in it: just the faintest hint of complicity, the minimal suggestion that he and I now understood each other and from now on were to be allies. Which is a lot to read in a smile, I know, yet something like this was there, and it offended me, because of its implication. And this was probably why, at that point, I blurted out a question which had not even been in my mind a few seconds before; I wasn't even thinking of anything of the sort. But what I said, so abruptly, was: "Charles: are you running for the Senate?"

And with this one, single, unpremeditated question, everything came apart. Everything.

Clearly, he hadn't expected it, it caught him off guard, and for just that instant he changed, and his face slid into an absolute neutrality of expression, an expression that was as controlled and careful as anything I'd ever seen, and as soon as I saw it I knew, positively *knew*—in the way that you can leap into certainty in a split second, skipping all intermediate steps—that he was lying. Or, if not lying, at least cleverly evading; the candor was gone, and in the same instant I knew that whatever its strangeness—or his strangeness—Phil's version was the truth!

"The Senate," Charles said. "Well, I just might. In due time. And even that could be reasonable, don't you think?" But it was too late, the harm had been done, the spell—to use a word that's too big—had been broken. I think he realized it almost at once. He looked hard right at me, he opened his mouth as if to follow up with something, then closed it without speaking. There was a pause, he shrugged once more, and then he smiled. "Well well," he said. "Okay, Jack. That's that."

And it was that: he stopped this line of conversation short, right there. He did not mention his own dependence on Phil, or Phil's misreading of his position, again. Clearly, all that was over now, and as Charles had said, he did not much like to waste time. He said to me, pleasantly enough, "I'll tell you what you can do, if you will. You can give Phil a message for me."

But I was wary now; I said, "One you'd rather not give him yourself?"

"No. One I've already given him myself. But I want to see that he gets it again. He didn't seem to believe me. I thought you might have better luck."

"All right." And then, even though now I didn't believe it could happen, or even that he wanted it to happen, I said, "Onc more peace offer? A last bid to come back?"

But it wasn't a serious suggestion, for me or for him, and he dismissed it, shaking his head impatiently. "No," he said. "I told you I was interested only in what was possible. Phil's not coming back. I know that. So does he. And so do you, Jack." He stopped again, and this time when he resumed speaking there was a change in his voice. Not a great change: just a shade harder, a touch colder, but quite enough for me to realize that the casual, almost indulgent phase of our talk was over. He said quietly but very deliberately, "Tell him this for me: tell him I want him to cut it out. Tell him that I want him to stop. That I want him to stop *now!*"

And of course I knew exactly what he meant—how could I help it?—but still I said, I suppose because I couldn't think of anything else to say, "Stop what?"

He looked hard at me again, he opened his mouth to answer, but before he could make a sound there was an interruption: unexpected, loud, violent. It was my Uncle Jimmy. All the time he had been sitting in his chair, and as I had gradually and unconsciously twisted more and more away from him, and had talked exclusively to Charles and had become increasingly absorbed in what he was saying, and as, moreover, my Uncle Jimmy had so miraculously refrained from taking even the slightest part in the conversation—apart from that one stifled snort in the beginning, I had ignored him: more than that, I had actually, and for the only time in my life, managed to forget that he was in the same room with me! Now, as if he were infuriated by such an affront, as well as by everything everyone else had been saying and, too, by the mere fact of his own unprecedented silence, he came crashing back into my awareness with a great roar of liberated impatience and anger, and at the same moment he leaped from his chair and now stood between us, looking down at me with a ferocity which seemed barely able to be contained. His mouth was working; he had spilled his drink; his glass lay on the floor; his stumpy little body was shaking with rage.

"Stop *what!*" he yelled. "I'll tell you 'stop what'! Stop all the God-damned bushwa! Stop acting like some thick-headed Mick son of a bitch! Stop sticking the shiv into his own brother! Stop double-crossing his own family! That's 'stop what'! Who the hell does he think he is? No son of mine can pull any two-bit squeeze play on me and get away with it: I'm his *father*. Listen," he shouted, "you listen to me and listen good! I've kept my trap shut long enough! You get over there and you tell that baby for me he's got one week—*one week*—to smarten up and ditch this crappy wise guy act or by God, son or no son, I'll come over there myself and put the blast on him so hard his ass'll turn to Jello! Now that's *my* message, Buster! Give him that for me! One week! *One week!* ONE WEEK!"

His voice had grown louder with each word, and by the end of his tirade the last "ONE WEEK!" was a bellow that must have been heard all through the house. I was thunderstruck, because even with all that had happened, I wasn't prepared for this. I had never seen him so angry, but not only that: never, at any time, in all the time that I had known him, had he spoken of any of his boys in this scathing, contemptuous way. There had been those storms of temper of long ago when all the boys in turn had got their "walloping," but these had come and gone in a minute, and they had even seemed quite natural in the context of my Uncle Jimmy's household. But this was something new and different: there was a bitterness here which I found frightening and sad. My Uncle Jimmy was still shaking in his rage, his eyes were bright and furious, all signs pointed to another explosion, but suddenly Charles rose and stepped over to his father, touching him lightly on the shoulder. "Come on, Pa," he said calmly. "This isn't helping much."

But my Uncle Jimmy shook him off. Not just the words, but Charles himself: one shoulder twitched and my Uncle Jimmy wrenched himself angrily to one side. "No no no!" he cried. "Don't try to con me! What the hell am I, some kind of a monk that I'm not supposed to talk? Listen, kiddo, I'll say what I have to say, and don't you forget it! It'll be a cold day in hell when you or anybody else stuffs a gag in my mush! Don't get funny with me!"

"All right," Charles said. He seemed completely undisturbed.

"You're the doctor. It's only that I thought we had an agreement. If we didn't, that's all right too. But I thought we did."

My original guess had been a good one, then: a decision had been made that Charles was to "handle" me. The reminder of this arrangement, now made so imperturbably by Charles, had a surprising and almost immediate effect on my Uncle Jimmy. The two men continued to look at each other, Charles as calm as ever, my Uncle Jimmy still glaring, but gradually the glare changed, my Uncle Jimmy seemed to relax, and his anger slowly diminished. Diminished, not disappeared, for at least a touch of truculence remained in his voice when he spoke. He said, "You still want to play it your way, right?"

"Oh, I don't think there's much more playing to be done," Charles said agreeably. "But I think I might like to. If it's all right with you."

My Uncle Jimmy continued to look straight at him, ignoring me, but obviously the fury was gone, and it was not with a kind of dutiful grumpiness rather than anything more serious that he said, "Okay okay. Play it any way you want to. It's your funeral."

"I'll try to remember that," Charles said. "To cheer me up on my bad days." He smiled at his father, then turned back to me. "So, Jack," he said, just as if there had been no interruption at all, "if you can do that for me, I'll be grateful."

I said, "Just tell him you want him to stop. Now."

He nodded. "That's right."

"In just that way?"

He smiled again. "I don't want to cramp your style," he said. "I know how sensitive you writers are. Variations are permitted: use your imagination. I just want him to stop."

I said, "I'll give him your message."

"I hope he listens," he said. And then his voice changed slightly, just as it had earlier; he said, "Because unless he listens to someone soon, there's going to be trouble. There'll have to be."

I said, "Charles, you're threatening, aren't you?"

"Not you, certainly," he said.

"No. But Phil?"

"Yes," he said quietly. "I'm afraid I am."

My Uncle Jimmy listened closely to this; he did not say a word. And after this, there was very little for any of us to say. The atmosphere was far too uneasy for general conversation, for the kind of talk I had always had in this room; the only thing left to do was to go, and when I said this Charles did not object. We left the room together; my Uncle Jimmy shook hands, muttered a perfunctory goodbye, but did not come downstairs with us. He remained seated, and as I left the room and turned back to look at him, I saw that he had not moved, that he was still sitting sunk back in his chair and staring straight ahead.

Jean and Marie were waiting for us below: I saw Marie look at me questioningly, even anxiously, but there was no opportunity to talk to her, for we did not linger. The four of us walked out into the front yard together; I was silent, but Charles was just as he always was, pleasant, amusing, and talking rather to Jean than to me. He said goodbye to me, though, just as if nothing in the least awkward had occurred between us; he did not mention Phil or his message again.

In the car going home, even before Jean had a chance to ask me what had happened upstairs, I questioned her about Marie: what she said, how she felt. I somehow felt that in Marie there might be just the possibility of a solution, if she were approached in the right way. She was angry at Phil now, but she was fond of him; Charles loved her, it just might be . . .

But not at the moment, certainly, for Jean said, "She doesn't know anything about it. Oh, a little, but not much: *I* know more than she does. And that's odd in a way, because you know Charles: he can be cosy enough with everyone else, but he always tells Marie everything. Only this time he didn't. She says that she thinks he wants to keep her out of it altogether, or as much as he can, and that makes her think it could get fairly messy. And I guess it could, couldn't it?"

"Yes. Very messy." And I told her all about our talk in the library: about Charles's persuasiveness, about my own wavering, about my Uncle Jimmy's sudden rage. I told her everything, and when I finished she didn't say anything for a moment, then she said practically, "I don't like the sound of that at all. What's Charles got up his sleeve, do you suppose?"

"I don't know. But something, you can bet on that."

"And then Phil will do something more?"

"Maybe. Probably. Although what I don't know."

"Oh me oh my," she sighed. "Jack, Jack, how's it going to end? Badly? I just have this awful feeling that Phil's going to be hurt. Maybe it's because I've always thought that Charles was a little bit of a snake. What do you think?"

And again all I could say was, "I don't know." Because I didn't: and I didn't see anything to be gained by telling her that I had her awful feeling, too. And so we rode home, and finally, just before we got there, she began to talk about Marie's baby, this happier theme providing at least a partial and temporary distraction from her gloomy thoughts.

It had been a long day. We went to bed almost as soon as we got in the house; both of us, in spite of all preoccupations, fell asleep quickly. But the day was not over, for some time later I was awakened, just as I had been this morning, by the steady ringing of the phone. I answered quickly, thinking it was Phil, but again, just as this morning, it was my Uncle Jimmy.

"I wake you?" he said.

"It's all right, Uncle Jimmy."

"Look," he said, and then stopped. He stopped for so long that I thought we had been cut off; I said, "Uncle Jimmy?"

"Yeah, yeah," he said. "I'm here, hold your horses. What's the matter, you can't wait to get back to that sack and cork off?"

There was the characteristic truculence in his voice, but there was also something else, something unusual: it was a note of gruff embarrassment. After a moment he said, "Look, all that guff I handed you about Phil tonight: you remember?"

"I remember."

"Well, forget it," he said. "You know how it is, a man gets tired and then he gets sore, and then he shoots his mouth off. You don't need to tell him what I said."

"I didn't think I would, Uncle Jimmy."

"What the hell, he's not the worst," he said. "He's one stiff pain in the tail to me right now, I can tell you that, but he's always been a pretty good kiddo. Smart as a whip. He's just been a little nuts lately. I don't know why. Talk to him, Jack. Beat a little sense into his squash. He'll go for your line. He always did."

But I didn't know what my "line" was; I said, "I'll talk to him, Uncle Jimmy."

"I'd do it myself in a minute," he said, as if apologizing for asking for help, "only I don't know what the hell he's talking about these days. I get Charles all right, every minute. James too, when he's around. But Phil . . . I start out okay and then it's like I'm talking to some half-assed Chinaman or something and I want to bust him in the snoot! My own kiddo! You get what I mean?"

"I get what you mean, Uncle Jimmy."

"It's a hell of a note when a kiddo can't level with his own father," he said. "I don't know . . . anyway, you talk to him, Jack. Get him back here! You can do it!"

Fight talk. I said meaninglessly, "I'll talk to him, Uncle Jimmy."

"Tell him to get back soon," he said. "Or else . . . well, you know Charles. He's a sweetheart, but you can't walk all over him. Or me. By God, I . . ." And suddenly his voice started to rise ominously, but then he stopped, the voice faded off, and he said, sounding tired, "Forget it. Just talk to him, that's all. Do what you can."

And he hung up. I did too and went back to bed. Jean was

asleep, breathing heavily; dead tired, she had slept all through this talking. So I lay there awake, at first wondering if this phone call had been still another "agreement" between my Uncle Jimmy and Charles, and then at once concluding it had not. This had been my uncle, all by himself. He was a deeply troubled man. It had never occurred to me before to think of my Uncle Jimmy as being in the least a pathetic figure, and yet here he was, alone in his bedroom on the other side of the city, reaching out desperately for possible comfort. Things were going on in the family—*his* family—that he didn't comprehend; one of his boys, whom he had raised and deeply loved, was against another of his boys, about whom he felt the same; here he was, still the father of the family, still nominally the boss of the tribe, and yet for the first time he was completely powerless: all the famous savvy and the old pazazz and the right hooks right to the button suddenly turned out to be, here, of not the slightest help at all.

So that, tonight, while I thought mainly of Phil and what might happen to him, I found that it was not at all hard to think of my Uncle Jimmy, too.

thirteen

Now we all waited for what was to happen.

For quite a long time, nothing happened. During the next month we saw very little of the family. A few days after my talk with Charles, I dropped in on Phil; he didn't seem curious about anything Charles might have said, but I gave him the message anyway.

"Charles must be getting old," he said. "He's repeating himself. That's the same thing he told me a month ago."

I said, "And . . ."

"And yourself," he said. "What am I supposed to do: go into shock just because Charles puts up his hand and says, 'Red light!' Come on, Jack, that doesn't sound like you."

"I'm just being the mailman. Then what are you going to do? And when?"

"I'm going to watch just a bit longer. Then, if things get worse, or even if they don't get any better, I'll move. You'll know when I do. You still think I'm way off base?"

"It's the old story: I'm with you but I think you're making a mistake. Whatever you're going to do, I wish you wouldn't."

"I know what they call that," he said with a smile. "It's prudence and it's a virtue. But it's too late. Too late, too late!"

After this it was weeks before I saw him again, although we

talked on the phone a few times; in that same period I neither saw nor talked to Charles. He had never called to inquire about the message to Phil: I think he probably assumed that I had delivered it, and that he knew Phil's answer. My Uncle Jimmy made no such assumption, or else he was hoping against hope: he telephoned, he asked if I had seen Phil, his voice was eager. When I told him what the result had been he swore briefly and hung up without saying goodbye; I think he may have held me partly to blame.

Jean and Marie continued to meet, usually for lunch, usually on some neutral ground—a restaurant in town, say, of which they were both fond. From Jean I learned that any hope I might have had that Marie would form a bridge between the separated brothers was now doomed. For whatever reason—possibly to prepare her for what was to come—Charles had decided to tell Marie the whole story: of course as he saw it. As a consequence she was now far more bitter toward Phil. Jean had responded by defending him, and I gathered that they had reached the point of sharpness between themselves. But then both of them had stopped; they had, without actually saying so, agreed to avoid altogether this dangerous subject; they now restricted themselves to safer themes, and their friendship was maintained. But no longer on quite the same easy, unfettered footing; something had changed; Jean knew it and was sad.

One day, late in the afternoon, Flossie came to call. She was full of apologies for having written to us in such alarm; she was contrite at having summoned us back prematurely; most of all she was worried. We told her over and over again that contrition was unnecessary, that she had done quite the right thing, that we had been coming back in any case. But—curiously for Flossie—I don't think she heard much of what we said. Ordinarily the most dutiful of listeners in any family meeting, her distress had made her eloquent. She knew very little of what was going on; unlike Charles, Phil had not yet chosen to inform his wife. And so, baffled, bothered, her pretty face looking for the first time strained and pinched, her large and lovely violet eyes filled with anxiety and wonder, she talked on and on of a Phil who was now strangely up and down—suddenly lively and happy, then down and very quiet—and who, always a considerate and affectionate husband and father, was now so oddly, *tender* so that it almost broke her heart. . . .

"Because he's so good and I so want him to be happy," she cried, "and I know that something awful must be going on! Something awful for *him*. . . ."

We agonized for her, but could do little to help: so little that it amounted to nothing; at the end of that week she and Phil left for Georgia, and after this I didn't even talk to him on the phone.

And, as my Aunt Gert remained in California, and as James was now somewhere at the Vatican where—it was reported—he was to stay for some time, that took care of the family. We settled back into our own routine, and for the next month I worked on my book, making the final corrections, and bringing the completed manuscript to the publisher's office one day in early November.

"Now this is . . . splendid news!" said Andrew Pout, heavily fingering the pages. "We'll get to work on this right away. I'm sure we all . . . look forward. And I think the public is ready for it, Jack. It's a good time for suspense stories. Just between ourselves I wouldn't be a bit surprised if this turned out to be . . . The One!"

"The one what?"

He gestured vaguely, indicating immensity without limit. "It could . . . take off," he said. "Who knows?"

"*I* know. Come off it, Andrew. My books all sell about the same and you know it. We'll do about as well as *Zagreb* with this one, maybe some better, maybe some worse. But not much better, and not much worse. And we'll certainly have no best seller in any case."

A smile of really extraordinary slyness appeared momentarily on the heavy face. "Well," he said, "you know how it is. Most authors like to hear . . . things." Then, deserting fun, he returned to the mainstream; he said, "I've been working very hard since you left. Do you remember that I spoke to you about the Governor? And the possibility of our getting a book out of him?"

I nodded; he said, "Do you remember that you said you thought there wasn't much chance?"

"Yes. I remember."

"Well," he said, "I wrote to him. His reply was most . . . interesting."

And this did surprise me; I said, "You don't mean he agreed?"

"Not in so many words," he said. "But his letter was quite cordial so I'm keeping right after him. What I really need at this point is someone close to the . . . throne. To urge him on. I thought perhaps I'd approach his brother Phil on that."

It was pure Pout. I said, "Andrew, I wouldn't do that if I were you. Not right now."

"Well, I've never really felt very friendly to him of course, but in a matter of this kind I've always believed in putting personal feelings to one side. Because I have a hunch, Jack, that what we may have here is more than a book." He looked at me solemnly and said, "It could be a . . . document."

There seemed nothing to say to this. I sat there and in a moment he said, "You don't feel I'm going over your head, I hope?"

"No no, not in the least . . ."

"Because when I first mentioned it to you, you may remember that you didn't show much . . . enthusiasm." He added with sudden practicality, "At least nothing happened. So I thought we might as well explore another avenue."

"All the same, I wouldn't be in a hurry, if I were you. This really isn't the best time."

At this there was another smile, not sly this time, but very small and somehow infinitely complacent. "I'm not at all sure of that, Jack," he said. "You learn one great thing about time in this business."

"That there's no time like the present?"

It was a feat of divination which, I think, genuinely staggered him; his heavy features wobbled. "Exactly," he said finally. "*Exactly. . . .*"

It was on the day after this that the first blow was struck—and it was struck by Phil.

It was a Tuesday morning: bright, clear, November blue. I was having breakfast and reading the paper. I was reading slowly, casually, not really paying attention to what I was reading, because half the time I was thinking about the rest of the day and what I would do with it. This was a feeling I always had when, after a long stretch of working on a book, the book was done, and then, just as if I had never suspected that one day it would be done, I suddenly realized—happily, unhappily, confusedly—that now there was nothing to do. It was a feeling that each time took a little getting used to. Jean had come down and was busy in the pantry; I had reached the editorial page and was skipping over the columns of the letters to the editor when I was stopped by the heading on the first of them. It read: PRAISE FOR OUR GOVERNOR? As I say, I wasn't paying full attention, and at first glance I missed the question mark, so that when I began to read I wondered what Charles was being praised for now. I had read no more than two sentences, however, when I saw that this letter was far from an encomium; on the contrary it was an urbane and extremely sharp attack on Charles for a recent appointment he had made to the bench of the Juvenile Court. In a way it was a fascinating letter: superficially courteous to both Charles and the new judge, it was murderous in its implications. It commended Charles for his continued concern for troubled youth, a concern which—it reminded the reader—had been stressed so repeatedly in his campaign addresses; it complimented him on his respect for the virtue of perseverance, so pre-eminently a part of the judge, and perhaps never better displayed than in his dogged early attempts to pass the bar examinations; it rebuked those opponents who suggested that the judge was unqualified for his new post by reminding them that he had perhaps the supreme qualification for dealing with the problems of the young: he had once been a boy himself. The letter closed by congratulating Charles on this ". . . bold and unorthodox appointment, the effects of which we will doubtless soon begin to feel."

It was signed simply "Edmund Burke"; instantly I knew that it had been written by Phil.

I handed the paper to Jean, pointing to the letter, saying nothing. She read it quickly, frowned, read it again. Then she said, "Phil?"

"I'm afraid so. The opening gun. A warning, I suppose, more than anything else—that's why the fake name. Just imagine what that letter would do if he signed it with his own name."

She said, "Oh dear." She sat down and read through the letter again slowly; she said, "Now what?"

"I don't know. I suppose the next move is up to Charles. If he moves at all, and I can't believe that he won't. But how or where I haven't any idea."

The next three days brought nothing new. There were no more letters from "Edmund Burke"; there were no answers to the first letter. There was, in short, no controversy whipped up in the correspondence columns, and this seemed to me to be good. I called Phil's house several times but no one answered: I didn't even know whether he and Flossie had returned from Georgia. Just after dark on the third day Jean and I drove over by their house; we saw that all the lights were on and, after a short debate, we decided to go in. But we were met at the door by the maid, who told us that Phil and Flossie had gone out to dinner and that she didn't know when they'd return—there had been some talk of going on to a movie. I asked if they had just come back to the city; she said they had been back for about a week. And so we left; as we did I left a message for Phil to call me when he got in that night.

We waited until midnight before we went to bed; there was no call. It came somewhere in the middle of the following morning.

"Hi," he said. "What's up? We're back."

"So I see. I also see that you've been writing."

"That's a switch," he said. "Isn't that what I'm supposed to say to you? Well, speaking as a pro, how did you like it? Did you admire my choice of pseudonym? I thought it suited the sinuous winding style."

He sounded lighthearted and also rather excited. I said, "Any reaction?"

"From Charles, you mean? Yes: one phone call. Would you like to hear a verbatim account?"

"Very much."

"It wasn't a long call: somehow we managed to skip the amenities. But he called that morning—it must have been right after he'd seen the paper. I'd told him what I was going to do, you see."

"You told him."

"Yes. Well, I didn't want to make too much of a sneak attack out of it. I didn't tell him what the letter was about or exactly when it would be coming; I just let him know in a general way that it was on the agenda. So that morning he called and said, 'Phil, that was you, wasn't it?' He wasn't in a rage or anything like that: just very businesslike. I said yes, it was me. He said, 'All right, Phil. No more. That's the end. I mean it.' I said, 'That's more or less up to you, isn't it?' He said, 'No no, we're done with that kind of talk. Just no more, that's all. I want you to agree to that. Now.' So I said, 'No. I'm sorry.' And he said, 'So am I.' Then, just before he hung up, he said, 'By the way, your timing is terrible.' And that was it."

"What does that mean? Terrible how? And for you or for him?"

"Who knows?" he said indifferently. "Anyway, that was the phone call, word for word, and nothing has happened since. I imagine he'll think of something, though. And then, so will I."

"I know. That's what I'm afraid of."

He laughed. "Don't worry. I'll keep you posted every step of the way. Listen, I can't talk any more: I've got to run." He laughed again. "Shades of the past," he said. "Do you know who I'm running to? The Abominable Abdominal. For the annual."

It was the name they had always given to the physician whom they had gone to since they were boys. His name was really Anthony Montgomery—Charles, James and Phil used to chant: "He's beautifully versed in medical flummery, the Abominable Abdominal Anthony Montgomery!" He was, roughly, my Uncle Jimmy's age and once, long ago, had cured him of some mysterious ailment; as a result my Uncle Jimmy had enormous confidence in him, and from the very beginning—despite the sudden proliferation of specialists and clinics in the city—he had sent the boys to him for all their ailments and for their annual examination. As they were seldom sick, this annual visit became their principal contact with Dr. Montgomery; I remembered now that for some reason it had always taken place in November; they used to joke about it in college, but apparently it had never been abandoned. I said, "Is that still going on?"

"Oh sure. The Abominable Abdominal is one of the family now. Well, keep in touch. And give my love to that pretty girl you're married to."

And he was gone. I told Jean what he had said, and for a long time we talked about him and his plans, guessing about them and worrying about them, and in the end coming back to wondering exactly what we had been wondering for the last three days: just how Charles would act, and when.

He showed us two days later. When his move came it was totally unexpected, it was swift, it was unbelievably harsh, and in the end—as it turned out—it was decisive.

We were at home; it was in the afternoon. I had been reading, Jean drawing. The telephone rang; Jean answered. I heard her say with just a touch of surprise, "Flossie!" There was a pause; then, first puzzled, then alarmed, she said, "Flossie? Flossie? I can't hear you. . . ."

I looked up quickly; she was beckoning me hurriedly to come and take the phone; I jumped up and went over, saying, "What?"

"I don't know, I can't make it out. Something about Phil, but I can't understand her. She's crying. . . ."

I said into the phone, "Flossie? It's Jack."

"Jack, Jack, Jack!" she said. "*Oh* Jack!" It was more of a moan than anything else, and then she began to sob so loudly and so uninterruptedly that she couldn't have possibly said a word and I couldn't have heard her even if she did. It was a terrible sound of apparently unstoppable heartbreak: she cried on and on.

I said, shouting, "Flossie! Please *tell me*. . . ."

"*Oh* Jack!" she said again, in the same moaning voice. "Oh Jack, I don't, I can't . . . it's not *true*. People don't do this . . . he came to the house this afternoon, this *dreadful* man . . . and I saw him and Phil saw him . . . and then he told Phil . . . it was awful, Jack, awful awful awful. . . ."

She was hysterical; I had no notion of what might have happened; I didn't know how Phil was or where he was; I said as urgently and as loudly as I could, "Flossie, let me talk to Phil!"

And suddenly she stopped crying for a moment and said, very clearly, right in the middle of her hysterics, "He's not here now. He said he was going out to walk for a while." And after this surprising, quiet, matter-of-fact statement she began to cry again. I felt slightly better; at least he wasn't injured or even worse—which was of course a thought that had immediately seized me. I said, as if I were gripping her by the shoulders, "Please, Flossie, I know it's not easy, but just *try* to tell me what's happened! Just try!"

And now, crying again, but less wildly now, she told me—and

when she did I understood why she wept. I was surprised that she could even talk with any coherence at all. For this afternoon, not half an hour ago, Phil had been notified officially, personally, that an application had been filed for his commitment to a mental institution. It had been filed by Charles Kinsella.

And then, while Flossie continued alternately to weep and to hurtle through words and phrases I now seemed to hear in only the dimmest way, and while Jean stared at me amazed and nearly frantic with curiosity and apprehension, I simply stood there, immobilized and dumb. I think that for that brief interval I was in fact completely and literally paralyzed, so that I couldn't move my body, I couldn't say a word, I couldn't even think. All I could do was repeat to myself the single catastrophic statement, as if somehow the sheer repetition would make it better, or more, might even make it go away. It was the kind of moment I'd had just twice before in my life: the first time when I was a little boy and had at last realized that I would never see my mother again; the second, just a few years ago and just a few feet from where I stood now, when I learned that Jean had left me. In rare and terrible moments like these I think a small annihilation takes place, so that a part of you is burned away and never quite comes back, although at the instant of its happening nothing at all is felt, but only a frozen numbness. And this is what happened to me now, not quite in the same way of course, not quite as powerfully, but still it was powerful enough so that there I was, standing still and stunned. I continued to stand there with the telephone in my hand, held against my ear; it was as if everything in me had come to a complete stop.

Jean was talking now, talking rapidly, asking questions; in my ear I heard Flossie's voice, not sobbing now but calling my name loudly, insistently—my silence must have struck this desolated woman as still another ominous development in the already unbearable situation—and finally I came to, I began to realize that I had to act, to do something, to help Phil, to comfort Flossie, to tell Jean, but first of all I had to tell myself. Because Charles was a determined man, I knew that, but to believe that he would have gone this far to protect his position, that he would even have thought of having his brother certified as *mad*—this was something new, something that took me into a different, bewildering, ugly dimension: one in which none of us—Phil, Charles, my Uncle Jimmy, myself—seemed to belong at all. I said, "Flossie, I'm coming over. Right now."

"Yes," she said dully. "Oh Jack, I'm so *frightened*. There was this man and he gave Phil this paper, this awful paper, and then I saw it . . . Jack, Phil's got to go to a hearing, a *sanity* hearing. . . ."

She began to cry again, and who could blame her? I said, "Flossie: where is Phil now?"

"Out walking," she said, her ravaged voice sounding hopeless. "He talked to me for a while, and then he said he didn't want to talk about it any more until he had a chance to think. So he went out for this walk, and I'm here in the house. He ought to be back soon. . . ."

I said, "Stay right there, Flossie. Don't go anywhere. I'll come over this minute. Then we'll talk, all of us. We'll talk it all over, and we'll fix everything. All right?"

I was talking to her as if she were a little girl; she replied as if she were. "All right," she said obediently. "All right, Jack. Only hurry because I don't know what I'm going to *do*. . . ."

I hung up, and quickly told Jean just what Flossie had told me. She flinched just as if she'd been hit, and her eyes closed; she said in a pained voice, "Oh *Jack*. He *couldn't*." And then, immediately, less certainly, she said, "Could he?"

I nodded slowly. "I guess he could. And from what Flossie said I guess he did."

"But what would make him do *any*thing like that? I mean, he was never my favorite, you know that, but he's not a monster. And to Phil, his own *brother*!"

I shook my head, because I didn't know. And yet already, although I was still telling myself that it was all incredible, that it couldn't be what it appeared to be, I had already begun to accept it as a fact, for suddenly, as we were getting in the car—Jean had decided to come too—I said, "But there's this: *of course he can't get away with it.* Hasn't anybody thought about that? He just can't do it: there are laws about these things. You can't put a man away simply because it's inconvenient for you to have him around during an election. It just isn't that easy!"

She said, "Not even if you're the Governor?"

"No, not even if you're the Governor. And especially if the man you've decided to railroad is someone like Phil, who's a good lawyer, a rich man, and has a few other things working for him as well. No, I don't see it at all!"

We talked along this line on our drive to Phil's; it was at least more encouraging than any other. The ride was not a long one, I drove very quickly, and perhaps not more than fifteen minutes had passed from the time I'd finished talking to Flossie until we reached the house. But we were not quick enough: when we got there we found that Flossie had gone and so had Phil. The maid said that Phil had come back from his walk, had talked briefly to Flossie, and then they had driven off together, not saying where they were going or when they would be back. And this was unlike Phil: as long as I'd known him he'd never deliberately evaded me, and I wished that now, of all times, he hadn't. Still, it was understandable, I suppose: this surprise tactic of Charles's, so flatly ruthless, must have shaken him severely, for I was sure that as well as this intelligent, imaginative man knew his brother, he had not been prepared for anything remotely like this. So then, he would probably want to be alone or with Flossie; with anyone else —even me—he would have to say something, to review the story, when now, almost certainly, all he wanted to do was not to talk at all.

We left and drove back home. We went into my study and sat

there; we didn't talk much. At first I thought a call might come at any minute: it would be from Phil, it would in a few clear sentences tell me everything I wanted so badly to know, it would suggest a meeting. But no such call came, and as the minutes went by I knew it was not going to come. For some reason I now began to grow apprehensive; I began to go over in my mind everything that Flossie had said to me, even trying to remember the different inflections of her broken voice. But there was nothing in this, nothing that I hadn't considered before, and so I told myself and I told Jean once again that there was nothing to worry about in the long run, that what had happened was cruel but essentially preposterous: a threat and nothing more.

It was true, and yet I found myself much more alarmed now than I had been earlier—why, I don't know. The afternoon was now almost over; I could look from my study window and see the autumn sun sliding down steadily behind the hills to the west, and then, suddenly, it was quite dark. I thought of Charles; I wondered if he would still be in his office, and thought it probable that he would—as Governor he kept long hours. I wondered what would happen if I put in a call to him now, and instantly I felt a strong desire to do just that, a desire that left me quickly as soon as I realized that now I wouldn't know what to say to him, I wouldn't even know how to begin. Because of course what he had done today had changed everything for all of us; nothing was the same any more; even a tone of voice that I had used to him all my life would have been unthinkable today. . . .

An hour went by, more than an hour. Occasionally we talked, but not often, and when we did it was always about the one thing. Tension grew; we both felt it; Jean said, "Jack, I can't stand it: call Phil."

I called him three times within the next half-hour; the maid answered each time; she had not heard a word from either Phil or Flossie. After this Jean decided to go upstairs for a while—I think just to help break the strain of sitting here, waiting—and after she went I made one more call. This time it was not to Phil; it was to an old friend of mine, a lawyer, a soft-spoken, sharp-minded man who—I now remembered—had done a great deal of work in the kind of thing in which Phil now seemed caught up. We chatted for a moment; then, after the preliminaries, I told him that I was working on a book and needed to know something about commitment procedures. I said, "If you want to put anyone away, isn't it apt to be a rather tricky business? Complicated, hard?"

"Oh no," he said. "Most people think it is, but it isn't. In fact nothing's easier. It happens all the time."

It was not what I wanted to hear; I said, "I thought there had to be a tremendous rigmarole. . . ."

"No no. If you want to put someone away all you need is a certificate signed by two physicians saying he's mentally ill. You file it with the court and you're on your way. Or he's on his way. It's very simple."

But I objected. "It's too simple for me. You mean to say he has no redress? Isn't there some sort of hearing . . . ?"

"Oh, there's a hearing. He's notified by the court that the application's been filed and that he has forty-eight hours to request a hearing. He can have his lawyer, other medical opinion, that sort of thing. It's all provided for."

"You sound as though you don't think much of it."

"I don't," he said. "These sanity hearings leave a good bit to be desired. Sanity, insanity, the area in between: no judge really knows too much about that. I've always found that the original complaint and the certificate from the two doctors can be fairly big medicine to most judges. No, I'm not happy about it. I've seen a good many people go off who in my judgment had no business going."

"Railroaded?"

"Not necessarily, although there's that too, of course. I'll give you a piece of advice, Jack: if anybody ever tries to put you away, make sure you have a very good lawyer."

I thought of Phil and his special gifts and felt better; I said, "So that if you're not crazy and you have a good lawyer on your side, you have nothing to worry about?"

"I didn't say that, did I? Because if I did I didn't mean to. No, it's more a matter of your chances being somewhat better. . . ."

It was in no sense a reassuring talk.

I sat in the darkness for some time, reminding myself that of course there were all sorts of safeguards, that Phil was in no danger, yet all the time my feeling of alarm continued to grow. I was troubled by Phil himself; I was troubled by Charles, who did not go in for empty threats; and then I think I was troubled most of all by a vague persisting fear of the word "madness" itself, applied to someone who was close to me, whom I had known so well. This was an old terror of mine; it came and went; it began I suppose in my childhood, when I didn't yet understand what it was, but knew that it had already played a part in my life. It was a suspicion that grew as I grew: it grew into a question that I had often asked myself, but one I had never asked aloud until I hinted at it with my father, literally almost in his dying moments.

It was in the hospital; it was in fact the day before he died. I remember that we were alone in his room: it was a day of sunshine and soft breezes; it was in the afternoon. By his bedside was a luncheon tray, untouched. He no longer bothered to eat. He was very thin, but strangely the thinness did not show in his face, so that when the covers were pulled up around him he did not look greatly changed. He was weak, but he wanted to talk: about me, my prospects. He had never talked much about money, but now, for the first time, he told me of what could come to me on his death. It was a surprising sum—his own resources were hardly a shadow of what they once had been, and I had simply assumed that there would be very little left to me: I was quite wrong—and while I was of course not in the same bracket as Charles or Phil, nevertheless this income, plus what I earned from my books, left me very comfortably situated. So it was good news, in a way, but sad news too, because I knew that my father was telling it to me only because he knew he was so close to the end. I got up from the chair and walked over to the window; I was very close to tears. In a moment my father called me back, motioning me to sit down again; he said, "Well, I'm pleased with you, Jack. That's all I want to tell you. And your mother would have been pleased with you too."

I looked at him and then I said, not even then quite asking the question, "About Mom . . ." I didn't complete it, and my father looked back at me for a long time: in all our lives together we had never talked about this. Then he said simply, "I don't know, Jack. I never knew. You see, she was so different from anybody else I ever knew. She had these times when she was so sad it would break your heart, but she always came out of them. You never saw her much then. The doctors used different words: 'unstable' was one. One of them once said I ought to put her in a place for a while; I almost killed him. Because I never wanted her away from me—from us—at all. I suppose that was selfish. Even worse. But I couldn't have stood that. Because, bad times and good, she was all the world to me, and when she went, I guess that was the end of the world for me. Except for you, Jack. You made it worthwhile. I thank you for that now." He grabbed my hand and held it; then I saw pain come into his eyes and he said, "But about the other: I just don't know. . . ."

And as it turned out, that was the last talk we ever had. I thought about it now; I thought about it for a long time. Later, when Jean came down, I didn't mention it to her.

We ate early: a quick and troubled meal. She said, "I don't like this. Let's go over there again. Let's just wait until they come back."

I was against this for several reasons. I told them to her, but she was unexpectedly stubborn. She said, "We can't just sit. We've got to do *something.*"

"Yes, but not *that*. . . ."

And so, ironically, provoked by the tension, in the middle of trying to help out in this family bitterness, we fell into mild argument ourselves. It did not continue long, however; it was interrupted by an unexpected visitor—a visitor miles removed from all our present problems. This was Arthur: he had taken to dropping in every so often, just to talk. He came at all hours, day or night, always unannounced: his schedule seemed to depend upon the availability of the married daughter who drove him. She sat outside in the car, refusing—or perhaps forbidden?—to come in while Arthur rambled through the past and told us his plans and discussed his duties around the property in the weeks to come. But these duties had shrunk vastly, even in the last few months, for Arthur had suddenly come to be a very old man—prematurely, it seemed to me; I sent him to a doctor, there was a diagnosis of circulatory trouble, the danger was not immediate, but there would be slow and steady retrogression—and so the visits ended mostly in talk about my father and my mother and the good old days, which to Arthur all might have taken place a minute and a half ago.

". . . so there I was and what was a man to do? Your pa was always a great one for that little airplane he had, Mister Jack. But your ma hated it. Well, she thought he'd kill himself in it. Or fall out of it. The reason you never went up in the air with him, or little Tommy neither, was she wouldn't let him take you. Once he tried but she started to cry so of course he didn't. Now, here's something I never told you. Not till this minute. One day, on a day just like this one, all bright and shiny and no wind, your pa and me . . ."

But he was wrong: he had told me, often. And as often as he'd told it I'd enjoyed hearing it: the story of the terrified Arthur and his one and only flight with my father. But tonight, as this good old man talked on and on about the only things that mattered to him and about what had always mattered so much to me, I could hardly bear it. Jean had left politely but quickly on some pretext; Arthur had not much noticed: he liked her, but she was not a part of these voyages into the past. I was; leaning forward, his old, smooth, cherry-bright face now close to mine, his eyes invaded with reminiscence, he watched me closely as he talked, it was important that I should miss nothing, not the slightest detail, and I, knowing the story so well, seemed to listen but did not, and against the background of the familiar words, against the vision of my young and eager father and the young reluctant Arthur towing the silver monoplane out onto the fresh green field, I could think only of what was facing us all now, tonight, and wonder with increasing desperation if somehow, some way, there wasn't something I could do.

And there was. It came to me almost as his story was ending. I could hear—or really, half-hear—the old voice building for the final moment, the big surprise, when suddenly I knew, with absolute certainty, that there was now just one thing for me to do. It would not be pleasant; it might not even help—but it had to be done, and I had to do it. I felt this so surely, so strongly that I could hardly wait for Arthur to leave; he had finished his story, he was ready to go, but he was lingering, and I think that for the first time in my life I hustled him out of the house quickly. Too quickly, I'm sure; I saw him look at me with some bewilderment as he slipped into the seat beside his waiting daughter. But I was too busy, too anxious to think about this now; I hurried back into the house and called Jean; when she came down I told her what I was going to do. I was going, right now, to Charles's house. If he was not there, I would wait until he came; if he was there, I would see him right away. Either way, at some point in the next few hours, we would have it out about Phil.

She said only, "I'm coming with you."

So then, we drove to Charles's together, just as a few hours before we had driven to Phil's. As we turned in toward the house I saw the official car parked in front of the house: in all probability, then, Charles was at home. We pulled up some distance behind it, and as we were getting out Jean suddenly touched my arm; I looked and saw that she was pointing down that section of the gravel drive which ran along the side of the house. Another car was parked there, which I hadn't noticed as we had come up. It was perhaps fifty feet from us, but even in the darkness I recognized it immediately: it was Phil's.

"Now what?" she said. "Does that change anything?"

I thought for a moment, and then said, "I don't think so, no. We're here; we might just as well stay. Besides, whatever this is, I think I want to be in on it."

We rang the bell; no one answered. This was odd, because there were the cars, the house was brightly lighted, and whenever any of the family were here the chauffeur or one of the maids was always around. But in the end, after we rang a second time, it was Marie herself who answered, and when she saw us I'm sure that for just a second or two she didn't know what to do. It was the first time I had ever seen her at anything like a loss; I saw the surprise on her handsome face, then dismay, then—I thought—a certain relief. And before she said anything I said, "Your problem is this: you can't very well say you're not at home, can you?"

She smiled faintly and said, "I'll tell you this: I wish we weren't. Come on in. I'm sorry if I didn't exactly glow but . . . it's not quite a normal night. As you know." We came into the hall; she closed the door behind us and said, "Everybody's upstairs."

"Everybody meaning who? You and Charles and Phil? Is Flossie here too?"

She nodded. "And Jimmy. Everybody."

"Does that mean you think everybody's there who should be there?" I said. "I hope not, because I'd rather like to be up there too."

She sighed and said, "Enough that's crazy has already happened around here. Do you think I'm going to start in now to tell you that you and Jean can't come into my own house? Or into any part of it? Go on up, Jack. We'll all go up, and with a little luck maybe we'll all come down. It may even be better with you there. God knows it couldn't be much worse."

We all began our walk up the stairs; for some reason I went first, with Marie and Jean following side by side. They said a few words to each other in low voices—what, I didn't hear. Near the top of the stairs I saw that the library doors were open; I could hear several voices all talking at once, then a pause, then Phil alone. There was no shouting: just voices. As I stood on the top step, Marie said, "Jack?"

I turned; she said, "Just one thing: don't gang up on Charles. I wouldn't like that at all."

It was half request, half warning; I said, "No ganging up. But you've got to know this: I'm not on his side on this one."

"Give me a little credit," she said. "I know which way the wind blows with you, Jack. It blows the same way it's always blown. But now don't let it blow too hard. I'm saying this to you only because I don't want what would happen then to happen. To all of us." She looked, not at me, but at Jean; then in a moment she said slowly, "It's not as simple as you think. Give Charles a little credit, too."

Then she motioned, and we went down the hall to the open doors. She led the way into the room: no one now was talking. First of all I saw my Uncle Jimmy. He was the only one in the room who was standing; he didn't see us immediately as we came in, for he was turned away from the door and from all the others and was staring moodily into the fire. Charles was seated by the fireplace, not far away from his father; he rose as we entered and came toward us, smiling slightly. We must have been a surprise to him as well as to the others; he gave no sign of this. Phil and Flossie were seated some distance away, much farther than was usual in such a small gathering—it was as if so much square footage of Chinese rug had been agreed upon as a no-man's-land; they were on the small couch directly under the large painting of my Aunt Mary. I thought Flossie looked dreadful: drawn, much older, obviously fresh from weeping. When we came in Phil did not get up but raised one hand and said conversationally, "Flossie told me about the phone call; sorry we couldn't wait around. I had an appointment."

He gave no further explanation; it was all implication. I noticed now that his other hand was holding Flossie's; she was sitting very close to him. Charles greeted us pleasantly, as if we had come to a dinner party, and asked us if we wanted a drink; my Uncle Jimmy had turned now and nodded shortly to us—nothing more. It was impossible to tell whether he was displeased by our arrival or whether he was merely sustaining the mood which had been there before we came. We sat down; so did Charles and Marie; everyone was now seated with the exception of my Uncle Jimmy, who still stood in his position by the fireplace, but now faced the room and the rest of us, still saying nothing, and looking neither furious nor glum, but peculiarly sour and blighted.

Then followed perhaps the most uncomfortable interval of my life. It could not have lasted long; it seemed eternal. For maybe a minute we simply sat there, and my Uncle Jimmy stood, no one saying a word or making a sound: it was as if we had all been forbidden to fracture this covering of unease, as if there had been some fearful penalty promised to anyone who dared interfere with the spirit of the ghastly occasion. And so we sat, simply looking at each other or at ourselves, like so many apprehensive children in an ogre's schoolroom.

And then, suddenly, this interval was over. It came to an end because Phil brought it to an end; still seated on the couch he broke the spell by speaking specifically to Jean and me.

"Just to put you in the picture," he said. "Before you arrived, we were having a little family discussion, in the most general terms, about the booby hatch."

I saw Flossie flinch; I saw too that Phil continued to hold her very tightly by the hand. He went on, talking as easily and pleasantly as if he were talking about a movie he had just seen or a plan he was suggesting for a family vacation; he said, "We found we couldn't agree. Well, that's understandable: we were approaching it from different ends of the stick. Charles represented society at large; on the other hand, I spoke as a potential inmate. It made a small difference. I suppose in a sense we were all interested parties; what we really needed was someone to come along to be neutral, to arbitrate. Someone who was uncommitted—although come to think of it I don't find that an especially congenial word at the moment. Anyway, here we were, talking away, but facing all the while a single basic difficulty: we were trying to conduct a rational discussion, the purpose of which was to establish that one of us was irrational." He looked across at Charles and said, "Wouldn't you say that was a fair statement of the case?"

Marie said, in a tired voice, "Oh, Phil . . ."

But Charles put up a hand, quieting her; he said calmly, "Tell it your own way, Phil."

"Enough rope, right?" Phil said. Then he turned back to me and said, "Background material, Jack. At the risk of boring the others. There I was, at half past three this afternoon, reading away in my study, bent on self-improvement, trying for the nine hundred and twenty-first time to get past the halfway mark in *Moby Dick,* when a man I'd never seen before, a middle-aged man of pleasant appearance, came in through the door and handed me a piece of paper which told me, among other things, that I was insane! Well, Jack, a thing like that can shake your day. Has it ever happened to you? I don't suppose it has, has it?"

He paused and looked at me expectantly. He was playing a game, he was playing it his way, and apparently I was to play too. He was waiting; it was impossible simply to remain silent; I said awkwardly, "It hasn't, no."

"Well, it might," he said earnestly. "It just might, Jack. After all, you know some of the same people I do, and one thing has a way of leading to another. And if it should, I haven't any idea of how you'd feel, but let me tell you how I felt. Just in case. I felt *surprised.* Genuinely surprised, and yet I guess I shouldn't have felt that way, because for most of our lives Charles and I have been giving each other surprises. You know, the way brothers do. We used to see which one could surprise each other the most; I'd say it was about even-Stephen all through the year. Until now, that is. Charles took all the marbles with this one. Because after all, if you really want to give your brother a surprise that's original, that's different, that's completely unexpected, what could possibly be better than a one-way ticket to the funny farm?"

And now he seemed to be addressing all of us, not just Jean and me, looking around the room with his manner a mask of polite inquiry, and with his attack on Charles mounting and becoming less oblique by the minute. I had no notion of what he was really up to at this point; all I did know was that whatever it was, I had no place in it: my plan of coming over to intercede with Charles, to somehow take charge and shape events now seemed a simple absurdity. Because I now saw very clearly what I had really known all along: that this was a matter for two men only, and that no one else counted at all—not even my Uncle Jimmy. It was all between the brothers. . . .

Phil continued to look around politely, as if asking if there were any comments, any questions; there was a moment when he looked straight at me and we held each other's eyes, and for just that instant I felt what I had sometimes felt before with Phil: a peculiar sadness which now was much stronger than ever before. It was like being a spectator at a drowning: a helpless spectator, unable in any way to prevent the tragedy that was to come, and yet at the same time feeling that this tragedy need not come if only one of the other spectators—a particular one—would merely raise his voice or lift a finger. But nobody spoke and nobody moved. My Uncle Jimmy's face was now pure stone. Marie was angry, clearly aching to move in against Phil, but just as clearly being held back by something—presumably firm instructions from Charles. Poor Flossie seemed to have shrunk back even farther into the couch, a constant in misery, her hand still held in Phil's grip. I did not dare to look at Jean. Charles had not changed a bit since we had come into the room: he sat in the chair, one leg crossed over the other; he was calm, not unfriendly, listening, waiting. He seemed absolutely sure of himself, confident of what was to happen, and looking at him now, I found it almost impossible to imagine that he could lose.

Phil went on, coming back once more to me.

"I'll tell you a funny one, Jack," he said. "This'll hand you a laugh. At first I thought the whole thing was a joke! I did, I really did. Well, I couldn't see what else it could possibly be. But then I read the paper again and then I saw that it wasn't a joke, that nobody was kidding at all. It was an authentic Coop-Him-Up-and-Right-Away certificate, duly signed by Charles, two doctors, and a judge. That's an interesting parlay, isn't it? But do you know what's even more interesting? One of the doctors was none other than my old friend and family medicine man, the Abominable Abdominal Montgomery himself. You remember I had a date for a physical earlier this week? Well, apparently Charles remembered it too." He looked at Charles with something that approached admiration; he said, "Fast work. You know it wasn't until I got that certificate that I understood your crack about my timing being terrible." He said to me, "I should explain: a certificate of mental illness, in order to be valid, has to be signed within five days of the actual examination. I got mine in two. Fast service. Incidentally, that exam was fairly peculiar; I thought old Montgomery and his quick stooge had both gone senile, but I guess it was only their brand of psychiatry. So there we had the doctors, and then of course there remained the judge. Well, Jack, I know you'll be pleased to learn that the judge who did the signing was none other than my old friend Probate Court Justice Charles E.

Kilrane! And once that was done, nothing remained but to wish me Godspeed and a safe ride to the bughouse. Isn't that tidy? So the only thing for me to do is say goodbye, and possibly to ask one little question. I'd like to ask you that question, Charles. If you have no objection?"

He paused again, this time as if it had become necessary for him to receive permission before he could proceed with his question: it was a parody of courtesy. For a second Charles did nothing; then I saw him give the faintest of nods, and Phil said in a clear, but flatter and colder voice, "What in the name of God makes you think I'll let you get away with it?"

So here it was at last: the challenge. The two brothers now sat looking at each other; the silence and tension in the room increased so that it really seemed that we all could hear each other breathing. I glanced quickly at Jean; she didn't see me. Her hands were gripped tightly in her lap; she was looking only at Charles. So was everyone else; so, now, was I. And he said slowly, "You see, it's the wrong question, Phil. I'm not trying to get away with anything. But I don't want to play word games with you. What you're really asking me is can I make the certificate stick. And I say of course I can. And without much trouble."

"You think so?" Phil said. "Think again, Charles. I don't know how you bamboozled this pathetic old clown Montgomery to sign this thing for you. I don't want to know. And of course Kilrane is contemptible. If you choose to play with him that's your affair, but don't for five seconds think that this shabby junta can put the boots to me. You just can't work it, Charles!"

Charles said patiently, "You're still using the wrong words. I'm not out to work anything. I could if I wanted to; I'm the Governor; it's a position not without its advantages. And if I found myself pinched I imagine I could throw a little weight around. But I don't have to here, because this isn't at all the simple frameup you make it out to be. This is on the level, Phil. I mean it. I filed that petition because it was necessary. And I didn't have to beat the Abominable with a rubber hose to get him to sign. You did all my work for me. I talked to him, yes, but what did the damage was the fact that you talked to him too. About me; I think he began by thinking you were slightly intemperate; I think he ended by thinking something else. You talked too much, Phil; that's sometimes a failing of yours. And so the Abominable signed, and so did his associate. And as for Judge Kilrane, I didn't go after him because I wanted a malleable judge. I didn't need to. Any judge would have signed this; any judge would have had to. There was my complaint; there were the signatures of the two doctors. It would have been automatic. I took Kilrane simply because he was the first judge I was able to reach, and in view of certain actions of yours I thought I'd better move quickly. And that's all there was to it."

"No soap," Phil said. "*Non credo*, Charles. Not for a bloody minute. I know exactly why you went after Kilrane. Don't hand me that fair-minded level-voiced garbage about his being selected simply because he was available. You picked him for two reasons. One, he'd sign fast and no questions asked; two, if he signed, he'd be the one who'd sit at the hearing. Judge Charles E. Kilrane would have the final say as to whether I did or did not go away. Didn't you think of that, Charles? Just a little? And if you did think of it, didn't you also—purely by chance, of course—mention to the judge, just in case he might have forgotten, that I was once the lawyer for Augie Benedictis? It did occur to me that you might have done just that little thing!"

And for the first time I saw a change in Charles's eyes; for a moment I thought the imperturbability might break, and maybe it might indeed have done so, but just then Marie got quickly to her feet. Her eyes were literally blazing; her face was filled with fury; and at that moment, even with everything that was going on, I found myself marveling at how really beautiful she was.

"I've had enough!" she said, her voice shaking. "I don't want any more of this! This is my house! You listen to me, Phil—"

"No," Phil said firmly. "No, I won't listen to you, Marie. There just isn't time. Don't you see that? You're a wonderful girl and I love you and all that and I'm sorry if I'm hurting you, but I won't listen to you now because this is all between Charles and me. And if you don't believe me ask your husband!"

Marie spun around to face Charles, who by now seemed perfectly cool and self-possessed again. He smiled at her and once more made that little quieting motion with his hand. He said, "I'll handle it. But thanks."

It was done quickly and pleasantly, so that while it seemed as if in this one instance he was really agreeing with Phil, at the same time he wasn't in the least rebuking or diminishing his wife. He seemed to be genuinely thanking her for what she had said, and to be indicating that now he would carry on from there. Certainly Marie seemed to understand, for she sat down, still angry, but saying nothing more, and Charles said to Phil, "There are two things you don't seem to understand, Phil. The first is that the ball game's over. I'm going to do what I said I'd do, and nothing you can do now is going to make any difference at all. It's too late for anything like that; you can't do a thing. And the second thing you don't understand is what I've done and why I've done it. You think it's a frame. You've got a story about the heartless politician who's suddenly willing to ship his own brother off to an asylum, simply because he's become a political inconvenience. Well, it's an appealing story, it makes good listening, but it's not true. Here's what is true, Phil. I'm doing this because you've forced me to. Quite literally, I have no other choice. I'm doing it because I have to do it, and because I also think it's the right thing to do. I'm not cynical about this; I'm not sending you away, all the while knowing that you're perfectly all right, that there's nothing wrong. Listen to me, Phil: the plain fact is that I believe something is wrong. I believe that you should be sent away. And I believe that you should be sent away for the reason that people are usually sent away. Now is that plain enough for you? Because that's what I believe!"

I heard Flossie gasp; I myself was not unaffected. Once more I realized how enormously convincing Charles was in these close-up encounters; it was extremely difficult not to believe him. And I saw that even Phil, who must have seen him so often with others in moments like this, was now looking curiously at him, as if trying to make up his mind, just for this instant, if there was or was not truth in what he heard. He shook his head quickly, and said, "I want you to say it in so many words, Charles. I want to hear you tell me that you think I should be confined. I want to hear you tell me, quite simply, that you really believe I'm mad!"

And again there was the great silence from everyone, and then Charles said slowly, "Mad, crazy: these are hard words to define, aren't they? I don't know what a really precise diagnosis would say about you, Phil. You don't tear your hair, you don't roll your eyes, you don't foam at the mouth, if that's what you mean. But I do know this: you've got an obsession. You've got an obsession that's been riding you hard for a long time now, and that obsession is me. You're obsessed with the notion that I've changed, that I've ruined everything we started out to do, that gradually I'm selling everybody downstream, and that because I won't do things the way you think they should be done, I've become a dangerous man who's got to be stopped. Now, that's all you think about, Phil. And no matter how many times I've told you why I can't do what you want me to do, and why nobody could do them because people and politics just can't be run that way, it's made no difference to you. You just went on thinking about me, and how to stop me. That was bad enough, but then you started to do something about it—something which, if I let it continue, would ruin me, and would ruin all of us. Well, I guess I think anybody who has that kind of an obsession, and who lets it push him the way you've let yours push you—I guess I think he's mad, Phil!"

Phil had been listening closely to every word; now everyone was watching him; he said thoughtfully, "All right. The trouble is that it's not quite like the old days, when I used to believe you, and you used to believe me. And that makes it hard for me to know whether you really believe I am, or whether you're just saying that because it's . . . convenient. That's possible too, isn't it?" And once more he looked away from Charles and took us all in, saying now, "You think it would be a good idea if I asked for an independent opinion? Am I or am I not nuts? I think I might. The problem is: who do I ask? Not Marie: she's got to stick with Charles, hasn't she? And not Flossie." He looked at his wife, whose hand he was still holding; he smiled at her. "She's stuck with me." Then he looked across at us, still smiling, and said, "I might ask Jack. Or Jean."

Jean said suddenly and clearly, "I'd answer. In a minute."

"I know you would," Phil said. "And I'd love to hear you. But you're prejudiced, Jeannie. And so is Jack. The right way, but still prejudiced, so I guess I really shouldn't ask you, should I? And so that leaves only Pa. Well," he said, turning to his father, "I think I'd like to hear that. What about it, Pa? You haven't said anything at all. Say this to me, Pa. Crazy? Or not? Which one?"

For the second time in my life I had almost forgotten the presence of my Uncle Jimmy in the same room with me, but as Phil asked his question we all quickly—and, I think, somewhat guiltily—turned to the standing little figure by the fireplace, not until now giving him the full attention to which, in all family gatherings, he had always been so accustomed, and which he had always been able so easily to command. He had been facing away from us, having at some point switched back to his morose examination of the fire, but with Phil's words he had slowly come around to us again, and now he stood there in his usual faintly belligerent stance, his feet wide apart, his eyes grim behind his small old-fashioned glasses, his jaw jutting out, and his whole body bending slightly forward, suggesting that at any moment he might spring.

"You want me to tell you what I think of all this?" he said, and somehow his voice seemed harsher than I remembered it. He looked now, not just at Phil, but back and forth at all of us, making sure that everyone was listening. "All right: I've got a message for you all. One year ago I stood right where I'm standing now and I told you what I thought then. I told you I was the happiest man in the world because I had the greatest family in the world! I drank a toast to myself in champagne because I was the proudest man I knew! Lucky Jimmy Kinsella: lucky in everything but luckiest of all because he had three of the greatest boys anybody ever saw, all sticking together like glue, all pitching in to help the family be what I always wanted it to be! Well, that was last year. Tonight I've got another message for you: forget it! Forget everything I ever said, because it's all done, it's all balls. I wouldn't drink a toast tonight if it was the last glass of champagne in the world! I was a man that used to talk about my family. I used to spend all my time bragging about my family. My whole life was my family! And now I can say only one thing about my family: to hell with it! Because I haven't got it any more. I've got one boy that's made me happy, that's doing a great job the way a boy of mine should, but he's the only one. I've got another boy that's turned out to be a fancy Dan priest that can chow down with a crowd of mealy-mouthed half-assed ministers every night in the week, but when I need him for something important, when I call him up to ask him to come here tonight to help out the family, then he's too busy for that, he can't get away, he's off to Africa in the morning because they're blowing the lid off some new coon saint! Well, to hell with him, too. I'm wise to him at last. He hasn't lifted a finger for his family in twenty years, because he doesn't give a damn about it! But at least," he said, now looking directly at Phil, "at least he's never tried to smash it to bits. The way you did. You're the one that knifed me right in the ticker, boy. Because you had more than all of them to begin with. You could have been a star! You could have helped make this the greatest family ever! But you were always a mystery to me, I never knew what you wanted to do, I never knew what you were going to do or how you'd end up! Well, now I know. You got sore as a boil because you got some bee in your bonnet about Charles, and then you did what I would have bet my life no boy of mine would ever do! You turned on us, Phil! You tried to blow us sky-high and to smithereens! You tried to do that to your own family! You tried to do it to Charles! And by God, you tried to do it to *me!* And now you've got the guts to sit here and look at me and ask me if I think you're crazy?" His voice had risen steadily; he was shouting now; his face was flaming red. "All right!" he yelled. "You want an answer so I'll give you one: *you bet your ass you're crazy!* Believe it or not, kiddo, you're as bughouse as they come!"

It was an awful thing to say, made even more awful by the explosive violence with which it was said. I was shocked; I heard Jean give a little cry; I think Marie and even Charles had expected nothing like this. As for Phil, his face had gone blank: maybe he had forgotten how savage his father could be, maybe he had never expected, whatever the circumstances, to be the victim of his savagery. But he seemed dazed now; looking at him, wondering what to do, I suddenly saw Flossie jump to her feet, freeing her hand from his. She ran, actually *ran* across the room to where my Uncle Jimmy stood. She stopped directly in front of him and I could see that her delicate body was trembling and that her face was dead white. She was as tall as my Uncle Jimmy, maybe even taller, and as she stood there confronting him, crowding him, so close to him that they were almost touching, for the first time in all her years with the family, Flossie screamed.

"You're a horrible old man!" she raged. "Really horrible! For anyone like you to say what you've just said to someone like

Phil you ought to be knocked down and beaten and if you weren't so old I'll bet you would be! You're a dreadful, horrible, insensitive, vulgar, stupid little tyrant! Nobody ever tells you that but that's what you are! You're a bully: you've been bullying me and frightening me ever since the day I married Phil, and I put up with it because I loved him so much and because as horrible as you are he always loved you. But you're too stupid to realize that! You're just a monstrous little maniac foaming at the mouth because in spite of everything you could do he's turned out to be kind and gentle and good instead of being as mean and cruel as you! That's your idea of being a father: to have someone around just like yourself! Well, you've got one, but you haven't got Phil. You stand there with your jaw sticking out like some gutter bully and you're furious because all your plans went wrong and you shout these terrible lies at somebody who's so good you don't even deserve to *know* him, let alone be his father! You're an awful father, a really horrible one, and you're a detestable man, and I don't pray much but tonight I'm going to get down on my knees and pray that after tonight neither one of us will ever be bullied by you or even talk to you or even so much as catch sight of you ever again!"

It was a fantastic speech, a fantastic moment. I think, I *know*, that nothing like this had ever happened to my Uncle Jimmy before—and it had been poor, shy, retreating Flossie who had done it! My Uncle Jimmy now just stood before her, stupefied, as though he couldn't even imagine hearing what he had just heard. And Flossie, having said it, now seemed aghast that she had; she looked around at all of us in a rather bewildered and even frightened way. Then Phil called to her; he said gently, "Floss: come on over here."

And she turned and ran quickly to him, beginning to sob as she did. He took her in his arms and held her while she hid her face against him and continued to weep. Again, as had happened so often during this evening, there was a pause when no one seemed to know what to say; then suddenly Jean, in her clear voice, said, "Good for you, Flossie!" And she got up and walked over to where Phil and Flossie stood, and took one of Flossie's hands.

Phil looked at Jean and just nodded; then he said, "I'll tell you what: would you mind taking her down to the car? I'll be down in a moment; I don't have much more to say."

And so Jean and Flossie slowly walked out of the library together, saying nothing to anyone. Jean, holding Flossie, guiding her, gave me a quick look which I took to mean that she hoped I understood; Flossie didn't look at anyone but just kept on going.

When they had left, Phil said, "Well. Flossie's upset. We all are, I guess. But I suppose Flossie's a little more so than the rest because she knows what I'm going to do."

I didn't realize, immediately, what he had said; then, when I did, I looked quickly at him, wondering: what now? Marie and Charles were looking, too; my Uncle Jimmy was not. He was sunk in himself now; I don't think he could have even heard Phil. But this made no difference to Phil, because now he wasn't talking to his father or to Marie or to me. He was talking only to Charles.

"You see, you *are* going to get away with it," he said, his voice easy and conversational once more. "And you're going to get away with it because I'm going to let you. You might be able to get away with it even if I didn't let you—as you say, you do pack weight—but I don't think so. The first thing I'd do is apply for a writ to take it out of Kilrane's court, charging prejudice; it's touchy, but I think I could do that all right. Then at the hearing it would be no trick at all to produce competent psychiatric testimony which would differ rather sharply from that stuff you got from those captive physicians of yours. And of course there'd be questions asked, and how long do you think the poor old Abominable would hold up under the rather embarrassing questions that I'd ask him? Because I'd be doing the asking, Charles; I'd conduct my own defense. Think about that for a minute; remember that I used to do quite a bit of that sort of thing. And in all modesty I'm not bad. In fact I'm a hell of a lot better than anyone you could hope to produce. So you'd have quite a little trouble there, Charles."

Charles shrugged. "Possibly. Although I don't think so. These things don't work quite that way; there are other factors. But in any case that doesn't matter now, does it? Since you're going to let me do it anyway? That's very generous. I do smell a small rat, though."

"Of course you do," Phil said. "That's what you do these days, Charles: you smell rats. In everything. You've become a very careful and suspicious man. But you don't need to be here. I'll tell you exactly what I'm going to do. I'm going to go along with the court order. I'm not even going to request a hearing. In other words, I'm going to agree to being sent away without a fight. No resistance, Charles. None at all. Any day you say."

Charles sat very still, looking at Phil for a long time. At last he said, "Why?"

"Because I want to show you something," Phil said. "I'm going to put you right on the spot, Charles. You're not fooling me. You don't think I'm crazy, any more than I do. You're doing this for the very reason you say you're not doing it: you have plans, I know about those plans, I could interfere with those plans, therefore you want me out of the way. Of course it's a frame, and just between ourselves we both know that, don't we? But it's a frame I'm not going to fight. Instead, I'm going to do something else: I'm going to put a little proposition to you. I'm going to put it in the form of two alternatives. On the one hand, you can go ahead, just as you planned, pursuing the court order, and having me committed just as originally scheduled. Now, you're perfectly free to do that—as I've said, I won't fight, there'll be no delaying tactics, if you want to go ahead with it there's absolutely nothing to stop you. On the other hand—and here's what's new,

Charles, so pay attention—on the other hand, you can order the commitment proceedings stopped, right now. And if you do *that*," he said slowly, "I'll tell you what I'll do: I'll stop too. I mean it: from now on in, no more campaigning against you in any form. No more letters to the papers, over my name or any other. No more attacks of any kind, public or private. I'll be as silent as the tomb. That's a promise, Charles: all hostilities from this end to stop as of this moment. That's your second alternative. It gets you what you've been saying all along, doesn't it? So what about it?"

And so, astonishing as it was to me—and saddening too, in a way—Phil had decided to give in. I felt what I suppose I had no business to feel: I felt oddly let down. I saw that Charles was regarding his brother thoughtfully, and then suddenly I saw him smile, just faintly, and I thought I saw in his eyes a look of . . . what? Satisfaction? Victory? Even slight contempt? But all he said, softly, was, "Well well well . . ."

But Phil said crisply, "No . . . Not 'Well well well' at all. I know what that means. You don't get it, Charles. This isn't the final craven capitulation. This is simply my new approach. I told you I was going to show you something, that I was going to put you on the spot. Well, now you're on it. Right now. You see, you're now perfectly free to do one of two things. You can coop me up. If you do that you'll be playing it safe: you'll never have to worry about me again. Not because I'll stay cooped up—because I won't, you know that: I'll spring myself almost as soon as I get in—but because you don't care if I stay cooped up or not. As a matter of fact you wouldn't care if I spent only five minutes inside. The big thing is to get it on the record that I was in fact once committed for reasons of mental instability, isn't it? Once you've got that, you've more or less eliminated me as any kind of witness against you. Who's going to take the word of an established nut, right? So that's what you can do, and of course I know how distasteful it must be to you, how much you must hate having to do a thing like that. So I've given you the option. The second alternative. Now that would be easier on everybody, wouldn't it? It would certainly be easier on me. It would be easier on Flossie and the kids. It would be easier on the family. And it would even be easier on you, Charles, because in this way you could get what you want without having to commit your brother. So isn't it much the better way? Isn't it the logical thing to do? I think so. The only hitch is," he said, "that of course there isn't even the ghost of a chance that you'll do it!"

And by now he had walked slowly over to where Charles was sitting and stood above him, looking down, and speaking with a kind of finality and a kind of sadness too, as if he were at last wrapping everything up for good, but in a way he had never wanted to.

"You see, I know you, Charles," he said. "That's why what looks like quitting or giving in on my part isn't that at all, because I know you won't accept the option. You should, but you won't, and you won't for only one reason: *it isn't quite as safe as the other way*. You know you can rely on the lockup, but you can't bring yourself to believe my word. Isn't that it, Charles? You don't dare to take the risk any more. That's another way of saying you don't dare to trust anyone any more. You can't believe anyone now—except Marie, and she's not a part of the politics. I told you the game would get you, and it has—isn't that clear to you yet? You haven't just sold us out: you've sold *you* out. At this point in your career your every move has to be insured in advance because it might damage your future. You have to have everything all wrapped up before you say a word. That's the way you operate now, Charles: you've become The Complete Pol. You can't do anything on trust any more because you've destroyed trust for yourself. And that's what I'm trying to show you now: just how much you've destroyed it, and how far you're willing to go without it. So that's why I've said to you: commit me or don't commit me; either way, you'll get my silence. The difference being that in one case the guarantee is a medical certificate; in the other it's my word. Now I know you'll think this over, and I know you'll weigh all the possibilities, and I know that in the end you'll make your decision in the same way you've made every decision for a long time now—and you'll commit me. You may not even like to do it very much, but you'll do it all the same. It's absolutely inevitable. Because that's the way you are now, Charles; that's what you've become. Well, all right. I'd like to say I know what's going to happen from now on, but I don't. I think you'll probably go very far. I don't see any way of preventing it. Except maybe one. It's just possible that you may, once in a while, remember what you did, remember that in order to be absolutely sure of getting what you wanted, you jobbed your brother, you shipped him away when you really needn't have done it at all. And when you remember that, if it ever shakes you up a bit, if it ever slows you down, if it ever brings you back even a little to what you used to be—well, Charles, I wouldn't be sore at that. I wouldn't be sore at all."

And then he stopped; the two brothers looked at each other in silence; in this final moment it seemed to me that once again I caught that fugitive flash of astonishing resemblance between the two—and then it was gone. For an instant I thought Charles was about to speak, but maybe he really wasn't or maybe he changed his mind, because he continued to look without saying a word. Then Phil said, "Well, I guess that's everything. So long, Charles."

Charles said only, "So long, Phil."

They did not shake hands. Phil turned to Marie; he said, "I'm sorry, Marie."

But she didn't answer him; her head was down; she didn't even look at him. We waited a moment but nothing happened, and so he came over a couple of steps to me and said, "Well, Jack."

I took his hand and said, "I'm with you, you know."

"I know you are." He smiled and said, "Well, how else could

it be? Didn't we once sign a pact? Aren't we the Fierce and Friendly Two? 'We will stay friends our whole lives no matter what happens. No matter how far away we are we will meet each other at least three times a year and probably a lot more. If anyone harms or wounds either one of us the other one will revenge him.' He quoted it all, word for word; then he laughed and said, "Remember?"

I remembered. I remembered with an ache the two small boys seated side by side in my Uncle Jimmy's castle long ago: it was the night before I was leaving for good with my father. It was midnight, and there in the stuffy room—for we had closed the windows and drawn the curtains so that our light could not be seen from the outside—we sat under the table lamp and jointly composed the two copies of our Pact: one for him, one for me. My copy had gone long ago—where, I haven't any idea—but now he took his wallet from his pocket, searched through it for a moment, and came out with an old folded piece of paper, pretty much held together by Scotch tape. He looked at it, and of course I knew at once what it was; he smiled again and handed it to me, saying, "Do you think this is a moment for sentimental gestures? I do. Have one on me." And he gave me the Pact. I didn't say anything; I couldn't have—I didn't dare to. He took my hand and held it; then he let it go and said, "Don't worry: I'll see you around."

He left me now to say goodbye to the one remaining person in the room—his father. My Uncle Jimmy was standing where he had been standing all the while; he was facing Phil. I had seen him watching his two sons as they talked and he seemed to be listening to them, and yet I was struck by, not so much his lack of excitement, as what appeared to be his lack even of any interest—it was as if he were still in a state of shock from what Flossie had said, or from something that had happened here tonight. But now he watched Phil coming toward him, and I had the peculiar and uncomfortable feeling that he was looking at his son exactly as he would have looked at any stranger, as someone he had never seen before and in whom he had no interest.

Phil stopped directly in front of him and about a foot away from him, he half lifted his arms and put them out tentatively, as if to embrace his father; he said, "Pa . . ."

But very quickly my Uncle Jimmy stepped backward two steps, evading the attempt to reach him, and at the same time looking straight at his son with the same terrible passionless neutrality. And Phil stood there, and then he dropped him arms. He gave a little shrug and said, "All right, Pa. I'm sorry."

And he turned and without looking again at any of us he walked toward the door of the room. Just as he reached it and was about to step out into the hall my Uncle Jimmy seemed to come to. I don't know whether he was calling after Phil, or whether he was appealing to all of us, but his voice came out now in a great agonized bellow.

"What the hell has happened?" he cried. "*What the hell has happened to my family?*"

And nobody said anything but Phil. Standing in the doorway, looking back now at his father for a second or two, he answered him.

"I don't know, Pa," he said. "I guess we all grew up."

And then he left. This meant that I was here with Charles and Marie and my Uncle Jimmy; it also meant that if Phil took Flossie home, Jean would be all alone, waiting for me. So I left too, going first to my Uncle Jimmy, shaking hands with him, saying goodbye, and getting in return a half-hearted grunt, an abstracted motion of the hand which said that no matter who came or who went, it made no difference to him now. I went next to Marie. She said briefly, "Goodbye, Jack," and that was all; to my surprise—because I'd never even thought of Marie as crying—I saw now that there were tears in her eyes. And then I went, last of all, to Charles.

It was a short, strained parting; as I went to go he said, "Jack?"

I turned back; he said, "Do you know what's going to happen now?"

I said, "Yes. I think so."

He looked at me for a moment, then said, "You're sure of that, are you?"

And I said, "Yes. Just about."

And he looked at me again, then nodded, and then I left the library.

Jean was in the hall downstairs; Phil and Flossie had gone. We went out to the car quickly and drove off. She told me that Flossie had said nothing when she had come downstairs; she had merely continued to weep. I told her what had happened upstairs, what Phil had done, and she listened to everything, at first with amazement, and then simply seeming to accept it all as it came along, as if amazement had been pushed far enough and could no longer go any farther. When I finished she sighed and said, "I feel as though I should be crying too, but somehow I just can't. I don't know why. Not now. Poor Phil. He's really pretty wonderful, isn't he?"

I said, "I think so."

She said practically, "And I think maybe a little crazy too. Just a little. But that doesn't bother me at all, because whatever they want to call it, I think it's just great. You think Charles will go ahead now?"

I nodded; she said, "But it's always possible he could do the other. Just possible. Don't you think?"

"It's possible," I said, but I really didn't think so. What I really thought was that it would happen just as Phil said it would happen, and that after it did, no one could be sure of anything. Except of one thing, and that is that my Uncle Jimmy and Phil and Charles and James and all of them were, sadly enough, as a family finished forever.

fourteen

There were no surprises: Phil was committed three days later.

Flossie called us when she got home late that day. It must have been the worst day of her life, yet either Phil had managed to calm her or else she was all cried out: in any case, she was not crying now. She said that she had called to thank us for all we had done, and to tell us that Phil was feeling well, seemed in good spirits, and was confident that he would get out very soon. Jean and I had talked about going to see him or trying to help him in some way, but when we mentioned this to Flossie she said more or less what we both expected: that Phil, right now, preferred to be alone, and that he was firm on handling everything for himself. So then we asked her to come and stay with us for a while, but she thanked us again and said that she was leaving immediately for Georgia, where Phil was to join her as soon as possible. When she hung up she was still thanking us; she was a good girl, a fine girl, and far more grateful than was necessary; we—or at least I—had done little enough to deserve this response.

Then we heard no more from her, although quite soon—it couldn't have been more than a couple of weeks—I learned that

Phil had been released. I learned this from the hospital, not from Phil. From Phil I heard nothing, not a word, and so I simply assumed that he had guessed correctly, that there had been no difficulty, no opposition from Charles—the fact of the commitment on the record was all that had been wanted—and that he had got out, left the city quickly, and gone directly to Flossie. As I saw, this was all assumption, and I didn't seek for further information anywhere. The whole matter of Phil's confinement had been managed most carefully, without any public attention; I did not want to run the risk of stimulating interest now.

So I said nothing, and I heard nothing. Not merely from Phil and Flossie, but from the rest of the family as well. Of course I had no trouble in keeping track of Charles: he was given the same ample coverage in the papers that he had been given from the first. He still seemed to win far more praise than blame, and I gathered—again, simply from reading the papers—that his position was now stronger than ever. It seemed to be taken for granted that he would run for re-election the following November; it seemed to be taken equally for granted that anyone who ran against him would commit an act of political folly. But all this was political news, public news—yet it was all I had. The private lines had been interrupted, cut off; in the weeks that followed Charles—as far as I knew—made no attempt to reach me, and I made none to reach him. There was no point; it was over; we both knew that.

Jean and Marie saw each other once. They had one of their lunches together; it was Marie who had suggested it, and Jean had accepted, but reluctantly, and yet with some hope, too. They had met on the usual neutral ground, but Jean came home far earlier than usual, and from her face I knew at once that it had not gone well.

"It was no good," she said simply. "We didn't fight, we didn't argue. Well, we were both nervous, and then we knew there were so many things we couldn't talk about any more that in the end we didn't talk much at all. So it was a washout, Jack, a washout all the way. I don't imagine we'll do it again in a hurry."

And they didn't: the lunch was not repeated. It was too bad, because while Jean was in no sense friendless—there were any number of women around the city whom she knew and liked—Marie had been her closest friend, the one she liked most to be with, and now she was never with her any more. She said once or twice rather wistfully that maybe one day, after a little time had passed, they might get back on the old footing and be easy with each other once again. I said I hoped so, but I didn't really believe it, and I don't think she did, either.

One day, one night, we heard from James. It was one of his unexpected telephone calls: he was passing through, there was no time for a visit, he wanted however to say hello. He seemed exactly the same: he talked entertainingly of his own activities. His television series, which had been temporarily discontinued in this country, was being shown on film in England to great advantage (". . . apparently of limited appeal to Youth, but I'm assured I fascinate the aging Nonconformist . . .") and he had recently made several visits to Spain, where he had had doings with the hierarchy there (". . . a remarkably obdurate old man, arthritic beyond belief, bent so far forward that when he walks his hips are higher than his head; he refers to the Era of Pope John as 'The Roncalli Madness' . . ."). He did not talk of Charles or of Marie or of my Uncle Jimmy or of any of the family, and when, pointedly, I asked him if he had seen Phil, he answered blithely, "It doesn't seem to be in the cards this trip; he's in Georgia with Flossie." And that was all. After the call I found myself wondering whether it was possible, just possible, that James could not have known exactly what had happened; I concluded that it was not. I was sure that he knew, just as I was sure that, knowing, he felt it all to be one of those minor tempests that now and then rose in minor teapots, whose effects were real, even regrettable, but transient, and which brushed faintly against, but did not really impinge upon, the great and swirling world of change which he had chosen for his own.

All through this period my Uncle Jimmy remained silent and unseen. In a way this surprised me, because I think that he was the one member of the family from whom I half expected to hear. I kept on thinking that any day now—or, more likely, any night, at some improbable and inconvenient hour—I would get a phone call, the familiar barking voice would again remind me that I was "all wet" and that I had better "wise up," and then, after the preliminaries, and with the usual mixture of truculence and concern, he would demand to know what I had heard from Phil. But no such call ever came. I had a hunch that he was still around, but it was no more than a hunch; he had always come and gone on a moment's notice, and for all I knew he might well have left the city weeks ago.

Then, one day, I saw him. It was just as the Christmas season began; Jean and I had gone into the city together and had remained there most of the day. Late in the afternoon I had finished with the last of my errands and had begun to walk over to the hotel where we had arranged to meet before going home. It was already dark enough for the street lights to be turned on; a few flakes of snow—the first of the winter—had begun to fall; the air was cold and unpleasantly damp. I hurried along; I stopped at an intersection to wait for the traffic light to change and, as I did so, suddenly I saw my Uncle Jimmy. He was alone in the back of the long Cadillac limousine—"What the hell would I want a Rolls for?" he had once, I remembered, replied to one of his boys: Phil, I think. "Listen, you babies are pushovers for those Jickey con men! What's so hot about a Rolls? A loud clock, lunch tables and a bar in the back, right? Well listen: when I want to know the time I look at my watch and when I want chow I go to a restaurant and when I want a drink I go to a saloon! And when I want to get across town in a hell of a hurry without breaking my ass in two, then I go to my Caddy and that's all there is to that!"—and he looked oddly small and isolated in the immense cushioned interior. I saw that there was a new chauffeur at the wheel; I was not surprised. My Uncle Jimmy seemed to be resting; he was slumped down in the seat and his eyes were closed. I raised my arm automatically, but he was in the second line of cars away from the curb, and even if his eyes had been open I doubt that he could have picked me out of the crowd. The lights now changed, the traffic started, and then, almost as if it were inevitable, as if it were done for my benefit, the Cadillac started with a great jerk—it felt uncomfortable even where I was standing. And the last I saw of my Uncle Jimmy he was sitting bolt upright, certainly resting no longer, but yelling at the back of still another chauffeur's neck.

So then, with the exception of Phil and Flossie, all the family were in town and so were we, and yet as far as we were concerned they might as well have been on the moon. Christmas came and went: we had a good day, a quiet one. Then we went off for a week of skiing, and returned shortly after the new year began. We stayed in the city for January and February; there was some snow, but not as much as usual; there seemed to be weeks of dull gray days and high winds and from time to time we talked about going somewhere for some sun, but we didn't: we stayed here. It was a curious time and, we both agreed, not a very satisfactory one. I was working in fits and starts; my book which I had delivered to Andrew Pout in the fall was soon to be published; I wrote one short story, then another: neither, I thought, was much good. So I was really marking time, moving slowly through one of those dead stretches that come along now and then, aware that I was in a kind of intermission which had somehow gone on too long, yet whose end I couldn't quite see.

The absence of the family played a part in this. We got a card from Phil and Flossie sometime in February; it did not say when they would be back and I had the feeling that perhaps they would not come back at all—that is, in any sense of coming back to *live*. And I found that as the weeks went by that I was thinking of them all more than I had expected to. It was natural enough, I suppose: they were the people I had known best from my childhood, and of all the people I had ever met—with the exception, of course, of Jean—they were the ones who were closest to me; there were old ties there I could hope to have with no one else. And although over the years we had often been separated, and sometimes a very long time would go by before we would see each other again, still, in a way they were always *around*, they were somewhere in the background, they had a vitality and a world of their own which, even though I touched it sometimes only at the edges, I had always felt was in some measure mine. They were, in fact, a part of *me*. And now this was no longer so: it left a gap, a hole, in my life. Here in this city, in their headquarters, so to speak, I found I missed the family.

Jean knew this; we talked about it. One day in March she said, "I don't think a change would be bad, do you? Let's get away: we could both stand it."

I said, "Now?"

"Why not now? What are we doing that keeps us here? Besides, if you're here when your book comes out Andrew Pout plans to give you a party. He told me; you're not supposed to know."

It was an argument of some strength. I said, "Where? Italy again? Do you want to greet the spring with Signor Barbettura?"

"No, I don't think Italy. Not this time. But I'll tell you where I might like to go." And then to my great surprise she now suggested Ireland—a country where we had been before (as I've said, on our honeymoon), where we had had a decent time, but a country which she had always thought of in terms of a rather pleasant way station: a place to pause on the way to some serious destination. But now she seemed fixed on going there and staying there for a while, and gradually I realized what I should have sensed at once: that she was doing this mainly for me, that she had a notion that this was really something I would like to do. In fact, I hadn't been thinking of anything of the kind, but once the idea had been proposed it seemed attractive; we talked about it with increasing enthusiasm; before the week was out we had begun making our arrangements to go.

On the weekend before we left, we had our first and only visitor from the family. It was Aunt Gert: she had just come back from the West Coast, driven all the way by the smiling tireless Ernie. She had a new car, but nothing else about her had changed at all. She told us of her pilgrimages along the Spanish Mission trail; she told us of her old friend Alice Leary who, it appeared, had not come back with her; she had chosen to remain in California where, if all went well, she would spend the rest of her days.

"Well," my Aunt Gert said, "why not, the poor dear? She's very feeble now, and she likes the climate. God bless us all, she even likes the kind of things they eat out there. Dates, you know, and stuff like that. And then there's a little church out there and she goes in and talks to the priests once a week and tells them if they don't watch out she might join up with Christian Science. God knows they couldn't care less what she joins up with, but the poor soul thinks she's got them terrified and that makes her feel good. Poor Alice has never been the same since she got put out of the Plaza. . . ."

It was just before she left that she talked about the family, although it was perhaps typical of her that she did not introduce the subject but waited for me to do so. When I asked her bluntly if she knew about what had happened she at once admitted that she did. She was in fact extremely well posted; I think she must have heard from Phil as well as from my Uncle Jimmy. I asked her what she thought about it, and she gave her great laugh.

"God bless my soul!" she said. "What difference does it make what an old woman like me thinks about anything? All the same, I suppose it's a little hard on Jimmy."

"On Jimmy," I said. "You don't think it's hard on Phil?"

"Well, of course no one likes to be put away, do they?" she said. "But that's all over now. People forget these things, even though they say they don't. And anyway half of my friends seem to be trotting in and out of places like that most of the time: it's all the fashion these days!" She laughed again and then, suddenly more serious, said, "And it's not the worst thing that can happen to anybody. Oh no. Look at Phil: he's out, he's a young man like yourself, he's down South now and he's fine. No matter what's happened, he's still got a good wife and a good big family around him. And look at Jimmy. He's old and he's got nobody now. He's lost all his boys. He spent all his life bringing them up and hoping they'd all be just like him. That's what he wanted: a house full of little Jimmies. Well, it didn't turn out that way, and anyone with half an eye could see it couldn't. First he lost James and now he's lost Phil, and the only one left is Charles. And he's really lost him too, only he doesn't know it yet. Oh yes, it's very hard on Jimmy. Because he's all alone. And that can be hard on anybody. But most of all when you're someone like Jimmy who's had no practice at it." Her tone had become, for her, almost somber, but then, suddenly, her spirits seemed to lift and I heard the familiar laugh. "Of course he's always got an old crock like me to stand by him," she said merrily, "but I don't think that's the way he had it planned at all!"

And then she left. Not for the first time, it occurred to me that my Aunt Gert was an extraordinary woman.

We were in Ireland three days later. We went to Dublin straightaway, and to the old hotel. Like the city itself, it seemed not to have changed essentially; there were touches here and there of new paint and polish, and inside ancient chairs had given way to others somewhat less ancient. It was only later that I discovered that in the back an entire new wing had been added; designed by Finnish architects, it was called the American wing:

spare, clinical, and charmless, its rooms were less than half the size of those in the main part of the hotel.

"The latest thing in public accommodation," said Mr. Guilfoyle, as he showed us around. "Half hotel, half hospital. The convertible room: you can sleep in it at night and be operated on in it in the morning. Not a change is necessary; if appendicitis strikes, stay where you are: the ether will replace the breakfast tea. Snip snip snip and the offending organ is removed! Oh yes, everything up to the minute in Holy Ireland. Ah ha ha ho!"

He spoke fluently and with consistent irony of the improved amenities of the hotel. He was no longer in active control, having been superseded as general manager some years ago, but he had been kept on as a kind of host in deference to the great number of long-established guests with whom he was enormously popular—and for whom, indeed, he was the hotel. He was now an old man—exactly how old I had no idea, but surely in his eighties—yet he in no way suggested great age. Even in his appearance he seemed almost identical to the tall bald baffling man I had first seen through the eyes of a little boy. The funny brown square of moustache had retained its original shape and color; his four-toned laugh still popped out of nowhere; his talk was as alert and as original as ever. He walked about more slowly now, and his one concession to age was a thick, warped, knobby stick which occasionally he used for support, but more often carried aloft, as if it were a weapon. While we were here in the hotel he came to see us every day; I loved to have him come and so did Jean. He usually arrived late in the afternoon, followed by two waiters who wheeled in a tea trolley loaded with sandwiches, cakes, cookies—enough to feed a battalion. Mr. Guilfoyle, who now took no strong drink, had cup after cup of tea and talked about his long years here in the hotel, and about the celebrated people who had visited here during that time. He had come to know many of them quite well; he talked about them politely but freely; he was far from being an idolater. . . .

". . . a very great writer, I'm told, with his plays on the stage all over the civilized world. I remember an American woman once saying to me, 'You must be very proud to have him under your roof, Mr. Guilfoyle. He has words that soar to heaven!' 'And checks that do the same,' I said. An injudicious thing to say, no doubt, but it was the hotelkeeper rather than the human being who spoke. He owed us three hundred and fifty pounds for bed and breakfast alone. . . .

". . . an outstanding politician in your country, I believe. A senator or something of the sort. A man of burning intellect of course. Ah ha ha ho. He came to us every year in friendship and to tell us how to behave. Oh yes, he felt very deeply about Holy Ireland. I remember that in the bar at night he frequently wept about what was wrong with us. In humble gratitude the Men of Mullingar once presented him with a marble ashtray. . . .

". . . a beautiful woman. I never go to the cinema myself but they say she was a great star. She used to visit us every now and then, each time with a different brother in tow. Or sometimes he was called a husband, I believe. Depending to some extent upon the probabilities: color, and so forth. She believed in ghosts, I remember, and one time when she was here with the underwater swimmer she came down in the morning with a black eye. Charity being the virtue it is in the Blessed Isle, I could only conclude that she'd been mauled by a poltergiest. . . .

". . . I knew His Eminence well. A man of exemplary piety. And generosity: he used to come over and share himself with us every two years or so. Popular with one and all, save possibly the waiters in the dining room. He'd give them his blessing instead of a tip, you see; no doubt it was his way of combating materialism. Ah ha ha ho. . . ."

And yet he had his great favorites; my father was one of these, and even more, so was my mother. He said to Jean one afternoon, "You never knew her, of course. She died well before you came along. Oh, a grand girl. Beautiful, you know, with a lovely voice, and enough charm to bring every last bird down out of the trees. And the best part of it was you could spend all the day long in her company, you know, and at the end of it she'd seem as fresh and as gay as if you'd walked up and said hello to her just ten minutes before. Oh yes," he said, "we had the good times when they were here. I remember one night when we all . . ."

But then he stopped talking, not abruptly, but his voice just softly diminishing and drifting away, and as I looked at him now I suddenly remembered that, after all, he was really a very old man in spite of all appearances, and that like all old men who have lived happily and well, he enjoyed the present most when it allowed him to slip back into the past.

"Great days!" he said now, finally. "Oh, great days entirely! Dum dee dee dum dee dee di di dum!" He hummed for a moment more, and then he said softly, "Ah ha ha ho."

It was here in the hotel, late one afternoon, that I had an improbable encounter with an old friend. I had stopped at the small newsstand in the lobby to buy some stamps for Jean; suddenly I felt a hard nudge in my right side and a voice said joyfully, "Well well well! Will you look at who's here!" In this setting, it was impossible, but I turned, and there he was: Walshie. This was a Walshie new to me, a sporty Walshie, a Walshie on holiday: he wore a small pork-pie hat with a bright feather in the band, a voluminous jacket of bright blue tweed, a very green tie. He seemed even smaller and more cadaverous than ever, and he was clearly delighted by this meeting: from the thin face the enormous false teeth clicked smile after smile at me. Mrs. Walshie was by his side; massive and severe as ever, she greeted me with prim restraint.

"You're a sight for sore eyes, Ralph!" Walshie said, hitting me on the shoulder. "I and the wife came over on the Tour!"

It appeared that a group from home had chartered the plane; they had been traveling around Ireland for three weeks; now, tonight, they were going back.

I said, making talk, "Was it your first trip?"

"Never before," Walshie said, "and never again! Give me home sweet home any day! Everywhere you go in this country the grub is lousy. And the hotels! Down in Parknasilla the wife found a bug in her bed!"

"Leo J.!" Mrs. Walshie said, reprovingly. To me she said, "I'm afraid I have very high standards of cleanliness."

I asked if Edso had come over on the Tour; Mrs. Walshie's soaring eyebrows and tightening mouth showed that her opinion of her husband's old friend had not improved; Walshie said regretfully, "He couldn't make it. The day before we left they had to take him to the hospital. I don't know what he's got. By God, whatever it is, I hope it's not what I had! I licked it, but there's damn few that do that!"

"I could tell them what's wrong with that one," Mrs. Walshie said. "It comes in a bottle."

Walshie nodded. "Edso takes a drink now and then." He added virtuously, "I've done my best to tell him, but he won't listen. Well," he said cheerily, "nobody's perfect! Isn't that right, Ralph? Tell me, is the Governor over here with you by any chance?"

I said that he wasn't; Walshie looked disappointed. "Because if he was," he said, "I could pay him my respects. Will you do that for me, Ralph? If you see him before me?"

I said I would; he said, "Just tell him Leo J. Walsh is with him all the way."

The bus that was to take him to the airport had arrived; I walked with him to the door, Mrs. Walshie preceding us sedately, inexorably. They got aboard; Walshie rolled his window down; as the bus pulled off he began to wave and as it turned the corner I heard him cry out the final reminder. "Leo J. Walsh!" he yelled.

It had been an absurd meeting, but for a moment it made me oddly homesick, bringing with it memories of the family and the city and the election night party and the Inaugural Ball. And when, upstairs, a few minutes later, I told Jean all about this, she laughed, but then she looked thoughtfully at me and said, "You almost sound like someone who wants to go home. You don't, do you?"

"No. Not at all." And it was true: I didn't. Not yet, anyway. I knew I would, certainly, some day, but just when that would be, or just how or why it would come about, I hadn't now even the faintest idea. . . .

Meanwhile, we continued to enjoy our stay, but now we decided to move away from the hotel and away from Dublin; for the rest of our visit we thought we would move out into the country: we would take a small house, preferably somewhere in the west—it was a part of Ireland that Jean had never seen. Here Mr. Guilfoyle proved to be of enormous help. This surprising man, who never willingly journeyed beyond the city limits of his beloved Dublin, had a prodigious and intimate knowledge of the available real estate all over the country, and when we came back from each of our house-hunting trips, perhaps through the cloud-dappled hills of Connemara, or out to the bleak magnificence of Mayo, or down to the improbable palm trees of the south ("Kissed by the benign breezes from the ever-present Gulf Stream," read the brochure, "these palm trees flourish in the approximate latitude of Labrador!"), bringing with us our list of possible accommodations, Mr. Guilfoyle was waiting for us, ready to assess, even readier to discard:

". . . know it like the back of my hand: a miracle in sunshine, a disaster in the rain. You might as well live out in the open air . . . handsome enough, I grant you that, but there's trouble with the drains. And the landlord is Tom McGee, a scoundrel from the time he was a child. . . . I wouldn't go near this one at all. Oh there's all the charm in the world, to be sure, but the electric light fails every second day in that part of the country. You'd be a madman in a week. Ah ha ha ho . . . this is the best of the lot, but you'd never get a soul to come in to wash a plate. There was a double hanging there last summer: a man and his wife. From the beams. With belts. A very low roof, but then, a very short couple. Oh no, I wouldn't advise that. . . ."

We settled, ultimately, on a small house that had been built for a friend of Mr. Guilfoyle's two years ago: it was modern, immaculate, just the right size, perfect for our needs. And it was beautifully situated, in country which was less dramatic than some we had seen, and certainly less rugged and spectacular than the desolate wildness which was less than a hundred miles to the north, but rural and quiet and pretty, ideal for living in day after day. There were sloping low green mountains to the east of us, while the long western horizon was formed by the Atlantic. Of all the settings we had seen, this one was the most familiar to me, because it was so like the one I had known as a boy here with my father, and I suppose this might have been one of the reasons for choosing this house now. In any case, here, as I worked every day—I had begun to work, rather tentatively, on an idea I had for a book—I could look out through the wide picture window and see the cattle wandering quietly over the long spread of fields that ran between the house and the sea, and as I did, especially on the sunny days, there were times when everything I saw—the cows and the fields and the narrow shining brook that spilled down from somewhere in the mountains—reminded me of nothing so much as the time I had ridden across Ireland in the small car with my father, so long ago now, and had stopped by the freezing pool in the meadow where, in the heat and sunshine, we had stripped off all our clothes and plunged in for the sudden, breathtaking swim. . . .

We lived in this house for five months. As we had in Italy the previous summer, we now spent most of the time by ourselves. It was a quiet time, a good time, a healthy time, a happy time—above all, a happy time. In this uncrowded green country of pastures and hills and sea, where on the brightest day clouds as huge as mountains could sail across the sun and storms which came in seconds could vanish as they came while great double rainbows rose behind the fresh and sparkling hills, all time slipped swiftly by: a week was gone and hardly seemed a day. I worked now quickly, surely, because I felt like working again; my book was well under way. Jean drew, she spent long hours preparing elaborate meals—she was an excellent cook whenever she chose to be, and she chose to be very often now—and above everything else she went back to her riding. She was something to see on a horse, and yet at home she rode very seldom—I suppose because the opportunities were fewer. But here she rode every day, always asking me to ride along with her, and sometimes I did—although always a little reluctantly, every minute aware of the staggering gulf that separates the carefully instructed, neatly competent rider from one who rode as naturally as she opened her eyes in the morning or went to sleep at night. So quite often she rode alone, and I always watched her until she rode out of sight, and watched her again as she came home, perhaps hours later, tired but happily so, and sometimes breathless with delight.

Then, one day, she did not ride. She gave no explanation, and I said nothing, not really thinking much about it. But when a second and then a third day went by and still there was no riding, I was puzzled. At dinner that night I asked her about it, and when I did she was silent for a few seconds, and then she looked at me in an odd way and said, "I was thinking I might not ride much more this summer. I was also thinking we might plan, sometime soon, on going home."

Startled, I said, "Why? How come?"

And then she told me, directly, quietly, but with a kind of trembling excitement which came shooting through—she told me what was so natural and so simple that I might have guessed it, I suppose, and yet the truth was that I hadn't even thought of it at all. Not even as a possibility. Because after all it had been a long time, and after so many years I imagine you can, automatically and gradually, not give up hope exactly, but just stop thinking about the things you thought about in the beginning. So that now I think I must have stared at her as if she were talking of wild improbabilities, as if she were telling me that she was contemplating murder or that she had learned to fly without wings—when of course what she was telling, now rushing her words and no longer able to control her own triumphant happiness, was that she was pregnant, she was going to have a baby, and that she wanted now, at last, to go home.

And I don't remember what I did then. But I do remember that my arms were around her and stayed around her, and that here in this small house, in the quiet and deserted Irish night, she was laughing and sobbing happily, and I felt exultant and bursting and as I had never never felt before.

We made our plans, then, to go home right away. We would not return first to Dublin; we would fly from Shannon; as we had few things to pack and very little to do, we could leave within days. Jean packed, the house was given a final cleaning, I got the plane tickets, and we made one phone call to Dublin: strangely but appropriately too, Mr. Guilfoyle thus became the first to hear our news. He seemed overjoyed; he talked to us for a long time; the call ended with his last cry in our ears.

"Come back, come back!" he said. "Come back to Holy Ireland! We'll all be waiting for you!"

I waited for "Ah ha ha ho!" This time it did not come.

On the day before we left, we made an odd and—up to the last minute—an unplanned trip. The house in which we had lived was really not very far from my Uncle Jimmy's castle—a little less than an hour's ride. We had several times talked about going over, just on the chance that he might be there—although we were by no means sure of our reception. We never did; now, however, it seemed somehow a good thing to do, and so on this last day, a rather sullen day with the rain clouds sweeping in from the sea, we decided to go. We drove off to the castle, reaching it in the middle of the dark and pelting afternoon. It turned out to be a trip made in vain. We saw thin smoke coming out of a chimney as we turned into the circular drive; as we came up to the castle—which seemed to me to be just the way I had always remembered it, with no changes at all over the last three decades—a limping dark-faced man whom I had never seen before emerged from the house and informed us, briefly and sullenly, that my Uncle Jimmy was not at home, that he had left the previous week, and that it was not known where he had gone or when he would return. I identified myself; this had no softening effect. The grim face and manner did not relax; there was a short nod and a sound which might have been a grunt of acknowledgment; then he turned abruptly away from us and limped back to the house. Whatever else my Uncle Jimmy had secured in his new caretaker, he had not secured charm—but about this, as, probably, about a great many other things in his life now, he may no longer have cared at all.

And so, the next morning, I left Ireland again, to go back to the city I had always loved, to the house which had always been my home, but now, for the first time, with my dear Jean, to a family of my own.